HELL DIVERS VI
ALLEGIANCE

BOOKS BY NICHOLAS SANSBURY SMITH

Copyright © 2019 by Nicholas Sansbury Smith
Published in 2019 by Blackstone Publishing
Cover illustration by K. Jones
Series design by Kathryn Galloway English

Printed in the United States of America

First paperback edition: 2019
ISBN 978-1-9826-6986-7
Fiction / Science Fiction / Apocalyptic & Post-Apocalyptic

1 3 5 7 9 10 8 6 4 2

CIP data for this book is available from
the Library of Congress

Blackstone Publishing
31 Mistletoe Rd.
Ashland, OR 97520
www.BlackstonePublishing.com

HELL DIVERS VI

ALLEGIANCE

NICHOLAS SANSBURY SMITH

BLACK STONE

PUBLISHING

To Arlo Wand. You're one of a kind, my friend.

"To fight and conquer in all our battles is not supreme excellence; supreme excellence consists in breaking the enemy's resistance without fighting."

—Sun Tzu

PROLOGUE

Michael "Tin" Everhart stood behind the red line on the deck of the launch bay as he armored up for his sixty-fourth jump. He had officially passed the threshold that earned him a spot as one of the most successful Hell Divers in history, and he was the youngest ever to reach the milestone.

It had cost him—and more than just an arm. He had watched friends and his own father lose their lives in the deadly task of jumping into the wastes. Not many veteran divers remained, but back at their new home, renamed the Vanguard Islands, a new generation had stepped up to meet the challenge. Between missions to find human survivors in the wastes, Michael was helping train them.

But today was not a training day in the sunny skies of the islands. Today, Team Raptor was diving back into the postapocalyptic hell world beyond the barriers.

Joining Michael in the launch bay were veteran divers Magnolia Katib and Trey Mitchells, along with a half-dozen support specialists. The divers watched the maelstrom of swirling black clouds outside while the technicians finished their diagnostic tests.

Alfred, the new lead tech who had replaced Ty, worked on Michael's wrist computer. The middle-aged engineer was a former computer technician on the *Hive*, with a wife and a newborn at home.

Michael thought of Layla, now pregnant with their son, Bray. In a few months, he would join their little family.

"Looks good," Alfred said. "Dive safely, Commander."

"Always," Michael said.

The technicians retreated as they finished their checks. Michael tabbed his wrist monitor, bringing the new drone online. A flurry of chirping came from across the room, where the robot was secured to the bulkhead.

Michael unlocked the safety bars, and the drone hovered over.

"Hey, there, Cricket," Michael said. "How you feeling, buddy?"

The former ITC utility robot chirped again. Alfred, the only technician left in the launch bay, walked over and confirmed that all systems were operational.

"Be careful with him out there," he said. "The new software might be a bit buggy."

Michael smiled at his new creation. The three-foot-tall robot flew across the space, its advanced hover nodes glowing red. Team Raptor had discovered the machine in a junk pile at an ITC facility four dives ago, and Michael and Trey had spent many days putting it back together.

Only three of the four arms attached to the base were functioning, but they would come in handy on the dive—from opening doors to hacking systems, to providing medical support. Michael had even managed to install a blowtorch on one mechanical hand, and a blaster on another. The smooth outer armor sported a freshly painted Raptor logo.

The drone didn't have the only fresh paint. On the port side of the launch bay, "*Discovery*" had been stenciled in glossy black.

Formerly the ITC *Deliverance*, the nuclear-powered airship had been completely gutted and rebuilt after a punishing battle with the Cazadores months earlier. This was her first journey back to the wastes, but it was Michael's twentieth dive since the fight that had cost the lives of so many.

Since then, the *Hive* had carried Team Raptor to locations to search for survivors, but so far, the only thing the divers had found, other than some much-needed fuel cells, was Cricket. Michael wasn't giving up hope on finding humans, though. If the Cazadores had found inhabited bunkers, then so could his divers.

The airship continued to transmit a message of hope over the radio waves: "If you're listening, don't be afraid. We are the last humans, and we are in the skies, looking for you. If you're out there, respond to this message. We will never stop diving for humanity."

Until a few days ago, they had heard nothing.

It wasn't until they transferred from the *Hive* to the repaired and refitted *Discovery* that they had detected a signal, coming from an island called Jamaica. It wasn't a message or even an SOS—just garbled noises in response to their own transmission.

According to Cazador records, their navy had never raided the location, which meant there could be survivors. But it was also dangerously close to Red Sphere—not even two hundred miles from where they had dropped the nuke on the facility.

The techs closed the launch bay's hatch to the hallway. As soon as it was sealed, a message came over the public address system from the airship's new captain, Les Mitchells.

"Green light to dive, Team Raptor," he said in a voice tinged with worry. "Good luck, and stay sharp."

Trey Mitchells seemed confident as ever. On the past few dives, he had taken some unnecessary risks to prove himself, which was probably why his dad sounded concerned.

"Keep tight once we land," Michael said. "There's nobody to impress down there, and anyway, the most impressive thing you can do is stay alive."

"I know," Trey said. "Don't worry, Commander."

Michael nodded and hit a button. The launch-bay doors opened to a dark sky. The platform extended away from the ship as the divers walked out into the wind.

He didn't waste a second studying the drop zone—just gave a nod to Magnolia. This time, she could yell the motto, but he was still the first to step off the extended platform, into the clouds.

For a moment, he felt the sensation of pure weightlessness, like a feather caught in a gale. The forces of wind and gravity seemed caught in a struggle over his body.

A glance over his shoulder confirmed that the other two divers had followed him out of the belly of the airship. Cricket, still hovering in the launch bay, would wait a few moments before joining them in the darkness.

Michael studied the cloud cover and surrendered to the pull of forces on his suit. Anxious to get a view of the ground, he stretched his arms and legs out into a hard arch, then broke into a stable free-fall position.

Could this really be the location of more survivors—a place where people had managed to scratch out a living from the toxic earth over the past two and a half centuries?

A wind shear slammed him, and the sky went topsy-turvy.

At the first dazzling flash of lightning, habit took over, and he straightened his legs and drew his arms in against his body, pulling himself into a nosedive. The electrical storm appeared to be a safe distance away, but he wasn't taking any chances in this turbulence.

Wind whistled over his armor as he broke through the mattress of cold air pushing up on him. Two beacons blinked on the translucent subscreen of his heads-up display, or HUD.

Magnolia and Trey were still above him but closing fast. After Michael, Mags was the most experienced diver in the world, but Trey was learning fast.

Over the past few months, the two young men had bonded, becoming closer than ever, and after protesting long and loud, the captain had at last agreed to let his son dive on this risky mission.

Watching Les say goodbye to Trey before the dive had reminded Michael of how he used to feel when his father dived over a decade ago.

But this would be different. Trey was coming back to his family. And Michael was glad to have him along for the dive. Cricket was also an excellent addition to the roster, bringing an entirely new element to the team. Still in his nosedive, Michael looked up beyond his feet to the red nodes of the robot plummeting through the clouds.

Magnolia had also maneuvered into a "suicide dive," as they called it, and was coming up fast. A moment later, she was rocketing down beside Michael, the glow of her battery unit illuminating her slender but muscular form. She glanced over, and though he couldn't see her face behind the mirrored visor, he knew she was grinning.

"This isn't a race," he said over the comms.

"Nope, but I'm going to beat you to the ground anyway." She moved her helmet downward and continued past him, blasting through a cloud that enveloped her in darkness.

At ten thousand feet, going this speed, they were

only a minute from the ground. Soon, he would be able to see the surface and their target—a former prison, according to the database on *Discovery*.

Michael remembered, as a kid, reading about the search for alien life on other planets. Now he had an inkling of what scientists must have felt back then when looking for evidence of life in the distant stars.

In a way, the divers had found modern aliens in the mutant creatures on the surface, which would have fascinated scientists from the past. But who would have thought that finding humans would be a far greater challenge?

At eight thousand feet, Michael checked over his shoulder again. Trey had angled into a nosedive as well, his lanky form spearing through the darkness. To the west, a flash lit up the belly of a storm cloud.

With the electrical storm moving in, Team Raptor would have to work fast. It was one of two reasons they had dived rather than risk taking *Discovery* down to the surface. The second reason was simple: Michael didn't want anyone to know they were coming, and three divers were harder to detect than an airship.

And Hell Divers were also easier to replace.

At six thousand feet, a web of lightning forked across his dive zone. He stared at the shifting clouds, trying to determine the best route through the hidden storm. With almost zero time to react, he cut left and was greeted by another wind shear that sent him spinning.

He fought to bring the heavy robotic limb back to his side, and finally managed to center his mass into a stable nosedive. At five thousand feet, he checked the digital map on his HUD and saw they were off target for the drop zone.

He adjusted his trajectory, cutting through the sky diagonally, working his way back toward the area indicated on his minimap. The altimeter was quickly ticking down to four thousand feet.

The clouds seemed to lighten as he closed in on three thousand feet. He was now slicing through the clouds at over 160 miles per hour. A few beats later, he got his first glimpse of the surface, which looked like a desert of black dunes.

Using his chin, he bumped on his night-vision goggles. After a few blinks, his eyes adjusted to the green hue, and he realized that the surface wasn't a desert at all, but rather the ocean.

The divers sailed toward the landmass once known as Jamaica. *Ja-may-ka*, he thought, trying to picture what this place had once looked like.

Blue light came up on his left as Trey joined him. Magnolia moved in on his right flank.

At two thousand feet, the divers maneuvered from their nosedive into stable position with their backs to the sky, knees and elbows bent at ninety degrees. Trey nodded several times at the shoreline as they prepared to sail over.

Michael peered down, trying to see what had caught his attention. He didn't see anything at first but finally spotted several large craft that looked like beached whales—ships anchored in a bay.

No way those have been there since the war.

The shoreline vanished as the divers sailed over charred and blasted terrain. There wasn't much to look at in the final seconds of the dive—just another dead, colorless landscape that dampened any hope of finding people here.

At twelve hundred feet, Michael reached down to his thigh and pulled his pilot chute, holding it out for a second before releasing it to haul out the main canopy. The other divers did the same, their suspension lines coming taut, giving them the sensation of being yanked back up into the sky.

He grabbed his toggles, careful not to squeeze too hard with the robotic hand. He steered toward fields of black that really did seem like a desert now that the divers were farther inland.

The black landscape undulated with mounds and humps as far as he could see. For the first few seconds under canopy, he didn't see anything in the desolate landscape. Flitting his gaze from the ground to his HUD, he finally identified their target.

The concrete prison complex was tucked away in the bleak terrain of seemingly endless bare dirt, and he picked it out only by matching up his view with the target on his HUD. Then he saw the radiation levels that Cricket was already reporting from the ground.

Michael swallowed hard at the readings. The sensors on *Discovery* had placed the area somewhere between green and yellow, but as he sailed toward the drop zone, he saw that the rad levels were closer to yellow, which lowered the prospects of finding anyone alive.

And it was likely his fault. The nuke they dropped on Red Sphere had caused the increase in radiation levels, perhaps dooming any humans who had managed to survive under the ground all these years.

Michael focused back on the digital map. There was no sign of the road marked on the translucent subscreen of his HUD, and the only buildings aside from their target were eroded down to the foundations.

Another bad sign was the rusted girders of larger buildings on the horizon—more evidence that a nuclear blast had torn through this area, killing everything in its path.

Michael wondered whether this signal, dubious from the outset, would prove to be a waste of time. But it was too late to turn around now, with the ground rising up to meet his boots. Magnolia and Trey were right alongside him, nose to the slight sea breeze. When they were about to hit the square of dirt, they pulled on the toggles to slow their descent.

Michael performed a two-stage flare. Dust puffed up under his feet on impact with the solid ground. He ran out the momentum and came to a stop. They were about a mile from their target.

Cricket flew over, red hover nodes whirling. At some point, Michael had to get the thrusters on the back working so it could fly faster.

The divers quickly stowed their gear and their chutes, which they would reuse on the next dive.

Once they were packed away safely, Michael pulled out his laser rifle and scanned the landscape for any sign of hostile life. Nothing came back on infrared besides insects and what was perhaps a rat. The small animal ducked into a hole.

"Place looks pretty barren," Magnolia said, checking the battery of her laser weapon. Trey palmed a magazine into his assault rifle. With their weapons ready, they covered their battery units with leather flaps—a design of Rodger Mintel's that helped lessen the glow and avoid detection by Sirens.

Michael thought of his friend back at the Vanguard Islands. Rodger's diving days were on hold due to injuries he had received from the Cazadores, but X had put him to work on other vital projects.

"Let's go," Michael said.

Cricket took point, and the three divers moved out, fast and low. There was nothing out here, not even the barbed plants or glowing trees that had spread across much of the terrain in other locations.

Michael flashed hand signals directing the team toward a hill. Then he used his wrist computer to give Cricket orders. The robot hovered up the rocky slope to do a scan.

It came back clear, and Michael motioned for the divers to follow him to the top. They crouched, and he raised binoculars to his visor.

The prison's exterior walls were still in fairly good shape. Above them rose multiple guard towers, their glass windows broken out and the paint long since stripped off. Only one section of barbed-wire fencing remained on the perimeter; the rest lay in tangled heaps on the ground.

Michael considered radioing *Discovery* to see if its AI, Timothy Pepper, had detected any exhaust plumes from the defectors. But he quickly decided it was too great a risk, and the airship was likely too high to pick up anything on the surface.

"Radio silence, everyone," he said.

If there were hostiles down here, Michael didn't want to give them a heads-up that Team Raptor had landed. The three divers and their drone were on their own now, without aerial support from *Discovery*.

He gave the signal to advance, and the team moved down the other side of the hill, weapons shouldered and pointed at the prison. Cricket kept behind them, moving apace and scanning for signs of life.

The three divers fanned out into combat intervals as they closed the gap between the hill and the former prison's outer concrete walls.

Michael felt the terrain change underfoot and stopped to brush dirt off the cracked asphalt of a road. It led to the front of the compound and a closed steel door covered in rust and pocked with bullet holes.

He checked the digital map on his HUD and this time managed to match it with another road coming from the east—the same direction as the ocean.

Michael gave more hand signals.

The team continued to the outer wall of the prison while he went to check this second road. His gut told him the best evidence of life would be any tracks he might find.

So far, he didn't see any footprints, hoofprints, or vehicle tracks. Nothing to indicate that anything bigger than a bug lived in this toxic wasteland. Cricket wasn't coming back with anything conclusive, either.

Magnolia and Trey took up position against the wall. He gave a nod to their mirrored visors before running out into the open with Cricket hovering after him.

Keeping low, he didn't stop until he got to the intersection. A crooked pole jutted up beside the road, two and a half centuries after the nuclear blast that should have blown it down. The directional sign, however, was long since reduced to flakes of rust.

Michael checked the ground and quickly found something that could be recent. Bending down, he studied the dirt and dust that had covered what looked like tire tracks.

He looked east, back toward the bay where they had flown in over the ships. The vessels could have belonged to Cazador pirates under el Pulpo's command, but there was no record of their coming here—which was part of the reason he had decided to check it out. More likely, the tracks and the ships had been left by someone else.

But they could not possibly have been here when the bombs fell.

A chill ran through him when a whistle of the wind sounded eerily like a Siren's wail. The noise passed, and again the landscape fell into silence.

He scanned the road for heat signatures and found nothing but small creatures that lived in the toxic dirt. Lightning forked over the western horizon. He faced south, where explosions of light inside a towering mass of cumulus looked like bombs going off. The storm was moving toward their position.

He hurried back to the wall, where Trey waited.

"Where's Mags?" Michael whispered.

Trey started moving along the side of the wall to the next corner. Around the edge, Magnolia stood behind a hunk of broken wall, looking inside the former prison yard. She was frozen like a statue.

"I've got a reading," she said without turning.

Michael considered sending Cricket in but decided to keep the robot back for now. He brought up his rifle and took a position on the left side of the wall. Then he glanced inside the rectangular prison compound.

A guard tower rose in the middle of the facility, its empty window frames overlooking concrete courts covered with the dirt and dust of centuries. Several basketball hoops remained, but where there had once been nets, Michael spotted something that looked almost like flags.

Movement at the base of the poles flickered across his night vision, but he couldn't make it out. He switched to infrared to see dozens … no, *hundreds* of small creatures on the courts.

"What are we looking at?" Trey asked, moving next to Michael.

"Rats," Magnolia replied.

"But what are they doing?"

Michael brought his scope back up to his visor but still couldn't see much.

"Hold here," he said. "I'll check this out."

Michael moved through the opening in the wall, careful not to snag his suit on a curl of rebar sticking out of the broken concrete.

Keeping low, he ran toward the guard tower, not stopping until he got there. He inched around the corner for a better view of the courts. The sound of thousands of clicking teeth grew louder as he closed in.

For a moment, he felt the sensation of something watching him, and he froze, scanning the buildings in the rectangular compound. The few windows and doors were broken and leading into darkness, where eyes could watch his team from the shadows.

Michael spotted a promising entrance that might lead to the guts of the prison, and the source of the signal. He looked back to the hole in the wall, where Trey and Magnolia were still waiting.

His hands told the story without a word spoken. Then he took off running, past the concrete fields, not slowing his pace even when he saw what the rats were feasting on.

Heart pounding, Michael took cover inside an open door, trying to keep from panting. But that was nearly impossible, and he found himself sucking in air.

When he looked back out the door, he saw skeletal remains of several humans in the courtyard. The rats meant they had to be recent kills.

He tried to slow his heartbeat. *You've got this, Tin.* He had told himself the same thing when he got scared as a kid.

He turned down the hallway to peer into the inky darkness. Switching from infrared to night vision, he made out the old passage. Ceiling panels hung loose, and sections of tile floor had sheared off.

But what the hell was the cylinder on the floor?

He brought the scope up to his visor and zoomed in on what looked an awful lot like a cryo chamber. Several were scattered in the hallway, with skirts of glass surrounding the vats.

There was no use going inside or sending Cricket in. Someone, or something, had beat Team Raptor here.

But that still didn't make any sense. If these chambers were holding survivors for 250 years, it was one hell of a coincidence their being raided within days of the team's arrival. More puzzling still, what on earth were cryo chambers doing in a prison?

Michael pushed aside the questions and moved back out into the yard. He ran past the rats, not looking at the remains they were feeding on. This time, a new sound replaced the din of nails and teeth—a screech reminiscent of baby Sirens.

Before he could react, a wave of black swooped away from the broken windows of the guard tower and slammed into him. A pair of wings wrapped around his visor, and he peered out at the deformed eyes of a bat the size of his head.

He flailed his arms, screaming as the creatures

covered his body like an adhesive that he couldn't get off.

"Hold on, and don't move!" Magnolia yelled.

Michael froze, knowing just what she was about to do. He felt the pressure lighten on his natural arm as she used one of her two crescent blades to cut through the flesh of several bats.

The hissing made him flinch.

"Don't move!" she shouted again.

Cricket hovered over their heads, using a blowtorch to burn the bats off Michael's armor.

The screeching rose into a strident cacophony around him as she went to work with her blades, hacking the beasts from the air and off his body.

"Run!" she yelled.

Michael didn't miss a beat. As soon as he had his bearings, he took off for the wall, where Trey opened fire. Rounds cut the air.

"Hold your fire!" Michael shouted.

But Trey kept shooting burst after burst.

Michael glanced over his shoulder at the same entrance he had hidden inside earlier. Orange eyes glowed from the open doorway, and a figure covered in bones and hide stepped outside.

"Get down!" Magnolia shouted.

Michael hit the dirt as a flurry of bolts singed the air.

Cricket chirped and moved for cover as bullets and laser bolts lanced through the air all around it.

Over the crack of gunfire came the shrieks of the bats and rats. Even the rodents were abandoning their meal to escape the killer machines. Not one but three defectors emerged from the interior of the prison, the skins of their recent kills still dripping blood.

"Run!" Michael shouted.

A flurry of laser bolts shot outward. Magnolia helped Michael up, firing her rifle at the same time. He turned and got off several bolts. Return fire hit Cricket, blowing off a mechanical arm at the joint.

Michael tapped his wrist monitor, ordering the drone to retreat as he ran for the exit. Trey had already escaped behind the wall, providing an opening that Magnolia leaped through.

Bolts pounded the concrete as Michael followed. Some broke through, streaking into the ground. He hit the dirt and Cricket sailed overhead, another arm hanging loosely from its socket.

Getting to his knees, Michael turned over to see Trey lying prone.

"Get up!" he shouted. "We've got to get into the sky!"

Michael grabbed the young diver and pulled. Trey rolled over, revealing a simmering hole in the center of his visor and his crushed booster pack, hissing out pressurized helium.

"No …" Michael choked. He pulled on Trey again. "Get up!"

The limp body didn't respond to his screams.

Michael stared for a moment, barely able to move. Trey wasn't getting up now or ever. Nothing they could do would change that.

A hand grabbed Michael and yanked him down as

more bolts sizzled through the concrete wall, streaking away into the desert.

"He's gone!" Magnolia shouted. "We have to move!"

She pulled an EMP grenade from her vest and lobbed it over the wall. Grabbing Michael, she leaned her face shield against his until they clacked together.

"We have to get in the air as soon as those machines are down," she yelled. "You got that, Commander?"

He fought free of her grip, bending back down to Trey. They couldn't leave him for the machines to parade around wearing his bones and skin.

"No, we take him with us!"

Cricket hovered over Trey and tried to lift the body with his remaining arm, but the weight just snapped it out of socket. Then the robot crashed to the ground, red hover nodes suddenly winking off. It took Michael a moment for the realization to set in.

The EMP grenade had fried the damn systems.

Before Michael could react, Magnolia punched the booster in his pack, and the balloon exploded out of the canister, filling with helium and hauling him skyward.

"No-o-o!" Michael wailed, reaching down.

He kicked his feet to no avail, looking down at Trey's limp body and the machines that had killed him. They jerked in the prison yard and then lay still, their systems fried just like Cricket's.

Magnolia bent down beside the drone and punched the booster they had mounted to it. The balloon pulled the limp machine into the sky, and she followed right behind.

Clenching his jaw, Michael held back tears as he was pulled higher. Their maiden dive from *Discovery* had dropped Team Raptor into a trap, right into the hands of the defectors.

But the machines didn't have a ship to escape on, and as soon as Michael got back to *Discovery*, he would urge Les to drop a bomb directly on the prison. It would mean obliterating his son's body, but it had to be done. They couldn't risk leaving the machines behind to repair one another and return to their mission of exterminating humanity.

ONE

Xavier Rodriguez clove-hitched the fishing boat to a pier piling and pulled the rope tight. He felt refreshed this morning, and strong. Over the past few months, he had recovered from his injuries and put on muscle mass by taking long daily swims and working in the sun.

Nearing a half century of age, he found it ironic that he should be in the best shape of his adult life. But he wasn't complaining. Age, after all, was just a number.

With the rope secure, he reached back into the boat for his backpack and motioned for Miles to hop out. The dog hesitated at the gap between the gunwale and the pier. He was wary of the depths ever since a snake pulled him under back in Florida.

"It's okay, boy," X said. "Come on."

Miles backed up, then ran and leaped onto the pier. He slid a foot before turning and wagging his tail.

X took an apple out of the bag and bit into it as he slung the pack over his shoulders. The fruit here was unlike anything they ever had on the *Hive*, and with fish added to his diet, X had added twenty pounds of lean muscle to his scarred frame. But he still wasn't used to the sun and had to protect his skin with lotion he bought from an old woman on the trading-post rig.

He bit off another chunk of apple and tossed it to Miles, and they set off down the long pier, past other boats bobbing gently in the afternoon sun. A light breeze ruffled his button-down shirt and shorts. He had traded in his Hell Diver gear for the loose-fitting clothing and sandals.

It sure beat the leather outfit Imulah had given him to wear.

"You are a king now," the scribe had said. "You must dress like one."

"You want me to dress like a court jester," X had replied. "Fuck that."

If it were up to him, he would have worn what was left of his old Hell Diver armor, but he had stowed it away in a locker, where it waited should he ever need it again.

Gazing out at the balmy skies, it was hard to imagine, but he knew there would always be a need for Hell Divers—and, more specifically, him.

He finished the apple and rested his hand on the pommel of the captain's sword from the *Hive*. He thought of all those who had carried the iconic sword before him. Their sacrifices had allowed him and so many others to experience life as it was meant to be lived.

But before he could truly enjoy the sunshine

today, he had to get something out of the way that he hated: talking.

Today, it wasn't just a talk. He was practically giving a speech, and the gathering of boats told him a lot of people had come to hear him. If that weren't bad enough, he had a council meeting later in the afternoon.

X halted at the sight of dark canopies sailing across the western sky.

The new Hell Divers deployed their chutes as they broke through the cloud cover on their training runs. Normally, they jumped at night to better approximate conditions in the wastes, but today the rookies were doing it in the sunlight.

He paused to watch as several veterans led the new recruits and volunteers. Many of the greenhorns, surprisingly, had come from the Cazador military. Who would have thought so many of them wanted to join the "sky gods," as they referred to his people.

His heart thumped with longing to be up there again.

But he was just a retired, grumpy old man now, and he had business to attend to this afternoon. Miles nudged up against him as if to say, *Keep moving, boss.*

"We're late, I know," X said.

Miles wagged his tail, and his crystal-blue eyes seemed to brighten in the mat of graying fur. The dog was only about twelve years old, but even with the genetic modifications, he was aging and, like any other creature, starting to slow down.

He wasn't the only one. Despite feeling great, X couldn't run quite as fast or jump quite as far.

"You and I are starting to geeze, old buddy," X murmured.

He reached down, and Miles lapped at his scarred wrist. There was nothing in the world like the love of a dog. He couldn't bear the thought of losing Miles like so many others he had grown close to over the years.

The clank of boots sounded ahead, snapping him out of his melancholy train of thought.

Several militia guards patrolled the docks ahead, keeping an eye on the boats. Two more guards stood in front of the elevator that would take X to the top of the capitol oil rig, from which el Pulpo had ruled his people. It was now under the militia's command, but Cazadores still lived here—mostly accountants, scribes, and wealthier merchants who kept the economy humming.

X continued toward the platform. The militia guards there wore black armor, but instead of the batons they had carried on the *Hive*, they had automatic rifles.

Red airship symbols with a "V" through the middle marked their helmet crests and their chests.

"Coming down," one of soldiers said.

The cage at the top of the lift rattled its way down to the marina while X waited. He turned back to watch the divers in the western sky.

A moment later, the elevator clanked and the door opened. Freshly promoted Lieutenant Lauren

Sloan, leader of the militia, stood there with her arms folded across her armored chest, clearly annoyed.

"King Rodriguez," she said gruffly. "You're *late*."

"No, *you're* late," X replied. "I've been here thirty minutes waiting for a ride up." He grinned and looked at the two guards. "Right, fellas?"

They exchanged a glance, then nodded unconvincingly.

"Whatever you say, King Xavier," Sloan said. "Now, can we get going?"

"When you stop calling me 'King,' sure," X replied.

"You are indeed a king," boomed another voice.

X turned as another soldier jumped from a boat onto the dock. This man was no militia guard. The dark, brawny fighter lumbered across the platform, the shaft of a double-headed spear gripped in his massive hand.

"You earned the title, Xavier Rodriguez," Rhino said.

The warrior also had a new rank, now that X had bumped him up from lieutenant all the way to general. The promotion had not sat well with Vargas, Forge, and Moreto, the three colonels next in line.

Rhino stopped a few feet away and tapped one point of his spear on the dock. Then he pounded his metal armor, which still bore the insignia of the Barracudas.

"It was your destiny to become king," he said.

X snorted. He didn't want to be a king or a leader of any sort. He just wanted to retire and live out his days with Miles, a fishing pole, and a mug of shine.

The only rest you're going to get is when you're dead, old man.

"King, Commander, Immortal, Xavier, X—whatever you want to be called, we need to get going," Sloan said. She stepped aside to let X and Rhino into the elevator. Miles moved inside between X's legs.

The gate closed, and the cage started up toward the airship rooftop. The vantage gave the occupants a view of the latest construction project in the Vanguard Islands.

"They're almost ready," Sloan said of the oil rig that had been retrofitted with a single platform. Two ships were anchored alongside, their decks, busy with cranes and other construction equipment.

The rig was one of twenty-one inside the territory and was about to become one of the most important. There were other rigs that also played vital roles in the darkness outside the Vanguard Islands, including a prison rig known as the Shark's Cage, and several fuel outposts that X had just learned about. The Cazadores had a manned facility in Venezuela, called Bloodline, and another, the Iron Reef, in Belize. Both outposts held their precious fresh gasoline and diesel fuel, thanks to a fuel stabilizer that ITC chemical engineers had developed before the war.

"I could never do that," Rhino said, looking at another team of Hell Divers sailing over the water. Their canopies were slowly spiraling down toward the ship waiting for them in the limpid blue water.

One of the divers narrowly missed the deck and splashed into the sea. A rider on a Jet Ski sped over the waves to fish him out before he could get ensnared in his lines.

"It's great training," X said. "Something I would have loved to have when I was just a greenhorn. When I first started, we dove blind as bats through storms."

Several of the divers on the decks had stowed their chutes and used their boosters to pull them back into the sky. *Discovery*'s belly poked through the clouds, the open launch bay sucking them up like a whale swallowing fish.

Back from its third journey into the wastes, the airship had yet to find a single survivor. The *Hive*, too, had been searching for isolated pockets of humanity, with nothing to show for its twenty-plus missions.

The only dive with real promise of finding human life had ended with the death of Trey Mitchells, ambushed in Jamaica by a team of defectors. The machines had beaten Team Raptor to the signal, killing the survivors living in a bunker under the prison, and destroying the cryo chambers that housed other people and animals.

Discovery had dropped a low-yield nuclear bomb that ended the threat, but X knew that more teams of defectors were out there, hunting humans. The Cazador logbooks documented several encounters over the decades.

X's most important job now was to make sure the machines never found the Vanguard Islands, and, if they did, to protect both sky people and Cazadores.

The battle for the islands, plus Trey's death, had

brought the sky people's numbers down to just 402 people—even with the recent births, less than half their numbers of only a decade ago.

And this was why X hadn't authorized a single mission since Trey's death two months ago. It was time to protect and defend what they had, not risk more lives in an effort to save potential survivors in the wastes.

The elevator cage clanked to a stop, and Rhino opened the gate to the rooftop. A line of palm trees swayed in the wind. Evidence of the pitched battle for the capitol rig was everywhere X looked: bullet-holed palm trunks, and gouges in the dirt where damaged trees had been blasted over.

Rodger Mintel had put all the wood to good use, though, in the new shop that his parents, Cole and Bernie, had started on the trading-post rig. They were two of the first people X saw on the rooftop when he stepped out of the cage.

The Mintels had gathered with a group of mostly former residents of the *Hive*, but some Cazadores were here as well, including wealthy merchants, scribes, and farmers.

Several of the people Katrina liberated from the Cazador container ship before the battle had also joined them on the rooftop. Among those rescued were Victor and Ton, the two leaders who had joined the militia. They had gained some weight over the past few months, but both men were still thin under their armor—especially Ton, who couldn't speak after losing his tongue to the Cazadores.

Victor had started to pick up English quickly, and spoke for both himself and the older African warrior. Despite all their tragedy and hardships, they always greeted X with a smile.

"Hello, King Xavier," Victor called out with a thick accent. The middle-aged warrior pounded his armor proudly, happy to fight alongside the people that had saved him.

X raised a hand to both men as he walked toward the crowd.

It was easy to tell who was who. The sky people wore hats and covered their sensitive pale skin that had never seen the sun until recently. The Cazadores, by contrast, wore little clothing over their bronzed flesh, save for the merchants, who dressed strangely in fancy trousers and vests over white shirts. On their heads, they wore round white cloth hats, of the sort worn by sailors in archives of the old-world US Navy, but with small silver fins affixed to the crown.

X was doing his best to assimilate the two societies, and events like today's were perfect opportunities. The scars from the battle were deep, and reconciliation had been painful and slow. A lasting peace on the islands was going to take a lot of work. But according to his own people and most of the Cazadores, only one person could do it. And it meant X being king.

He cursed under his breath and strode over to the crowd with Sloan, Rhino, and Miles. Seeing the fresh mound in the graveyard caused him to slow. This one was different from the others. Though it had the same engraved wooden plaque, it was empty. Trey Mitchells was just ashes now.

X couldn't imagine how painful the order had been, but Les had executed it, dropping the bomb that obliterated both his son's remains and the machines that had killed him. That hard decision had proved he was the correct choice to replace Katrina DaVita as captain of the airship.

Les was in the crowd today, standing almost a full head taller than anyone around him. No wonder they called him "Giraffe." Most of the people were busy watching the Hell Divers floating back up into the airship as their training for the afternoon ended, but Les saw X approaching.

"King Xavier is here," he said in a commanding voice.

X shook his head as he walked. He would never get used to the ridiculous title. The crowd parted to let him through, treating him as if he were indeed the Immortal that Janga had promised them all in her prophecy. But he knew what he was: just a flawed man with a very high pain tolerance.

Familiar faces turned to watch him as he made his way toward the crew of *Discovery.* They waited in their white uniforms with the red embroidered Vanguard logo.

Absent was their AI, Timothy Pepper, piloting the ship for the Hell Divers so that its crew could be here for the ceremony.

Les gave a sharp salute, and X returned the old-world gesture. Lieutenant Ada Winslow, the new XO, also greeted him with a salute and a dimpled smile. Ensign Eevi Corey also raised her right hand sharply over her brow. The former militia investigator and Hell Diver was now an officer on *Discovery* while her husband, Alexander, remained a diver. Also present was Michael's girlfriend, Layla Brower, now seven months pregnant. She stood with a hand on her swollen belly.

She smiled warmly at X, and he smiled back as he walked to a platform built onto the hull of the ancient airship that served as the oil rig's roof. He gripped the warm metal rail in his calloused hands. Miles, sitting on his haunches, nudged up against him again.

John Wynn, the new militia sergeant, stepped over, holding a walkie-talkie to his ear. The former communications expert from the *Hive* was now Sloan's right-hand man.

"Almost ready, sir," Wynn said.

With his hand again on the pommel of his sword, X turned to face the crowd, taking a moment to scan the familiar and not-so-familiar faces for a moment.

"Today, we gather for a pivotal moment in our history," he announced after a pause. "But first, I'd like to take a moment to remember all those we have lost over the past few months, many of whom are buried here."

Les held his head up high, so far holding back the tears. His daughter, Phyl, and wife, Katherine, were at the front of the crowd, their pale faces looking up at X.

X waited a few more seconds in silent commemoration of those who had perished. His gaze flitted to

Katrina's grave. Now he too was holding back tears. He could feel them welling up, and he didn't especially give a shit whether anyone saw. Shedding a tear for Katrina was the least he could do to honor her memory.

"Captain DaVita made the ultimate sacrifice so we could have a home here," X said. He drew the sword and raised it skyward. "Today, we honor her and everyone else who gave their lives so that humanity could survive and thrive together, in the sun."

Wynn put the walkie-talkie back into a pouch and nodded—they were ready to proceed with the next part of the ceremony.

X lowered the sword and looked to the west. *Discovery*, with its belly full of Hell Divers, began its descent through the clouds.

It wasn't alone. To the south, another airship hovered below the clouds. The whir of turbofans carried in the still air. The hull seemed to pop out of the cloud cover.

Seeing the smooth beetle shape of the *Hive* brought with it a pang of nostalgia. X straightened his back, sticking out his chest with pride at the sight of the airship he had spent most of his life protecting.

At the helm was Chief Engineer Samson, who had also been doubling as captain for the past few months while they figured out what to do with the ancient airship.

X had finally made his decision a week ago. It was time to put her to rest.

The *Hive* was officially being decommissioned

and would be put down on the oil rig that el Pulpo had planned to turn into a prison for the sky people. Over the airship's curved top, a platform would be added for gardens and maybe even a tropical forest, like the one on the capitol rig.

Rodger Mintel had worked with Samson and the lead technician, Alfred, on the massive project that required multiple ships, cranes, and dozens of workers.

X nodded, and Rodger joined him on the platform.

"You sure this is going to work?" X murmured.

Rodger pushed his glasses up farther on his nose and grinned. "What are you going to do to me if it doesn't?"

"I'll tell Magnolia you soiled yourself on one of your dives," X said.

Rodger laughed deep and hard. "Try harder. She already knows, and still seems to like me."

"Okay, then I'll make you fight in the Sky Arena again. But this time, you won't be wearing any clothes."

"Oh," Rodger replied quietly, his smile vanishing. He looked out over the water. "This better work, then, and if it doesn't, I blame Alfred."

X clapped Rodger on the shoulder and turned back to watch the *Hive* descend slowly over the oil rig in the distance.

If all went according to plan, the inside quarters would be reclaimed by many of the sky people currently living in community housing on a rig guarded by militia soldiers. Soon, they would wake up every morning to a view that none of them would have dared dream of only a few months ago.

For 250 years, the airship had done her job, keeping the remnants of humanity alive above the storm clouds. Now she could finally rest in paradise.

But for X and many of the other survivors, there was no rest. They had to find a way to produce more food, strengthen the economy, keep the peace, *and* protect their borders. If that weren't enough, X hoped someday to continue the missions to the wastes, to find human survivors still out there—people who had no idea the Vanguard Islands existed. People the Hell Divers would save and bring here as humanity slowly rebuilt.

The whir of the turbofans rose to a high whine as they eased the airship's mass down onto its final resting place.

X glanced at Rodger.

"It'll hold," Rodger said without taking his eyes off the *Hive*.

Samson slowly lowered the belly over the top of the rig. Cranes swung over from the anchored ships to clamp on to the hull. Long steel arms filled the deck of one of the large ships. Eventually, they would support a platform that the cranes would place over the top of the airship.

The distant clanking and clanging began as workers started bolting the *Hive* to the rig's steel superstructure.

Rodger stepped closer to the railing. "*Please* hold," he said. "Please ..."

Wynn held his radio to his ear, listening to a transmission that X couldn't make out over the noises. A smile broke across his craggy face.

"Alfred confirms that the ship is secure on the pad, sir," he reported.

The crowd burst into applause, and X joined in the celebration. More clanking noises sounded as beams were bolted and welded into place. But that was just the first part of today's decommissioning.

X raised the sword again. "Today, with the official decommissioning of the *Hive*, we reflect on our past and look to the future," he said. "A new generation of Hell Divers has been training to ensure a safe future for Cazadores and sky people alike."

X nodded at Rhino and the other Cazadores who had helped, including Imulah. The scribe stood in the crowd with his hands clasped behind his back. He had proved to be a valuable asset in helping the sky people understand how the Cazador culture worked—a key factor in peacefully assimilating the two societies.

Others, too, had helped, including Sofia Walters, the happy widow of el Pulpo. The feisty raven-haired woman was one of a dozen rookie Hell Divers preparing to jump through the clear sky with the vets.

She wasn't the only Cazador to volunteer. Hector Rivera and Alberto Ortiz, two former soldiers who had served as mechanics on wasteland missions, had also joined up. They had assimilated well so far, thanks to Sofia's help.

Many new divers came from the ranks of the sky people. Ted Maturo and Arlo Wand were *Hive* mechanics who had received Samson's blessing now that the *Hive* was being decommissioned. Lena

Clayton, a young militia enforcer, had also stepped up. She was fast and agile, but without the snarky attitude that Magnolia had at her age.

"They dive so humanity survives!" X yelled.

A team of Hell Divers leaped out of the belly of *Discovery*. They pulled their chutes almost immediately and flew their canopies toward the roof of the *Hive*.

He spotted the red glow of Magnolia's and Michael's battery units. They were the first to land on the smooth top of the airship. The ceremonial dive was Michael's idea—a fitting tribute to the home that had kept one of the last bastions of humanity alive.

After all that had happened, X never thought he would see two dozen divers aloft at the same time. He smiled and swallowed to fight back the emotions.

But not everyone appeared to be impressed by the sight.

Across the water, Cazador civilians had gathered on the decks of other platforms to watch the ceremony. Unlike the people here and on the airship rooftop behind X, they didn't appear to be clapping or cheering. Many of them surely saw the Cazador Hell Divers as traitors.

It was another reminder of just how fragile the peace was at the Vanguard Islands. The job he had inherited was, in some ways, even more difficult than his former job of keeping the airships in the sky.

X looked past the *Hive* and the other rigs to the darkness beyond. It wasn't just the tensions of two vastly different societies learning to live together that had him worried. Far more concerning were the threats that lurked behind that swirling black wall.

The biggest threat to humanity wasn't other humans or even mutant monsters—it was machines.

TWO

Two hours after the decommissioning ceremony for the *Hive*, Magnolia was taking the elevator to the top deck of the capitol rig with Rodger. She was more nervous about the council meeting than about the low-altitude dive.

As the cage rattled upward, she looked out at the workers securing the *Hive* onto the rig in the distance. From here, in their new yellow jumpsuits, they looked like bees at work on a comb.

All the banging and construction noise had attracted a pod of spinner dolphins, which were jumping playfully and doing barrel rolls in the air.

She smiled, soaking in the magnificence of nature that she had never known during her life in the air. This place was a miracle that humans might not deserve after what they had done to the planet.

A dolphin leaped out of the water, spinning on its axis, and splashed back down.

"Pretty awesome, right?" Rodger said. But he

wasn't paying attention to the dolphins. His eyes were on the second phase of construction.

"Those cranes are securing vertical beams to support the platforms we're adding," he said. "In time, the people living there will be able to open hatches to balconies for a view of the water, and soon we'll add an entire new platform above the curved roof, for a garden and rain catchment system."

Magnolia leaned in to give him a kiss on the cheek.

"Nice work, Rodgeman," she said. "Color me impressed."

"Color you … *what?*" Rodger tilted his head, then chuckled.

Magnolia realized he was checking her out. "It's a phrase from the Old World, you know?"

"Not that one, but I do like the hair."

Magnolia pulled on a strand to look at the new color. A major change from the old blue and purple, the fiery red streaks matched her new Hell Divers battery unit.

"I wonder what that's about," Rodger said.

Across the rooftop, near the grove of trees, a small group lingered. X, with Miles beside him, stood in the shade with Rhino, Michael, Layla, and Les, listening to Ada. The young XO used her hands to emphasize whatever she was saying.

X saw them over Ada's shoulder and waved for them to join the group, moving to the stairwell hatch as they approached. Miles's tail whipped when he saw Magnolia.

"Hey, buddy," she called out.

Imulah walked up the interior stairwell and stepped through the open hatch. Seeing Magnolia, he moved his hand behind his back. She still hadn't apologized for sticking a knife through his palm, but he hadn't exactly apologized for helping imprison her, either.

The tension between them was still palpable, and months after the battle for the islands ended, there were still plenty of problems from fresh wounds, both real and imagined. As a member of the new council, she was about to hear many of them.

"Meeting starts soon," Imulah said. "Everyone, please follow me."

They took the stairs down through the residential levels, one of which had served as Magnolia's prison.

Sofia was waiting outside the large chamber doors on the fifth floor. She too had changed out of her Hell Diver jumpsuit, and wore a thin white cotton dress that clung to her slender frame. She was in her late twenties—older than Magnolia had thought, though her features showed no signs of aging. With mild annoyance, Magnolia thought of the crow's-feet that she herself was getting now that her skin had been exposed to the sun.

"What a rush, Mags!" Sofia said with dimpled grin. "I can't wait for the next dive."

"They aren't all fun like that," Rodger said.

Sofia flashed a seductive smile at Rhino.

Magnolia had found a partner in Rodger, although they were taking it much slower than the two Cazadores, who seemed to disappear anytime they managed to find a few minutes.

X stopped outside the large metal doors engraved with an octopus. A militia soldier and a Cazador soldier, both armed with swords, stood guard outside the chamber. Magnolia didn't like it, but it was part of the peace deal X had negotiated with Cazador leadership. The warriors would retain their weapons if they swore allegiance and promised to keep the peace.

"Let's go," X said to Rhino. "I want to get out on the water before we lose the sun."

Rhino pushed open the double doors to a long room with high ceilings and the platform where el Pulpo had once held court.

Miles trotted ahead of X and up the stairs to the platform, where he sat in front of the throne. The dog knew where he wanted to be.

The rest of the council filed down an aisle past a wooden bench where three scribes sat waiting to record the meeting. A pleasant smell of freshly hewn wood was almost as potent as that of the fruit trees on the sun deck above.

"Again, got to say I'm impressed," Magnolia said quietly.

Rodger smiled proudly. "I must confess, my dad did most of the finish work on the table while I helped Samson prepare the rig to receive the *Hive*."

The chief engineer sat at the table now, using a handkerchief to mop the sweat from his forehead. Along with Magnolia, Les, and X, he was one of the four sky people on the eight-person council.

They all sat but X, who remained standing on the throne platform.

Colonel Carmela Moreto, a fifty-year-old Cazador warrior, sat across from Magnolia, next to an even older soldier, General Diego Santiago. After the battle, both had kept their rank by swearing loyalty to X and promising to help avoid more bloodshed.

Magnolia didn't trust Santiago. She scrutinized him as she walked to her seat. A thick white beard clung to his lantern jaw but failed to mask the scar carving a diagonal line across his weathered face.

She didn't trust Carmela, either. The older woman wore a turquoise necklace and copper wrist guards engraved with sharks. The feathers of the cockatoo on her shoulder matched her braided white hair. The annoying bird kept cackling and looking at Magnolia.

"Shhhhh," Carmela said. "¡Silencio, Kotchee!"

The cockatoo stopped squawking but continued eyeing Magnolia with eyes as black as coal.

I fucking hate birds.

Magnolia wasn't the only one. Miles didn't seem to like Kotchee, either, probably seeing it as a miniature version of the vultures that nearly killed him at the Turks and Caicos Islands.

On the platform, X had pulled out a tablet from his backpack and was tapping the screen. "Piece of shit," he grumbled.

The glow from Timothy Pepper's hologram spread across the dimly lit room.

"There we go," X said.

Several latecomers came through the open doors as the AI walked onto the platform. A group of six merchants entered, all of them men, and all of them dressed in silly finery. They took off their sailor hats, revealing lighter skin than most Cazadores, who worked in the sun as laborers or warriors. These men lived a life of ease in the shade.

Their leader, Tomás Mata, maybe fifty years old, with a full head of wheat-colored hair, walked down the aisle while the other merchants took seats in the gallery. With his own fleet of trawlers, the wealthy businessman owned a chunk of the most profitable business aside from war: fishing.

A group of Hell Divers, including the new Cazador recruits, took seats in the gallery. Two more Cazadores followed—officers, with their black capes and shiny swords. Armored soldiers with red capes, the symbol of the legendary Praetorian Guard, accompanied the two men.

Magnolia recognized them as they walked down the center aisle. Colonel Ken Forge and Colonel Pablo Vargas were both part of the infamous Black Order of Octopus Lords, which had served under el Pulpo.

The order also included General Santiago, General Rhino, and Colonel Moreto. Everyone else above the rank of lieutenant had been killed in the battle for the Metal Islands, except for one Cazador colonel who had refused to acknowledge X as the rightful ruler. Rhino had executed the man two days after the battle ended, tossing his body to the order's monstrous namesakes that lurked in the depths.

General Rhino continued to prove his loyalty to King Xavier and played a vital role in keeping any underground rebellions from getting traction. But it was hard to believe that somewhere among the twenty-one rigs plus the outposts, Cazadores weren't planning an attack.

Hell, the militia had had a difficult enough time putting out rebellions on the *Hive*. Magnolia wasn't sure how they could ever stop one here.

The double doors clanked shut, and X cleared his throat.

"For those of you who don't know, this is our AI, Timothy," he said.

The Cazadores all looked skeptically at the hologram. They had done their best to run the islands with as little technology from the former world as possible, even radios, and had certainly never dealt with an AI.

"I'm at the council's—and your—disposal, King Xavier," Timothy said.

X sighed loud enough that Magnolia heard it. He clearly hated the title, and she found it a little corny, but according to Imulah, the Cazador tradition had to continue.

"Tomás is first on the agenda," X said.

The merchant stood and bowed slightly. He spoke nearly perfect English. "I'm pleased to announce this was a very good week for fishing. Even with our devastated fleet, we should have an adequate supply to feed our new friends."

"And the farms?" the king asked.

Another merchant stood up in the gallery. He was bald, with a gray beard, and spoke Spanish.

"He says we need rain," Imulah said. "Or we will have to start using recycled drinking water on the crops."

"Then we shall hope for rain," X said. He looked down at General Santiago and gestured for the old warrior to speak.

Santiago spoke quickly in his deep, gruff voice while Imulah translated as fast as he could.

"General Santiago requests the Sky Arena be opened immediately," he said. "Our people thirst for blood, and they are growing impatient with these new laws."

"These new laws are meant to keep humanity alive," Magnolia reminded the old general. "We all have suffered great losses, and reopening the Sky Arena would reduce our numbers even more."

Imulah explained her words to Santiago, who glared back at her. He clearly didn't appreciate the opinion of any woman on the council who wasn't Carmela.

That was fine. Magnolia didn't appreciate sitting on a council with a man who had served in the army of a sadistic cannibal.

"You kill each other so often, it's amazing there are any of you left," Samson said to back up Magnolia.

"Perhaps there is a way to have fighting that does not result in death," Les added.

Santiago's gaze flitted to the tall, fair captain as Imulah continued to translate.

"Would you consider fights that do not end in the taking of life?" X asked. "I really don't have a problem if you want to beat each other silly, but cutting off heads and dismembering one another seems a bit counterproductive at this point."

"That would go against our customs," Imulah said, answering for Santiago.

"The fight is always to the death," Rhino added.

"Maybe it's time to end your barbaric tradition," Sofia said from the gallery. "Like eating people. We've stopped that. Don't forget where you came from, now that we're free."

Rhino clenched his jaw but did not respond. He was having a harder time than Sofia in letting go of the warrior mentality learned over a lifetime of fighting.

When Imulah explained what the other Cazadores had said, the old general snorted, making his nose ring quiver. He stood up from his chair and spoke, looking at X.

Carmela also joined in, and her bird made a clucking sound that so grated on Magnolia's nerves, she considered taking out a blade and cutting the damn thing's head off.

"General Santiago says that if we want to kill each other, we should have that option, King Xavier," Imulah said. "And Colonel Moreto agrees. She says we aren't asking *your* people to fight."

"That is true," Samson said.

Magnolia nudged him in the gut with her elbow, earning an angry glare from the old engineer.

"What?" he said. "If they want to kill each other, who are we to stop them?"

X folded his arms over his open white shirt. "Perhaps, before jumping into this topic, I should have brought up the report Lieutenant Winslow gave me earlier."

The room fell silent.

"The crew of *Discovery* has detected a radio signal like the one Team Raptor discovered in Jamaica," X said after the pause. "However, there is one major difference."

This was what Ada had been talking to them about outside, Magnolia realized.

"There is also a message with the signal," X said. "From survivors who need our help."

Carmela folded her hands together, copper wrist guards clanking, while Imulah interpreted. She replied, and Santiago nodded.

"There is a reason we use radio jammers and have warned you not to send out messages," Imulah said. "The metal gods have never found these islands, because we are a grain of sand in a desert, thanks to the storms forming a barrier around our home—and thanks to the great lengths we have gone to in not using old-world technology."

Carmela spoke again, and this time both Colonel Vargas and Colonel Forge stood up in the audience, pounding their chests.

Imulah waited for the noise to subside. "Colonel Moreto said that if the metal gods are there, we should send out warriors to crush them."

Kotchee let out a cackle, as if in agreement.

"Could you please tell that baby buzzard to shut its beak?" X said.

Imulah hesitated.

"On second thought, don't," X said.

Carmela glared at X, clearly sensing that he was insulting her bird. Magnolia couldn't help but smirk.

"We crush," Santiago said in broken English. He smacked his open palm with his fist. "Crush metal gods."

Vargas and Forge again pounded their chests. Magnolia turned to look at them. Both were middle-aged and had clearly seen their share of fighting over the years. Forge had short brown hair the color of his skin, and even darker, unwavering eyes. He was older than Colonel Vargas, but age had been kinder to Forge, whereas Vargas's protruding dark eyes and scarred features made him look half-mad and decades older.

"Metal gods?" X said. "I appreciate your eagerness, General, but the defectors are killing-machines, not mere cans to crush."

Imulah started to translate but hesitated again.

"If I could cut in," Magnolia said.

Santiago glowered at her, but she wasn't intimidated. She had survived el Pulpo, and the old warhorse was nothing compared to that mean, ugly son of a bitch.

"The most important thing we have to do right

now is keep our home safe," Magnolia said, "and that means removing the threat of the defectors. Not fighting amongst ourselves over stupid shit like who can lop off someone's head in the Sky Arena would be a good start."

The old general raised a gray hedge of brow at Carmela, who gave a half nod after Imulah had relayed Magnolia's words. If the Cazadores had gone to such lengths as creating radio jammers to keep the location of the islands secret, it was clear enough that they feared the defectors.

Also, Magnolia had read their logbooks about several encounters they'd had with the machines over the decades. Encounters that did not end well for the Cazador warriors. Perhaps having a mutual enemy was a good thing, she thought. It might bring the two societies together in a way that nothing else could.

"I volunteer to check out that signal," she said.

X thought about it and shook his head. "Not yet, Mags. I need you here."

"We should send a warship," Rhino suggested. "We can spare one of the three currently patrolling the barriers. Two others are undergoing repairs, and there is still our training ship, *Elysium*."

X seemed to prefer this idea to Magnolia's.

"Why not send *Discovery* out again?" she asked.

"Because that leaves us vulnerable, and because we have already lost too many souls," X said. "I will not risk more if—"

"We're already vulnerable," Michael interrupted.

He stood in the audience. The other Hell Divers rose as one, a wall of red suits around the commander.

Magnolia saw many fresh faces in the group. She had helped train them all, and while some were ready for a real dive, most were still rookies like Ted, Lena, and Arlo.

Arlo Wand showed the most promise of all the new divers. But the well-built kid with dark eyes didn't just have long curly blond locks hanging over his shoulder. He had a chip on it and was a little too eager to prove himself.

"If we hope to defeat the defectors and keep our home safe, we need forces in the air and on the sea," Michael said. "If the machines are lying in wait at the location of this signal, then I say we send as much firepower as we can spare and destroy them before they can destroy us."

"He's right," Magnolia added. "We can't be on the defensive forever and hope this place stays a secret. If you and I found it, then the machines can, too."

Her words led to a moment of silence.

Michael raised his robotic arm. "I'll go, too."

Layla looked shocked at his suggestion. X seemed caught off guard, too. He started pacing, his finger rubbing the gray stubble on his square jaw.

Magnolia suspected that his reluctance to send out *Discovery* wasn't just because he didn't want to send out his friends and family. It was because he wanted to go and couldn't.

X was stuck here, whether he liked it or not.

Without his leadership and reputation, Magnolia had a bad feeling the Cazadores and sky people would tear each other apart.

* * * * *

"You want to go back out there after what happened to Trey?" Layla asked. Her back was to Michael as she folded their freshly dried clothing.

He put a hand on her shoulder. "I'll be careful if I do."

Layla pulled away and walked over to the open window in their small quarters. She brushed her face against her shoulder to wipe away a tear. Then she put a hand on her belly and looked out over the ocean.

Michael followed her and gently put his hand over hers. It was the most glorious feeling, to know that the life inside her was part of him. The little guy was getting more active by the day.

"I can't believe you're even considering this," Layla said.

"I want to stay here with you and Bray, but you and Bray are why I have to go."

The breeze was up this afternoon, creating whitecaps across water as clear as a sapphire. Michael sometimes found her here, just staring, lost in her thoughts.

Katrina's death had hit both of them hard, but she and Layla had been especially close.

"Everything's going to be okay," Michael said. "Katrina wanted us to live out our lives here and raise our family. That's why she did what she did with the USS *Zion*."

Layla lowered her head. "I know," she said. "I just miss her. She never got to experience being a mom, and I know she wanted that with Xavier at one point."

Michael had never heard this, but it didn't surprise him. Katrina had always loved X.

"She never got to see all this," Layla added. "The way the world was meant to be."

Michael gave a quiet sigh. "A lot of people gave their lives so that we could have a second chance."

"That's what I'm worried about, Michael. That *you'll* be next. Trey didn't get his second chance."

The guilt Michael felt about Jamaica gnawed at him. "If I end up going, everything I do will be with you and Bray in mind."

She clutched him tight. "You promise?"

He gently took her hand and put her palm over his chest.

"Maybe we should make this official," he said.

"Official?"

He shrugged. "You know, like, get married."

"Well, *that's* romantic."

"Sorry, but …"

"It's fine," she said. "I don't love you because of your charm. You are the guy who took me on a 'date' to the weapons operation room or whatever it's called, back when *Discovery* was *Deliverance*."

He laughed. "Yeah, but that was fun, right?"

"It's very possible Bray was conceived there."

Michael leaned down in front of her stomach. "You hear that, little guy? You were conceived in the weapons operation center, which means you're going to grow up to be a badass!"

Layla shook her head but had to laugh. She pulled Michael up straight, and he kissed her again.

"I'd better get to the library," he said. "X is going over the Cazador maps."

"Okay, I'll just stay here and do …" Layla looked at the pile of unfolded clothing. "House stuff, I guess. Never thought I'd say that."

"I'll make it up to you when I get back tonight. How does dinner in the hall and then stargazing sound?"

Layla shrugged a shoulder and grinned. "Maybe you are a romantic after all," she said.

"Don't get your hopes up."

Michael chuckled and left their small quarters and went to the great hall where the council chamber was located. The Cazadores had turned this fortress into an impressive place, but it lacked the technology the airships had.

Part of the reason, Michael suspected, was that they didn't need to fix things with the same sense of urgency. Their lives didn't depend on staying in the sky, and they had far more access to food sources here on the sea.

The bigger part, though, had to do with keeping this place a secret. So far, their lack of tech had kept them safe from the machines and everyone but his people.

Vaulted ceilings rose above Michael as he crossed the

tile floor. A militia soldier and a Cazador soldier stood sentry beside the steel doors of the council chamber.

Michael walked down a passage lined with paintings of Cazador warriors. The men, and a few women, were dressed in armor and holding their weapons of choice.

General Santiago was there, gripping an axe with a blade the size of his head. Dozens of other generals, living and dead, seemed to watch the young commander's progress, assessing his worthiness. But one section of wall was blank—the picture of el Pulpo, removed by the sky people.

Soon, there would be a picture of the man who killed him—assuming someone could get X to stand still long enough for a portrait. So far, he had been "too busy."

Sconces with burning candles guided the way to the study. Michael passed several doors, one of them open to reveal an armory turned museum. Inside were glass cases full of swords, spears, bows, and old-world rifles that looked like antiques. On the walls hung suits of armor, helmets, and chain mail.

Around the next corner, he spotted the open doors to the study, or what his people called a library. The long room was far more than a library, though. Above the level furnished with hundreds of bookshelves was a meeting area with round wooden tables and several offices.

He had spent many hours in this place, going over records of the Cazadores' travels, most of which had been limited to the Caribbean and the eastern coasts of the Americas. Only a few warriors had led expeditions across the Atlantic Ocean to West Africa or Europe. None had returned.

The library's few patrons sat at tables, reading under lamps with orange shades. At the front desk sat Jason Matthis, the former librarian on the *Hive*, who had taken a beating from the militia during the dark days under the tyrant Leon Jordan.

The door shut behind Michael with a click, and Jason looked up with cloudy eyes.

"Who's there?" he asked.

"Michael Everhart, sir."

Jason rose from his seat and turned toward the voice. "So good to hear your voice, Commander. King Xavier is expecting you."

"Thank you, Jason. It's good to see you, too." Michael walked down the rows of tables and stacks. The place had an academic vibe that didn't really fit the Cazadores' Spartan warrior culture, though the paintings on the walls helped bridge the gap—scenes of battles in the Sky Arena, on the open seas against mutant sharks and giant serpents, and on the mainland with Sirens and killer birds.

A voice called out from the balcony above. "Come on, kid," X said. "I still haven't gotten my daily swim in."

Michael took the stairs two at a time up to the second level. X motioned him over to a large rectangular table draped with maps. Magnolia stood with her arms folded across her purple jacket.

Les was also here, in uniform. "Commander," he said.

"Captain, how are you?"

"Worried," Les replied.

X leaned with his palms on the table, looking down at the maps and then up at Michael. The concern in his gaze told Michael there was more to this meeting than simply discussing the SOS signal and the message, which he still hadn't heard.

"We discovered something else after the council meeting," Les said.

"This stays between us," X said. "Got it? No one in this room says a word."

Michael, Magnolia, and Les all nodded.

At a sudden movement under the table, Michael backed away. Miles stuck his head out to see what was going on.

"You, too, buddy," X said. "Not even a growl."

The dog whipped its tail and went back under the table.

X spread out a map. It showed eastern South America and a dead old-world city called Rio de Janeiro, where the signal originated.

Then he flattened a rolled-up square of paper on the table. It was a Cazador expedition log.

"What's it say?" he asked.

"It's a record," X replied. "The Cazadores have been to this city before. Ten years ago."

"And did they find anyone?"

"We don't know."

Michael scanned the log, realizing it was incomplete. "They never came back, did they?"

X shook his head. "Nope."

"This message could be a trap from the defectors," Les said. "The same one that got my son killed."

The words stung Michael's ears. He glanced at the captain, then looked away. Michael knew that Les blamed himself, but he also put some of the blame on Michael, who had led the mission on the ground.

"It could be a trap, yes," said X. "But this time we know for a fact that there are survivors. We heard their voices before you got here."

Les placed an electronic tablet on the table. "The original audio is in Portuguese, but Timothy has translated in his own voice."

Michael stepped closer and bent down to listen as Les touched the screen.

"We have women and children. Please, if you're out there, we need help. Our water system is failing, and our last crop yielded only half the normal rations. We are slowly starving, and if we can't fix our water system, we will die."

Les let it play twice before hitting the off button.

"This is what we've been waiting for," Michael said. "*Real* survivors that need our help."

"We also know that the Cazadores have encountered defectors before," X said, "and if they never came back from this area, those machines could be why. It's possible the machines are already there, and thanks to our signal, now they know the survivors' location."

"That's why I'm requesting to take *Discovery*, sir," Les said. "We have to eradicate the threat before they also find us."

Everyone stared at Les in surprise.

"If there are survivors, I'll bring them back here," Les said. "And if there are defectors, I want to be the one to destroy them."

"*Discovery* is grounded, Captain," X replied.

"Please, X," Les said. "Don't make me beg. Let me take the airship and avenge my son."

"I'll think on it," X said. "In the meantime, Commander Everhart, get your divers ready."

"For what?" Michael asked.

"We're doing another training run, but this time it's going to be outside the barriers, in the storms."

THREE

Captain Les Mitchells returned to his quarters on the capitol oil rig right after the council meeting. He wanted to see his daughter and wife before heading back up to the skies. The new training mission would take the greenhorn divers into storm clouds for the first time.

After his son's death, Les had considered temporarily stepping down from captain to spend more time with his wife and daughter.

"We can find someone else," X had said. "Take time to grieve your boy."

In the end, though, Les decided that his duty was not just to his family, but to all humankind. And knowing that the defectors were out there and programmed to obliterate all human life made the decision an easy one.

Now was not the time to grieve. Now was the time to go on the offensive and fight.

"Daddy!" Phyl called out as he shut the door. She ran over from the table facing the sliding door to their balcony. Katherine was there, too, but she did not get up to greet her husband.

Les bent down to hug his daughter. He averted his gaze from the open door to the quarters she had shared with Trey.

Katherine got up from the table, but instead of coming over to greet him, she moved into the small kitchen area.

"Are you hungry, Daddy?" Phyl asked. "We're making dinner."

"Starved," Les lied. "It takes a lot to feed a giraffe."

Phyl grinned, and he followed her past the other bedroom and the tiny bathroom, into the space that served as both kitchen and living room.

Katherine had her back turned to him and was chopping up carrots on a plastic board.

"What are we having?" Les asked.

"Fish chowder," Phyl said enthusiastically. "Are you still taking me fishing later tonight? That's when they bite the best, right?"

Les could have kicked himself, remembering his promise. The smile on his young daughter's face quickly turned to a frown when she sensed he had forgotten.

"I can't tonight," he said. "I'm sorry, but I will take you soon, I promise."

Katherine looked over her shoulder and raised a brow at him before turning back to finish cutting the vegetables.

I know, I know. I can't keep breaking promises.

He had already broken the most important

promise in their twenty years of marriage, by failing to bring Trey home alive—or at all.

He swallowed hard at the image that kept popping up in his mind's eye, of the flash and then the mushroom cloud from the bomb that incinerated his son's body. It had destroyed the defectors that killed Trey, but that was small consolation. Bottom line: he had not been there on the ground to save his son.

His wife must have sensed his moment of weakness, and put the knife down, but she stopped shy of coming over to give him what he needed most: a sign of love. A kiss, a hug, a soothing murmur … *Anything.*

He longed to have her support again, but he didn't blame her for the resentment in her gaze. He had failed his son and his entire family.

Nothing he could do would bring Trey back, but he would be damned if he didn't track down and eliminate the defectors before they could destroy what was left of his world.

Leaving his wife and daughter to finish making dinner, he went out to the balcony. When they had first moved in here, he would sit with his family for hours, looking out over the water and watching the sun rise and set each day.

But tonight, he hardly even looked at the tangerine glow in the west. Instead, he set his backpack down and fished out his tablet. Sitting on a plastic chair, he touched the screen and pulled up the data he had on Rio de Janeiro.

The beachfront city was vast and, according to records, had not sustained a direct nuclear hit during the war. The nuke had instead hit the ocean, creating a massive tsunami that washed away much of the city, but it had also crushed the reactors of a power plant there, causing a meltdown.

The logs from a Cazador scouting mission showed radiation readings of a yellow zone, but the team that was eventually deployed never came back to give a firsthand report.

Les put in earbuds and clicked the audio file. He had already listened several times but wanted to hear it again. Timothy's clear, soothing voice filled his ears, translating the SOS.

A finger tapped his shoulder, and he turned to find Phyl, beaming at him and holding a bowl of soup. He took out his headphones and smiled at her. Katherine was already sitting at the table.

"Dinner, Daddy," Phyl said.

He had to smile. "Okay, please set it down for me on the table. I'll be right there."

She set the bowl down at his spot as he gathered up his things. He left the sliding door open so they could eat in the cool breeze.

His wife avoided his gaze when he sat, and he avoided looking at the empty spot where Trey had sat. His family had changed so much in a few short months.

Les swallowed, but the lump in his throat remained. He looked out over the water, watching the sunset fade to a purple bruise over the horizon.

Trey had hardly gotten to enjoy the sunshine and the water.

A tear glazed his eye, and he discreetly turned and wiped it away while pretending to scratch his nose. His family didn't need to see him like this. He had to be strong.

He held out his hands for his wife and daughter to take. They always gave thanks for their food, but tonight Les had something to add to the usual blessing.

Katherine took his hand, but her grip was limp. He squeezed her hand and Phyl's while thinking of the survivors out there starving in the darkness.

"Tonight, we give thanks for being together in this place where we have food, water, shelter, and safety," Les said. "And we thank Trey for giving his life so that we and others can have these things."

Katherine squeezed back. It was a start, but he had a lot to do to help his wife heal. He let go of their hands and picked up his spoon.

"What were you listening to out there?" Katherine asked.

"An SOS from survivors," he replied.

Phyl tilted her head slightly. "What's SOS?"

"A message from people asking for our help."

"There are more people out there?" Katherine asked.

Les nodded. "We mustn't tell anyone, though, okay?"

Phyl no longer seemed interested in her meal. She had too many questions.

"Eat, kiddo," Les said. "After dinner, we'll go fishing for an hour before I have to go back to the sky."

* * * * *

At midnight, two dozen newly minted Hell Divers huddled outside the fence of tropical trees on the rooftop of the capitol oil rig. The growing canopy, still a bit tattered from the hail of gunfire during the battle with the airships, swayed in the light breeze.

X stood behind a bullet-scarred coco palm, watching as they waited for their ride into the sky. None of the new divers had been outside the barriers of the Vanguard Islands, and he knew they could never be truly ready for what awaited them.

But others were ready. Silhouetted against the rising moon, four veterans stood in front of the greenhorns. Michael and Magnolia were flanked by Edgar Cervantes and Alexander Corey, two of the three surviving members of the USS *Zion* team. Alexander's wife, Eevi, had also lived through the *Zion*'s epic sea battle but was now an ensign on *Discovery*.

X moved closer for a better look at the four veterans who had taken the leadership mantle of Teams Raptor, Angel, Phoenix, and Wolf. They all looked skyward for the airship being piloted by Timothy.

"Captain on deck!" someone shouted.

Les ran out in uniform, apologizing for being late. If he had his way, he would take them all on a machine-hunting mission. But X knew from experience that a mission of revenge, especially with so many rookie divers, was a sure recipe for mistakes—and unnecessary deaths.

He knew because he had seen it happen many times before.

If anyone was going, it would be the vets and perhaps a small handful of the best new divers. Tonight, X would learn who the standouts among the greenhorns were. They weren't diving through the fluffy white clouds of the Vanguard Islands, either. They would be tested in a way they have never been tested before.

X had approved the mission even though he wasn't sure they were ready, because he had no choice. The only way to get them ready was to throw them in the meat grinder—the same thing the Cazadores did by sending their trainees to an island they called the proving grounds.

The whir of the airship made a gradual crescendo, and he could make out a red light blinking in the sea of stars. X remained in the shadows, unseen by the divers and captain. He would've liked to be out there giving them all a talk before this important dive, but that was no longer his role and would undercut Michael and the other commanders.

Still, X wanted more than anything to join them. Just thinking of torpedoing through the clouds warmed his blood.

A voice spun him about to face the darkness of the forest. His sword flashed.

"Easy, man," said a familiar voice. "I got enough scars."

X lowered the blade but didn't sheathe it as the figure approached, hands up. The man stepped into the drip of moonlight, revealing a bearded face, glasses, and a grin.

"Rodger," X said. "What are you doing here?"

"Watching, like you. I always worry about Mags."

X sheathed the sword and turned back as the airship lowered over the forest. *Discovery* wasn't even a tenth the size of the airship that the Cazadores had mounted atop an oil rig and turned into the Sky Arena and gardens, but it still made the ground tremble when its feet touched down on the dirt pad.

The launch-bay doors hissed open, and a ramp extended downward. Michael gestured with his robotic arm for the divers to follow him inside.

X resisted a powerful urge to move, as if a force were tugging him to join the divers and plummet through the unending chaos of the storms.

"I hope they all make it back," he said.

X unsheathed his sword again, this time handing it to Rodger.

"Hold this for me," he said.

Rodger took the sword and looked at it, clearly at a loss what to do with it.

"X ... what are you doing?"

"Going where I belong. Tell Miles to hold down the fort while I'm gone," he said with a grin. "He's sleeping in my quarters."

"Wait …" Rodger reached out, but X was already running toward the retracting boarding ramp.

"Hold up!" X yelled.

The turbofans kicked up a cloud of dirt that formed a hazy halo around the landing zone. X covered his face with a sleeve.

"Wait!" he yelled.

The airship began to pull up.

A rear thruster fired, and the ship moved toward the edge of the rooftop. X ran after it, still shouting and partially shielding his eyes from the gusting wind.

Someone must have heard his voice, because the ramp stopped retracting and started to extend back down. But the ship continued to move, as if whoever had heard his shout hadn't gotten the message to the captain.

X ran harder, and when he was under the platform, he jumped and grabbed for the ramp. His fingers closed around the metal bar at the end. The airship pulled over the side of the roof and rose into the sky with X dangling from the retracting ramp.

When it was just shy of disappearing fully into the ship and squeegeeing X off into the sea, it stopped, and a diver scrambled over from the launch bay. X looked up to see Michael's frowning face.

"You just couldn't help yourself, could you?" Michael said.

"Just pull me up!" X yelled over the turbofans' loud racket. His sandaled feet kicked for traction against the hull, but he couldn't reach it.

Discovery rose higher into the air, leaving the capitol tower behind. A glance down revealed a black desert of water, and it occurred to X that this would be one stupid freaking way to die.

"Come on!" he yelled.

Michael grabbed him and yanked him up and onto the platform, ripping his shirt. Magnolia took his other arm and helped him to his feet.

Together, they retreated inside the launch bay as the doors sealed shut.

Panting, X nodded at Michael and then Magnolia. "Thanks for the help," he said.

Magnolia took off her helmet. "You just love to keep testing that whole 'Immortal' crock, don't you?"

"No one said anything about you coming," Michael added.

"Because I wasn't planning on it—sort of a last-second decision."

When X turned away from them, every eye in the launch bay was on him. All the new divers, Cazadores included, wore the same confused look.

Even Alfred, the lead technician, had stopped working on Cricket. X avoided the curious gazes and looked at his locker.

But he wasn't here to dive.

The hatch to the room opened, providing a welcome distraction as Les reentered the launch bay. He looked as baffled as everyone else.

"Sir, what are you doing?" he asked.

"Decided to come along and watch," X said.

Les paused, then said, "Suit yourself. We're climbing to thirty thousand feet and heading to the drop zone. Should be there in twenty minutes. The ship and rescue craft are already in position to make sure it all goes smoothly."

"Good," X said. "I'll meet you on the bridge soon."

"Okay," Les said in a tone almost of resignation. He turned away, and X noticed how thin he looked from the side. It wasn't just his normally confident voice that had diminished. He had lost more weight despite having access to more nutrition than ever before in his life. X hated seeing the man like this, but there was nothing to be done. He had to grieve in his own way.

The hatches closed behind the captain, leaving X with the divers and technicians. Alfred finished up on Cricket and moved to help Alberto and Hector with their wrist computers. The Cazadores weren't familiar with the technology.

Another tech helped Sofia with her booster pack. Arlo was still stuffing his long, curly hair into his helmet. Lena, the quiet former militia enforcer turned Hell Diver, held the helmet for him while he muttered profanities.

X couldn't even really remember what he was like at their age. That was half a lifetime ago and seemed even longer. He watched them from afar, studying their tense features.

Arlo had been a good friend of Trey Mitchells and had joined up after his death. He finished getting his hair tucked away, and there was the trademark rakish grin as he flirted with Lena who was still holding his helmet. He brushed back a lock of her hair to whisper something in her ear that made her smile.

"*That's* why they call you Thunder?" she said loudly enough for X to hear.

I hope you're as good at diving as you are at charming, kid.

Arlo looked his way and nodded as if he could read X's mind.

X smirked.

He liked this kid already, but would his instincts and his boldness with women translate into what he would need to dive through dark skies and electrical storms?

They would find out soon enough.

The other divers prepped their gear and performed last-minute checks on their armor and systems. Some chatted in hushed voices and flashed suspicious looks at X. Hector and Alberto stuck with the other Cazadores, while the sky people clustered together.

The King had not expected them to mingle freely, but he hoped they would soon learn to dive together. He would teach them about having each other's backs—the most important part of being a diver.

Michael finished talking to the technicians working on Cricket. The robot chirped, the hover nodes flashed red, and it rose off the launch bay's deck and followed Michael, who flashed a proud smile.

"Nice work," X said. "Reminds me of that vacuum bot you put back together when you were just a kid. Remember that?"

"Of course," Michael said. He pulled X aside and, in a serious tone, said, "X, what are you *really* doing here?"

"Look, Tin, I know you got this under control, but I wanted to be here for the first dive outside the Vanguard Islands." X kept his voice low. "I'm worried some of them aren't ready."

Michael looked over his shoulder. "Everyone's passed the jump test in clear skies, but I am a bit concerned about a few of them, primarily—"

"Ted Maturo," Magnolia said, joining them.

Michael half frowned, as if he didn't quite agree but couldn't really argue with her choice.

"Silver Fox is terrible," she said. "No way he makes it to five dives. I'll bet my poker bankroll on it. Chances are good he hurts someone else, too."

X looked at Michael to get his reaction but got nothing.

"Not everyone is cut out to be a diver," Magnolia said.

"Maybe hold him back," X said, trying not to make it sound like an order.

"Agreed," she said. "Have him dive a few more times in clear skies before you give him the green light for the storms."

"Only way to learn is to dive," Michael said. "But if you both think he isn't ready, I'll go let him know."

X appreciated that Michael listened to advice. He was a lot wiser than X had been in his twenties. Hell, X was still crap at taking counsel.

"This should be interesting," Magnolia said, folding her arms over her armor.

Ted was crouched down, working on his gear with his back turned. X went for a better view and saw the rookie was actually taking a drink from a silver flask.

He stood up with a smile as Michael approached. The smile vanished in an instant.

"No, I'm ready," Ted said, loud enough for everyone to hear.

Michael shook his head. X couldn't hear his words, but everyone could hear Ted's reply.

"Commander, please, I can do this."

The other divers looked up from what they were doing, and the ritual clicks and clanks stopped. Michael patted him on the shoulder and walked away.

Ted turned, glaring at Magnolia as if he knew that she had something to do with this. Then he turned and walked away, kicking at the air in a fit of frustration.

"What are you all looking at?" Michael said to the surrounding divers. "Finish your gear checks."

As they returned to their work, the wall-mounted speakers crackled. "Prepare for slight turbulence," said Les. "We're entering the barrier. We will hit the DZ in approximately T-minus-eight minutes."

The divers donned their helmets and lined up in teams behind the veterans: Michael, Edgar, Magnolia, and Alexander.

"System checks," Michael said.

The teams went through the final steps to confirm

that their HUDs were working properly and their suits were sealed.

A red light strobed from the corners of the bay, and a siren sounded, warning of the imminent launch. The divers all faced the launch-bay doors in anticipation.

All sense of movement ceased a few minutes later as the airship reached dive altitude over the drop zone. The speakers crackled again.

"Team leads, report," Les said.

The newly reassigned leaders acknowledged.

"Raptor One, online and ready to dive," Michael replied.

"Angel One, good to dive," said Alexander.

"Phoenix One, locked and cocked," said Edgar.

"Wolf One, online," Magnolia said. "Let's see what y'all got."

The dozen new divers reported in, confirming that their systems were operational.

"Dive safe, everyone," Les said when they had finished. "Remember your training."

"Team Raptor goes first," Michael said.

The launch-bay doors hissed open, and he stepped up with his team, waiting to lead the first new boots into the black void.

A cool blue light swirled from the corners of the bay. X had always found it calming before jumping into the hell that awaited them.

Lightning forked across the black skyline like a misshapen sword stabbing into flesh.

X retreated from the blast of freezing air to the center of the launch bay. The platform extended outward, and Michael led his team toward the dull, pitted metal. Cricket hovered after them and then dropped like a rock into the darkness, to get into position for aerial video of the new divers.

"We dive so humanity survives!" Michael called out.

"Hell yeah, we do!" shouted someone behind X. A figure darted past him and sprinted around the diver teams.

"Wait!" X yelled out.

Before anyone could stop the idiot, he ran onto the platform and leaped into the black abyss. At first, X thought it was a technician or some crazy crewman who had decided to get creative with suicide.

Then he realized that the guy *was* likely committing suicide.

A glance into the corner where Ted had been sulking told him the rest. And if the kid was as bad as Magnolia said, chances were that he was now taking his last few breaths in this life.

FOUR

"Everyone else but the team leads, stay put!" Magnolia shouted.

Michael and Alexander had already dived off the platform, and Edgar followed her into the black, leaving the new divers inside the launch bay with X, who had run over wearing nothing but his ripped T-shirt, shorts, and sandals. The doors sealed the other new divers inside with the living legend.

If he'd had his chute on and was suited up against the negative five degrees Fahrenheit, she had no doubt that he would have jumped out to see that Ted made it safely to the ship.

The reckless greenhorn had already gotten a few seconds' head start, and Magnolia couldn't see him in the darkness below. At thirty-two thousand feet, they had only two to three minutes to make sure he wasn't in a tailspin and could deploy his chute properly.

She could kick herself for even letting him onto the airship in the first place.

Scanning the black emptiness, she saw no sign of his battery unit.

Shit, he must be in a suicide dive.

"Ted, get into stable fall position NOW!" Magnolia shouted into the comm.

"I got this, Mags! See you on the ship!"

This time, she cursed out loud. "Stupid son of a bitch."

There was no denying that Ted had cojones, but big balls coupled with inexperience was a dangerous mix that got people killed. Still, she couldn't deny that he was a bit like her rebellious younger self.

What Ted didn't have, however, was speed and agility like hers, on the ground or in the air. She just hoped he could hold the dive all the way to the surface. If he hit turbulence and spun out of control, there wasn't much they could do unless they caught up to him fast.

Lightning raked the clouds in the distance, and her HUD flickered from the disturbance. She checked the digital map and reached down to her wrist computer to switch from Team Wolf to Team Angel.

Four other beacons blinked, representing the heartbeats of the three team leads above her, and Ted, a thousand feet below.

They crossed the twenty-two-thousand-feet mark—a third of the dive already behind them. Magnolia was almost to terminal velocity, her arms tucked back against her sides, body straight as a Cazador spear.

Thunder cracked like a rifle shot in her ear, distracting her for a moment. Her eyes flitted to a dazzling display of lightning to the east. Here on the edge of the storm, the new boots could get a sense of what a real dive was like, without getting zapped. But Les had maneuvered them close enough to test their nerve.

Another skein of flashes lit up the sky. Magnolia searched the black anvil below, hunting for the glowing blue dot of Ted's battery pack.

"I don't got eyes," she reported.

Michael came up alongside her in a nosedive. Alexander and Edgar spread out, flanking them. Static broke over the comms, then a scream.

Magnolia felt the first jolt of turbulence tugging her sideways. Biting down on her mouth guard, she pulled the falling dart that was her body into a horizontal position.

She finally saw the erratic blue strobe of a battery unit—Ted, cartwheeling through the sky. Catching up to him would require serious skills and extreme caution.

She had to maneuver carefully, or the turbulence would throw her off course too, and send her crashing like a fish on a cresting wave.

"I've lost it!" Alexander shouted over the comms.

Magnolia could see in her mind's eye what was happening. The turbulence had knocked him out of his dive. Edgar was next, tumbling out of control, but Magnolia managed to keep her orientation through the shear.

Michael shot past on her right, his armor glowing red from his battery unit.

A hundred feet out, another red light caught her attention. Cricket was tracking the tumbling bodies, but there was nothing the two-armed robot could do now. Maybe if Michael had been able to replace the other two missing arms ... Without them, the bot could only monitor, not assist.

The blue light of Ted's unit vanished as the cloud cover thickened and, with it, the turbulence. Magnolia tried to maintain her core tension but finally succumbed to the forces lashing and tugging on her body.

She held in a scream as she pitchpoled sideways, end over end.

The lightning seemed to come from all directions.

Perhaps it was a good thing, Ted doing what he did. If the other greenhorns had hit this pocket, it could have resulted in crashes and potential deaths.

She fought her way back into stable position, belly down with knees and elbows bent at ninety degrees. Her suit rippled violently in the wind.

"Ted!" she shouted into the comms. "Ted, where are you?"

The blip representing Ted on her HUD was blinking sporadically, which told her he was still spinning. Worse, he was over two thousand feet wide of the DZ. No way in hell would he make it to within a quarter mile of the target ship.

Ted was going to land in the black ocean, and even if he managed to get his chute open, he could easily drown, entangled in the shroud lines, or be easy pickings for all sorts of voracious sea creatures, while waiting for a boat to pick him up.

She resisted the urge just to give up on the rescue and let fate take its course. And the Magnolia of twenty years ago might have done that—maybe even the Magnolia of ten years ago.

But diving was in her blood now, and despite Ted's flagrant insubordination, she couldn't just let him die if there was a chance of saving him.

Straightening her legs and pulling her hands in to her thighs, she became an arrow again, angled to meet his runaway trajectory. Another glance at her HUD told her she didn't have much time.

"Ted, listen to me!" she shouted. "Put your arms and legs out and arch your back, just like we taught you!"

The muffled reply was indecipherable.

She checked her HUD again. Six thousand feet to the surface, but she had closed the gap between herself and Ted. The glow of Michael's battery unit confirmed that he, too, was gaining on the out-of-control greenhorn.

"Alexander and Edgar, continue to the DZ," Michael ordered.

"Copy," Alexander said.

After a slight delay, Edgar acknowledged.

"Mags, stay back," Michael said. "I've got this."

"But …"

"That's an order."

"Roger that," she replied through gritted teeth.

A moment later, she got a visual on Ted's battery unit. He was tumbling and not responding to Michael's hails.

Holy wastes, is he unconscious?

Another wind shear sent both her and Michael spinning out of control.

At three thousand feet, it occurred to her that the rookie diver may have doomed them all.

"Mags, pull your chute as soon as you're in stable position," Michael ordered.

"You pull yours!"

She could see that they would never get to Ted in time now. The best they could do was to save themselves by deploying their chutes as soon as they could.

Michael was the first to recover, and Magnolia managed to get steady a few seconds later. At two thousand feet, they broke through the cloud cover and had their first view of rough seas.

Lights blinked on the surface where the ship and motorboats waited. One of them seemed to be moving toward their location.

"Pull your chute NOW!" Michael yelled.

She pulled the pilot chute from the pocket along her right thigh, held it out, and let it go. It caught air and dragged out the main chute, yanking her out of free fall.

Michael went next, and as their parachutes seemed to pull them skyward, they could only look on as Ted tumbled toward the endless expanse of whitecaps below.

"*Ted!*" Michael shouted.

It was no use. The diver was out, insensible to his impending doom.

At just over a thousand feet, Magnolia closed her eyes, unable to watch him slam into the ocean.

"What the …!" Michael gasped.

Her eyelids popped open to see a green light shooting diagonally through the dark skies. She nearly spat out her mouth guard when she realized it was X.

He had somehow managed to suit up *and* catch up to them. But how was that possible unless he had somehow held the nosedive through the turbulence?

Cricket swooped down to document the miracle.

Moments later, X pulled his legs in and extended his arms, slowing his approach speed toward the unconscious diver. At eight hundred feet, he wrapped his body around Ted, clipped his carabiner to Ted's harness, and pulled his own pilot chute.

Magnolia let out the breath she hadn't known she was holding.

"Got 'im," X said over the comms.

She looked over at Michael, who was steering his canopy toward the ship below. X was trying to do the same thing, with his left hand on the steering toggle, and the other arm wrapped around Ted.

The ship's deck rose up to meet Magnolia's boots. She performed a two-stage flare over the rusted old Cazador ship. Right before touching down, she glimpsed X and Ted in the distance.

They splashed into the water as she stepped out of the sky and onto the deck.

She spilled the air from her chute, released it, and handed the wad of bright-yellow nylon to a crewman. Then she hurried over to the edge of the boat, where someone had already tossed a buoy into the water.

Magnolia gripped the rail. She was furious at Ted for almost killing himself and others, but mostly she was elated that X had saved the young idiot. Maybe the "Immortal" thing wasn't a crock after all. Maybe the king was indeed the sky god that some of the Cazadores believed him to be.

* * * * *

Rhino had never liked his Cazador nickname much, but it was better than the first one they had given him: Perrito, or Small Dog. He had known another name before that, but his birth name, Nick Baker, was abandoned after the Cazadores captured his and several other families living in a bunker.

The name sounded weak, and the boy he had been was weak. But the only thing that Cazador warriors respected was strength.

Strength was how Rhino had risen through the ranks. He was no Nick Baker, and he was no Small Dog.

As a teenager, he used physical strength and cunning to best fighter after fighter. In his twenties, he continued to climb the ladder from grunt soldier to sergeant, eventually becoming one of a dozen lieutenants commanding a platoon of soldiers. Then, after the battle for the Vanguard Islands, X had bumped him all the way up to general.

He had proved himself many times over in the wastes, slaughtering beasts that would make most men piss inside their armor. But it had never been enough to earn him the degree of respect and loyalty that el Pulpo had from his ranks. Nor had Rhino earned the respect of Colonel Vargas and the other officers of the Black Order.

Maybe he didn't deserve it.

Rhino hadn't been strong enough to protect his team of Barracudas on their last excursion to fight the monsters. They all were dead now, including Wendig, the toughest warrior, male or female, he had ever known.

Rhino stepped into his private training chambers inside the rusted hull of *Elysium*. The huge vessel was the biggest in the entire armada. It served as the training ground and barracks for new warriors and also as military headquarters.

Colonel Forge, Colonel Vargas, and Colonel Moreto would meet with him at the command center later to assess the new recruits. But first he had his morning training.

He lit the candles on sconces mounted to the bulkhead. The glow spread over a raggedy old mat, a rusty rack of weights, and a wall of mirrors, most of them cracked.

Wearing only a loincloth and sandals, he walked into the center of the space and went to work with the double-headed spear.

The mirrors reflected his movements as his callused hands twirled the spear over his head. He closed his eyes, picturing two enemies trying to flank him on the deck of a boat. The blades slit both men's throats in a single swipe.

Then he swiped upward at a third imagined enemy, opening a gaping line from pubis to chest and spilling viscera onto the deck.

The vivid images in his mind were not fantasy. They were memories of the time a squad of Cazador assassins tried to kill him so their leader could take his spot as lieutenant. It had happened on a coastal foray to a place once called Georgia.

And but for Wendig, the assassins would have succeeded in their mission to kill Rhino. The ferocious woman warrior had saved his life, fighting by his side against six men.

The memory of the ambush prompted a little surge of adrenaline through his veins. He continued training, recalling almost every swipe, thrust, and parry of that fateful day.

Rhino lost track of time as he reenacted the fight. When he stopped to check the clock, he was bathed in sweat. He opened his eyes, and the memories vanished like footprints before a wave.

Chest heaving, he finally lowered the spear. If he didn't hurry, he was going to be late.

After putting on his armor, he picked up the spear and climbed the companionway to the weather deck. There, in the faint glow of a crimson sunrise, a group of two hundred had gathered. They ranged in age from fourteen on up to their midtwenties.

Most of them looked like Rhino did at their age: thin and weak. It wasn't until el Pulpo started feeding the growing Cazador human meat from their hunting trips that Rhino had grown in size. But these young men and women would not be eating human meat anymore. Their diets would consist mostly of vegetables and fresh fish. Their training would be rigorous, six days a week from dawn to dusk, in the baking sun or out in the wastes.

Some of them would never see their families again.

Rhino looked to the west, where the sky was still dark, and glimpsed the blinking red light on the last flying airship in the world. Its launch bay was also filled with young men and women.

Unlike the Cazadores, they worked mostly in the darkness, diving into the abyss to simulate what they would face out beyond the barrier surrounding the Vanguard Islands. Today they were returning from their first mission outside that barrier.

Seeing them reminded Rhino that the sky people had a lot more in common with Cazadores than he had ever thought. To fend off extinction, the Hell Divers, too, had fought on extreme terrain against mutant beasts—maybe even more than his own people had. Unlike here, where there were no electrical storms or radiation, living on an airship required constant maintenance just to keep from falling out of the sky to certain death on the poisoned surface.

He looked away from the airship and walked out onto the deck. A group of veteran Cazador soldiers in armor waited for him.

Colonel Vargas had also shown up to look at the new recruits. He remained in the command center in the ship's island tower, watching like an eagle from its nest. The man was known for observing, with his own eyes and through the spies under his command.

Rhino had warned X about that, too, but as long as the spies stayed off the capitol tower, X was satisfied. And so far, the militia had kept any unwanted visitors away.

Vargas's protruding eyes met Rhino's. The colonel didn't even bother trying to hide his resentment.

Rhino turned away to have a closer look at the newly recruited teenagers talking amongst themselves. Some of them sat on the deck with their heads propped up in their hands, trying to grab some sleep.

He woke them up with his booming voice.

"Get up, shark bait!" he yelled in Spanish. "You got two seconds to get into position before I start tossing you overboard!"

All side conversations stopped as the youngsters snapped to attention. All but one.

Rhino immediately gravitated to the biggest recruit, a kid with tattoos all over his muscular arms and legs.

A hideous crab image covered his shaved head from the widow's peak to the nape of his neck, its stick eyes just two inches above his own.

The young man was Felipe, son of Whale, who had perished with the rest of the Barracudas. Rhino could almost hear Whale's spirit screaming from the hereafter at his disrespectful son.

"Get in line!" Rhino yelled.

Felipe ignored the order.

The other teenagers watched, eager to see whatever was going to happen.

So this is how it's going to be …

"Did you not hear me?" Rhino said "You got crabs *inside* your head, too?" He strode up to where the young man sat. Felipe showed his sharpened teeth.

Rhino sensed that this was due to bad blood, and he was right.

"Why should I listen to you?" he asked. "You got my dad killed."

"You'll listen to me because I will feed your nuts to the crabs if you don't."

Felipe unfolded his arms and stood up. "You could try, but you're past your prime, old man."

Rhino would have laughed, but Felipe was half right. Now in his thirties, he was indeed past his prime. Sofia, almost six years younger, didn't agree when he worried about his age, but she didn't know what it was like to fight against fit, cocky young men like Felipe.

They were quicker and more agile and had the fearless heart of youngsters who thought themselves invincible. Over the years, Rhino had seen hundreds of Felipes perish in the wastes for that very reason.

"Fall in line," Rhino said.

"Fuck you."

Rhino swung a left hook, but the boy easily ducked the blow. He then jumped into the air and kicked Rhino in the chest. The force of the blow knocked him backward, but he quickly regained his balance.

Laughter erupted all around as the recruits fanned out in a circle to watch the fight.

The Cazador veterans moved in, but Rhino shook his head. He tossed his spear to one of them, then unbuckled his chest armor. He let it clank to the deck and quickly shucked off the rest of his armor.

Vargas, who Rhino had expected to challenge him long before someone like Felipe, had moved out of the command center and stood at the railing, looking down.

Felipe smiled as he bobbed and weaved, throwing punches like an old-world boxer.

Cocky little shit …

Whale would be ashamed, and now Rhino was going to teach the kid to respect the old-fashioned way.

Felipe strode forward and threw a punch that Rhino allowed to land on his clenched jaw. The crack was audible, but Rhino just laughed and spat on the deck.

Several voices broke out around them.

Rhino feinted with his right, then threw a left uppercut that caught his opponent under the chin, knocking him to the deck.

The kid got up faster than Rhino had expected. Now it was Felipe spitting blood. He wiped a smear off his face.

Rhino moved in to finish the fight, but the younger

warrior jumped and kicked at his face. Raising an arm, Rhino deflected the blow.

Felipe moved quickly to flank him, but Rhino went low and threw an elbow, narrowly missing Felipe's ribs. He kicked Rhino in the back of the knee hard enough to bring him down on his other knee.

A kick to the back of the head nearly knocked Rhino to the deck.

Head spinning, he staggered to his feet.

The onlookers went wild, but Rhino ignored them. Felipe was dancing again, moving quickly, and for a fleeting moment, Rhino worried that he might lose this fight.

If he did, he was doomed. No one would follow him into battle.

He needed just one well-timed blow to knock the kid on his ass, where he belonged.

Felipe came at him again, kicking air. Rhino hammered down on his thigh, stuffing the kick, and threw a roundhouse punch, which Felipe ducked.

A golden rind of sun peeked over the horizon, making Rhino squint. In that instant, he took a blow to the diaphragm, knocking the air from his lungs. He gasped for air, and Felipe moved in.

That was his mistake.

Rhino was not as shaken as he looked, and as Felipe cocked his leg for another flashy jump kick, Rhino strode forward and threw a punch that caught him in the ribs.

The blow sent the young man flying. He hit the deck hard and stayed there.

Rhino loomed over him, chest heaving. When he looked up at the railing, Vargas had folded his arms across his chest.

"You want to dance, too?" Rhino shouted up.

Vargas flashed his sharp teeth.

The crowd quieted, and a sergeant brought the spear over. Rhino took it and held the tip to Felipe's throat. Blinking, the boy tried to move, then gave it up and settled on his back.

"I didn't get your dad killed," Rhino said. "But if you don't shape up, you're going to follow in his footsteps."

Felipe bared his sharp teeth as Rhino pressed the edge just enough to draw blood. Then he pulled the spear back, twirled it, and said, "You have to decide. Will you fight and die with honor like your old man, or keep being a shithead until it gets you killed?"

Rhino let Felipe think on it a moment and then reached down. After a moment of indecision, Felipe grabbed the offered hand.

"Good choice. You will do much better as a warrior if you learn from your mistakes." He hauled the boy up onto his feet, gave him a good hard pat on the back, and pushed him back into the crowd.

The recruits had stopped watching Rhino and Felipe. Some of them were pointing at the sky. Rhino squinted at a green glow descending toward the ship. The light trailed a Hell Diver in free fall.

A parachute blossomed and began to spiral gently down toward the deck.

"*¡Viene el rey Xavier!*" Rhino yelled, repeating it in English. "Here comes King Xavier!"

Everyone fell into orderly rank and file, including Felipe.

Rhino walked over to greet his friend and their ruler as X touched down gracefully on the deck. He quickly released his chute, grabbed it up, and stuffed it back into the pack. Then he took off his helmet and walked to the assembled recruits.

Many of the youthful faces eyed X suspiciously. Rhino knew what they were thinking: *How could this old man have killed el Pulpo?* Many of them probably thought it was luck, but Rhino knew better. Scanning faces, he noticed several gazes locked on the new king, showing the same anger and bloodlust that he had seen in Felipe a few minutes ago.

Before long, Rhino wouldn't be the only one with a challenger.

The question was *how* challengers would go about trying to take X down. Would they come at him like the assassination squad that had come after Rhino years ago, or would they challenge him to a match, as Felipe had just done?

Time would tell, but Rhino knew one thing for certain: King Xavier Rodriguez didn't need luck to fight his enemies. He had the heart of a lion, the skills of a seasoned warrior, and, when he needed it, the ferocity of a shark.

The fool who challenged him would be the one needing the luck.

FIVE

"How'd the dive go?" Rhino asked.

He and X stood on the platform outside the ship's command center. The sun glinted off the windows, but storm clouds were moving into the clear skies to the east.

"It could have been a lot worse," said X, "considering that one of the divers jumped ship and tried to get himself and a team killed."

"Is Sofia …"

"Fine."

Rhino wiped a drop of blood away from his eye.

"Looks like you've had a rough morning, too," X said. "Figured I'd stop by since I was in the area. Show the fresh meat what a Hell Diver looks like up close and in person."

They watched the new warriors on the deck of *Elysium*. The veterans had started to move the recruits into groups based on their size and age. Eventually, they would be judged on their fighting ability before being placed on a team and, finally, in a platoon.

X looked out over the youngsters, picking out the weaklings and the showboats. The group had more than a few Ted Maturos.

He was still shocked at the kid's stunt. After Ted regained consciousness, the team leaders had given him a serious ass-chewing, stripped him of his armor, and reassigned him to his new job: mucking out the livestock pens for the next month.

"Soon, they will be tested, like your divers," Rhino said of the trainees below.

"Not too soon, let's hope. Looks like some of them are just kids."

"They're all of age, and this is part of their culture," Rhino said. "When they complete the first round of training, we'll weigh anchor and set off for the proving grounds, where mutant beasts and poisonous flora will test their skills."

"What doesn't kill them makes them stronger, eh?" The adage was generally true for Hell Divers, too.

"Most of them already know how to fight, as you may have noticed with Felipe on your way down," Rhino said. "Now we figure out who the real warriors are."

The distant roll of thunder drew their eyes east, where lightning flickered from the dark base of a towering cloud bank.

"That doesn't look good," X said.

The clang of metal on metal signaled the start of the first matches. The sparring brought shouts and cheers. These youths would join an army of over a thousand warriors spread out over the oil rigs, outposts, and remaining fleet of warships.

X couldn't see them, but the *Lion*, *Mercury*, and *Star Grazer* all cruised outside the barrier of the Vanguard Islands. Each was manned by a hundred sailors and soldiers, patrolling for defectors and other threats.

The clank of metal and wood on the deck was another reminder of how outnumbered X and his people were. Lieutenant Sloan and her new sergeant, Wynn, were doing a fine job. Recruiting sky people who needed jobs since the *Hive*'s decommissioning, they had grown the militia's ranks to just under a hundred, but the disparity was still huge. Even with almost a fourth of the sky people serving in the army, if the Cazadores decided to break the truce, they would have an overwhelming advantage in numbers.

A boat pulled up alongside the warship, and a dozen more Cazador warriors climbed a rope net to the first deck. These weren't just grunts, either. The rest of the Black Order of Octopus Lords had arrived.

General Santiago, Colonel Forge, and Colonel Moreto set off across the deck with a squad of warriors in full armor. Black capes fluttered behind Forge's and Moreto's shoulders. Santiago's cape was blazing orange.

Escorting the officers were eight Praetorian Guards in black armor.

"What are they here for?" X asked.

"To have a look at the 'fresh meat,' as you called them," Rhino said.

X suddenly didn't feel so safe. He hadn't even told

Sloan or Wynn he was coming here. But a glance at the sky eased his mind.

Discovery hovered at three thousand feet above the water. The ship could strike at a moment's notice with a variety of missiles, bombs, and twenty-millimeter Minigun fire on any Cazador ship that might threaten it.

And X had made sure all antiaircraft weapons on the islands were under his control. The thirty-millimeter cannons were now manned by several of his most trusted militia soldiers.

The Cazadores had the numbers, but the sky people had the firepower.

"So, you going to tell me why you're really here?" Rhino said.

"You don't miss much, do you?" X said. "That's why I like you."

"Thank you, King Xavier."

X sighed, wondering whether he was making the right decision. The only way to know was to ask for advice—and then try to listen to it, for once.

"We fought together to take this place back from a mad king," X said. "You helped my people even when it meant fighting your own, and now I need your help again."

"I serve at your pleasure," Rhino said, bowing slightly.

"I appreciate that."

"I saw, and see, a great warrior in you, Immortal. You are the only one who can lead both our peoples to prosperity. Tell me what I must do, and I will do it."

"I want you to lead an expedition by sea to Rio de Janeiro."

The thick brows squeezed together. "King Xavier, I am honored to be considered for this mission, but I do not think leaving your side would be a good idea."

"I know I have enemies," X said, glancing at the officers on deck. "I see the way some of them look at me. Even the new warriors are suspicious."

Colonel Vargas joined the other officers on the deck. They all were looking out over the rail at two speedboats flanking a fishing boat. The three vessels appeared to be heading for the warship *Elysium*.

"Who's that?" X asked.

"The first challengers."

"Challengers …" X spotted cages on the deck of the fishing boat, and he wasn't surprised to see the pale, dead-looking flesh moving inside them.

Rhino said, "I will have to oversee this personally, King Xavier."

X nodded. "We can discuss this mission later. Meet me at the capitol rig when you finish here."

Rhino thumped his chest. "I'll make sure you get to a boat safely."

X laughed at that. "Brother, I'll be fine."

"I know, but I'm coming anyway."

They walked back to the deck where the two hundred youngsters, some of them bloody now, stood at attention. A crane had lowered chains to the fishing boat. Once they were secure, the first cage rose from the boat.

The Cazador officers walked over to watch. They nodded to X—all but Vargas, who looked away.

A muffled screech came from the Sirens inside the rising cage. The veterans operating the crane swung the load onto the deck.

"Back, back!" Rhino yelled.

The trainees didn't need to hear it twice, not even Felipe. But like the Cazador officers, the boy wasn't looking at the Sirens. They were staring at X.

He took in a deep breath, filling his lungs. He would never grow tired of the fresh salt air. After a decade in the wastes, this was as close to heaven as he had ever been.

And it was why he had to do this.

X gave Rhino his helmet. "I'll take the first one," he said. "Tell them to hold the second cage on the boat below."

"¿Qué?" Rhino said. "I mean, what?"

X gestured for the sword on the belt of a veteran standing a few feet away. The soldier unsheathed it and handed it over.

"The knife, too," X said.

He tucked the knife under a strap on his armor, then walked toward the cage as two veterans guided it down.

Rhino called out orders in Spanish.

The cage clanked onto the deck, and the veterans picked up the same black electrical cattle prods they had used on X back in Florida.

He readied his sword and nodded at the two men.

Neither looked to Rhino for approval. At least *they* respected him. Now it was time to earn the respect of these youngsters.

All the trainees were hanging on his every move, and while the eyeless female Siren couldn't see him, it could hear and smell him just fine.

It sniffed the air, tilting its head as he moved. Listening, sensing, anticipating.

They were matchless hunters, designed to survive in a postapocalyptic world—the ultimate *cazadores*.

Dropping to all fours, the beast moved with his steps, sinewy muscles flexing under pale, leathery skin.

The gag in its mouth would prevent it from screaming or sinking those jagged teeth into his flesh, but there was nothing to stop the long razor-edged claws from slashing his throat or spilling his guts on the deck.

The beasts hadn't been fed in a month, though, and this one was clearly weakened, its ribs and bony back protruding. Even these genetically modified human descendants had to eat.

One of the guards unlocked the cage, attracting the Siren's attention. X raised his sword. The instant the lock clicked, the monster slammed into the door, swinging it open.

X would have finished the beast right away, but he had to put on a show, and the recruits needed to see how these creatures fought. So he pinked it on the arm, just enough to draw blood and piss the thing off.

The monster slashed at the air, dangerously close

to the crotch of his armor. X jumped back, prompting cheers and shouts from those assembled. He would have loved to see the look on Rhino's face.

A gust of wind sprayed X with rain as he drew the Siren away from the center of the deck, toward the bow. It followed him upright instead of on all fours, moving faster than he would have thought considering its weakened condition.

The creature sprang through the air.

X ducked and raised the tip of his sword from a squatting position, opening a gash in the creature's belly as it vaulted over him.

A muffled screech of agony followed as the beast landed and spun back toward him.

X got up, wincing from a searing pain where a toe claw had slashed his forehead. With one eye closed, he retreated from the flopping monster. It struggled up onto all fours, then reached down with one hand to keep in the loop of intestine that bulged from its midsection.

X felt the cut above his left eye—just a nick compared to the gash in the variant's visceral wall.

Panting and grunting, the creature struggled to remain on all fours. At first, X thought it was going to collapse, but then it must have gotten a whiff of something. All its muscles seemed to flex in a ripple across its body. The powerful hind legs sprang the injured beast upward, on top of a shipping container.

X suddenly wondered whether starving these things had been the best idea. He moved backward with his sword up, ready for the monster to jump off the container.

The rope of intestine flopped out from the open abdominal wound as the Siren leaped down onto the top of the crate. But instead of attacking X, it darted toward the youngsters. The crowd scattered, with screams and shouts in all directions.

"*Shit*," X muttered, pulling the knife from the armor strap at his hip. Closing one eye, he threw the blade by the hilt, end over end. The point sank into the beast's right leg, and it crashed in a heap on the deck.

X ran over to the thrashing monster, then sprang backward to avoid a slashing claw before bringing the sword tip down hard below the thickly armored forehead, right where an eye should be. The cracking sound merged with a peal of thunder, and when the noise passed, the deck was silent.

Blood pooled around the dead Siren.

"Bring up the other cage," X said.

Rhino nodded at the man on the crane, and the second cage clanked up over the railing and swung around.

Sheets of rain quickly rinsed away most of the blood on the deck. X touched his scalp wound. It wasn't just a nick, after all, and would probably need a couple of sutures. *Another scar.*

Rhino shouted for everyone to back away from the new cage. Inside was a male Siren with its wings strapped down.

X plucked the sword from the female's skull and held the bloody blade flat to the rain.

"Who's next?" he shouted over the din of thunder. He held the sword out, offering it to each of the Cazador officers.

Colonel Vargas grabbed the hilt and held it up to the sky, looking down the blade. He handed it back to X, then drew the sword from his own sheath.

The colonel's bulging eyes flitted to Rhino, and the sharp black teeth grinned.

X half expected him to challenge Rhino. But instead, Vargas moved over to the cage and tapped the side with his blade.

For now, Rhino and X seemed to have put to rest any potential challenges, but X had no illusions. It was only a matter of time before some crazy, ambitious bastard like Vargas tried to kill him and his loyal general.

* * * * *

First Ted's dangerous little stunt, and now an intense storm that continued to strengthen.

Magnolia just wanted to go back to her quarters and sleep with the rain pounding the shutters, but she was stuck on the container ship used for Hell Diver training.

Waves slapped the vessel, and the pouring rain washed away the red chalk X had used to mark the landing spot for the Hell Divers in training.

Discovery had rushed back to the islands several hours ago to avoid the lightning after taking a hit to its new shields. The explosion of sparks had been visible even down here.

She walked over to Ada Winslow. The young lieutenant was helping make up for the lack of available officers while Timothy took her place on *Discovery*.

"Hell of a storm," she said.

"Hell of a *dive*," Magnolia replied. "Ted was just about shark bait."

"Probably the best use for that guy. Maybe X should have let him splat."

"*What?*" Magnolia said, glancing over.

The lieutenant kept her gaze on the bow as it cleaved the waves. The darkness ahead seemed to lighten as they approached the border between their little paradise and the terrors of the outside world.

Ada didn't reply to her question, so Magnolia asked again.

"You think X should have let Ted *die*?"

This time, Ada looked over, her freckled features uncharacteristically hard.

"No, not really, but I do think he should have killed the Cazadores when we took this place. If it were up to me, I would have killed every last soldier. I still don't understand how X could let them keep their weapons."

The bow pushed through the barrier, and two oil rigs appeared in the distance. Magnolia felt a shiver of memory from her captivity, when she was in a cage on a ship, looking at these same two rigs.

"Take us wide around those," Ada told the officer at the helm.

"No," Magnolia said. "Let's go right by them. I want to see something."

As the ship approached the rigs, Magnolia wasn't sure what she wanted to see. Perhaps she was curious to see what had changed since the sky people took over, or perhaps it was just the human fascination with things different. Either way, they were about to get a good, close look.

The large container ship sailed by the two outlying rigs, giving everyone on the bridge a view out the starboard portholes. Tarps fluttered in the wind and rain. Some were tied down over leaky shack roofs; others shaded crop seedlings that grew on the platforms. But by far the most important use of tarps was as catchment areas, sluicing rainwater into thousand-gallon cisterns, which stored it for drinking, bathing, and cleaning. The intricate system of reservoirs and pipes reminded her that these people weren't barbarians, despite their appearances and violent culture.

When Magnolia had sailed underneath them months ago as a prisoner, hundreds of people were staring down at her from a bridge that stretched between the two rigs. She remembered their heavily tattooed bronze flesh, the clacking teeth, and the stares. It was like discovering an alien race, and she had been the alien.

Now most of the Cazador people were sheltering inside their shacks. Only a few came out to watch the ship pass. Ada folded her arms over her chest and watched a group that had gathered on the fifth level of the open platforms. The men held spears, and one woman had a pitchfork.

They stood at the edge of the platform, looking as if they were about to be invaded.

"Barbarians," Ada muttered. "X should have taken every weapon at the very freaking least, and he should have killed the warriors, especially the Black Octopus Gods or whatever bullshit they call themselves."

Magnolia didn't necessarily disagree with Ada's assessment, but X had made his decision in hopes of keeping the peace, aware that other threats still lurked out there. If the defectors did find this place, they would need every Cazador to help in the fight.

"We need them," Magnolia said quietly.

"For what?" Ada said. "What can a woman with a pitchfork do against one of those machines?"

"They don't all have pitchforks, Lieutenant."

"Yeah, well, *she* does," Ada said.

The woman continued to watch from the platform as the boat sailed by. At the sight of the next rig, Magnolia's breath caught. She remembered this place well. The two-story structure was a warehouse and salting and drying rack for fish and livestock the Cazadores butchered.

But there would never again be dolphins hanging from those hooks. One of X's first royal decrees had been to outlaw the killing of those intelligent creatures.

A chill rushed through her mind as she continued

reliving the day of her capture. After the boat had passed the rigs, she recalled seeing a container ship with a deck full of caged Sirens—the same container ship she was on today.

The crackle of radio static snapped her out of her reverie.

Ada moved over to the comm station.

"Lieutenant Winslow, it's Captain Mitchells," said Les. "What's your location? Over."

"About twenty minutes southwest of the capitol tower, Captain."

"The storm's getting worse, and I've got new orders from King Xavier," Les said. "Meet me back at the capitol tower. We've been ordered to take *Discovery* beyond the barrier, to check on the Cazador ships patrolling the frontier."

She paused, holding the receiver up to her lips.

"Lieutenant," Les said.

"Copy that," she said. "We'll be there."

Ada put the receiver down and shook her head. She muttered under her breath, but Magnolia heard every word.

"Waste of fuel checking on those dumb ships," Ada said. "Makes me wonder whose side X is really on."

SIX

The wail of an air-raid siren rose over the howling wind and the rain pounding the docks.

Michael hated that sound as much as any other sky person. In the air, it awoke the visceral fear of crashing to the surface, but on the oil rigs, it meant war or a hurricane. Luckily, today it meant the latter—if a hurricane qualified as lucky.

"How did we not see this coming?" Rodger yelled over the howling wind.

"The sensors outside the barrier didn't pick it up until too late," Michael yelled back.

They stood with Cricket inside the protected boat harbor, watching the rain pound the rising waves. A small flock of gulls and terns had taken refuge under the overhang. Birds knew better than to fly in the violent wind, but it hadn't stopped X from sending *Discovery* to check on the warships.

And now, thanks to a busted satellite, they had lost contact with the airship. Michael was part of the team preparing to get it back online.

He took off his goggles and pulled his wet hair into a ponytail, wishing he had stayed in his Hell Diver armor and helmet. At least he had Cricket and his wrist computer. Bringing it up to his mouth, he called X.

"I'm inside."

"On my way," X replied.

Cricket chirped as it hovered behind them. Michael checked the robot while they waited. He had replaced the electrical system fried by the EMP grenade at the prison in Jamaica, but he still needed to find two new limbs.

The machine used one of its two remaining arms to hit the port's door lever, sealing them inside. With the sirens and howling wind suddenly muted, the clatter and hum of machinery filled the enclosed space.

"Come on," Michael said.

Rodger and Cricket followed him inside the port. Graffiti and mural art—images of fish, birds, and monsters—covered the massive concrete pillars that held up the overhead and the levels above. The Cazadores had decorated every part of their home, just as his people had decorated their home in the sky.

Around the next pillar, several Cazador mechanics worked on a long cigar-shaped speedboat that had once belonged to el Pulpo. Samson barked orders at two of his engineers wearing the traditional light-blue coveralls.

"Ah, Commander Everhart," Samson said. "About time you showed up."

"Sorry," Michael said. "I was helping secure the tarps over the gardens, but I brought Cricket along just in case we need it."

Samson turned his attention to Rodger. "And what's your excuse? Been playing grab-ass with Magnolia again?"

"I wish," Rodger said.

The two engineers laughed, but Samson was a tougher audience. "I need all trained hands on this boat. X wants it ready as soon as possible."

Rodger jumped into the cigar boat and ducked down to remove an electrical panel. Now that the *Hive* had been secured to the oil rig, he was back to getting damaged boats up and running again.

All the smaller vessels were stored here, but the container ships and warships were anchored by an oil rig retrofitted as a massive warehouse. The rig was completely controlled by Cazador workers, with a catch—the militia had an outpost there that allowed Lieutenant Sloan and Sergeant Wynn to keep a close eye on the repairs.

It was part of their plan to monitor the Cazadores on all the rigs.

Two militia guards were present today, each armed with an assault rifle, watching the Cazador mechanics.

"No!" shouted one of the men. He waved at Rodger, who held a panel in his hand on the boat.

"What?" Rodger asked. "What'd I do now?"

The Cazador spoke in Spanish while Rodger pushed his glasses farther up on his nose.

"I think he's saying the electrical panel needs to be replaced," Samson said. He looked at the Cazador mechanic. "Well, why didn't you tell me earlier?"

The hatch to the harbor inside the rig opened, and the Cazador guard standing with the militia soldiers pounded his chest when he saw that it was King Xavier.

"We ready to go?" X asked, striding out onto the pier with a blood-soaked bandage on his head.

"Sir, we have a problem with the boat you requested," Samson said.

"So find me a new one," X said. "I need to get that satellite back up and running pronto, Samson. It's the only way to contact *Discovery*."

"We have others, but do you really want to take them out in this weather?"

"I don't *care* what we take," X said. "Just give me something that runs."

Samson looked to the Cazador engineers and tried to speak in Spanish to them. He had already picked up the basics and was doing better than Michael in this new and necessary language.

One of the men pointed at the back of the boathouse. X peered into the shadows and then smiled, and Michael saw why.

The man was pointing at the *Sea Wolf*.

"*That* thing?" Samson said. "I'm not taking it out in this."

"Relax, I'll take the helm," X replied.

"Oh, that makes me feel *so* much better." Samson

pointed to his bag of tools, and Rodger picked them up. Then he and Michael followed the chief engineer and X down the platform, toward the boat.

"She didn't sink on our journey here," X said. "And I pushed her through storms just as bad as this one, so don't get your oversized undies in a bunch."

Samson patted his gut. "I take exception to that after all the weight I've lost."

"Just messing with you," X said, clapping him on the shoulder.

Michael took the access ladder down to the deck and went through a hatch to the bottom level. Cricket followed them into a brand-new command center with a new windshield and dashboard.

X sat in the captain's chair and fired up the engines.

"All right, old friend, let's see if you still got it," he said.

He steered the boat through the choppy water and around the neat rank of moored boats in the protected port. When they reached the big exit door, one of Samson's engineers pulled the lever.

The metal hatch opened slowly into a violent storm.

Sheets of rain pounded the windshield.

"You all know I can't swim, right?" Samson said.

X clenched his jaw, all business now that they'd left the safety of the port. Swells lifted and lowered the boat as they moved out into the open water, leaving the capitol tower behind them.

"Have a seat," X said to Samson. "You're making me nervous."

The chief engineer slumped down in one of the padded leather passenger chairs. Michael felt like doing the same thing. After the morning's training mission, he was running on fumes. All he wanted to do was get into bed with Layla and sleep for a day, but duty called.

"You decide what you're going to do with Ted yet?" Rodger asked.

X kept his eyes on the controls. "I should make *him* climb this crane in the storm, wearing metal armor, but I don't trust him, so he's shoveling shit at the livestock pens."

"He's lucky you saved him," Michael said.

"We got bigger problems than Ted," X said. "The last transmission I got from *Discovery* before the satellite went down was that the *Lion* is smack in the eye of that hurricane."

"With the new shields I added to the exterior, *Discovery* should be fine," Samson said.

"I'm not worried about the airship," X said. "I'm worried about losing a warship and her crew. We need every Cazador soldier to defend the frontier."

The rain continued drumming on the windshield as the *Sea Wolf* climbed and dipped through ten-foot waves, toward the unmanned oil rig. Cricket chirped when they finally reached the isolated platform.

The winds had reached a steady twenty-five miles per hour.

"The satellite dish is at the top of that crane," Samson said.

Michael couldn't even see the dish through the sheeting rain.

X pulled the starboard side along a concrete pillar, trying to keep the boat steady in the rising swells.

"Son of a bitch," he muttered.

A wave knocked them against the pillar, with an audible crunch.

"I don't feel so good," Rodger said, holding his stomach. X nodded toward the head, halfway down the passageway.

"Good thing we got Cricket," Samson said, "because we can't count on Rodge."

"Michael, send out the bot and get us tethered up," X said. "I'll hold us steady."

Using his wrist computer, Michael directed Cricket to follow him outside. They moved past the head, where Rodger was embracing the toilet.

"Tin," X called out. "I mean, *Commander*."

Michael stopped at the hatch and turned.

"Be careful," X said.

"Always." Michael put on his goggles before opening the hatch. The wind and rain hit him so hard, he stumbled back a step.

Samson stood in the passage, shielding his face from the wind. Michael gave him a thumbs-up and then closed the hatch. He turned to look at the rig looming above them. He still couldn't see the satellite dish, but he could see the boom of the crane.

"All right, Cricket, moment of truth!" Michael shouted over the wind. He moved over to the starboard rail and braced himself as another wave pushed them closer to the concrete pillar.

Grabbing the bow rope, he uncoiled it and prepared to throw it over to a cleat, then realized they could not tether safely here.

Michael wrapped the rope around his chest and tied it with a bowline, then brought up his wrist monitor. "X, I'm heading up with Cricket!" he shouted.

A reply came just as Michael climbed onto the rail and jumped into the water. He sank beneath the waves and kicked back to the surface. Then he swam over to the ladder running down the concrete pillar and started up the rungs.

He could hear the angry replies on the wrist monitor as he climbed, and looking over his shoulder, he saw the *Sea Wolf* pulling away. X raised a hand behind the windshield, probably unleashing a stream of curses in two languages.

Michael's robotic hand clamped down on each rung while Cricket fought the wind and hovered up to the first level of the rig. From there, they took an interior stairwell up to the fifth level. Michael stopped just inside the protected access to look up at the satellite dish. It was still pointed at the sky, and he didn't see any external damage.

Using his wrist computer, he directed Cricket to check out the dish. The drone rose into the air, battling the wind and rain. Several moments later, it was in position. Using one of its two arms, it reached out and opened the panel to the dish. Then it deployed a small metal finger into a slot to run diagnostics.

Michael cursed when he saw on his monitor that the problem was electrical. Cricket didn't have the tools to replace electrical cables, but Michael had them in his pack. He unslung the rope and, keeping his head down, crossed the deck to the crane.

Cricket flew back down and met him there. With carabiners, Michael clipped one end of the rope to the drone, and the other end to his belt.

If he fell, Cricket would at least be able to hold on to him.

That was the idea, anyway.

Michael looked up at the crane, thinking twice about the plan. He pushed his fear aside and started climbing the diagonal boom, keeping the metal between himself and most of the wind. Cricket rose back up to the dish, the rope paying out until little slack remained.

If not for Michael's robotic hand, he could not possibly have made it up the slick wet steel. Halfway up, he looked down. The *Sea Wolf* rode about five hundred feet out, disappearing behind a wave, rising again on the next one.

Michael continued the ascent, hand over hand up the steel latticework, not stopping until he got to the dish. Cricket had the panel off now, exposing the guts of the dish. Michael hooked his robotic arm over a metal crossbeam, got a good footing with his boots, and dug into his tool kit.

Carefully removing three different colored spools of insulated wire, he placed them inside the open dish. Then he found the proper tools and went to work.

Cricket swayed in the wind ten feet away, its red hover nodes glowing in the gray sky. When Michael had the time, he would finally fix the machine's thruster so it could fly and maneuver faster in conditions like these.

It took fifteen minutes to replace the wires. Not as bad as he had thought. He brought up his wrist computer and yelled, "Now try hailing *Discovery* on the encrypted line!"

Michael brought the device to his ear but kept the mechanical arm gripped tight on the crossbeam. The wind pushed and tugged his body as he waited for a response. It came a moment later.

"We're through!" X said. "Now, get your *culo* back down here!"

Michael looked down and felt his gut sink. This wasn't like diving into the sky. Unlike in a dark storm over the wastes, he could actually see what was below him.

Cricket moved back over to button down the panel over the new wiring as Michael started off down the boom, keeping three points of contact, thanking all the gods for his robotic hand.

A quarter of the way down, a violent gust ripped both feet loose, and he flapped like a pennant in the gale. Once his heart slowed, he continued down, making sure both boots had a firm purchase.

Five minutes later, he was safely on the platform,

where Cricket joined him. After coiling the rope—a precious commodity—they moved back down the enclosed ladder and came out at the bottom, where he flagged the *Sea Wolf*.

X maneuvered the boat toward the ladder, and again Michael dived into the water. He swam the rest of the way and climbed the boarding ladder to the deck. Only then did Cricket fly down onto the boat.

"Good work, buddy," Michael said.

The hatch opened, and Rodger was there, wiping his mouth on his sleeve.

"Did you do it?" he groaned.

"Piece of cake," Michael said. "Now, let me in."

Rodger moved out of the way to let Michael and the robot into the passage. The hatch clicked shut behind them, sealing out the howling wind and making the voices in the command center audible. From the sounds of it, X was talking to Captain Mitchells.

"We're still searching for their last known location," Les reported. "I'll let you know as soon as we find them."

"Copy that," X said. He cradled the handset on the dashboard and looked back at Michael.

"Ballsy, kid," he said.

"Like you with Ted this morning?" Michael replied.

X touched his bandaged head. "I haven't even told you about the Siren yet."

"Siren?" Samson said, looking over from behind the wheel.

X laughed. "It's a long story."

"I don't have any pressing appointments," replied Samson.

"We got time," Rodger said, slouching in a chair and holding his stomach.

Michael took the seat beside him.

"You best get cleaned up, Rodger Dodger," X said. "Don't want Mags seeing you like this, do you?"

Rodger managed a shrug. "I don't think anything I do will win her over. I've carved her animals, saved her life, and she's even seen my butt. Few women can resist that."

Samson chuckled. "You're forgetting about the rest of you."

"Give her time," Michael said, punching Rodger on the arm.

Rodger sat up. "I am, but she's really playing hard to get."

"Layla was that way, too," Michael said.

X and Samson leaned forward as the boat approached the capitol tower.

"What in the unholy wastes is going on here?" X muttered.

The bow of the *Sea Wolf* cruised into the open boat port and a scene of chaos.

Two militia soldiers had a Cazador mechanic pinned down on the dock where the cigar boat was tethered. Meanwhile two Cazador soldiers were shouting, holding their spears in a fighting stance.

"Is that DJ?" Samson said, standing for a better look.

The *Sea Wolf* motored closer, and Michael saw the engineer crumpled on the dock. His head looked like strawberry jam.

X cursed long and evenly in a low voice.

"So much for that peace, King Xavier," Samson muttered.

SEVEN

The nightmare was always the same. Les stood on the poisoned surface in Jamaica, in full Hell Diver armor and gripping a laser rifle. The defectors came storming out of the former prison, firing bright-red bolts that sizzled through the air.

Trey ran with Michael and Magnolia while Les held his ground and covered their retreat. He went down to one knee and fired three bursts at the closest machine—humanoid in shape and wearing a vest of human skin. Red eyes glowed from a metal face also covered in hide.

Les aimed and pulled the trigger, melting an orange hole the size of his fist through the titanium exoskeleton. He followed with a bolt to the cranium, and the machine slumped over, raising a poof of dust from the fractured pavement. Two more defectors strode out through the prison's destroyed western wall. One dropped to all fours, charging like a lion.

"Get in the air!" Les yelled. "Go!"

He punched his booster, and the balloon fired from its canister, filling with helium and yanking him off the ground. As he was being pulled into the sky, he fired at the hurtling machine. It leaped into the air, reaching for his boot.

The dreamscape shifted, and he was on the bridge of *Discovery* with Michael and Magnolia. They both were dripping with sweat and screaming about the machines.

"You have to drop a bomb!" Michael said. "We have to finish them!"

"Before they take Trey and use …" Magnolia's words trailed off.

Trey. Where was his son? Les looked around him on the bridge and saw the horrified faces of Ada and Eevi looking back at him. Timothy was also here, looking as solemn as ever.

"Les," Michael said, grabbing him. "I'm sorry beyond words, but we have to drop a bomb on the prison and destroy the machines."

The nightmare then would transfer back to the surface, outside the prison. Les stood in the open; staring at the smoking helmet of a Hell Diver lying on the cracked earth. He choked as he walked toward his son.

As he approached, something came whistling down from the sky. A thump sounded, then a beeping noise. The walls of the prison vanished in a burst of dazzling white. The fire engulfed Trey's armor and rushed toward Les in strangely slow motion.

Through the wall of flames, Les could see something moving. A human figure. Burning.

Les brought up his hand to shield his visor from the brilliant glow. Between blinks, he glimpsed a figure striding out of the wall of fire. Not a man, but a machine. The exoskeleton glowed orange in the all-consuming heat. Even as it began to melt, it kept walking, reaching out for Les with long metallic fingers.

"No!" he shouted. "TREY!"

Les jerked awake from the dream.

The beeping of a weather sensor reminded him that he was on the bridge of *Discovery*, sitting in the captain's chair. He shook off the nightmare and tried to forget the image of his son's smoking helmet. Each time, the scene was the same, and each time, he couldn't reach the body.

Les sat up straight, blinked, and looked at his watch. He had been out a half hour since talking to X about the mission to locate the Cazador warship *Lion*.

"Timothy, got a twenty on that ship?" he mumbled.

"No sir, we still haven't located them." The AI's impeccably dressed and groomed hologram cast a glow over *Discovery*'s dimly lit bridge and its skeleton crew of Ada and Eevi.

The ship rattled from a lightning strike below. Les leaned over his monitor to see that they were coasting a few thousand feet above the heart of the massive storm. He reached for the cup in the holder by his chair. Even cold, Cazador coffee was a thing of beauty.

He downed the last of it, trying to banish the fatigue so he could focus. Aside from the catnap, he had been awake almost twenty-four hours. But that was fine with him. The nightmares were a far worse torture than sleeplessness.

"Sir, the storm front is expanding," Eevi reported. "It is now almost eighty miles long, with winds capable of gusting over seventy knots."

She continued rattling off data, but Les, even fortified with coffee, had trouble focusing on anything but the past. He should have dived with his son. He should have been down on the surface instead of up here, in this prison.

He took a deep breath, trying to fend off the darkness. It was getting worse, and it wasn't just from the lack of sleep or the grief.

Maybe X was right. He needed a break.

"No, you have a duty," Les said out loud.

Ada and Eevi looked up from their stations.

"Sir, are you okay?" Ada asked.

"Fine. Sorry," Les replied.

Timothy walked over and said, "Captain, I'm happy to take over in the search if you would like to go to your quarters to rest."

"I'm *fine*," Les said. He got up from his chair and walked over to the porthole. Blue fire burst in the clouds below them.

They were fifty miles east of the Vanguard Islands, on the final leg of their mission to check on the *Lion*. The hurricane had barreled into the area with almost zero warning, thanks to the electrical storms, and the crew hadn't reported in for several hours.

This was again likely a result of the electrical disturbance, but he wanted to be sure. Losing one of their three warships—especially now, with the message from Rio de Janeiro and the threat of the defectors, would be a terrible blow to their small fleet.

"Hail them again, Lieutenant Winslow," Les said.

"Aye, aye, Captain."

Even in his exhausted state, Les could tell that his XO didn't agree with coming out here. He wasn't the only one changed by death. Ada, too, knew the trauma of loss. Her peppy, selfless attitude had darkened, leaving her prickly and angry. Most of that anger was directed at the people who had killed her mentor, Captain DaVita.

She continued speaking into her headset and brought the channel up so everyone on the bridge could hear.

Les peered outside but saw only the rain pummeling the glass and filling the bridge with a soft, percussive white noise.

"They aren't responding, sir," Ada said.

"Ensign Corey, do you have them on radar?" Les asked.

Eevi checked her screen. "I don't see anything yet, sir, but we're nearing their last known location."

"How about this hurricane?" Les asked. "Still looking like the worst of it will miss the Vanguard Islands?"

"I think so," Eevi said, "but we all know how unpredictable these systems can be." She checked her console again. "You see anything I'm not seeing, Pepper?"

The AI crossed the bridge. "From my estimates, the Vanguard Islands will see increased wind and more heavy rain, but unless the path of the storm changes, there should be only limited damage."

"Good," Les said. He stepped back up to the porthole window, listening to the barrage of thunder below them. He had seen a lot of bad weather in his day, but this wasn't your garden-variety electrical storm.

"I've got something on radar," Eevi announced.

Les hurried over to her station. "Is it the *Lion*?"

"Yes," Timothy replied.

"Good," Les replied. "At least, we know they haven't been taken down by a storm wave."

"So we can go home now?" Ada asked.

Les saw the fatigue in her eyes too, but he still wanted to confirm that they didn't need assistance. "Hail them again," he said.

Ada did as ordered, but again lightning static crackled over the channel.

Les stared out at the brilliant display. "We should descend for a closer look."

He caught the unease in the glance that Eevi and Ada exchanged. And he understood it well. He also felt conflicted about helping the people who had shot both him and his son in the fight for the Metal Islands.

But the war was over, and the Cazadores hadn't

killed his boy. The machines had, and if Les wanted the rest of his family to survive, he needed to work with the Cazadores to secure the Vanguard Islands.

"Take us down," Les said before his crew could object. "Twenty degrees down angle."

"Descending," Timothy reported.

The hull groaned in reply.

"Winds out of the northwest at almost seventy knots," Timothy added.

Eevi and Ada tensed, grabbing the arms of their chairs.

"All due respect, Captain," Eevi said, "but why are we risking our ship to check on them? We already know they're down there."

Ada looked at Les for his response.

"Because it is our duty," he replied. "Do you have a problem with my order, Ensign?"

"It's just …" Eevi began to say. Her words trailed off, but Ada, who held rank over the ensign, picked up the thread.

"This is one of the ships that attacked the USS *Zion*, is it not, sir?" Ada said. "One of the ships that murdered Captain DaVita."

Les licked his dry lips. She was right, damn it, and he hated that some of the warriors on that ship may have fired the very rounds that killed her.

Still, he had a duty—and orders from X—to make sure the warship was not in trouble.

"Those Cazadores have sworn an oath to fight for King Xavier Rodriguez, and he has given us the task of checking on the warship as part of our patrol. Do you understand, Lieutenant?"

Her freckled brow scrunched, and she nodded.

"We are all human and should work together," Timothy said.

The other officers didn't acknowledge the AI or correct him, but Les nodded. Part of Timothy still believed he was human, and maybe, somehow, there was a bit of him left in all that artificial intelligence.

What Les knew for certain was that Timothy had been a good person. He had died taking care of his family and had suffered terribly since then, yet he still did everything in his power to help his species.

The hull creaked and groaned as the airship lowered through the storm.

"Turn on frontal beams," Les ordered.

The bright lights activated, cutting through slanting rain that looked like knives hitting the bow. Lightning flashed, followed a few seconds later by a thunderclap loud enough to rattle the hull.

"We're at four thousand feet," Timothy said. "The *Lion* should heave into view in a few minutes."

Les stared ahead, trying to see through the storm. The ship held steady, withstanding the storm better than he had expected. She was a solid ship, built to last, and she had spent only a tiny fraction of the *Hive*'s time in the sky.

"Two thousand feet," Timothy said.

The beams raked the surface, hitting what looked like a sloshing tub of water.

"Dear God," Les whispered.

Even from this height, the waves appeared gigantic. And down there, plowing through them, was the bow of a small Cazador warship, bobbing like a toy.

"There they are," Les said. "Eevi what's their bearing?"

"Due west, sir."

"Ada, try hailing them again."

This time, Ada received a garbled reply in Spanish.

"They are taking on water," Timothy translated. "The captain is making a run for the islands to try and escape the worst of the hurricane."

"That's fifty miles away," Les said.

"Forty-nine now, to be precise," Timothy replied.

Les watched in dismay as the *Lion* seesawed over the monster waves. A crate on the deck snapped free of the chain holding it down and slid down the deck as the ship climbed over another wall of water.

"They aren't going to make it," Les said. "We have to do something."

"What can *we* do?" Ada asked.

"Timothy, approximately how much does the boat weigh?" Les asked.

The AI raised a brow. "The *ship*, sir? Far too much."

"Not the ship—the ship's *boat*," Les said. "Maybe we could lift them up and carry the boat back to the islands."

"In these winds?" Ada said, looking at Les as if he were crazy.

He did feel that he was starting to go off the rails, but most of that had to do with lack of sleep.

Get it together, Mitchells. Lives, and the airship, are on the line here.

He picked up the radio and called the launch bay. "Alfred, I need your team to lower the cables. Proceed to the lower bay, ASAP."

The lead technician came back on the horn. "Sir, for what reason?"

"Just get down there," Les said. He cradled the handset and crossed the bridge, but Ada moved to block his way.

"Sir," she said, "You're risking *Discovery* by doing this. You heard what Timothy said about the winds."

"The ship can handle it, and we need their help, Lieutenant," Les said.

"*Why* do we need their help?"

"Because the battle between our two societies is over, and the war with the machines will require every single man and woman," Les fired back.

As if in reply, the hull gave out a long groan.

"You're on the ragged edge of insubordination, Lieutenant," Les said. "Now, step aside."

Ada clenched her jaw but moved aside and let him pass.

The passages were deserted, all crew members either at their stations or in their shelters. *Discovery* could take much more punishment than the *Hive*, especially since Samson had it retrofitted with stronger shields against the lightning.

Les ran to his locker in the launch bay and got into his suit and armor. Helmet in hand, he took a ladder down to the lowest deck, where the belly of the airship opened under the turbofans.

The divers never jumped from this spot, but the cable system was here, and it was built to carry heavy cargoes.

The wind howled through an open hatch in the deck, where three technicians were lowering the two hoist cables.

Alfred looked up. "Sir, due respect, but what are you doing here?"

"Helping." Les put his helmet on and secured it with a click. Moving over to the technicians, he gripped the handle and peered down into the water while the cables lowered.

Les opened a channel to the bridge. "Timothy, do you copy?"

"Copy, sir."

"Tell the captain to get all crew into that …" His words trailed off when he saw that the ship's rescue boat was no longer mounted in its davits on the side of the warship.

"Did they already abandon ship?" Les asked. He saw movement on the deck—several Cazadores leaning into the steady wind, waving their arms in the air.

"Sir, I did not catch your last," Timothy said, "but the secondary rescue boat was lost in a wave."

Les scanned the warship. A half-dozen containers were still chained down on the deck. The bow climbed over another mountain of seawater, then vanished for a moment.

The wind pushed on the hovering airship, jolting it slightly. He gripped the handle harder and shouted, "Hold us steady!"

The wind roared in the open hatch, and rain clattered against his armor. He strained for a better view, spotting the *Lion* as it rose onto another wave.

"Timothy, tell the captain to get every sailor and soldier aboard into one of the containers," Les said. "We will pull them up and transport them back to the islands."

"Sir, the weight could be too much," Alfred protested. "Especially in this storm."

"Do it," Les said.

Alfred gave a reluctant nod to the two other technicians. They went back to work, and Les bent down to watch. Another wall of water hit the hull of the warship, but the containers all held.

A moment later, the Cazadores aboard the *Lion* streamed out toward the cluster of containers. He thought of the container that Katrina had found before reaching the islands, where the Cazador crew had stored human captives for their flesh. Ton and Victor, two of the survivors, now fought in the militia. Like Ada, neither man seemed to have forgiven the Cazadores for what they had done.

For a fleeting second, Les considered letting the bastards all drown. But doing so would make him no better than they, and if the Cazadores back home found out, it would ignite another war.

Static crackled in his helmet. "Sir, you're not going

to believe this, but I'm picking up another message from the source of the signal in Rio de Janeiro," Eevi said.

"What …" Les stuttered. "What are they saying?"

"They're asking for our location, sir."

The message made Les freeze in place. "Do not respond yet," he said.

"Roger that, sir."

His mind raced with the possibilities. Was this real? Was it a trap?

He pushed them aside to focus on the lowering hoist cables. They had reached the deck of the *Lion*. Les bent down and watched the technicians using an automated system to clamp on to the top of the container at both ends.

"It's secure, sir," said Alfred.

The last personnel on the *Lion* ran out onto the deck, sliding and falling and then pushing themselves back up before clambering into the container. They closed the doors to keep out the wind and rain.

"Bring them up," Les said. "Timothy, hold us as steady as you can."

"Will do, sir," replied the AI.

The clank of the cable windlass echoed in the room. The container rose off the deck, leaving the *Lion* to drift aimlessly—a ghost ship with no one at the helm.

Another wave slammed into the bow, inundating the weather deck.

Les gripped the safety handle again, holding tight.

The container was halfway up now.

"It's a lot of weight," Alfred said.

"The cables will hold," Les said. He opened a line back to the bridge. "Hold us steady, Timothy. Once the container is locked into place, we head back above the storm."

The load swayed slightly, and the hull groaned and creaked.

"Sir, I'm having a hard time keeping us steady," Timothy reported.

"Too much weight," Alfred repeated.

"I said it'll hold," Les said. "The cables can carry far more than that."

"But the storm—"

The ship lurched, cutting the AI off.

"Shit!" one of the techs yelled.

"Oh, God, no!" cried the other.

Les looked down in time to see the container splash down into the sea. The ocean swallowed it in an instant, as if it were nothing more than a pebble.

The cables swung loosely in the wind.

Les yelled, "What the hell happened!"

The technicians all shook their heads. "That wasn't us," Alfred said.

"The cables didn't just *snap*!" Les shouted.

Another voice came over the comms channel in his helmet, hard and flat.

"Let them drown," Ada said. "They deserve worse."

EIGHT

The storm beat the shutters covering the council chamber windows. X sat on the ridiculous throne, his hands folded into a pyramid that covered the gray stubble on his square jaw.

There was much to contemplate tonight, despite the fatigue weighing on him. His joints, his muscles—everything hurt, even his *liver*. And he hadn't even been drinking—not the hard stuff, anyway, although he was starting to enjoy wine. "It's basically fruit juice," he kept telling everyone.

This wasn't the first time he had stayed up for two days straight. In the wastes, he had survived days on end without more than a few hours' sleep.

Miles, on the other hand, needed his rest now more than ever. The old Siberian husky hybrid slept on the tile floor in front of the throne, his fur rising and falling gently with each breath.

Having the dog with him kept X calm in the face of an uncomfortable reality. In a matter of hours, the truce between his people and the Cazadores had been threatened not once, but *twice*, by the actions of two criminally stupid individuals.

Everything he had worked so hard for over the past few months was suddenly on the verge of crashing down like an airship into the wastes. It had started when a Cazador mechanic smashed in the head of DJ, an engineer on Samson's crew, with a length of pipe.

Then Lieutenant Ada Winslow had dropped a shipping container full of Cazadores into the ocean. And all this while they were still facing humanity's greatest threat of all: the defectors. The machines were out there, and X had a feeling it was going to be a race against time to save the survivors in Rio de Janeiro from them. Indeed, the defectors may already have reached the shores of Brazil and begun looking for the bunker. It was also possible they had been there all along and the message was from *them*. The implications filled X with dread.

He looked up as the double doors at the end of the chamber creaked open. Rhino walked inside, bowing slightly.

"King Xavier," he said, "I've gathered the people you requested."

"Bring them in."

Rhino motioned for the group to enter. Leading them was Captain Mitchells, still in his white uniform. Lieutenant Sloan, Sergeant Wynn, and three militia soldiers followed, their armored bodies surrounding Lieutenant Ada Winslow and Ensign Eevi Corey.

X rose from his seat, resting his hand on the pommel of his sword. Miles glanced up and then let out a sigh and rested his head back on his paws.

Michael, Magnolia, and Samson walked in, and the doors closed behind them. They were the only ones who knew the truth about the events aboard *Discovery*, but X knew he couldn't keep this a secret forever.

The group stopped in front of the steps, and X moved to the edge of the platform, looking down on Ada, who continued to avoid his gaze. Her youthful features were in shadow, but he could tell by her posture that she was nervous.

Rhino stepped onto the platform and stood beside X, cradling his double-headed spear so that it rested against his chest and shoulder. He was the only living Cazador who knew about what had happened beyond the dark barrier, and X trusted he would keep it that way.

X walked to the edge of the platform and looked at Ada.

"Why, Lieutenant?" he said. "Why did you kill them?"

He knew the answer. Hell, he should have known something like this would happen. Not only in the sky but also in the boat port.

"I'm sorry, sir. I just …" Ada's words trailed off, and she bowed her head.

Magnolia looked at X, but he didn't return her gaze.

"The crew of the *Lion* helped kill Captain DaVita," said Eevi. "We all know what some of them did to Katrina once they boarded the USS *Zion*."

X wanted to close his eyes and block out the image, but he kept his gaze on Ada.

He too had heard that some of the Cazadores dragged Katrina's body onto the deck, where they held her up like a prize. Edgar Cervantes, the soul survivor, had witnessed it when the Cazadores took him into captivity.

The warrior had stayed with Katrina until the end—an almost certain suicide mission. But not only had he survived the Cazadores who boarded the ship, he had killed three of them before they finally subdued him.

Knowing that the courageous diver had been with Katrina in the end helped ease some of the pain X felt. But it didn't bring her back.

"Captain DaVita sacrificed herself so we could live here in peace," he said. "So that we could have a home. You just jeopardized it all—*everything* she died for."

Ada glanced up, her eyes glazed with tears. "You don't think they're waiting to kill you, sir? You don't think they'll do the same thing to us when they get the chance? Parade our bodies on boats or hang us from the rigs? And *eat* us?" she said.

He had considered everything she was saying, but what was he to do? Commit genocide? When the human race was already facing extinction?

That would make him worse than el Pulpo.

He had to keep the big picture in mind. Sometimes, young people didn't consider all the ramifications of their actions. When X was her age, he couldn't think beyond a bottle of shine.

"She's right, you know," Samson said.

It seemed the older generation was also having a problem with the bigger picture.

"That mechanic killed DJ in cold blood, over a stupid boat," Samson said. "And then the asshole stuck a screwdriver through my other mechanic's eye when he tried to pull him off DJ."

"Cold-blooded murder is also what Lieutenant Winslow did to those people in the crate," Les said, glowering at his former XO. "You murdered them when I was trying to save them."

"I couldn't forgive them, and they deserved to die," Ada said.

"So that gives you the right to disobey a direct order, commit mass murder, and put us all at risk?" X snapped. "Guess what? El Pulpo captured and tortured me when I was clinging to life by my teeth in Florida. This was *after* Captain Jordan abandoned me on the surface for nearly ten years. I had a hell of a lot more to forgive than you will ever know."

The chamber fell into silence.

"The Cazadores aren't the only humans to have sinned," X went on. "We have also sinned, and I was trying to move past all that, to forgive the past and look toward the future." He waited for Ada to look at him again and then said, "You just severely fucked all that up, Lieutenant."

"If the Cazadores find out about the *Lion*, it will start another war," Les said.

"Maybe they don't have to know," Samson said.

"I mean, none of them survived, and they didn't send any radio transmissions, right?"

"None that we know of," said Eevi.

Rhino spoke up. "Colonel Vargas has spies," he said. "If he or any of the other members of the Black Order find out, war is a given."

X resisted the urge to sit back down on his throne. He needed to think.

Maybe he should have had Rhino execute Colonel Vargas and the rest of the Black Order, along with the Praetorian Guards who protected them. But Vargas had taken the vow with the others, and X had let them serve.

In hindsight, maybe that wasn't the best idea.

If they found out about the *Lion*, it would mean Ada's and X's heads at the very least; at worst, another war. He couldn't afford more spilled blood. They had too many other problems and threats to worry about.

But how could he keep these events secret? He couldn't silence everyone who had been on the airship. Alfred and the other technicians who had helped Les lower the hoist cables didn't know exactly what had happened, but they knew their equipment. They had surely gone over every plausible accident scenario and come up with nothing.

X bent down and rubbed Miles's neck, mulling his options. *What should I do, boy?*

The dog rolled on his side—an invitation to rub his belly. X almost smiled, but that would have been disrespectful under the circumstances.

He patted Miles again and stood.

His people looked to him for guidance. And a decision. This duty he had inherited was way above his pay grade. He didn't want to be king, captain, or even a commander. He was just an old Hell Diver.

It was the only thing he was ever good at. And now he couldn't even dive.

"I spent ten years in the wastes," he said, "wandering like a crazed cockroach, thinking I was the last man on this poisoned planet, only to discover that not only were my people still alive, but there was a habitable goddamn paradise waiting for all of us. Then we fight for it, win it, and two idiots put it all at risk."

He looked at Ada with a frown. "I should throw you to the wolves, kid. I should let them kill you for what you did. Or perhaps I should send you to the wastes—exile you from paradise and leave you, just the way Jordan left me."

"You can't," Magnolia said. "That would be killing her."

"*I* didn't die."

"True," she replied, "but that's why you're the Immortal."

"I'm not Jordan, and I'm not a Cazador, that's for sure," X said. "I'm a Hell Diver. My job is to save people, not kill them."

Ada let out a small sigh of relief.

"Honestly, I'm not sure what I'm going to do with you yet," he said.

He saw Rhino stiffen.

"What I am sure of is that we can't delay any

longer on sending someone to check out that signal in Rio de Janeiro. I've made up my mind. I'm sending *Discovery* and deploying *Star Grazer* to take out any defectors and save the humans there."

He turned to Rhino. "General, I've changed my mind about having you lead that mission. You'll stay here and help me keep the peace. I want you to put together a team of men and women you trust, just in case our friends decide to do something stupid like Ada did."

Rhino nodded.

"I want eyes and ears in the sky and on the sea for this mission," X continued. "Mags, you know how to sail. I want you to start the mission on *Discovery*, and when you arrive at the target, you'll use the *Sea Wolf* to accompany *Star Grazer*."

"Aye, aye, sir," Magnolia said.

"Captain Mitchells, you are in charge of the mission in the sky," X said. "Commander Everhart, you're going, but I want only two of the best Hell Diver rookies going with you."

Michael and Les both acknowledged their orders.

"Once you arrive at the target, you will scan for the defectors. If they are there, you will destroy them. Then Team Raptor will dive from the sky and rendezvous with Magnolia and the Cazadores to search for the survivors requesting our help. Splitting up will give you the best chance of reaching and rescuing these people."

"Sounds like a good plan, sir," Michael said.

"What about the council?" Les asked.

"Disbanded until the mission is over," X said. "No way in hell I'm meeting with just Moreto and that fancy pants merchant Tomar."

"Tomás," Rhino corrected.

"Whatever," X said. He looked at Lieutenant Sloan.

"Lieutenant, you make sure our security is airtight by the time *Discovery* and the warship depart," X said. "I don't want any surprises here at home while our divers are away."

"And what about the Cazador that killed DJ?" Wynn asked. "You aren't just going to let him go free, are you?"

X had decided to go with his gut on this one. It would be tossing the Cazadores some red meat while dealing with the problem in a way they would understand.

"General Santiago is spoiling for a fight in the Sky Arena," X said. "I say we let this Cazador murderer fight for his freedom. If he wins, he goes free. Otherwise, justice is served by his death."

Rhino nodded and said, "That is a wise decision, King Xavier."

"Glad you agree," X said. "'Cause once this storm passes, you're the one who's going to kill the bastard."

* * * * *

"You really have to go?"

Magnolia flinched at the unexpected voice, and out came the pistol on her belt. She looked up from her work on the deck of the *Sea Wolf* to see a figure on the dock.

A man stood in the shadows, away from the glow of the torches, not far from where DJ got his head bashed in.

"Just me, Mags," said Rodger, walking into the light with his hands up.

"Jeez, Rodgeman, don't scare me like that." She holstered the pistol and took out her tin snips.

"Sorry, didn't mean to."

"It's okay, I'm just finishing this roll up."

She used the snips to cut through the roll of razor wire she was adding to the boat's rail. Then she set the coil down and waved him aboard.

The storm outside had weakened, but she could still hear the wind rattling the door of the boat port. The sound gave her the creeps, and she was glad Rodger had shown up.

Not that she was new to violence or monsters, but the dark water slurping against the tethered boats made her uneasy. There was no telling where the Cazadores' famous human-eating octopuses were right now. No one had seen them since el Pulpo took his last breath.

Rodger took the access ladder to the *Sea Wolf*'s deck and stood with his hands in his jumpsuit pockets, head bowed slightly.

"I really wish you didn't have to go," he said.

"I know. Honestly, I wish I could stay, but X needs me out there, and I want to be ready for whatever we might face on the seas and at the city."

Rodger looked at the mounted harpoon gun, the razor wire, and the crates of supplies she had yet to take belowdecks.

He pulled a small cardboard box out of his pocket, looked at it, and handed it to her.

"What's this?" she asked.

"Gee, I guess you'll never know unless you open it."

Magnolia untied the string and opened a flap. Inside was the head of a wolf, carved in exquisite detail. It looked just like the Hell Diver team logo, and the figure Samson's team had added back to the deck of the boat after the Cazadores painted over it.

"Wow," she whispered.

He raised a brow above his glasses, a half smile on his face. "You like it?"

"No, Rodge, I don't like it," she said, pausing a second before adding, "I *love* it!"

She reached out and gave him a fierce hug, then kissed him on his cheek. Rodger tilted his head, no doubt expecting another kiss, this one on the lips. But romance was the last thing on Magnolia's mind.

Not with recent events.

She was staggered by the news that Ada had dropped the container of Cazadores into a watery grave. But learning of DJ's murder had hit her even harder. The forty-year-old engineer had left behind two kids and a wife.

Magnolia's heart hurt just thinking about it.

"I'm sorry," she said, pulling away. "It's not that I don't want to be with you, Rodge. It's just everything that's happened, and the uncertainty of the future."

"I understand. Trust me, I do."

She held the wolf carving up to the light and smiled. "It's going to look great next to my elephant. They're so realistic, I hope they don't scare each other."

Rodger returned her smile, but she could tell he was disappointed.

"You really have a knack for this stuff," she said. "Maybe you should open your own shop and try selling it to the Cazadores."

"Maybe," he said, slipping his hands back into his pocket. "Hey, I was thinking maybe we could have dinner with my mom and dad later tonight. They want to get to know you better."

"Sure, I'd love that," she said. "Maybe I'll see if you get your humor from Bernie, or Cole."

He smiled and looked at the razor wire coiled on the deck. "I've got something I need to finish for DJ's funeral, but I should have a spare hour right now if you want some help."

"Yeah, actually. Would be nice to wrap this up and get some rest before we ship out."

"When's that?"

"Two days," Magnolia replied.

There was a lot to do before then, and she worried about what could happen when she left. She tucked the wolf carving into her bag and put her gloves back on.

"You got to look after X when I'm gone, okay?" she said.

"I'll have his back, don't worry."

Magnolia snipped another section of wire and glanced up. "I'm serious. I'm really worried someone might try and knife him while he's sleeping."

"You're talking about the Immortal, Mags. You think someone's just going to waltz into X's bedroom, somehow get past Miles, and stick him while he's sleeping?"

Rodger had a point, but that didn't mean someone wouldn't try to ambush X when he was alone on a swim or in a dark hallway.

"I'm just worried, okay?" Magnolia turned to make sure no one was eavesdropping from the dock. "I'm worried about Ada, too. She's young, and dumb like I was at that age. I doubt she really understood the repercussions of her actions."

Rodger kept his voice low. "Did she really kill all those Cazadores?"

"I wasn't there," Magnolia replied. "I only know what Les said happened."

"What do you think X is going to do to her?"

"I don't know."

"You think he's going to banish her from the islands?"

"Like I said, I don't know."

Rodger must have realized he was annoying her, and stopped with the questions. He politely asked if he could borrow the tin snips.

After handing them over, Magnolia tapped her wrist monitor and pulled up the collection of music she stored on it. She scrolled through until she found her favorite album.

"You like rap when you're working, right?" she asked.

"Depends on what I'm doing. If I'm using a hammer, sure."

Magnolia laughed. "I don't mean the verb, silly. I mean the music genre."

"Oh." He shrugged. "Sure, it's okay."

"Good."

She hit the button, and hip-hop music crackled from the speakers built into the computer. To her surprise, Rodger started singing along with the ancient beat.

He wasn't bad, either.

"I'm a bad bitch," he sang. "A bad bitch with supernice tits."

Magnolia chuckled as Rodger continued improvising the words.

"Them Sirens think they bad, but they never met a bad bitch diver like me ..." He shook his chest like a dancer and broke out in a huge grin.

"Nice one, Rodge."

"Thanks, Mags."

When he finished singing, he twisted a roll of wire around the rail and she helped, trying not to look at the black water over the side. Not much in life scared her more than dark water.

They installed razor wire for the next hour and then took the crates down to the enclosed lower deck.

"That's good for now," Magnolia said. She turned off the music and pulled off her gloves. A faint noise came over the slap of water on the piers and boats. It sounded a lot like a Klaxon.

Rodger walked to the edge of the boat, hearing it too.

"What the hell is that?" he asked.

Magnolia had her pistol out, and Rodger bent down and grabbed the small semiautomatic from his ankle holster.

"What?" he said when he saw her staring.

"How many bullets does that hold, two?"

"No," Rodger said. He released the magazine, looked, and reseated it. "Six."

Magnolia rolled her eyes before taking the access ladder to the pier. Then she set off for a hatch that led from the rig's protected boat harbor to the docks outside.

"Hold on," Rodger said, opening the hatch and stepping through first.

The rain had mostly stopped, though clouds still blocked the stars and moon over the capitol tower. On the horizon, just outside the barrier, the clouds flashed blue from the outer edge of the storm, which had finally passed.

The water was mostly dark, with a few lights from boats moving between the rigs.

Magnolia glanced up at the platform where el Pulpo had once sat and watched his wives lying out on the sundeck near the pool. Several militia soldiers and sky citizens stood there looking out over the water.

"What the hell is going on?" Rodger asked.

She unslung her backpack and pulled out her binoculars. Then she motioned for Rodger to follow her to the elevator cage.

She hit the lever, and the chain started pulling them skyward. When they were a few floors up, she looked through her binos, zooming in on several Cazador boats.

Dozens of people stood on the deck of each vessel. But it was the massive container ship that caught her attention. On the deck, hundreds of Cazadores held torches in a circle.

"Well, what do you see?" Rodger asked.

"Trouble." She could hear the fear in her own voice. Her gut told her that the Cazadores knew about the crew of the *Lion* and were coming for revenge.

Why else would an entire fleet of boats be sailing in the open water while Klaxons blared from the other rigs?

The cage clanked to the top, and Magnolia shoved the gate open and rushed out. She found X standing with several militia soldiers, looking out at the flotilla gathered below.

"What in the wastes is happening?" she asked.

Miles rushed over, tail wagging, clearly not worried about the boats or anything else.

X leaned against the railing, and Magnolia relaxed a degree. His casual attitude told her this wasn't some war party coming to kill them.

"X, what are they doing?" she said.

"Mourning."

Magnolia followed the deep voice to the hulking figure of General Rhino, standing in the shade of a fig tree and watching over his king.

"So if that that's not a war party, why the Klaxons?" X looked to Rhino for the answer.

"The gods are angry from this tragedy at sea," he said. "So many of our warriors have been lost all at once to the depths. We now must summon the Octopus Lords and ask their forgiveness."

Magnolia recalled the shell whistle that el Pulpo had worn around his neck. The Klaxon wasn't a call to arms; it was to beckon the underwater beasts the Cazadores worshipped.

"We must offer a sacrifice," Rhino said. "If we don't, the Octopus Lords will destroy everything we have built here, before any of us have a chance to."

Magnolia looked down at the spectacle on the water. The belief about the Octopus Lords turning against the humans if left unappeased was probably just superstition. But standing here in this miraculous paradise that was the Vanguard Islands, she wasn't so sure.

NINE

Michael awoke to the clank of shutters. He reached over instinctively to Layla, but his hand touched empty sheets. He shot up, squinting at the sunshine streaming in through the open window. He had overslept.

And where was Layla?

He swung his legs over the bed and placed them on the cold tile floor. His Hell Diver jumpsuit, freshly pressed, hung on a hook from the bulkhead. On the breast, just over the white arrow symbol, was a note.

Michael plucked it off and read it aloud. "Meet me at the fruit trees."

Relieved, he reached outside and latched the open shutters against the bulkhead. Two days after the loss of the *Lion*, the skies had finally cleared, but a thousand Cazadores were still out on the water, offering sacrifices and prayers.

From what Michael had heard, the underwater beasts still had not surfaced to claim their offerings of animals and fish. So far, the Cazador leaders were not blaming *Discovery* for the loss of their warriors. They thought the airship had been coming to the warship's aid.

And it was not altogether a lie. Les had tried to save the *Lion*.

Michael noticed another vessel on the horizon. Grabbing the binoculars from the windowsill, he zoomed in. It was *Star Grazer*.

The Cazador warship, back from patrolling outside the barrier, would dock at the capitol rig for provisioning before the mission to Rio de Janeiro. He had seen the ship only once, but X had told him it was the one that captured him in Florida. If X could forgive the Cazadores for that, then so could Michael.

He put the binoculars back on the windowsill. He was more worried about the Cazadores forgiving the sky people if they ever learned the truth about the *Lion*. Especially if he should be away when it happened.

Leaving Layla here, even on the heavily defended capitol rig with X, had him on edge. And that reminded him that he didn't want her off on her own.

He threw on his Hell Diver suit and grabbed an orange from a bowl in the kitchen. Then he took the stairs up to the airship rooftop.

With each step inside the enclosed stairwell, the guilt ate at him. Layla deserved a husband who would be around to help her raise their child—not a Hell Diver who was constantly risking his neck on missions.

Since Trey's death, Michael had thought a lot about his future. Over the past few days, he had been away from Layla almost every waking hour, working on *Discovery* and supervising new Hell Divers. Today, he would select the two rookies to join Team Raptor on the mission to Rio de Janeiro.

And today he would be saying goodbye to Layla.

At the top landing, he walked into the sunshine, searching in the glare for the soon-to-be mother of his child.

Discovery hovered above the oil rig with the *Sea Wolf* already secured to her belly, nestled between the two rows of turbofans. The ship was low enough that Michael could hear the hum over the wind, but high enough that the drafts didn't disrupt the tropical canopy on the roof.

In a few hours, the crew would board it for the flight to the only known location of human survivors outside the Vanguard Islands.

Michael crossed the little forest, tossing his orange rind into the compost bin. He spotted Layla at the far edge, carrying a basket brimming with tangerines.

"Morning," she said with that smile that always made him feel a little weak in the knees.

"Why didn't you wake me up?"

She plucked another tangerine off a branch. "Because you need your sleep for the mission."

Layla gave him the elevator eye treatment, up and down.

"Wow," she said, "I don't think I've ever seen you in an unwrinkled suit. Guess I've gotten pretty good at the laundry. Farming too, but I do miss diving."

"I'm glad you're retired."

"Not quite," she said. "There's something I need to tell you, Michael."

He waited for it, heart skipping a beat for the second time this morning.

"I'm coming with you," she said, setting down the basket of fruit. "I won't be diving, but I'm taking Ada's spot on the bridge. Les asked me, and X agreed—well, technically, he said he agrees if you agree."

Michael massaged his forehead. In truth, he wasn't all that upset. The bridge on the airship was probably the safest place she could be.

"Okay," he said.

"You're not mad?"

"Not at all." Michael walked over and put his hand on her stomach. "I'm glad you and Bray are coming along. After what happened with the *Lion*, the ship might be safer than the islands."

"Good, because I was coming regardless."

"I have no doubt about that."

"There's something else," she said.

"I'm listening."

She reached up and gave his ponytail a flick. "I think it's maybe time to cut this off."

"No longer listening."

A grin broke across her dimpled cheeks. Something over his shoulder caught her eye.

"Hey, Commander! When you finish picking fruit, we got some guns to check!"

It was Arlo yelling. The young rookie diver was really starting to get on Michael's nerves.

"Kid is way too excited about those guns," he said.

Layla chuckled. "Like most boys. Better get over there. I'll see you at the launch."

Michael kissed her and went over to the edge of the rooftop, where the new Hell Divers were starting to assemble. Veterans Magnolia, Alexander, and Edgar were already there with Cricket, who hovered above them, monitoring the deployment of weapons.

Ton and Victor stood in their militia uniforms, guarding the weapons crate. Michael had a lot of respect for those two. Not only had they fought to take the Vanguard Islands, but they were also some of the hardest-working people around.

"Hey, Victor," Michael said, raising a hand. "How you doing, Ton?"

"We are good, Commander," Victor replied in near-perfect English. He gave a broken-toothed smile, and Ton made a noise with what was left of his tongue, and grinned.

Arlo was smiling, too, looking as excited as a kid at the candy-jam shack on the *Hive*.

"Attention!" Magnolia shouted. "Commander on deck."

"Good morning," Michael said.

She flicked a swatch of newly red hair out of her eyes.

The divers all straightened, and Michael took a long look at the dozen-plus rookies. Only two of them would join Team Raptor, and it was a tough decision. They had already weeded one out—Ted was currently hosing down a deck strewn with fish guts.

He scanned the first six quickly. None of them had stood out to him on the training mission.

His eyes stopped on Lena. She looked eager, and she was talented in the sky, but she was shy and nervous. He had no idea how she would do on the perilous poisoned surface.

Next were Hector and Alberto. The lean, muscular young men, both covered in tattoos, were trained fighters and had served on several missions to the wastes. But they weren't great with the gear yet, and both had missed the boat landing on their training run in the darkness—partly due to not reading their HUDs properly.

No, they needed more training on equipment and in the air before they could be trusted on a mission this important.

Michael and Magnolia had met after the last training dive to discuss the greenhorns, focusing not just on the best divers, but on those who seemed mentally and emotionally fit in a combat situation. And as much as Michael didn't want to admit it, the cocky kid with long curly locks and a handsome grin was the best man for the job.

"Arlo," Michael said. "Welcome to Team Raptor."

"Hell yes!" Arlo said, throwing up a fist in victory. "I fucking knew it!"

Several other divers slapped him on the back as he lugged his gear over to the veterans. Edgar gave Arlo a nod, and Alexander did, as well.

"Do I get to pick my gun now?" Arlo asked.

Michael shook his head.

"What about a nickname? I get one of those, right?"

"I thought your nickname is Thunder," Michael said.

"Yeah, but that's boring. I want something new. Something worthy of—"

"So earn it," Sofia said.

Arlo frowned. "Hey, can't be too eager, though, right?"

"Eager beavers end up dead divers," Magnolia said.

Arlo's smile vanished, and he dropped his duffel on the dirt. "I ain't planning on dying, Katib. In fact, I plan on diving more times than King Xavier."

This got a laugh all around.

"You ain't even making it into that launch bay if you call me Katib again," Magnolia said.

Arlo stiffened like a board and threw up a salute. "Yes, ma'am."

"Don't make me regret picking you," Michael said.

The kid was, without a doubt, the best of the new boots, but he was also the cockiest. Though he wasn't the first diver with an outsized ego. X, Magnolia, and many others had been unbearable assholes at one point or another in their careers.

And there was nothing like diving to the toxic, mutant-infested surface to humble someone. If Michael had to guess, Arlo "Thunder" Wand would be an entirely new man if he made it back alive from the mission.

Magnolia scanned the new divers one by one, then went back through the line before making her decision.

"Sofia," she said. "Welcome to the mission."

Sofia stepped out with her duffel, showing zero emotion. She wasn't the best rookie in the sky, but she had already proved she could fight once she got to the surface, which made her the right fit for this mission.

"All right, the rest of you will stay behind and will spend your time here on the capitol rig, training and keeping the peace," Michael said. "For now, everyone pitches in and helps us get ready to lift off at o-nine-hundred hours."

He activated his wrist computer and ordered Timothy to lower the airship. Cricket chirped, holding out both arms to back the divers away from the landing zone.

Discovery set down in the clearing between the Sky Arena and the tropical forest.

Michael watched the legs extend and press down into the dirt. The shields that Samson had installed gave the ship's exterior a scabby look, a bit like the outside of an old-world hand grenade. *Discovery* had saved his people from an uncertain fate, and now she was heading back out to keep his people and their new allies safe.

As always, the bustle of mission prep gave him a little buzz of adrenaline. He had listened to the transmission from Rio de Janeiro a dozen times now, and the sooner they got *Discovery* into the air, the better their chances of saving what survivors remained.

Morning became afternoon as Hell Divers and crew loaded the airship. Michael spent much of that time working on Cricket in the launch bay, improvising and installing some spare parts that Samson had somehow "happened to find."

Not only was the robot being fitted with two more arms, it was also getting additional armor and several new cameras. There wasn't time to finish, though, and by midafternoon, Michael called it quits to help with the other divers.

"Almost there, buddy," he said to Cricket. "I'll get you fully operational once we take off."

The robot chirped and followed him to the oil rig's safety railing. Magnolia and Rodger were there looking down at the water, where Cazadores loaded *Star Grazer* with fresh supplies.

By early evening, both groups had finished their work. Timothy confirmed that *Discovery* was ready to fly, all systems checking out.

Michael tied the red bandanna with the Raptor logo around his head and put on his Hell Diver armor, clicking the red battery unit into its chest slot.

Finally, he grabbed a blaster from the crate and holstered it on his thigh.

The other divers chose their primary weapons, and Michael took one of the two laser rifles. Magnolia took the other, and Arlo selected an assault rifle with a new stock and barrel.

"She's beautiful," Arlo said, kissing the barrel.

"Careful where you point that," Magnolia said. "Don't want you to mess up that pretty smile."

Several divers laughed, then stopped at the sound of distant shouting.

"Hear that?" Michael said to Magnolia.

"Yeah, I do," Magnolia said. "Must be coming from the deck of *Star Grazer*."

The shouts became more rhythmic, turning into what sounded like a chant.

Michael and Magnolia walked over to see what was going on. Edgar and Alexander were already standing on the platform where X had held the ceremony decommissioning the *Hive*.

The four veteran divers looked at the deck of the warship to see the most decorated veteran of all.

"What the hell is X doing there?" Michael said.

The other divers shook their heads. No one had been informed about their leader's plans to board the warship.

X climbed the access ladder onto *Star Grazer* with Rhino and a small team of militia soldiers. They made their way around fifty Cazador warriors standing in ranks before the stacked containers on the deck.

All the soldiers wore thick armor and held gas masks and a primary weapon in their hands. Mechanics and deckhands were busy loading spearguns and feeding ammunition into the machine guns protected by armored turrets.

The warriors tapped their spear butts against the steel deck as they chanted.

"*¡El General de la Muerte!*" they yelled.

"What are they saying?" Alexander asked.

"'The General of Death,'" Magnolia replied. She pointed at the observation platform overlooking the lower deck and frowned. "General Santiago, my favorite Cazador general, is leading them into battle."

The old warrior stood on the platform dressed in full Cazador armor with a bright-orange cloak draping his back.

"And you're going into battle with him, right?" Edgar asked.

"Yeah," Mags said, raising her laser rifle. "And if anyone tries anything, they'll get a nice bolt to their pearls."

"So, who's *that*?" Alexander asked.

Michael squinted at a husky naked man being led up an access ladder from the piers below. Two Cazadores led him on a chain that connected to shackles around his ankles and hands.

"That must be the bastard that killed DJ," said Edgar.

"His name's Javier," Magnolia replied.

The Cazador holding the chain pulled hard, forcing Javier to his knees. Now Michael could see that he wore a loincloth.

General Santiago held up a hand, silencing the chanting and the beat of spear shafts. X and Rhino climbed to the top of the upper platform, where the general waited for them.

"Well, this ought to be good," Magnolia said.

Michael let out a sigh. "What in the wastes are you doing now, old man?"

* * * * *

The last time X had seen a Cazador company this big, he was part of it and heading out on a monster-hunting mission. But he was no longer a slave. He was their king, and he was hiding a terrible secret about the fate of another Cazador company.

The paranoid part of his brain wondered whether Santiago, now standing beside him, suspected his people of having something to do with those deaths. But his gut told him the old general didn't know shit.

What X did know beyond a doubt was that the warriors on the deck below him wanted blood. He could smell it as surely as a Siren could smell fresh meat.

More Cazadores filed onto the deck as he waited to address them. Carmela, wearing her battle armor and feathers in her braided hair, led a group of them. Her annoying parrot, Kotchee, perched on an armored shoulder pad.

Six Praetorian Guards flanked the Black Order. Next came Imulah, leading a group of scribes in brown robes. Finally, a Cazador accountant in a faded green suit walked onto the deck, carrying a clipboard under his arm. He put on his spectacles and began to count heads while the scribes began recording what they witnessed today.

Imulah joined X, General Santiago, and General Rhino on the top deck while everyone else, including the militia, remained below.

"I am here to interpret, my king," Imulah said, bowing slightly.

Rhino moved out of the way so the scribe could stand beside X.

X raised his hands in the air. "I stand before you tonight to discuss several things," he said. "First, my sincerest condolences for the loss of the *Lion* and her crew. I know what it's like to lose warriors in battle, and tonight I join you in mourning those men and women."

It wasn't entirely a lie, although his heart didn't feel the loss the way it did when sky people died. Ada was right about one thing: the Cazadores on that ship had indeed been part of the crew who killed Katrina. And that was exactly why he had decided to keep it a secret—not only to save Ada's life, but also to keep the islands at peace.

What he had to do now was extend a peace offering that would also distract them.

When Imulah had finished interpreting his words, X said, "Second, I'm offering Javier a chance at redemption for murdering a sky engineer."

X gestured to the guards holding the Cazador mechanic on the deck below. They got him to his feet and brought him forward.

Imulah finished interpreting, and X continued with his speech.

"General Santiago has requested that I reopen the Sky Arena, and that is exactly what I'm going to do tonight. I've already made the arrangements with Colonel Moreto, who has put together a lineup."

When Imulah translated this, cheers rang out from the assembled ranks.

"You want your human sacrifice for the Octopus Lords?" X shouted.

Imulah spoke, and the warriors all shouted their response.

"*¡Sí!*"

"You're going to have several by the end of the night!" X yelled. He pointed to Javier, who stood below. One of the guards kicked him to his knees, where he remained, head bowed.

Every Cazador on the deck raised his weapon in the air, chanting something about the Sky Arena.

Well, that was easy.

He had come here to appease the Cazadores and divert their attention from the loss of the *Lion* and its crew. That goal was now accomplished, but he still had to rally them for their mission to the wastes.

X held up his hands again to silence the crowd. When the chanting had died down, he lowered his hands, and the two soldiers led the murderer away.

"In a few hours, you will depart for an old-world city, Rio de Janeiro," X said. "For the first time ever, Cazadores and sky people will fight together on a mission to protect what is left of humanity."

Imulah relayed the words. This time, there was no chanting, no raised weapons. Not even a single shout.

"This mission is long and dangerous," X continued. "*Star Grazer* will first stop to refuel at outpost Bloodline in Venezuela. Then it will proceed south to Rio de Janeiro, where warriors will begin the first part of the mission: to seek out and destroy any machines there."

This time, Imulah's words met with a few grunts.

"Second, we are searching for survivors we believe to be hiding in an underground bunker or shelter of some sort," X said. "When we find them, we will evacuate them and bring them here."

He waited anxiously to hear what these men and women thought of that idea. In the past, el Pulpo would have ordered his army to enslave the survivors and, in some cases, eat them.

But things were vastly different now that X was in charge.

After Imulah finished translating the second part of their mission, some warriors exchanged glances and talked in hushed voices. X could tell right away they weren't excited about the prospect of saving people. To them, it just meant more mouths to feed.

"We must do this to help replenish our ranks," X said. "To help rebuild the great Cazador army so we can meet the challenges and threats of the future."

Imulah again relayed the words. This time, several Cazador warriors nodded, and one raised his rifle in the air.

"We crush the metal gods!" Santiago yelled in broken English, pounding his armored chest.

The warriors raised their weapons to their general and gave a loud grunt in unison.

X's work was done. He had baited the hook, and the Cazadores had responded well to the reopening of the Sky Arena, and the idea of adding warriors to their ranks.

Over the noise, he heard the engine of *Discovery* activate with a loud *vroom*. Timothy was testing the engines, which meant the ship was nearly ready for takeoff.

X looked up again at the rooftop, where he could see the smooth back of the airship. He couldn't see the *Sea Wolf*, but he knew she was already attached to the underside—by the same cables that had dropped the container of Cazadores into the ocean.

He swallowed hard at the thought.

But it was the thoughts that followed, the memories of his crazed years trekking through the wastes, that gripped him hardest.

He suddenly felt alone, far away from his home and his people. *His* people were setting out on a mission to the wastes, and he wanted so badly to join them, he could taste it.

He stepped away from the railing, ready to return to the rooftop so he could help with any last-minute issues, and so he could spend some time with Michael and Magnolia.

To his surprise, General Santiago reached out and gripped him by the forearm—the handshake of a Cazador warrior.

"Very good, King Xavier," Santiago said.

"*Gracias,*" X replied. He nodded to Rhino that it was time to leave, and they went back down to the lower deck. Every face seemed to focus on the two men as they departed.

The Cazadores began to chant again. This time, they were saying something that X didn't understand at all.

"What are they saying?" he asked Rhino.

"All hail the Immortal," Rhino said.

X scratched his growing beard, not knowing how to respond.

"Most of them think you're a god," Rhino added. "But I'm pretty sure some of them would still love to kill you."

TEN

The capitol tower was alive with activity tonight. The Cazadores and the sky people had finished preparations for their dual mission to the wastes. But it wasn't just warriors and Hell Divers that had gathered. Cazador citizens from other oil rigs had boated over to the rooftop to catch the first fights in the Sky Arena since the sky people won the battle for the islands.

Rhino had the honor of fighting in the main event. But he wasn't thinking about that. His mind and heart were with Sofia, standing beside him in front of the airship. She helped tighten the leather guards on his wrists—the only protection he wore tonight.

"You sure you don't want your battle armor?" she asked.

"No need," he said. "Javier may have fought in the army, but I don't need armor to best him in battle."

"Don't get cocky," Sofia said. "You still haven't recovered from the fight against el Pulpo."

She pulled the strap tighter.

"Javier is not el Pulpo, and that's too tight."

Sofia loosened the strap.

"Good," he said.

She went back to work on the other strap. "I know he's not, but you can't let your guard down for a second in there."

"I never let my guard down with any enemy."

As she moved to the next strap, he gazed at the dark eyes, long black braids, and dexterous, knowing fingers.

God, you are beautiful.

She finished with the straps and stepped away, hands on her hips. "Good?"

"Perfect."

Sofia picked her helmet up off the dirt and took a moment to look him over.

"I better not catch wind of any other ladies lookin' at you while I'm gone, or there will be hell to pay when I get back."

"Almost ready, Sofia?" Magnolia called out, passing them by with a basket of fruit.

"Be right there," Sofia said, not taking her eyes off Rhino.

He laid his hand on her dimpled cheek. "I love you, my queen. Please, be careful."

"I'll be fine. You're the one I need to worry about, back here with that madman." Sofia glanced at X, who was eating an apple and talking to Michael inside the dark launch bay. Miles sat by his master's side, looking down at Rhino.

"X is one of the best I ever met," he said.

"Yeah, well, he's still crazy. Maybe not el Pulpo crazy, but bat-shit nonetheless."

Rhino chuckled. "I suppose we all are, in one way or another, aren't we?"

She looked past him to the Sky Arena, where hundreds of Cazadores were starting to take their seats.

"I'm glad I won't have to watch you gut Javier," Sofia said. "But he does deserve it."

Rhino could think of someone else who deserved to die: Lieutenant Ada Winslow. But his duty was to the king, and Xavier had told him to keep it a secret— one that he had kept even from his woman.

A horn sounded from the arena—the first notice of the impending fights.

"*Te quiero*," Sofia said.

"I love you, too."

He kissed her goodbye, and she hefted her duffel and started up the ramp.

Inside *Discovery*'s launch bay, Rhino could see X hand Michael a handgun. Then he gave the young man a hug. X embraced Magnolia next. When they parted, she hunched down to Miles, who licked her face.

She stood and waved at Rhino. "I'll take good care of her, don't worry."

"You better."

Rhino picked up his spear and stepped to the platform. Ton and Victor crossed their spears in an X, blocking his way.

"It's okay," said Lieutenant Sloan.

Both former prisoners of the Cazadores hesitated, but not for lack of understanding. Victor knew what she had said.

"Let him through," Sloan added.

They pulled their spears back upright.

Sloan's lazy eye wandered Rhino's way, and she grumbled something.

"Good luck, and dive safely!" X said as he walked down the platform. "I'll see you all soon."

Miles barked once, tail thumping.

In the open launch bay, the divers looked stoically out—no waving or departing words. Even Sofia kept her arms at her sides, but her eyes were on Rhino.

His heart thumped as the launch-bay doors closed. He had always longed to be with Sofia, and now that he finally could, they were once again pulled apart by the realities of war.

"You ready for this?" X asked.

"Always ready for a fight," Rhino replied. "But I'm afraid this won't be much of one."

"That's what I'm counting on."

X set off with Miles running ahead.

"Move it, lug," Sloan said, elbowing Rhino in the biceps. She cracked a sly grin that made him wonder whether she was flirting with him. The gruff woman would have made a good Cazador like Wendig.

"Ton, Victor, with me," Sloan said, gesturing for them to follow. They ran to catch up, eager to protect their king.

Hundreds of Cazadores stood in the stands around

the recessed stadium while more streamed in through the heavily guarded access door. They wore their best clothing and jewelry to watch once again the spilling of blood on sacred ground.

Unlike the other Cazadores, Rhino hated the Sky Arena. Even when he was a younger man, the cheers and bloodlust had felt unnatural. Fighting the monsters in the wastes was one thing, but he had never enjoyed taking another human life.

As a child living underground, he had learned to value life as a precious gift. But living on the islands had taught him that life here was anything but precious. Here, they glorified death. He would perform his duty tonight, but he would not enjoy it.

He closed in with the other soldiers to form a phalanx around the king. Here, with so many Cazadores who had lost loved ones, X had security threats aplenty.

Families stopped to look, some baring their sharpened teeth in a show of respect. A man bent down next to his four-year-old daughter and pointed at X, whispering something to her that made her smile.

Rhino scanned for threats and moved into the elevated booth from which el Pulpo had watched the battles during his reign. Sergeant Wynn was already there.

"Area is secure, King Xavier," said the brawny soldier, pulling back a drape to the booth. Today, there were no slaves serving wine, broiled chicken, or skewered shrimp. Just two boys and a woman Rhino didn't recognize, but judging by their fair skin and their clothing, they were sky people.

X spoke to them quietly and gestured toward Rhino. "General, this is Mallory and her sons, Rhett and Keith."

Rhino didn't need to ask who they were. Both boys and their mother had swollen eyes from crying.

"Tonight, they will watch you kill the man who killed their father," X said.

Rhino walked into the booth and stopped in front of the kids. The oldest couldn't be much past puberty, the youngest nine or ten. Skinny boys with long, wild hair.

"I will avenge your father," Rhino said.

A second horn silenced the crowd in the recessed stadium. Everyone stood and looked down at Jackal, the announcer, with his spiked hair and thick, curled mustache. He wore his trademark faded blue pants and bloodred shirt. In one hand, he carried a megaphone; in the other, a handgun.

Rhino couldn't stand the guy, but the crowd roared as he strutted to the center of the stadium. He brought the megaphone to his mouth. "*¡Buenas tardes, señoras y señores!*" he yelled. "*¿Están listos para ver un poco de sangre?*"

The stadium erupted in clacking teeth and excited screams.

Jackal pumped the megaphone into the air and brought a hand to his ear. "I can't hear you!"

The audience yelled louder as Jackal raised both arms higher and higher.

But not everyone in the arena shared the exuberance.

Mallory stared blankly downward, and her boys watched the spectacle with the same hatred in their eyes that Rhino saw in the gazes of some Cazadores who looked up at the booth and their new king. It was a look he had seen on the deck of the training ship *Elysium* when X first went there to meet the youngster warriors.

"Since you all have been starved of blood, Colonel Moreto has decided to quench your thirst," Jackal said. "Tonight, Warthog comes out of retirement to deal with two thieves we caught stealing fish."

Rhino looked across the arena at another booth reserved for nobility. Inside stood Councilman Tomás Mata with several other wealthy merchants. They huddled in the shade of an awning, drinking wine and smoking cigarettes.

In the next booth was Carmela, with her parrot on her shoulder. She waved to the crowd and then gestured down to a gate.

"Here comes Warthog!" Jackal yelled.

Rhino hadn't seen the warrior fight for almost two years. The sixty-year-old former soldier, who had fought under the leadership of el Pulpo, had gone into retirement after a long and impressive career in the army and as a gladiator.

The last Rhino heard, he was living on a fishing boat.

Warthog ducked under the gate and strode out wearing a helmet topped with the spiked crest of a bone beast—the same monster that had killed Whale and Fuego in the wastes before Wendig finally brought it down. Only a handful of the nightmarish things had ever been killed.

Warthog wore the trophy and carried the spear that had killed it in the wastes twenty years ago. It was also the reason for his nickname—the bone beast had clawed off half his nose in the battle, leaving him with a porcine snout.

Hollers and clicking teeth greeted the warrior. Jackal scampered away and climbed a ladder to the stands while two gaunt, half-naked Cazadores were shoved out onto the dirt. Though the men had some military training, they were still fishermen, and a far cry from skilled warriors.

The thinner and older of the two turned and tried to run back into the gate before it closed. A Cazador standing guard kicked him to the dirt. Laughter rang out from the stands.

The man brushed his long gray hair from his face and looked around, disoriented. He got up and stumbled over to pick up a sword that a warrior had tossed down. The other prisoner picked up a second rusty blade.

Jackal fired his handgun into the sky to kick off the fight.

Rhino had a feeling this was going to be fast.

The only way the two men stood a chance would be if they worked together, and that didn't happen. They split up, and Warthog decided to pick one of them off right away.

He threw his spear at the older fisherman, impaling

him through the chest and pinning him like a bug to the wooden wall of the arena. It happened so fast, the crowd didn't immediately react. He squirmed for several seconds before going limp.

Then came the shouts.

Warthog threw his arms up in the air, feeding off the excitement.

The second thief, seeing his only opportunity to dispatch Warthog while his spear was stuck in the wall, ran at him. He swung his dull blade, but the veteran gladiator ducked it easily.

The edge hit the bony skull crest with a loud crack.

The man staggered past Warthog, his balance off. He swung the blade backward, but Warthog was already on his feet and backing away. The swipe missed his arm by a good two feet, and the prisoner wobbled again.

Warthog used the opportunity to move forward and punch the man in the back, knocking him to the ground. But the scrappy fisherman managed to hold on to the sword and swiped again, nearly slicing Warthog's boot.

The gladiator again backed away, letting the man get to his feet with the sword. He crouched in a defensive position and motioned for Warthog to advance. Perhaps he was more than a fisherman after all.

Most Cazadores knew how to handle a sword, but few had the skills of a veteran like Warthog. He moved forward and then, instead of attacking, kicked dirt into the thief's face.

Though momentarily blinded, the man fought viciously, slicing the air. He got lucky on one stroke, slashing Warthog in the side as he moved in for the kill.

Warthog reached down, and his hand came back bloody.

The thief wiped the dirt from his eyes, looking as if he couldn't believe he had actually drawn blood. A scream of excitement came from his mouth, and he raised the sword high above his head. Too high.

Warthog lunged forward and punched him in the throat, breaking his windpipe as the rusty blade arced downward. The sword crunched into the top of the mounted skull on Warthog's head, where it stuck between two bony knots.

The thief slumped to the ground, holding his throat and choking. The arena went quiet, the sound echoing as Warthog stood watching the man struggle for a last few seconds of life.

Rhino looked over at Mallory, who clutched her younger son, Keith, against her breast, shielding his eyes from the violence. Rhett stood watching every move.

Jackal jumped back into the arena as Warthog pulled his spear from the first kill. The corpse slid down to the dirt, and a cleanup crew dragged the two bodies out.

"*¡Qué divertido!*" Jackal said into the megaphone. He repeated in English: "That was fun! But fear not, we have much more excitement to come. For tonight, we bring you a story of potential redemption."

He walked in a circle and continued in Spanish.

"Two days ago, Javier killed a sky engineer named DJ. Now he gets a chance to win his freedom!"

Another gate opened, and into the arena walked the husky shape of Javier. He had his thinning hair slicked back and wore a leather vest over his considerable belly.

X glanced over at Rhino.

Rhino nodded and went down a ladder to the dirt, where Jackal introduced him to the crowd. Not that he needed introducing, but he was surprised when the spectators did not give him the same applause they had given Warthog. Some even remained in their seats.

"They don't like you," Warthog said, laughing. He stood behind a gate, his hand still on his side where the fisherman had cut his flesh.

Rhino ignored him and twirled his spear. He stuck one end in the dirt and watched Javier walk out to meet him, holding an axe in one hand, a sword in the other.

Unlike the two fishermen, Javier knew how to fight. He had deployed on several missions to the wastes before being transferred to work as a mechanic. But he was still no match for Rhino.

He reached for his spear, gripping the shaft and preparing to pull it from the ground, when a voice shouted from the stands.

Rhino turned to see Colonel Carmela Moreto standing in her booth. Colonel Vargas was there with her, arms folded over his chest, bug eyes leering at Rhino.

Jackal gestured toward the two colonels.

"I invoke my privilege under the law of the Black Order of Octopus Lords!" she shouted in Spanish.

The crowd gasped, and Rhino clenched his jaw.

"I select Warthog to join Javier in the fight against Rhino!"

Vargas's lips parted in a wicked grin that exposed his black teeth.

It was happening, Rhino realized. They were striking first.

X rose to his feet in his booth. He probably had no idea what was about to go down, but Rhino knew exactly what it meant. Being a former soldier in the Cazador army, Javier had more rights than the normal Cazador citizen, and if someone on the infamous Black Order of Octopus Lords wanted to save him from fighting, they could.

In this case, Carmela was granting him a partner in the fight, but Rhino had a feeling it was Colonel Vargas behind the orders. He was killing his rival the easy way.

But there was nothing easy about killing Rhino.

The gate clanked open, and Warthog walked out, laughing.

"You're fucked, Small Dog!" he said.

Vargas picked up a weapon from the booth and tossed it down onto the dirt. Warthog picked up el Pulpo's prized double-bitted axe.

"Let's get this over with," Rhino said.

Jackal fired the gun into the air, silencing the crowd.

When the echo faded, Warthog and Javier were already moving on Rhino. He grabbed his spear and backed away, wishing he had worn his armor. This fight had suddenly gone from simple to challenging.

Warthog advanced beside Javier, the two working together, just as Rhino had feared. If he had a shield, he would have been able to deflect the spear that Warthog launched through the air. Rhino jerked sideways and felt the missile whistle past his neck.

He jabbed with his own spear as far as he could reach, his hand on the very butt of the shaft. The blade darted toward Javier's chest, but the husky mechanic deflected the blow with his sword.

Rhino spun, swiping the spear in a wide arc to keep Warthog back. It worked, and Rhino then turned to Javier, who approached defensively.

A raucous *vroom* sounded as *Discovery* lifted off from the rooftop, though no one but Rhino gave it a glance. They all were riveted on the fighting.

He thrust the spear at Javier, and again Javier parried the blow with his sword, this time nearly knocking the spear from Rhino's grasp.

Warthog attacked from the left, slashing with el Pulpo's axe.

The blade slashed Rhino on the shoulder, opening a gash that made him cry out in agony. He jumped backward to avoid a second blow. Then he turned and ran to get some distance.

"Don't run, coward!" Warthog shouted.

Rhino gritted his teeth, halted, and turned,

twirling the shaft of his spear at the prowling opponents, trying to anticipate their next move.

"Time to meet the Octopus Lords!" Warthog yelled.

"Time to lose the rest of your face!" Rhino shouted back.

Warthog charged, snorting out of his snout. But instead of striking, Rhino gave Warthog a taste of his own medicine by kicking the dirt up into his nostrils.

A muffled cry of pain and confusion followed. Rhino jabbed the spear at the blinded warrior's leg, sinking the blade deep into his exposed calf. Blood welled out from the wound when he plucked it out.

Warthog let out an animal roar of agony.

Javier moved in, swinging his sword, and Rhino deflected the blow with the steel shank of his spear. He pushed the smaller man backward, then threw a right hook that smashed into Javier's cheek, breaking teeth and knocking him to the dirt.

With both men down, Rhino strode forward to finish them off.

The rumbling of the airship distracted him for a second as it climbed into the sky. He took a moment to glance up, wondering whether Sofia could see him in his moment of victory.

Warthog limped away, axe in hand, and Rhino took out his other leg with a slash to the Achilles tendon. He crashed onto his back, and the skull helmet rolled off his head.

Rhino kicked Javier in the gut, lifting him a good

few inches off the ground. He rolled over after hitting the dirt. Spitting blood and gasping for air, he glanced up at Rhino, eyes pleading for mercy.

"Forget it, murdering shithead," Rhino said.

He recalled his training and walked over to Warthog.

Take out the biggest threat first.

The gladiator was trying to crawl away.

"Tell the Octopus Lords hello for me," Rhino said.

Warthog turned over, and Rhino made good on his earlier promise, swinging the spear low and parallel with the ground. The front of Warthog's face, including the lips and what remained of his nose, slopped onto the dirt.

The crowd went wild, but Rhino saw at once that it wasn't because of his kill. A boy was running across the arena. X jumped down from the booth to the dirt, but he was too far away.

It was Rhett, the elder son of the murdered sky engineer. He came running at Javier with a knife in his hand, screaming about his father.

"No!" Rhino shouted as Javier got to his knees and brought up his sword.

The boy leaped.

An anguished scream followed as X came running across the arena. Rhino got to Javier first and flicked the spear point under his jawline, slicing him from chin to ear.

X slid on his knees to where the boy lay crumpled with a foot of bloody steel jutting between his shoulders.

He took two more breaths, gave a rattling gasp, and fell limp in the king's arms.

X closed the staring eyes and looked up at Rhino.

"What have I done?" he moaned. "What have I done …?"

ELEVEN

The encrypted radio channel crackled with a message from *Star Grazer*. Les could make out snippets of General Santiago's words, but not enough to string into anything meaningful. Not so much because it was in Spanish, which Les had gotten tolerably good at, but the warship was twenty thousand feet below them, and the electrical storm was chopping up their comms.

The Cazadores were nearing the first stop on their journey: a fuel depot that no sky person had ever seen. Known as Bloodline, it was one of two such hidden outposts.

Les glanced at the map on his monitor again to confirm that they were almost to the coastline of a country once named Venezuela.

"I always wondered where they got their oil," he said.

Timothy had explained how, before the war, ITC scientists had developed a stabilizer to preserve both gasoline and diesel fuel indefinitely. The sky people had never needed gasoline to power their airships, which ran on nuclear fuel cells. Other than parts and medical supplies, the only other thing they needed was helium, to keep the ships in the air.

The Cazadores, by contrast, needed petroleum-based fuels for practically everything, including this mission. Since the depot was on the way, the ship had left port without refueling from the dwindling reserves back at home. Without stopping to refuel now, they wouldn't have enough diesel to get to Rio de Janeiro and home again.

The Iron Reef was in the opposite direction, two hundred miles west of the Vanguard Islands, at a place called Belize.

Another message broke over the channel.

"Timothy, you get any of that?" Les asked.

"Some of it, sir," he replied.

"Well, enlighten us."

Eevi and Layla looked over from their stations.

"Sir, they are asking for our assistance," Timothy said.

The speakers popped again with another message from Santiago. This time, Timothy was able to translate in real time.

"General Santiago said they sent an advance team," the AI said, "but the outpost has been damaged severely. He's worried there could be defectors or … something else."

"Or maybe it could have been the hurricane," Layla said.

"Highly unlikely," Timothy replied.

"So what's he want us to do?" Les asked.

"To lower *Discovery* and check it out from the sky—or send a team of divers." Timothy's voice caught slightly, as if he understood the perils implicit in such a request.

"Could be a trap," Eevi said.

Les frowned at her cynicism.

"Let's give them the benefit of the doubt," Layla said. "If they wanted to kill us, they could shoot us out of the sky pretty easily with the ordnance they have."

Les appreciated having Layla back on the bridge. She had always been a voice of reason, much as her mentor, Katrina DaVita, had been during her time as captain.

"Look, I think we all should be suspicious," said Eevi. "My husband is one of the divers they want to go down there." She paused and then added, "Has it occurred to you that they might want our ship?"

"Yes," Les said. "It has, actually. If they could steal *Discovery*, they would have the upper hand in both numbers and firepower. But that isn't going to happen."

"No, it won't, because you have me," Timothy said, smiling.

Les would have smiled, too, but the airship shook viciously in a pocket of turbulence.

"Going to get rougher before it calms down," Eevi said, checking her monitor. "This storm is growing, so I hope you aren't seriously considering descending. "What about sending Cricket?"

"The drone will never make it through the storm,"

Layla said. "But maybe if we do descend, we could deploy it. Assuming Michael has finished his modifications. I know he's been working on the thrusters."

Les took a moment to consider his options. The hurricane had already pummeled *Discovery* during the first leg of the flight. And the threat of lightning made this storm even worse.

As if to emphasize the danger they were still in, thunder rattled the hull.

"Timothy, do you have a map in the database of this facility?" Les asked.

"Negative, sir," Timothy replied. "All we have is an old map of the surrounding area, and the current readings from our sensors."

"Pull them up on the main monitor."

"One moment, sir."

Les unbuckled his seat harness and walked over to the mounted wall screen. Eevi and Layla joined him there.

"No wonder General Santiago wants our help," Eevi said. "It's a red zone."

"And they have a team that actually *lives* here full time?" Layla asked. "How could they survive?"

It wasn't just radiation that had Les concerned. "Those toxicity levels are sky-high," he said. "A minute without an air filter, and you'd be dead."

"Definitely a hostile environment," Timothy said.

Ten minutes later, another message broke over the open channel.

"General Santiago's advance team has returned from

reconnoitering the facility," Timothy reported. "He said they can't access the piers or the facility, and is again asking us to recon from the sky for a separate route."

Les could tell right away that Eevi didn't like the suggestion, and Layla didn't seem too fond of it, either. But their preferences didn't really matter. What mattered was that they do their part, because when they reached the main target, they would need every warrior they could get, and without fuel, *Star Grazer* wouldn't make the journey home.

"Prepare to take us down, Timothy," Les ordered. "I want to see what we're dealing with before I commit to sending in Team Raptor or Cricket."

Timothy nodded. "On it, sir."

"Layla, ready the weapons. I want to be ready for any hostile contacts."

"You got it, Captain."

Les pulled the handset off the dash and opened a channel shipwide.

"This is Captain Mitchells. We're heading to the surface, and things are going to get bumpy. Please report to your shelters or buckle in wherever you are."

He returned to his chair, strapped in, and fingered his monitor to make sure their exterior shields were fully deployed.

All but one of the fifty panels flashed operational. As long as they didn't take multiple lightning hits, the shield over that sector of the hull would hold.

"Execute, Timothy," Les said. "Forty-five-degree down angle."

"Aye, aye, Captain," the AI replied.

The bow slowly dipped, and the airship cut through the clouds, accelerating. Lightning arced across flight path. A strike hit but was absorbed by the shield.

Layla shot Les a concerned look.

"We're fine, Lieutenant," he said.

Halfway to the surface, the storm intensified, and Les almost choked on his words. The ship took multiple strikes, resulting in several alarms.

"We've sustained damage on the starboard side," Layla reported. "Two shields are at ten percent. Another hit, and we could see some internal damage."

Les clicked out of his harness and moved over to the controls. He grabbed them and slightly altered the angle of descent. Then he fired the six rear thrusters.

"Everyone, hold on," he said.

Purple flames streaked from the boosters, propelling their descent. Les grabbed the armrests and gripped them tightly. As in diving, sometimes the best way through a storm was the fastest way.

The altitude monitor ticked down and their speed rocketed to one hundred miles per hour and increasing. Les finally backed off just below *Discovery*'s two-hundred-miles-per-hour maximum, not wanting to risk it if they should hit a major pocket of turbulence.

The hull groaned, and the airship jolted before steadying back out again. All around them, the forces were testing the bones of the airship.

"Hold, baby, hold," Les murmured.

He looked back at the main monitor. Forks of lightning sizzled vertically, one of them grazing the airship. Another warning beeped.

Through the last of the descent, Les thought of his boy. He had tried to bury the painful memories and remember the good times, but his heart broke for his son. Trey had served time in the brig and came out a man, dedicating his life to his people and, in the end, sacrificing it for them.

Les would see to it that he had not died in vain. He would honor Trey's memory and avenge him.

At five thousand feet, lightning blitzed from all sides, setting off alarms.

"Almost there," Timothy said.

At three thousand feet, Les eased off power to the thrusters and slowed their descent with the turbofans. Random flashes of lightning splashed across the skyline, leaving behind a blue residue that lingered on the retina.

"Timothy, turn on our front beams," Les ordered.

The lights clicked on, cutting through the inky bottom of the storm. Only sporadic lightning crossed their flight path.

At two thousand feet, the surface coalesced before his eyes.

"There she is," Les said.

The warning sensors ceased, and an eerie silence fell over the bridge. Les gave Timothy control of the ship and walked over to the windows to see the old-world coastal city with his own eyes.

Not really a city, he realized. Not anymore.

The refueling station was one massive facility on the shore, with several buildings surrounding a central tower. The piers extending out into the water were broken away, only hunks remaining where *Star Grazer* would have docked to fill its tanks.

A beach separated the fuel depot from the piers, but the land was too fogged in for them to see any bridges or roads leading from the docks to the central station.

He did spot a lighthouse on a peninsula not far from the main facility, but unlike the other Cazador lighthouses he had seen in the past, this one was not glowing to attract Sirens or human survivors.

"Timothy, scan for life-forms," Les said.

"Already did, sir," the AI replied. "I'm not detecting signs of any animal life bigger than Miles on the surface, or any exhaust plumes from the defectors. But there are some very large creatures under the water."

"Take us lower," Les said.

Timothy brought them down to under a thousand feet—so close, they could see some of the faded letters on the central tower. The top floor was an observation deck with shuttered windows.

"Take a look at this," Timothy said. He switched the feed on the main monitor to a camera under the ship, and Les moved back from the windows to take a look.

What remained of the vehicle bridge from the piers to the main station lay scattered across the beach. Something else was odd down there, too.

"Zoom in," Les said.

Timothy magnified the view, revealing razor-wire fences, and black craters where mines had exploded on the sandy beach.

"I don't think a storm did this," Layla said.

"Then what did?" Eevi asked. "The defectors?"

"Pardon me for interrupting," Timothy said.

The officers all turned from the screen to look at him, but he pointed back at the screen, which flickered to another image.

"Those life-forms in the water," he said. "They are feeding."

Fish bobbed in the black surf on-screen. Hundreds of thousands, perhaps millions of them—so many that it looked as if the water had a rippling white skin. But not everything down there was dead.

The camera zoomed in on a dorsal fin cutting through the water. And another.

Dozens of sharks fed on the easy pickings.

"What killed all those fish?" Layla asked.

"Oil," Timothy said. "The refueling station appears to have sustained either an attack or severe storm damage. I'm not sure which, but the pipes have been breached and much of the fuel released into the ocean."

Les walked back to the windows, his hands clasped behind his back.

"There is a secondary pumping station, but it's a few miles inland," Timothy said. "Other than that, the only other fuel outpost is in Belize, in the opposite direction from our destination."

Les pressed his face against the porthole. He could

see a road below, but getting there was going to be the problem.

"You think it was the machines that did this?" Eevi asked.

"I don't know, but I'm going to find out," Les said. "Timothy, you have the controls. Layla, you have the bridge."

"Where are you going?" she asked.

Les paused just inside the bridge door. "To the surface."

* * * * *

X wondered what was hiding in the Cazador history books. The archaic society had kept pretty good records chronicling its journeys into the wastes—so many, in fact, that he still had barely made a dent.

But there wasn't much about the raiding excursion to Rio de Janeiro other than a few pages about a ship that was deployed and never came back.

Tonight, he sat in the library, trying to find more information, something that he might relay to *Discovery* on the encrypted channel before they arrived in a week. It was his way of feeling as if he was helping—that and an attempt to keep his mind off the recent string of tragedies.

But how could he ignore the pointless deaths?

The battle for the Metal Islands had been costly for both societies, and while he had hoped to avoid further bloodshed, he could see now that it was impossible.

Holding the limp body of a boy who died trying to avenge his father had taken another piece of X, and he didn't have many more pieces left to lose.

He shut the book, sending up a little puff of fine dust. The noise attracted the attention of the only other person in the library. Imulah sat at another table, combing through the archives for information about Rio de Janeiro.

Reaching over to the stacks, X grabbed the next book filled with stories of monsters the Cazadores had encountered in the wastes and human survivors they had taken captive.

The drawing of an airship helped distract him from the painful thoughts. Taking a closer look, he saw that it was the same airship the Cazadores had mounted to the roof of the capitol tower and converted into the Sky Arena.

"Imulah, come here," X said.

The scribe walked over.

"Read this to me."

X moved the book over so Imulah could read it from the chair beside him.

"These are the records of the airship that came before yours," Imulah said, holding up the book. "Almost a year after the missiles and bombs fell from the sky, an airship called the ITC *Jupiter* discovered the Metal Islands."

X had never heard of the ship.

"Yes," Imulah said. "The record goes on to talk about the events that followed—primarily, a peaceful landing.

The people of the airship assimilated with those who had fled here when the bombs destroyed the Old World."

"So there was no fighting?" X asked.

Imulah shook his head.

"This was a very long time ago, when things were much different."

Imulah kept reading, but X's thoughts drifted to the conflicts and resentments of today—to DJ, his son Rhett, and the crew of the *Lion*. A few floors above him, Ada Winslow sat in a cell, just as he once had, awaiting her punishment.

X still hadn't figured out what to do with her. He had thought that reopening the Sky Arena would slake the Cazadores' thirst for blood. But it had only resulted in the death of an innocent boy trying to avenge a father murdered over a stupid boat. Now he had two dead sky people, and a situation that was quickly spiraling out of control.

Fur brushed against his legs under the table. The warmth of Miles lying at his feet reminded him there was still much to be thankful for. A year ago, he had been trekking across the wastes with this dog, crazed, exhausted, and dying of cancer. Now he was the freaking king of a paradise that his people could call home forever, as long as they didn't kill each other first. Maybe things weren't as bad as they seemed.

The doors to the library screeched open. Sergeant Wynn and Lieutenant Sloan walked inside. Their rifles were slung, so this wasn't likely an emergency. He walked away from the tables and spoke softly.

"Sergeant, Lieutenant," he said. "Please tell me you have good news."

Sloan looked to Wynn.

"I've spent the day talking to our Spanish-speaking militia soldiers on all the rigs and have ordered them to keep an eye and an ear out for any talk of rebellion," Wynn said. "So far, they haven't heard anything."

"How about *Discovery*?" X asked. "Have we heard anything from them?"

Sloan shook her head. "With those storms, it's possible we won't hear from them again until they return."

"Keep trying. Maybe we will get lucky. If you do get through, I want you to tell me ASAP. I don't care what time it is."

"Understood."

"Keep up the good work," X said.

The soldiers left, and he returned to the table.

Imulah closed his book. "King Xavier, I'm sorry," said the scribe, "but the failed mission to Rio de Janeiro seems to be one of the operations with little documentation."

"Why? For every other mission, you have the records of how many soldiers deployed, on what ship, all the way down to how many freaking bullets were sent and how many came back."

Imulah licked his lips—a new nervous tick.

"What aren't you telling me?" X asked, stepping closer.

"King Xavier, we have many customs that you still do not understand."

"For example?"

The scribe brought his scarred hand up to his beard. "For example, we do not keep detailed records of failed missions, because the warriors who failed are not glorified in their deaths."

"So what happens the next time a mission is sent out to the same place? Those warriors are left in the dark about the dangers? Just like *this* mission?"

Imulah nodded. "It is a challenge and a rite of passage."

"It's also stupid."

"With respect, King Xavier, 'stupid' could apply to many of your customs as well."

"Oh, yeah? Name one."

"Jumping out of airships into electrical storms."

X chuckled and cracked a grin. "Okay, fine. Touché, scribe man. But just remember, you guys worship a *mollusk*. And you followed a man that you called Octopus Lord."

"And now I follow you, King Xavier."

X narrowed his gaze, trying to gauge Imulah's sincerity. The scribe hadn't forgiven Magnolia for pinning his hand to a door. Not that X blamed him for harboring some resentment, but the man was lucky to have his balls after what he did to Magnolia.

"So you're telling me you have absolutely zero details on the last mission to Rio de Janeiro other than the fact that a warship left and never came back?" X asked.

Imulah sighed. "There doesn't appear to be any record of that mission other than what you have already read about the ship and the warriors deployed," he said. "The only way there would be anything about this place would be if there was a successful journey there in the distant past that I'm not aware of."

"Would have been nice to know earlier tonight, before I wasted my time coming here."

"I'm sorry, but I'm not sure there ever was another mission. I will have to dig deep in the archives."

"You do that. I've got someone I need to talk to."

"Very well, King Xavier."

X left the scribe to his work. He'd had enough of the library for the night. He whistled for Miles, who followed him out the doors and down a passage displaying pictures of former kings and great generals.

"No way in hell they're putting my mug up there," he said.

Miles wagged his tail.

"Oh, so you want your picture on the wall, boy?"

The dog's tail whipped harder.

"Okay, maybe someday," X said. The thought made him sad, knowing that someday, perhaps soon, Miles would pass over the golden bridge.

When that day came, X wouldn't feel like sticking around much longer himself. In many ways, the dog was the closest friend he had known in the past decade.

He shook away the morbid thoughts on his way down the corridor, where he saw another loyal friend. Rhino stood guard with Ton and Victor. X was glad to see that Victor and Rhino had been talking. He trusted all three men with his life, and it would be good if they too became friends.

"Are you finished with your studies, King Xavier?" Rhino said.

X resisted the urge to laugh. He just couldn't quite get used to being called "King" and having a bodyguard the size of an old-world power lifter.

"Yeah, I'm done and heading up to talk to Lieutenant ... to *Ada* Winslow," X said, correcting himself.

Rhino's nostrils flared, moving his nose ring. This small reaction told X all he needed to know about the man's feelings toward the young woman who had murdered his people.

X nodded at Ton and Victor, then gestured for Rhino to walk the halls with him.

"What would you have me do with her?" X asked.

Rhino took a moment to reply. "It is not my place to say, King Xavier."

"I'm asking your opinion."

Again Rhino hesitated.

"Speak freely," X said. "I seek your counsel."

"I'd keep what she did silent forever—by killing her."

X studied Rhino and then turned away.

"If what she did ever gets out, it would likely mean civil war," Rhino said. "You can't risk it, for the sake of both our peoples."

"I know."

"Then you know what you must do."

"What are you saying? That I should kill her right now?"

"That is your decision as king."

X pondered their conversation on the flight of stairs up to the brig. A single militia soldier stood guard outside the dimly lit passage leading to three cells.

"King Xavier," the guard said, coming to attention as he approached.

"Evening," X said. "Please open the gate and give me the key to prisoner Winslow's cell."

The soldier found the key and opened the door, then handed X the ring of keys. X went inside and stopped at Ada's cell. She was sitting up on her bunk, knees up to her chest.

"Sir," she said.

He opened the door and stepped inside to look out the window over the water.

"How old are you?" X asked with his back to the young woman.

Ada stammered. "Twenty-five, sir."

She wasn't much older than Michael and Layla. He turned toward her and sighed.

"You had your entire life ahead of you," he said, "with a promising job on *Discovery* and a home in the sunshine—something so many of us literally fought and died for."

"And I killed to protect it."

X sat down in the chair across from the bunk.

"I was evening the playing field for the war that is inevitable," she said. "You're much older than I, and I know your gut tells you this won't end well for our people."

"So, we shouldn't even *try* to live in peace? We're supposed to fight to the last people standing?"

Ada shrugged. "I don't regret what I did for myself, but if it hurts anyone else, then I'm sorry for that."

X was gratified to know that she had done the crime for her people and not just to avenge Katrina.

"I loved Katrina," X said. "I miss her terribly. But I know in my heart she would have wanted us to assimilate peacefully with the Cazadores."

"I disagree," Ada said. "She was a warrior. She would have wiped out their soldiers or, at the very least, never allowed them to keep their weapons."

"You think she would have executed everyone who could fight?"

"I think she would have considered it."

Ada got off her bed and walked over to the window.

"Are you going to kill me?" she asked with her back turned. "Maybe the way Javier killed DJ? Bash my head in like an animal?"

X could hear his knees complaining as he got off the chair. *Getting too old for this shit.*

"I still haven't decided what the hell to do with you, kid. You have put me in a very bad spot."

"The Cazadores are killers and cannibals," Ada snarled. "They killed our captain and executed many of my friends, including Bronson, an old man who could hardly *walk*! We can't trust them. *You* can't trust them."

She turned from the window, her pretty freckled face illuminated in the moonlight. All trace of the innocence X had once seen in her gaze and joyful smile was gone.

It wasn't the first time X had seen a young person transformed by death and despair.

"I don't trust them, kid," X said.

"Good. Because if I were you, *King* Xavier, I'd be a lot less worried about what to do with me than about what Santiago plans to do with the crew of *Discovery* out there in the wastes."

TWELVE

Captain Les Mitchells stepped into the launch bay, where the divers were suiting up.

"The refueling station on the coast has been damaged," he announced. "And it appears the former crew is dead. General Santiago has no way to get his tankers ashore without our help."

Magnolia knew what this implied, though Arlo clearly didn't.

"What's that mean?" he asked. "Without *our* help?"

"It means we're going to give them a ride," Michael said.

Yup, Magnolia thought. *Maybe this time, we don't drop 'em to their deaths.*

"Look, this sucks for them," Edgar said, "but we already took some damage descending through that storm, and this is a red zone. Why we got to risk our skin?"

"You don't," Les said. "I need only two divers for this mission, and you're not one of them."

The captain looked at Magnolia. "Mags, I want you to join me."

"Wait. *What?*" she said.

"I need someone fast and agile and experienced on the surface," Les said.

Arlo raised a hand. "I'm the first two things, Captain," he said.

"You're also the greenhorn," Michael said. "But—all due respect, Captain—why are you going? Shouldn't you stay on the bridge?"

"Because I owe them," Les said.

Magnolia grumbled under her breath. The captain felt responsible for the crew of the *Lion*. They had trusted him to pull them into the sky, and he wanted to atone for their murder, which had happened on his watch.

"Fine, I'm in," she said after only a slight hesitation.

"Thank you," Les said. "Grab your gear and meet me in the hoist bay. The rest of you, be ready in case we need a team for support."

"Captain," Michael said, "I think we should send a few divers down to that tower to see what happened to the crew that was—or *is*—stationed here."

"Absolutely not. We're here for fuel, and that's it," Les said. "I will not risk a team for data collection."

"What about Cricket?" Magnolia asked.

The robot chirped, and Michael frowned. He obviously didn't like the idea of sending out his robot, armed with just a blaster. But it was safer than sending in divers.

"You okay with that, Commander Everhart?" Les asked.

"I'd rather go with Cricket," he said with a sigh, "but I guess I can send it out alone."

"Good." Les walked toward the door, then stopped. "Absolutely no diving unless I give the order. Anybody who jumps the gun won't get the luxury of shoveling shit with Ted."

"Aye, aye, sir," Michael replied.

Magnolia nudged him with her elbow as she walked past, grinning.

He didn't grin back. "Be careful down there, Mags," he said in his all-business voice. "I got a bad feeling it wasn't a storm that destroyed this outpost and killed those Cazadores."

"We think alike, Tin."

He handed her one of the laser rifles. "Just in case."

Magnolia crossed the open launch bay, feeling the other divers' eyes on her. No one seemed to like this mission, but there was nothing they could do to change the captain's mind.

And part of Magnolia understood his decision. Not that she liked it, but she respected it. They had made a pact with General Santiago, and she would uphold their end.

Cinching down her helmet, she headed below-decks, where Les was already getting the hoist cables down. Alfred and another technician pulled open the hatch levers. Both wore protective suits against the toxic air.

"Timothy, retract turbofans four and six," Les ordered over the open channel to the bridge. "Be careful of the *Sea Wolf*."

"Don't worry, sir," replied the AI. "*Sea Wolf* is secure."

A deep rumble sounded underfoot as the two fans were retracted into their compartments. Les threw the strap of his laser rifle over his shoulder and bent down to help the technicians.

"Move us into position and tell General Santiago to have his men secure the cables to the first tanker," Les ordered.

Magnolia peered down through the opening.

Star Grazer was directly below them now. On the deck were two old-world trucks with tank trailers. A third vehicle, which looked like a troop transport, was also there. A dozen soldiers in full armor waited to board.

The cables lowered, and Cazador mechanics jumped up to secure them to the four loading points on the troop transport. Magnolia put a harness on over her armor. Les, already in his harness, moved over to an open hatch in the hoist bay. The narrower cables here were meant for smaller cargoes.

"See you down there," he said.

Les went first, clamping his descender onto the hoist cable before sliding downward into the darkness.

Magnolia had done this only a few times and would have much preferred diving to using the harness system. It spooked her every time she slid down past the turbofans, knowing that if those whirring blades were ever reversed, they would turn her into shark chum. She bent down and watched Les touch down on *Star Grazer*'s deck.

She put her legs through the opening and locked into the cable system.

"You good?" Alfred asked.

She nodded and slid out, using the brake lever on her harness to slow her descent. The wind wasn't bad, though it did rock her body slightly.

For a moment, she took in her surroundings without the aid of her night-vision goggles. Like most of the poisoned surface, this place was the color of rust. The ocean lapped a shoreline rimmed with fish poisoned by the petroleum spill.

The piers had broken away, leaving slabs and concrete pilings protruding from the water like broken bones. The beach was littered with pieces of a bridge and the craters of exploded land mines, but she saw no evidence of Sirens or other monsters.

She pulled on the brake lever again, slowing her descent to barely a crawl. Her boots hit the deck a moment later.

After getting out of her harness, she gave a thumbs-up, and Alfred's team began winching the cable toward the ship.

"Mags, let's go!" Les yelled from the back of the armored troop transport, which rode on tank tracks instead of wheels.

"Where's General Santiago?" she asked.

"He must be staying belowdecks," Les said with a shrug.

A Cazador opened the back hatch to the troop transport, and she ducked inside. Les joined her on a bench facing the warriors already inside.

Magnolia nodded to them, but looking back at her through their oval eyepieces, they may as well have been machines. Several more Cazadores squeezed into the vehicle before the hatch banged shut. The troop transport jolted, then swung slightly coming off the deck.

The front windshield provided the only view in the armored truck. Magnolia watched them rise past the warship's command island. They rose above it, swaying slightly.

On the shore, tendrils of lightning illuminated the brown central tower of the outpost. *Discovery* pulled them higher until even the tower was out of sight.

The cables brought them all the way to the docking area underneath the airship, where cargo brackets locked the transport into place. Alfred used remote arms to secure the vehicle.

"Cargo secured," Timothy said. "Proceeding to target."

The ship's thrusters kicked on, and the AI piloted them across the water, up the beach, and over the tower. They hovered there for a few moments while Team Raptor launched the drone.

"Cricket is deployed," Michael confirmed over the channel.

"Stand by for landing," Timothy said.

The cables lowered, and the troop transport's stiff suspension jolted as the tracks touched down. The path they were on wound through a ravine that had to be on the north side of the refinery.

The hatch opened again, and two Cazador soldiers got out to unhook the cables. As *Discovery* lifted away to pick up and deliver the first of the two tanker trucks, Magnolia could see the road now, or what was left of it. Cracked red dirt covered most of the asphalt. The winding path led back to the shoreline and the central tower of the outpost.

Discovery pulled away and flew back out to sea.

An hour and a half later, both empty fuel tankers were on the ground and convoyed with the transport between them.

"Good luck, Captain," Timothy said from the bridge of *Discovery*. "And good luck to you, Magnolia."

She grinned at that. "Thanks for remembering me, bud."

"Keep the airship in range," Les said. "Just in case."

"Roger that, sir," Timothy replied.

The soldiers slammed the hatch, and Magnolia looked ahead through the windshield as the transport set off. Tracks crunched over the battered roadbed. The tanker ahead blocked most of the view, but what she could see was mostly barren wasteland.

Purple vegetation grew along the path and snaked over the road. A few minutes into the drive, the convoy had to stop for the Cazadores to clear the dense flora.

Flames shot away from the lead truck, and a soldier with a flamethrower walked into view. He raked the fire over the dense wall of foliage, which sizzled and curled back from the heat.

The troop transport drove on, the man with the flamethrower walking alongside.

A transmission from Timothy crackled over the encrypted channel.

"Captain Mitchells …" The voice was barely audible through the white noise.

It came again a moment later. "Captain Mitchells, do you copy?"

"Lots of interference, but I copy," Les replied.

"We're picking up some *very* big life-forms in your sector," said the AI. "Do you have eyes on anything?"

Magnolia could hear the transmission well enough to catch the emphasis he put on "very." Les moved with her for a better look out the windshield.

"You guys see anything up there?" he asked.

The driver said nothing, either not understanding English or not pleased at having guests in his vehicle.

"Timothy, where do you see them?" Les said over the channel. "Sky or land? I can't see shit."

"Any of you speak English?" Magnolia asked the Cazadores sitting in the troop hold.

One of the men replied, "*Un poco, nada más.*"

"Ask your buddies if they can see anything up there," she said.

The soldier shook his helmet. "*No comprendo.*"

Magnolia grunted, then reached up and turned the spin wheel to open the top hatch to the turret. Before anyone could stop her, she climbed up for a view.

A mounted machine gun with a large barrel was attached to the armored turret. She unslung her laser rifle, preferring its proven firepower to the archaic machine gun.

Ahead of their convoy, she spotted several low warehouses, a row of silo-shaped structures, and a three-story brick building that had taken some damage over the centuries. She didn't study it long enough to determine whether the destruction was from Mother Nature or something else. Right now, other matters took precedence.

She brought up the laser rifle and scanned above for male Sirens.

Seeing nothing, she watched the surface for movement. Through her scope came a familiar view from other tropical wastelands: spindly purple vines, bushes with fishhook barbs, and the occasional thorn tree.

Nothing moved in the green hue of her optics. Switching to infrared, she picked up several small heat signatures, but nothing that would be a threat from this range.

Magnolia opened the channel to *Discovery*. "Timothy, I've got nothing in view besides a few oversized insects."

The reply hissed into her ear. "That's odd," said the AI. "The scans are now showing nothing. Must have been a glitch."

Magnolia felt like sliding back down into the shelter of the vehicle. Something was out there. She could feel a presence, but she couldn't see anything.

The brakes screeched on the oil tanker ahead of them. It turned off toward the row of silos that contained the diesel fuel the Cazadores needed for their warship.

"Mags, you got anything up there?" Les asked over the channel.

"Nothing but poisoned earth and some truly nasty-looking plants."

"Get back down here, then," he said.

She did another scan of the cracked earth surrounding the settlement. The terrain here was mostly flat and barren but with a few random thickets of barbed purple bushes, and a lone tree whose skeletal branches reminded her of arms raised in prayer to an uncaring deity.

Lightning speared the horizon. The boom of thunder rattled the turret, but she stayed there, watching what appeared to be something slithering across the cracked earth.

"Wait a second," she said into her comm.

Bringing the laser rifle's scope up to her visor, she aimed at the first mutant creature and then almost laughed at what appeared to be a snake with two heads.

It wasn't small—probably four feet—but didn't really qualify as a threat.

Bumping on the channel to *Discovery*, she said, "I think I found your hostile contacts, Timothy: just your garden-variety two-headed snake."

The creature slithered into a hole and vanished.

"Copy that," replied the AI.

The first truck stopped at the silos, and two soldiers jumped out. The driver in the troop transport remained behind the wheel as the passenger got out to open the back hatch.

Magnolia stayed in the turret, watching for threats while the transport disgorged Cazador soldiers. A total of twelve moved out to form a perimeter while two teams of three went to work hooking up the tankers' feed hoses to the silos and mounting generators to power the pumps and the arc lights that would let them see potential threats before they arrived.

Voices called out in Spanish, and three more men climbed down from the tanker behind the transport. Two of them carried only spears, and they flanked a man with an orange cape hanging over his oval neck guard. Instead of oval eye slots, the soldier had a face shield like those of the Hell Divers.

"Oh, shit," Magnolia said. Bumping her comm, she opened a private channel to Les. "General Santiago is here, Captain."

"Ah, glad to see him risking his neck alongside ours," Les said.

The general shouted orders at the soldiers standing guard, and they set off into the wastes with their machine guns and flamethrowers.

Six men fanned out into the dirt off the road, three moved behind the rear tanker, and three more held security near the first truck.

Santiago cradled a double-barreled shotgun and looked up at Magnolia. Then he walked away to monitor the fuel transfer. The generators kicked in with a loud chugging.

She looked back to the patrolling Cazadores who had walked out onto the barren rust-colored terrain. The two on point moved out cautiously, armed with a flamethrower and a machine gun. The two-headed snake she saw earlier wouldn't stand a chance.

Lightning flashed over the ocean to the east, and in the glow, she glimpsed *Discovery*, hovering over the central tower that had once been a Cazador outpost.

A chill traced her spine when she thought about it.

Something was off about this place.

The generators continued to hum, and she rotated in the turret to check the loading status. Les was standing beside General Santiago, overseeing one of the teams.

A flicker of motion caught her attention, and she brought her scope up to the low rocky hills west of their location, just to the right of the three-story brick building.

She stopped and moved the scope back for another look. The red humps in the ground seemed to be *moving* slightly. She blinked to make sure her eyes weren't playing tricks on her.

What in the wastes ...?

The ground was definitely moving, the dirt humping as whatever moved beneath it pushed upward. She bumped on the channel to *Discovery*. "Timothy, are you picking up anything on your scans?"

"Negative," replied the AI.

She cursed under her breath. The airship was likely out of range now. She switched back to the channel with Les and said, "Captain, I've got something moving east, toward the oil tanker behind my location."

The underground creature was moving faster now and appeared to be moving right toward the chuffing generator. Two Cazadores had stopped patrolling to look at the mound of rising earth.

"Watch out!" Magnolia shouted.

An explosion of dirt made her flinch and blink. In that fraction of a second, one of the soldiers vanished in the cloud of dust. When it cleared, his comrade ran over to a hole in the ground.

He aimed his rifle downward and fired a burst. A blur of red shot up from the ground, and a crocodilian head swallowed half his body. It lifted him into the air, and only then did she see the second massive head connected to a red, rubbery neck as thick as a full-grown palm tree.

The first Cazador was now a bulge in the neck the two heads shared.

Magnolia aimed the laser rifle, but before she could get off a shot, the two-headed beast pulled the second man back into the hole.

Screams and gunfire seemed to ring out from all directions.

Les came running around in front of the troop transport, laser rifle at the ready. "What the hell was that!" he shouted.

"The mom or pop of the snake I saw earlier!" she yelled back.

The Cazadores on patrol made a run for the trucks, but three of them were a good distance from the road. Another explosion of dirt geysered into the air between the men and the vehicles.

Two more heads climbed into the air on a thick neck, swaying back and forth like cornstalks in a breeze. The heads suddenly shot toward the three stranded Cazadores.

One man tried to roll away, but too late. He and another soldier were snatched into the air. The third warrior turned and fired his flamethrower, setting the snake's hide ablaze.

Both heads screeched in agony, dropping one of their victims back to the dirt. The man crawled away, pushed himself up, and ran. But the other man in its mouth was gobbled down whole even as the creature burned.

The line of soldiers on the road opened fire on the dozen yards of snake still writhing aboveground. Purple blood leaked out of the burning rubbery hide, and a guttural screech rose over the crack of gunfire.

Magnolia tried to aim, but the troop transport jolted hard, slamming her forward into the grips of the machine gun. She nearly lost her laser rifle.

"Captain!" she yelled as the ground around him humped upward from another snake circling the truck.

Les jumped up, and she reached down, catching his wrist and hauling upward as he clambered on top of the troop transport.

"Timothy! We need air support!" Les shouted.

"On my way," the AI replied.

The snake behind the vehicle broke through the road in an explosion of dirt and broken asphalt. The first head that emerged grabbed a man with a flamethrower and rose into the air. The other head, now visible, snapped at the Cazador in the other pair of jaws, ripping off an arm.

The man's other hand squeezed the trigger of the flamethrower, releasing a blast of fire, so that, for a few seconds, the snake became a fire-breathing dragon. The jet of fire zigzagged erratically through the air and then swung right toward the troop transport.

Magnolia ducked inside the vehicle with Les, who pulled the hatch shut just as burning liquid coated the armored turret.

THIRTEEN

Michael stood on the bridge of *Discovery*, watching through a porthole as the ambush unfolded. At the airship's altitude of a thousand feet, the vehicles, soldiers, and bizarre reptiles looked somehow not entirely real, but he had no illusions—humans were dying down there, and Magnolia and Les were right there in the thick of it.

Flames shot away from the perimeter the Cazadores had formed around their precious oil tankers, but even fire didn't seem to deter the two-headed leviathans.

Both heads of another snake grabbed a Cazador and tore him in half as they pulled in opposite directions. Another line of liquid fire jetted up from the road and engulfed one of the monsters.

"They're getting slaughtered!" Michael yelled. "We *have* to do something!"

Layla watched a screen displaying the feed from the ship's cameras.

"What can we do?" she said. "We can't fire on

those things without risking the lives of Captain Mitchells, Magnolia, and the Cazadores."

"She's right," Timothy said. "I have to tell the captain." The hologram walked several steps and vanished. "Captain, we can't get a clear shot from our current altitude, and going lower would put the airship at risk."

Michael knew there was only one way to help. He took over the comms. "Captain, this is Commander Everhart, requesting permission to dive!"

Layla shot him a concerned look, but it was the captain who said no.

"Hold your position, Commander," Les said. "Timothy, if you can't get a shot, then lower those damn hoist cables. We have to get at least one of these tankers airborne!"

Michael looked back out the porthole. "How the hell are they supposed to attach the cables with those things picking them off?" he said.

He hurried over to Layla, kissed her on the forehead, and put a hand on her stomach. "I love you, and I promise I'll be back."

She held his hand to her and nodded. "Go save our friends."

Michael rushed belowdecks, opening up a channel to Team Raptor on his way down the ladders as he realized that the only gun he had on him was the Beretta M9 that X had given him right before they took off.

It was a beautiful weapon, with a cursive engraving on the slide that read, "*Face your future without fear.*"

But he was going to need something with more firepower if he had any hope of killing the reptilian monsters down there.

He bumped on his headset to Hell Diver Edgar Cervantes. "Get everyone to meet me in loading dock two, and bring me a rifle with at least two magazines of armor-piercing rounds."

"Copy that, Commander. We're on our way."

By the time Michael arrived in the lower compartment, the other divers were already there helping Alfred's technicians lower the hoist cables.

"What the hell is going on down there?" Alfred asked.

Everyone looked to Michael.

"Just get those cables down." He moved over for a look out a porthole. The view here was angled and not as good as from the bridge, and he went from window to window for a better view.

At the last porthole, he glimpsed the silos and a few of the Cazador workers still holding the long rubber hoses attached to the front tanker.

"Shit, they aren't done fueling," he mumbled.

It wouldn't matter in a few minutes, if those snakes or worms or whatever the hell they were got any closer.

Michael reopened the channel to Les. "Captain, we have to get down there!" he said.

A voice came through the static. "I said *hold* position, Commander! I don't want to risk any divers. We have this under control."

Michael's eyes told him that was utter bullshit. Another two-headed beast broke through the ground near the road to snag a Cazador with a machine gun. As it pulled him into the air, the weapon sprayed bullets in all directions.

A round penetrated the hull of the ship. An emergency alarm blared, and an automatic message broke over the speakers.

"All nonessential personnel, report to the nearest shelter."

"I've got a leak in compartment fourteen," Layla said over the comm. "Sealing it off."

Glancing over his shoulder, Michael saw Edgar and Alexander standing and ready to dive. Arlo and Sofia, however, were hunched down. He couldn't see behind their mirrored visors, but judging by their posture, they were terrified.

It was then that Michael realized why Les didn't want to risk letting them dive in this chaos. The meat grinder below wasn't a fitting drop zone for the new boots' first real mission. But that didn't mean Michael had to stay put.

"We doing this, Commander?" Edgar asked.

Michael shook his head. "Change of plans. You all stay here. I'm heading down on my own."

"What!" Alexander said. "Commander, all due respect—"

"That's an order," Michael said, feeling like a hypocrite.

He bumped on his comm channel back to Les.

"Captain, this is Commander Everhart. I did not catch your last transmission, over."

He grabbed a harness and nodded to one of the technicians. Alfred moved over to an open hatch in the deck and locked Michael's descender onto a cable. A moment later, he was sliding toward the surface.

Glancing up, he saw the *Sea Wolf*. He bumped off his comm system and whispered, "I love you, Layla and Bray."

The wind jerked and buffeted him on the way to the surface. The harness held him in place, but he kept the prosthetic hand on the lever, governing the speed of descent. That proved to be a mistake when a gust of wind caught him, and the titanium-alloy hand snapped the lever off the lowering device. He picked up speed, zipping down the cable now, his guts floating upward with a queasy feeling.

"*Shit, shit …*" He looked down at the battlefield, where one of the bizarre reptiles had spotted him. Both mouths opened as the sinuous neck moved them into position to swallow him whole. Even from several hundred feet in the air, he could see the swordlike teeth.

An arrow of flame from below hit the creature in the neck, and it dived back into the hole it had emerged from.

Michael did the only thing he could think of. He grabbed the cable with his robotic hand and squeezed. Metal screeched against metal, throwing sparks as he slowed to a near stop just twenty feet from the surface.

Easing his titanium grip on the cable, he slid the

rest of the way down, his boots thudding into the dirt. Then he unclipped his harness, unslung the assault rifle, and crouched down.

A few feet away, a body lay in the dirt. It looked untouched, without so much as a scratch or scrape. But when he lifted away the broken-off palm frond that had fallen over it in the fighting, he realized that the man's lower half was simply gone but for a ropy pile of viscera. One of the arms twitched, the fingers flexing and then going limp.

Michael felt the burn of bile in his throat as he moved around the corpse with his rifle shouldered. He had landed on the south side of the road, between the troop transport and one of the tankers. *Discovery* had lowered overhead, and four cables were down, but no Cazadores moved out to grab them and attach them to the tanker's load points. Most of them were dead or dying.

Another Cazador, helmetless, lay sprawled on the ground. His bloodshot eyes looked skyward, and pink foam bubbled from his mouth.

Gunfire and screams came from the north side of the road, where the Cazadores continued to battle the monsters. Michael kept low on his way over to the vehicles. One of the beasts rose over the troop transport and then slammed a coil of its body against the side, careening the truck precariously onto its right wheels. As he watched, a figure emerged in the turret, and the machine gun barked to life.

High-caliber rounds punched through the thick

neck and up into one of the heads. Blood spattered in a bright violet arc across the tank trailer, but the creature kept coming.

The turret machine gun fell silent as the gunner scrambled to feed a new belt of ammo. Raising his rifle, Michael fired off a burst into the already wounded head, aiming for the eyes. He hit one with the second burst, and the creature reared away, screeching in agony.

That gave the gunner in the turret a chance to finish reloading. In the glow from the raging fires on the ground and the back of the armored transport, he saw that the gunner wasn't a Cazador—it was Magnolia.

The snake slumped to the ground on the other side of the transport, and Michael ran over to the back hatch of the transport. It had opened, and Les was helping a Cazador with a broken leg and a badly burned arm inside.

"What the hell!" Les yelled when he saw Michael.

"Sorry, sir, but I figured you could use some help getting these rigs back in the air."

Without warning, Les reached out and grabbed Michael by the chest armor, yanking him into the vehicle—not exactly the greeting he had expected. He fell to the floor just as a crunching sounded behind them.

Turning, Michael saw that one of the snakes had slammed into the side of the tanker behind them, pushing it onto its side. The filling hose's head broke off, sending diesel fuel spurting through the air.

Les reached around Michael and slammed the hatch shut just as the spewing fuel caught fire. The explosion of superheated air and gases smashed into the armored vehicle, moving it several feet.

Magnolia had foreseen the inevitable explosion and ducked back inside, closing the turret hatch. The fireball enveloped the vehicle, but the armored and heat-shielded sides protected its occupants from the blast.

"Tin," she said. "What are you—"

"Disobeying orders," Les said.

The captain climbed into the front seat, leaving Michael and Magnolia with the moaning Cazador. He cried out in pain as the vehicle jolted again with another body slam from one of the whipping serpentine coils.

The red flesh of the beast slithered past the windshield before going back underground. Les grabbed the shifter and double-clutched the transmission but couldn't get it back into gear.

He cursed a blue streak—an unusual event—and Michael moved up to help. A moment later, after a light and brief grinding of gears, the vehicle jolted, and the heavy tracks rolled forward, toward the remaining tanker.

Several Cazadores were still holding their ground there, firing assault rifles and a flamethrower at a snake that had just broken through the ground.

"Someone get back in that turret!" Les yelled.

Michael pushed the hatch open and climbed up. Two of the reptiles had surfaced on the north side of the embattled Cazador warriors while a third tunneled beneath the road to flank the men.

The mound of dirt moved fast, and he swung the machine-gun barrel in hopes of stopping the monster before it could reach the Cazadores. Leading the rising mound just slightly, he pulled the trigger. Green tracer rounds cut through the darkness and punched into the soil, kicking up dirt.

The beast veered left, away from the silos and the Cazadores.

A flash from the sky hit the dirt twenty yards in front of the transport and detonated, forcing Michael down. Hunks of earth and snake blew into the sky.

Michael hunched down in case *Discovery* should fire another rocket.

"Target eliminated," said Layla's voice over the comms.

Michael smiled as he climbed back up into the turret. Smoke curled up from a four-foot crater lined with snake gore, purple in the light of the arc lamps.

"Good shooting," Michael said. He swiveled the machine gun back toward the silos, where the remaining tanker continued to take on fuel. Two Cazadores had climbed to the top of the tanker and attached the four cables from the airship to the load points, front and back.

The remaining snakes had retreated underground, but one burst through the surface to snag one of the five Cazador warriors guarding the tanker.

A man strode out from between the cab and trailer, firing a shotgun into the thick flesh of the beast. Whoever the hell it was, he had ice running in his veins.

Both heads shot toward the soldier, one of them knocking him to the ground. The heads pulled upward and both mouths opened, letting out a long, warbling screech.

Michael seized the moment to fire the turret machine gun. Rounds punched through the shared neck that was in the process of gulping down the first Cazador it had snatched.

Another beast suddenly slammed the under-carriage of the troop transport, lifting it several feet off the ground. Michael fell back inside, landing on Magnolia.

"Tin!" she shouted.

The snake struck again, and this impact sent the vehicle rolling. The world went topsy-turvy, and Michael hit the ceiling, then the deck, then Magnolia again. The transport continued to roll, the hatch slamming shut, popping open, and slamming shut.

They finally came to a stop with a loud crunch.

Les crawled out of the cab, gripping his helmet and mumbling.

All four of them were on the ceiling near the closed hatch to the turret. The badly hurt Cazador lay at the rear of the vehicle with his back to the bulkhead, chest armor heaving.

He gasped for air, the muffled sounds resounding through the enclosed space. He reached up for a severed oxygen line and then put both hands on his helmet.

"No!" Michael yelled.

But it was too late. The soldier pulled off his helmet, to reveal not a man, but a young woman. Her face turned pink at her first gulp of toxic air.

The comm channel fired, but Michael hardly listened to the transmission—he was too horrified at the sight of the woman in front of him to respond.

Her eyes bulged, turning bright red as capillaries broke. Blood trickled from her nose, and pink froth bubbled out from the corners of her mouth. She reached out to Michael, trying to speak, and then slumped to one side, convulsed several times, and lay still.

"*Fuck*," Les said, again resorting to uncharacteristic language. He looked to Magnolia and Michael.

"Are you guys okay?" he asked. "How are your suits?"

Michael managed a nod.

"I'm …" Magnolia gave up finishing her sentence and made an O of her forefinger and thumb.

"Timothy has the tanker airborne, but our cable snapped," Les said. "We have to get—"

Another coil of reptilian flesh bashed the side of the capsized transport, sending it skidding across the ground. The next blow dented the armored side and knocked Michael against the bulkhead.

"We have to get out of here," he said, wincing. "Get ready."

Les and Magnolia checked their laser rifles, and Michael slapped a fresh magazine into his assault rifle.

"After the next hit," Les said. "Then we go out the hatch and sprint for the tanker."

Michael and Magnolia nodded.

The next impact was not long in coming. The transport vehicle rolled again. Michael hit the floor and used the bench to pull himself up.

Disoriented, he took in several breaths and looked for the back hatch.

The monster shrieked again outside, and he braced for another impact, but all he heard was the boom of a gun firing. A wail of agony followed, then two more booms.

"Now!" Michael shouted.

Les turned the handle and pushed the hatch open. A Hell Diver moved into view before any of them could get out of the troop hold.

"Come on!" yelled the diver outside, waving.

Les jumped out, and Michael followed, wondering which diver had broken his orders after he broke the captain's. The armored man stood near a harpoon as long as he was. The head was buried in the ground, and a rope trailed from its aft end up into the sky.

If Michael didn't know any better …

He glanced up, following the rope to the bottom of the *Sea Wolf.* The remaining oil tanker was already secured to *Discovery*'s hull, beside the boat.

"Shake a leg, people!" shouted the diver.

Michael had a hard time hearing his voice, because he wasn't using the comm channel, but it sounded familiar.

When he turned toward the diver, he saw why. It wasn't a member of Team Raptor.

"Rodger?" Michael said.

The diver threw a slovenly salute and said, "Rodger Dodger, reporting for duty!"

Plum-colored blood poured from the half-severed neck of the snake curled across the road. Three Cazadores stood guarding the beast. One of the three held a double-barreled shotgun.

General Santiago, Michael realized.

Rodger hadn't saved the divers all alone. He had worked with the Cazadores who stayed behind to fight the beasts, to give the crew a chance to get the tanker off the ground.

Magnolia grabbed Rodger. "What are you doing here?" she yelled.

"Just enjoying saving your arses."

"We can talk about it later," Les said. "We have to get out of here!"

Michael looked up at the airship. There was no way they could get the three Cazadores back there using their boosters, and Rodger didn't even appear to have one. Or a chute. Had he really slid down a cable to get here, without a way back up? And had he been stowed away in the *Sea Wolf* this entire time?

Whatever—it didn't matter right now. What mattered was getting back to the ship before any more of those infernal snakes surfaced.

"Timothy, send us another cable down," Les said. "We'll get the transport attached again. The rest of you, form a perimeter. We hold our ground right here."

Michael raised his rifle and scanned the terrain

for more threats as Alfred's technicians worked on lowering more cables to bring the disabled transport back up to the airship. *Discovery* would be seriously overweight, but she could probably do it.

Flames from the tangled wreckage of the tanker down the road provided a grim view of Cazador bodies and parts lying where they had fallen. A severed snake head the size of an oil drum protruded from a hole in the ground, and shreds of another beast hung like moss from the tree branches around Layla's rocket crater.

Michael's boot slid on a hunk of scaled flesh in the dirt. He had never seen creatures remotely like these or even read about them in the archives. But he knew that the Cazadores had encountered them before. The men who held this outpost for years had to know they were out here.

General Santiago broke open his shotgun and reloaded with shells from a bandolier slung over his shoulder. His mirrored visor turned to Michael and then looked away.

When they all got back to the airship, Michael was going to find out why the old warrior hadn't warned them about the snakes. And if they were lucky, Cricket would be able to shed some light on the fate of the Cazador crew manning this outpost from hell.

FOURTEEN

Moonlight made a soft carpet of the whitecaps below. The view reminded X of the moving snowdrifts in Hades. Trekking through those wastes seemed like a lifetime ago.

At his feet, Miles lay happily chomping on a pig bone. The crunching suddenly stopped at the sound of a distant high-pitched whistle. The dog looked up, with the bone still between its forepaws.

"The time has come to see if the Octopus Lords accept our sacrifice," Rhino said.

He wore his armor tonight, covering the healing gashes he had gotten in the Sky Arena and on the deck of *Elysium*. X, too, had a bandage covering a recent injury, from the Siren he fought on *Elysium*.

The two warriors stood on the roof platform of the capitol oil rig. Not far from the piers, a fishing vessel prowled the waters. In the bow, visible in the full moonlight, stood Carmela, parrot on her shoulder, whistle in her mouth.

X didn't have to wait long to see the summons answered. And while he was too far up to see the octopus's warty mantle, he could make out the dark tentacles writhing through the chop. They reached up toward the boat like the arms of a child begging for a treat.

"Looks like the Cazadores have been forgiven," X said. "Let's hope the goodwill extends to us as well."

"If only the Octopus Lords knew the truth," Rhino said. The unfinished words told X there was deep resentment there, but he still could not bring himself to kill Ada.

More whistling floated over the water, and two men on the boat deck pushed the corpses of Warthog and Javier into the water. The tentacles wrapped greedily around the bodies and pulled them beneath the surface.

A horn followed, and the onlookers began to chant.

X turned away, unable to stomach any more Cazador rites today. Miles got up and trotted after him, away from the platform's edge, while Rhino remained behind for a few moments.

Finally, he followed X around the pool and gardens, to the stairs, which they climbed to the airship's roof—the highest point in the Vanguard Islands. Flickering lamplight illuminated the canopy of tropical trees growing on the airship.

They strolled past the Sky Arena. The bloodstained dirt was a painful reminder of where he was heading and why.

X steeled himself as he approached a group of sky people who had gathered on the other side of the forest. Ton and Victor stood guard, their spears resting on their shoulders, eyes scanning for threats.

He wondered how they felt about what was happening here. The two men had seen more suffering than anyone should have to see, which was no doubt part of the reason they were so happy to be living as free men at the Vanguard Islands.

X walked past them, toward people holding candles and huddling around two fresh graves. Both were dug in the same area they had buried Captain DaVita and their other fallen friends.

Tonight, they were here to honor two more sky people who had lost their lives. DJ and his son Rhett had been laid to rest. Widow and mother Mallory clutched her remaining child, Keith, in front of her.

X walked past the row of buried officers: Katrina, Bronson, Dave. With them were the Hell Divers and civilians who had lost their lives in the battle for the oil rigs.

Seeing Katrina's grave made X wonder again what she would have thought of his leadership.

Was Ada right? Would Katrina really have sanctioned killing all the Cazador soldiers after the battle? X couldn't bring himself to believe that.

He nodded at familiar faces as he moved through the small crowd. While he knew everyone here to some degree, he wasn't really close with anyone besides Bernie and Cole Mintel, Rodger's parents. His family and most of his dearest friends were either dead or off risking their lives on *Discovery*. For a moment, dread curdled in his gut—the same dread he had felt seeing the airship pull away yesterday.

Miles brushed up against his leg as if to say, *Don't forget about me.*

X bent down and said, "You're my best friend of all, boy."

Cole Mintel opened a box and pulled out two newly carved wood plaques. "Rodger made these before he left," he said. He handed them to Mallory.

"Left?" X said softly. He looked around, not seeing Rodger in the crowd.

Mallory took them in a shaky hand.

"Here, sweetheart," Bernie said, and helped Mallory lay the plaques on the graves.

X watched the ceremony silently from the shadows. Mallory sobbed while her son just stared at the grave. Friends took their turns approaching. Some threw flower petals onto the dirt.

Les's wife, Katherine, walked by with their daughter, Phyl, in tow. They both scattered flower petals and then moved on to Trey's grave to do the same.

Seeing two mothers who had lost their sons ratcheted up the feeling of guilt, never far from the surface. The darkness was worse even than it had been in the wastes—a crushing, debilitating feeling that made X want to step over to the rail and jump off.

Everyone thinks you're some badass warrior, X thought, *but they don't know.*

Taking a few breaths to fortify himself, he walked over to Mallory and Keith to pay his respects.

"I'm so sorry for your loss," X said. "If there is anything you need, please let me know."

She turned toward him, rage in her eyes.

He understood the glare, but he wasn't prepared for the slap across the face. The sting didn't bother him; he was used to pain. What hurt more were the words that followed.

"My son died because of *you*," she growled. "He died in that filthy arena with those barbarians all because you decided to reopen it and give that murdering demon a chance at freedom. Now my husband *and* my son are dead."

Rhino stepped forward, but his towering presence didn't deter the woman one bit.

"And you!" she shouted at the Cazador general. "You *promised* you would kill Javier. Instead, you let him kill my boy."

"I'm truly sorry," Rhino said.

"You both disgust me," Mallory shot back. She wiped a tear from her eye and looked again at X. "I knew Janga, and I believed her prophecy about a man leading us to a new home on the sea. You may have been that man, but this ..." She waved her hand outward, encompassing the rooftop and the surrounding sea. "This is not the home that we deserve." Mallory poked X in the chest with her finger. "And you are *not* the leader we all deserve. A real leader would have killed all these animals and never given them the chance to kill my husband and son."

Mallory looked Rhino up and down. Then she spat in the dirt between his sandals.

Rhino did not say a word, though his muscles flexed for an instant.

"X saved us all," said Cole. "It's not his fault what happened in the arena."

"Saved me just yesterday," came a voice.

X looked for it and saw Ted Maturo, his silver hair seeming to glow in the moonlight. He nodded at X, and X nodded back. Maybe the young man had actually learned something from his dumb stunt.

"The Cazadores should not be allowed to have weapons," said a farmer.

"Yeah, and the warriors should be banished at the very least," a woman added. X was surprised to turn and see that Katherine had spoken the words.

"Listen, everyone, we're here to pay our respects tonight," X said. "Not debate the peace treaty we have with our …"

He stopped short of saying "friends," even though the man next to him was indeed his friend.

"Allies," X finished. "This is no different from how things were in the Old World, when enemies became allies after fighting each other for years."

"This is not the Old World," said a mechanic. "Allies don't bash each other's heads in like they did to my friend DJ."

"Your peace treaty is as dangerous as diving through the storms," said a familiar gruff voice.

X turned to see that it was Marv from the Wingman, the bar where X had spent far too many hours drinking far too much shine. Marv had lost an eye in the battle for the islands, and the one he had left was pinned on X.

"Eventually, every diver ends up dead," Marv said. "And eventually, this treaty will fail and the Cazadores will slaughter us all."

"X survived all the dives, and he won't fail us," Cole argued, his voice louder now. "We have to trust him."

Mallory shook her head and walked away. Her son looked over his shoulder, his glassy gaze locked on X. The rest of the group dispersed, but X couldn't bring himself to meet their eyes. He deserved this shame.

Mallory was right. Her son's death was indeed his fault. If he had never reopened the Sky Arena, the boy would still be alive.

"She's wrong," Rhino said as if reading X's thoughts. "Rhett's death wasn't your fault. It was mine. I should have killed Javier faster, before the kid could jump in."

"Doesn't change anything." X bent down and patted Miles on the head. The dog had brought his bone with him and was chewing it once more.

The last of the people who had come to the graveside vanished around the trees. Only Ton and Victor stayed behind to guard the area. X felt better with them there.

He looked up at the sky. "Leave me," he said to Rhino.

"King Xavier, I—"

"I said leave me," X said. "I am fine on my own."

Rhino didn't seem convinced.

"Go to bed. Or, if you're not tired, go put together that team I told you we need."

When Rhino didn't respond, X's eyes narrowed. "Don't tell me you can't find anyone you can trust," he said. "The Barracudas followed you into battle, and I know you've got plenty of others who would, too."

"They are all dead," Rhino said coldly. "Or they have turned on me because I now serve you."

"I'm sorry," X said, not knowing what else to say.

"I do not regret anything, and there may still be hope," Rhino said. "I just need time to go visit an old friend who might be able to help."

"Take as much time as you need. Until then, I've got these." X gripped his sword in one hand and cinched up his belt of weapons with the other. A blaster was holstered at his thigh, a pistol on his waist, and a hatchet hung from the back of his belt. The weight made his shorts sag.

"Good night, King Xavier," Rhino said.

When Rhino was out of sight, X whistled to Miles. The dog picked up the bone and trotted after him. They returned to the graves, and X knelt beside Katrina's plot. He put a hand on the mound and bowed his head.

"What would you do with Ada if you were in my shoes?" he whispered.

He kept his hand there, trying to imagine her voice and what she would say to him. All he knew for sure was that she wouldn't kill Ada as Rhino had recommended.

But he was less sure about how Katrina would handle the Cazadores. Perhaps Ada was right. Perhaps Katrina would have killed all the soldiers or, at the very least, banished them.

"King Xavier," said a voice.

X rose to his feet, his hand instinctively going for his sword. He relaxed when he saw Ted step out of the shadows. He held a silver flask in his hand and held it out.

"Thought I'd thank you for saving my hide," he said.

"You're welcome, but my days of shine are over."

Ted shrugged and brought the flask to his lips, then hesitated. He frowned and put it away.

"I'm sorry for what I did, and I hope someday I will have the opportunity to train again with the Hell Divers," he said ruefully. "Seriously, sir, I know how stupid that was. It put everyone at risk."

"You're damn right it did," X replied. "Kid, we're all stupid at times. You were lucky, like I've been many times in my life."

"Lucky you were there … I just hope you will someday forgive me and give me the chance to serve again."

A female voice rang out before X could respond. He turned from Katrina's grave, half expecting to see her ghost. Instead, he spotted Lieutenant Sloan running across the rooftop. Rhino was right behind her.

"Sir," she said, stopping to pant. "I've been looking all over for you."

"Why? What's going on?"

"It's *Discovery*, sir …" She took another breath and added, "We received a transmission."

"And?"

"They ran into trouble at the fueling station."

"What kind of trouble?" X asked.

Sloan finally caught her breath. "When *Star Grazer* reached the shore, they discovered the fuel outpost had been damaged," she said. "*Discovery* descended to take a look and found it was destroyed."

"Shit," Rhino said. "They won't have enough fuel to get to the city and back."

"No, they did manage to get some," Sloan said. "*Discovery* helped haul two tanker trucks inland to fuel up, but they were attacked by giant snakes."

"Is everyone okay?" X asked.

"I think so. Apparently, *Rodger* helped kill the things. I didn't get much more after that; the line cut out."

"Rodger?" X said, then growled with realization. When Cole said his son had "left," he meant he had gone on the mission.

"Reckless idiot," X muttered. He looked to Ted. "See, stupid people doing stupid shit."

"Glad I'm not the only one," Ted replied.

X sighed, shaking his head. "Lieutenant, I'll meet you in the command center in five. Rhino, you'd better inform the other Cazador officers on *Elysium* about the transmission," he said. "Report back here tomorrow morning."

Rhino lingered after Sloan and Ted left.

"Did you hear me?" X asked.

"Yes, King Xavier, but there is something I want you to know."

"What's that?"

"I've served many men in my life, but unlike most of them, you have the heart and the mind of a good man. You are the leader your people deserve, the leader we all deserve. And I know you will make the right decision about Ada."

He stepped so close, X could smell his breath.

"But if you don't, it will be the end of your people and mine." He clapped X on the shoulder and then turned, twirling his spear once before tucking it under his arm.

If X didn't know better, Rhino had just followed up a compliment with a veiled threat.

* * * * *

"Prepare to intercept Cricket," Timothy said.

Several hours after the ambush at the fuel station, *Discovery*'s crew was finally retrieving the drone from the tower of the destroyed outpost. Les had just finished the detox procedures to ensure he hadn't brought any dangerous chemicals or microorganisms back from the surface, and he was now back on the bridge of the airship.

An acid rainstorm had moved into the area, and it was coming down in sheets so thick he could hardly see the dark silhouette of the tower in the distance. But he could see the beam from the robot flying toward the airship with the new thrusters Michael had installed.

Sitting bolt upright in the captain's chair, Les waited anxiously for the robot and for a chance to talk to General Santiago about the monsters they had encountered.

"Sir, I got through to Lieutenant Sloan and informed her of what happened," Layla said. "Unfortunately, this new storm is playing havoc with outgoing transmissions."

"Keep trying," Les said. "I want to talk to X."

"Will do, sir."

"Cricket is preparing to dock," Timothy said. "Alfred and his techs are on standby."

"Good. How's the radar looking, Ensign Corey?"

"This storm doesn't seem to be getting worse, but I've got my eye on another front moving in," Eevi replied.

"Keep me updated."

She nodded, and Les checked the main monitor, which gave a view of the central tower. He had plenty of questions about this outpost—not only what had happened to the crew, but why the hell Santiago had never warned the Hell Divers about the snakes.

The hull rattled from a nearby peal of thunder.

Les took them off autopilot and manually kept the ship steady while it received Cricket. He watched the robot on his screen, and when it was safely inside, he put the ship back on auto.

Les, Magnolia, Rodger, and Michael had gone through detox along with General Santiago, a lieutenant named Alejo, and a third soldier named Ruiz. And now that they had the drone, and Timothy had dropped the damaged Cazador troop transport and the remaining fuel tanker back onto the deck of *Star Grazer*, the hard part was over.

Les still wasn't sure they had taken on enough fuel for the journey back to the Vanguard Islands. If not, the trip had been a waste of lives and equipment. The Cazadores had suffered ten casualties from a team of sixteen and lost one of their tankers.

The mission had also cost *Discovery*. On his screen, he pulled up the damage assessment from the storm and the battle. They had damage across multiple sectors of the ship, from both lightning and random shots out of a flailing machine gun when they lowered toward the surface. But the ship was still operational, and Les was just happy they hadn't lost any divers.

"Timothy, transfer the data from Cricket to the briefing room," Les said. "Layla, you have the bridge."

He caught up with the divers outside the launch-bay doors. Some were watching through the windows as the drone went through detox. Alfred and three technicians, all in hazard suits, sprayed the robot with chemicals.

Rodger and Magnolia sat farther down the passage, leaning against a bulkhead and talking quietly. Seeing Les, they both stood.

"Captain on deck," Magnolia said.

Michael, Edgar, Sofia, Arlo, and Alexander all turned away from watching the robot's cleaning ritual.

"Where are the Cazadores?" Les asked.

"Our militia team is with them in the med bay," Michael said. "Ruiz got hurt."

Les ordered Timothy to have the Cazadores escorted to the briefing room. Then he told the divers to follow him. When they got there, Timothy was already inside. His hologram cast a glow over the long table and dozen chairs.

Three militia soldiers showed up a moment later with General Santiago and Lieutenant Alejo. Les had never seen the old soldier without a helmet. He had pale skin, a thick head of brown hair the color of his short beard, and only one ear.

"Captain Mitchells," Santiago said in his thick accent. "How are you?"

"*Bien*," Les said, using Spanish as a sign of respect. "*¿Cómo está usted?*"

The general's reply made no sense to Les, so Lieutenant Alejo took over. "Captain Mitchells, General Santiago says he is grateful for your support."

Alejo spoke nearly perfect English, which told Les he was like Rhino, a survivor whom el Pulpo had captured from a bunker or shelter and enslaved.

"I'm glad you speak English," Les said. "Maybe you can explain to me and to my divers what the hell those snakes were."

The divers all remained standing behind their chairs.

Alejo and Santiago both looked around at the unsmiling faces that far outnumbered them. And while the general couldn't understand Les, he couldn't miss his angered tone. But Les didn't care. He was sick of these people keeping secrets that endangered lives.

"Well?" he asked.

"We call them the oil serpents," Alejo said. "They live in the old pipeline here, but they rarely venture this far."

"And you didn't think to warn us about them?" Michael said, stepping up beside Les.

Alejo glanced at the diver as if sizing him up. "Like I said, they don't usually venture to the outpost. I guarantee, whatever caused that damage and killed our crew was something else."

Les searched the man's face for a lie but saw none. "We're going to find out," he said.

Alejo translated to Santiago, who nodded.

"Have a seat," Les said, gesturing toward the chairs. "Timothy, pull up the footage."

"Aye, aye, Captain."

The divers and Cazadores sat, and the AI walked around the table, massaging his neatly trimmed beard while they waited for the first footage from Cricket. Les hadn't even asked Timothy what he had discovered, but he hoped it was enough to solve the mystery of whatever happened to the facility and its crew.

The footage transferred to the main screen, and everyone scooted their chairs so they could see. Timothy walked up to the wall-mounted monitor.

"Cricket was able to access the tower directly, through a broken hatch on the east side," he said.

"What you are seeing is from directly after the drone entered."

The robot's new cameras had switched to night vision. Its hover nodes allowed it to fly through the open room, and the multiple cameras provided a nearly panoramic view of the space on multiple smaller screens.

"Looks like a living space," Michael said. He pointed at the bottom-right box on the monitor and told Timothy to pause the frame. Sure enough, there were several bunks, and a bank of radio equipment in the corner.

"How many men did you have posted here?" Les asked.

"Probably twelve," Alejo said. "Maybe a bit more, but I don't have the information on me at the moment."

Cricket continued into another room, whose floor was covered with puddled water. Les had hoped they might find a survivor somewhere, until he saw the broken hatch. Anyone inside here was dead.

The robot hovered into a common area that looked like a mess hall. Cans of food and drinking glasses were scattered across the surface. A plate seemed to be moving in place.

"Zoom in on that table," Les said.

The camera captured an image that made his stomach churn. Hundreds of red maggot-looking larvae were eating whatever rotting food was on the plate.

Cricket pushed onward, but there were no bodies. The divers were getting visibly anxious.

"Where are the corpses?" Michael asked.

"Would you like me to fast-forward?" Timothy said.

Les held up a hand. "No, I want to see everything you found."

"Very well, sir."

Cricket hovered through a storage room that had been ransacked and was now overrun with more of the red insect larvae as well as some wiry bluish worms. It went on into more sleeping quarters.

Hatches sealed off the glass windows in the next room, which seemed to be some sort of command center. Several chairs faced a display of computer equipment.

On the floor, a mug had fallen and shattered. The drone turned and moved through a passage where Les saw the first signs of a struggle.

He had expected to see the holes from laser bolts but instead found long scratch marks and spattered gore along the walls.

"This is where Cricket found the crew," Timothy said.

The robot buzzed around a corner, passing over a steel door that had been battered down. A bathroom came on-screen, with showers on the far wall, toilets, and sinks.

"I don't see anyone," Michael said.

Cricket shined a light on the ceiling over the showers and then on a wall around another corner. Several corpses were plastered to the tiles.

"Sirens," Les whispered.

Alejo shook his head. "No," he gulped.

"Sirens didn't do this," said the AI. "Actually, there is no evidence of their being here at all."

The beam raked over what looked like dried skin manually stretched over human bones.

"Holy Siren shit," Magnolia breathed, cupping her hand over her mouth. "Is that what I think it is?"

Les swallowed hard at the ghastly images.

Several human eyeballs, noses, and lips had been stitched onto a skin blanket that was then stretched over a frame of limb bones. It looked a bit like a worn and wrinkled map.

"Defectors," Les said.

"I don't think the machines did this, either," Timothy said.

Cricket hovered into another room, whose hatch had also been broken off. The light hit a balcony and two more displays of skin stretched over human bones. Unlike the earlier remains, these sculptures were hardly recognizable after exposure to the elements.

The remains reminded Les of a scarecrow in a book he had read as a kid.

Then it dawned on him. These weren't sculptures.

They were a warning.

He glanced to the two Cazador officers to see their reaction.

To his surprise, General Santiago seemed uncharacteristically agitated, as if he had seen something like this before. He turned to Alejo and said something in a hushed voice.

"All right," Les said. "Shut the footage off, Timothy."

The screen went dark.

Les put his hands on the table and looked at the two Cazadores in turn.

"Before you return to your ship, one of you is going to tell me what the hell did that to your comrades. No more secrets."

Alejo translated to Santiago, who began speaking fast.

Les looked to Alejo, waiting.

Santiago spoke faster, growing more agitated.

"Well?" Rodger said. "Someone going to tell us what turned those people into human scarecrows?"

"So, I'm not the only one," Les said.

"Scarecrows are supposed to warn birds away, right?" Magnolia said.

The general looked at Les, raised a hand, and then pointed at his chest.

"What's he saying, damn it?" Les asked.

Alejo didn't seem to want to explain.

"What did that?" Les said. "Spit it out!"

The lieutenant hesitated for another moment before saying, "*We* did."

FIFTEEN

Magnolia shivered in her bunk. The images of framed human-skin canvases were seared in her mind. Rodger sat in the bunk across from her, his knees pulled up to his chest under a blanket.

"I really want to know what the hell Lieutenant Alejo meant when he said 'we' did this," she said.

"Maybe one of the guys living on the outpost got cabin fever and decided to turn his pals into upholstery," he replied. "I'm sure a few divers thought about doing that to me back in the day."

"Not funny, Rodge."

"We'll find out soon, I hope."

"I'm guessing they're still talking, since we haven't lowered to drop them off on *Star Grazer* or climbed above the storm yet."

She rested her head and tried to calm her beating heart. She should be sleeping but was still riding high on adrenaline from an eventful day.

Just when she thought she was going to get some

answers in the briefing room, Les had kicked out all the divers expect Michael. It left her and the others wondering what secrets the Cazadores had kept from them this time.

Even with a vault full of records, there was still much they didn't know about these people and their past.

Rodger groaned. "First the snakes, then whatever bizarre, ghoulish stuff we saw in the tower, and we're not even halfway to our target yet. Now I'm *kind* of wishing I hadn't stowed away on the *Sea Wolf*, but I couldn't let you come alone."

"You were supposed to be guarding X."

Rodger gave her a wry smile. "Mags, did you somehow miss seeing that six-foot-five badass that's guarding him? I'm pretty sure he's safe with Rhino. Guy is pure muscle."

"Yeah, yeah, but he could still use more eyes with all the enemies he has back at the islands. For the record, you don't have to come on this mission once we get to the target."

"Mags, you can't get rid of me," he said with an extended grin. "I'd ride the back of a mutant whale if you were on it."

Magnolia forced a smile back, but she wasn't in the mood for romance, which was what Rodger had in mind, judging by his gaze.

She pulled the blanket up over her bra.

"You shouldn't have come, Rodge. X needed your help, and I can take care of myself."

Rodger seemed a bit taken aback by her response,

and for that she was sorry. After all, he had helped save her on the surface. Who could say what might have happened if he hadn't ridden the cable down to help.

"Look, it's not that I don't want you here," she said. "I just worry about X."

"I understand. With flawless hindsight, I see that I should have stayed behind. I'm sorry."

"It's okay."

Rodger laid his head back on the pillow. "We'd better try and get some sleep," he said.

"I wouldn't count on that," said a voice.

Michael's head poked through the open hatch.

Wearing jumpsuit and armor, he looked ready to dive.

Rodger was wearing nothing but tight-fitting shorts similar to those he had worn in the sky arena. He hopped out of bed and stretched, his face distorting from trying to suppress a yawn.

"Man, what's going on now?" he moaned.

Michael looked away from Rodger. "Rads and Sirens, man! Get some clothes on and meet me on the bridge."

Magnolia laughed and threw off her blanket as soon as Michael had closed the hatch. She didn't mind giving Rodger a quick peek. He deserved that much.

Rodger swallowed and pushed his glasses up.

"Your hands are shaking," she said.

"What?" he said. Then he put his hands behind his back. "Oh, sorry."

Magnolia walked over to him in her underwear,

kissed him on the lips, and then left him standing there, quivering, while she changed.

They met Michael on the bridge a few minutes later. The other divers were there, too, but General Santiago and Lieutenant Alejo were gone.

Acid rain continued pounding against the portholes of the bridge.

"All right, listen up," Les said. "We've got a massive storm front bearing down on us, so we're going to stay below it and follow *Star Grazer* east and south, the rest of the way to Rio de Janeiro."

Timothy nodded and said, "Ready to lower the Cazadores back to their ship, Captain."

"Get it done."

The airship began to descend toward the warship on the seas.

"So, what's this situation?" Rodger said. "The storm?"

"No," Les said. "The skinwalkers."

"*What?*" Magnolia asked.

Les walked over to the portholes.

"Apparently, there are more Cazadores than we thought," he said. "The defectors and mutant life-forms aren't the only things we have to worry about out here."

Timothy joined Les at the windows and whispered something that she couldn't make out. The captain nodded at the AI.

"Lieutenant Brower, you have permission to fire on my mark," Les said.

"Fire at what?" Magnolia asked.

Les kept his gaze out the porthole, his hands cupped behind his back. She crossed the room to join him with the other divers.

"Mark," Les said.

A thump sounded belowdecks, and a missile streaked away. The vapor trail curved away from the ship and over the ocean. It hit the central tower of the outpost a moment later, a bright explosion blooming in the darkness.

The fiery blast lit up the tower as it collapsed into a pile of debris. Hunks of glowing shrapnel rained down onto the coastline.

"Fire again, Lieutenant," Les said.

Another missile roared away from the ship, this time going past the flames of the tower. Two more beats passed before it exploded.

"Is that the fuel station?" Magnolia whispered.

Layla looked at her screen. "Both targets destroyed, Captain."

"Good," Les said. He returned to his captain's chair. "Now we can focus on the real mission."

Magnolia stared out the windows, watching the distant orange glow. "What if we need to come back here for fuel?" she asked.

Les tabbed his screen, not looking up. "We won't ever be coming back here. The location was compromised, and we can't allow the precious fuel to fall into enemy hands."

Magnolia recalled Santiago's words about his

people being responsible for what happened in the tower.

The skinwalkers weren't a new group of humans on the surface. They were another faction of Cazadores that had split off and destroyed Bloodline.

"Timothy, set the course to Rio de Janeiro," Les said. "Time to see what's really waiting for us there."

* * * * *

A day had passed since *Discovery* and *Star Grazer* departed, and Rhino was going crazy with worry about Sofia. In less than a week, she would arrive at the target and jump from the sky to look for survivors and possibly battle the metal gods.

Rhino would bet his monthly rations that no one was alive there. If the metal gods had intercepted the transmission, that put everyone at risk and could result in a Jamaica-style shit storm or worse.

He tried not to think about Sofia on the ride from the capitol tower to *Elysium*.

With the loss of the fuel outpost Bloodline and the decimation of their fleet in the battle for the islands, things weren't looking good for their once powerful armada.

If his subordinates knew the truth about the *Lion* and her crew, he would have enough swords sticking out of his back to get mistaken for a bone beast. Worse, he still hadn't recruited for the Cazador team X wanted.

The ride from the capitol tower to *Elysium* was long, giving him plenty of time to think about it. There were so many places he would rather be. In bed with Sofia, for instance, or at one of the ale shacks where he could soak his worries into submission— even the trading-post rig that he so despised.

The thought had given him an idea.

The only surviving member of the Barracudas lived there now. Mac had retired from service after multiple injuries all but killed him on a mission six years ago, long before Rhino took over the team. It had been a while since he last saw his old friend, but no matter. Mac was someone he could trust.

Rhino watched the capitol tower receding in the boat's wake.

Moonlight illuminated the little tropical forest and the gun emplacements that the militia manned to protect their new home. X was inside his command center, still trying to raise *Discovery* on the encrypted channel.

Rhino had thought he needed some time away from the sky people, but that was before he gave much thought to the time he was about to spend with his own people.

But what *were* his people? He was not a Cazador. Nor was he a sky person. Hell, he didn't even feel like part of the family he was born into back in the Texas bunker.

You're a mutt. Nothing more.

He tried to relax on the back of the speedboat, letting the cool breeze wash over him. The pilot kept his eyes on the water, but his son, the boat hand, kept staring at him.

The kid was maybe ten years old, with long hair, eyes the color of the ocean, and a tattoo of a fish on his wrist. Even under a nearly full moon, Rhino couldn't make out what kind of fish.

The boat thumped over the waves, faster now that they were past the no-wake zone around the capitol tower. Rhino tried to relax, but the rocky ride and the kid's stare finally got to him.

"What?" he finally said to the boat hand.

In reply, the kid held up his arm in the moonlight, revealing the tattoo of a barracuda. He nodded proudly at Rhino.

This kid wanted to become a warrior on the legendary team that Rhino had once led into battle—a team that no longer existed.

"Sorry, kid, but if I were you, I'd stick to fishing with my dad," Rhino said in Spanish.

Rhino thought of his old teammates. Whale, Fuego, Wendig. Having them by his side now would have made things easier—and safer. But now he was a general without any soldiers he could truly trust. He also held a secret that could lead to another war.

Picking up his spear, he stood and grabbed the rail as the boat slowed. A dozen smaller craft, including some merchant vessels and troop transports, were anchored alongside *Elysium*.

Rhino thanked the pilot and gave him a coin. Then he slapped the boy on the shoulder.

"Hunting fish beats hunting men and monsters," Rhino said. "And it has a better future."

He stepped up on the gunwale and onto the warship's ladder.

Clanking blades and shouting from trainees and instructors greeted him on the deck. A drill sergeant stood at a chalkboard, keeping tally of the young warriors sparring in the moonlight.

A scream cut through the general clamor, and a young man dropped to the deck, clutching a broken leg. Two corpsmen splinted the leg and slipped a stretcher under the kid and hauled him away. For the near future, his training was over.

Rhino walked over to the chalkboards. Felipe had already racked up several wins, and he was fighting now. With his staff, he swept his opponent's legs. Then he pounced like a Siren.

The drill sergeant let Felipe get in a few punches before finally calling the match. Felipe jumped to his feet, arms raised in victory. Then he saw Rhino watching.

Rhino offered a nod of approval and beckoned him over.

Felipe ran over, panting. "*Mi general*," he said politely.

The kid's change in attitude caught Rhino by surprise. "*¡Muy bien!*" he said. "You look good out there, but next time maybe keep your staff ready before pouncing like a tiger, just in case he's got a knife."

"Right," Felipe replied. "I will be more cautious next time."

Rhino gave him a slap on the back. The young man turned back to his training, then hesitated.

"General," he said, "my mom said my dad loved you and that he would be pissing on me from the afterlife if he saw how I behaved the other day."

"Is that an apology?"

Felipe swallowed. "*Sí. Lo siento.*"

"Your dad was a good man, and you'll be a fine man, too. Now, go kick some more ass."

Rhino stuck around for a few more fights. These youngsters were the future of the crumbling Cazador army and, perhaps, the human race. Soon they would be sent off to the proving grounds to test their mettle against the mutant beasts that prowled the surface. But maybe they should be training to fight the metal gods instead.

He finally left the young warriors and climbed the ladder to the command center for a meeting he was dreading.

Several Praetorian Guards patrolled the deck with rifles. Seeing Rhino, they came to attention, and he gave them all nods. He could have his own detachment of warriors following him around, but he wasn't Colonel Vargas.

On the bridge, several officers worked the graveyard shift in the open space. They looked up at him from the glow of their workstations and exchanged nods with Rhino as he continued to the briefing room.

Carmela was the first person he saw inside, with that ridiculous bird perched on her shoulder. Flanking her were Colonels Forge and Vargas.

"Ah, General, so nice of you to join us tonight!" Carmela said. "Did King Xavier grant you a bathroom break?"

Normally, such disrespect would have cost a lower-ranked officer's head, but Carmela knew she could get away with it because the king had shown mercy.

"I'm here to deliver an update on General Santiago's mission with *Star Grazer*," he growled. "But you may want to tidy up first, Colonel."

The smirk evaporated from Carmela's weathered features as she looked down at the small white and gray blob on her armored shoulder.

Rhino walked over to the wide metal table with maps draped across its surface. He stood at the head while the three colonels took their seats.

He looked at their faces in turn. Colonel Forge locked his iron jaw, revealing no emotion. Forge had once been a good friend, a man Rhino respected on the battlefield just as much as at the table of Black Order of the Octopus Lords.

But it was obvious in Forge's smoldering gaze that he resented being passed over for a promotion. Perhaps he was yet another Cazador who thought Rhino had betrayed his people by serving X in such a manner.

Of the two men, it was Vargas who really hated Rhino. With his beakish nose, protruding eyes, and Mohawk hair, he looked a lot like the bird on

Carmela's shoulder. He kept his gaze on Rhino, trying to show strength.

It didn't work.

Vargas was known and feared for his viciousness on and off the battlefield, but Rhino had seen him fight, and he lacked skill, making up for it with brute force. It was one of the main reasons el Pulpo had liked him—both men were psychotic.

Rhino would have executed Vargas after the battle that killed el Pulpo, but X had decided to let him serve after he swore allegiance. In his view, killing Vargas would cause more problems than it would solve.

That had been a mistake.

Carmela finished cleaning off her shoulder. "We can dispense with the big-dicking," she said, seeing the men staring. "Tell us about the mission, *General.*"

The officers took a seat while Rhino went to the maps and put his finger on the fuel outpost. "Bloodline has been destroyed."

"*What!*" Carmela jerked in her seat, causing the bird to flap its wings. "How?"

"We don't know yet," Rhino said. "I only know that when General Santiago arrived, the station was destroyed, and they had to airlift tankers inland to fuel up. They were attacked by the oil serpents that live in the pipeline."

"They came that far inland?"

"They did."

Carmela stared down at the map. "How bad is it?"

"We lost a tanker and ten soldiers."

"Then we're down to three warships, not counting *Elysium*, and just under a thousand soldiers," Forge said.

Kotchee squawked.

"The bird says we're fucked," Vargas said. "I think it's right." He let out a cackling laugh that made Kotchee move to Carmela's other shoulder, away from the demented man.

"You're failing us, Small Dog," Vargas said. "King Xavier was wrong to make you general."

Rhino stepped around to Vargas's side of the table.

"The only thing he got wrong was not slitting your neck from ear to ear," Rhino said. "You want to take my place, feel free to challenge me. I'll take your face and swap it for Warthog's."

Vargas stood up to meet Rhino's gaze. "Your time is coming, you half-blood fish-fucker," he snarled.

The insults didn't bother Rhino as much as they probably should.

"You already used your rights under the Black Order to try and take me out," Rhino said. He glanced at Carmela. "Look how that turned out. Guess you'll have to stab me in the back instead."

"Let's all just ease up," Colonel Forge said. He eyed the other officers in turn, stopping on Vargas last.

"You may not like it, but General Rhino isn't the only one who signed a peace treaty with King Xavier," Forge said. "General Santiago also shook on the deal."

Carmela gave a resigned nod, but Vargas didn't seem to care.

"General Santiago is a Cazador, but Rhino here is

worse than a half-blood," he said. "You are in bed with the sky vermin, Perrito."

Forge's nostrils flared in anger. Even he knew that Vargas had gone too far.

The tension in the air was palpable, and Rhino thought of flicking out his knife and jamming it through one of those crazed eyes. But if he did, Carmela—and probably Forge too—would jump in. He didn't want to risk fighting all three officers here, especially without the blessing of the king, who had the final say on executions. But the time would soon come when Vargas and Carmela again tried to kill Rhino—if not through the Black Order, then while he slept or shat. God, what he would give to have Whale, Fuego, and especially Wendig at his side right now.

Before Vargas could react, Rhino had a hand wrapped around his veiny neck. Leaving his knife hand free, he lifted the colonel off the deck.

Carmela and Forge both moved closer, but neither went for a weapon.

"I should break your windpipe and toss you to the Octopus Lords," Rhino snarled, his spittle flecking Vargas's face. The smaller man's feet kicked uselessly in the air, and he gripped the massive forearm with both hands as it clamped down tighter around his neck.

The eyes bulged even more.

"Put him down, General," Forge said. "This is not the way to victory."

"Fuck that," Rhino replied as Vargas's face went red. "Showing disrespect to a superior officer is punishable by death. You should keep that in mind too, Colonel Moreto."

Vargas gagged, struggling to take in air.

"We need him," Carmela said. "We've already lost too many of the Black Order."

Vargas's eyes rolled upward. Rhino wanted to break his windpipe and drop him like a sack of crabs on the deck. But he was just trying to scare the man into submission.

Mercy might make you look weak now.

"Let him go," Carmela said.

Vargas's hands fell away from Rhino's forearm, and his feet gave one last feeble kick.

"Lump of whale shit," Rhino said.

He let go of Vargas as if dropping a bag of refuse. Now was not the time to kill him. He stepped away as the man lay gasping on the deck.

"Test me again, and I'll have those goggle eyes staring out your ass," Rhino said.

He returned to the maps as if nothing had happened. Carmela and Forge joined him while Vargas gulped air on the deck. Rhino kept him in his field of vision, just in case Vargas got stupid again.

"General Santiago managed to fill one tanker with the help of the Hell Divers," Rhino said. "I hope it's enough to get to the target and back, but in the meantime, we should send out an expedition to check on the Iron Reef, in Belize. We can't afford to lose both, and our reserves are dwindling back here."

"Agreed," Forge said.

"This must get the okay from X first, but I will recommend sending *Mercury* to escort a tanker to the Iron Reef," Rhino said.

"I'll help," Carmela said.

Rhino shook his head. "I want you in charge of getting *Renegade* and *Shadow* back into the fleet. Whatever destroyed the outpost could be coming this way."

Carmela nodded. "I'll see that *Elysium* is ready, too."

"Let us hope that General Santiago returns victorious soon, so we can focus on rebuilding our army and armada," Forge said. "The Octopus Lords will forsake us if we do not."

Vargas pushed against the deck, coughing and laughing at the same time.

"You all forget what happened with the last ship that sailed to Rio de Janeiro," he said. Staggering to his feet, he massaged his neck. The sharpened black teeth grinned.

"No Cazador warrior has ever returned from that place," he said. "And when General Santiago doesn't come back, the blame will fall on you, *Perrito*."

SIXTEEN

X tossed and turned in his bed for hours. Unable to sleep, he had decided to call another dive with the rookies, waking them all before dawn. There was something about diving that always seemed to clear his mind. At first light, he took Miles to the marina and boarded a boat with his trusted guards, Ton and Victor. In the gray predawn, they sped toward a location between the decommissioned *Hive* rig and the capitol tower.

Two container ships had already anchored in the water, with large white drop zones marked on their wide decks where containers had once been. The rookie divers and support teams had arrived and were finishing their gear checks.

X joined them on the deck, the orange glow of the sunrise illuminating their helmetless features. Most of them looked exhausted, but all appeared annoyed, and not because of being woken early.

Lena, Hector, Alberto, and the other greenhorns

weren't wild about diving with Ted again. X didn't blame them, but he had decided to give the young man a second chance to prove himself.

X walked over to Ted.

"Don't make me regret this," X said.

"I won't, sir, you have my word," Ted replied.

Satisfied, X scanned the other rookies. With all the veteran divers aboard *Discovery*, it was up to him to help train them, and while he had a packed day, he decided to start it with a few dives.

X finished putting on his gear, secured his helmet, and walked around with the technicians. They double-checked all systems, and once everyone had confirmed they were operational, he bumped on the comm channel.

"Hector, Alberto, Lena, and Ted will go first with me," he said into his headset. "The rest of you, watch and keep out of the way on the deck."

Nods all around.

"Follow my lead to fifteen thousand feet, release your booster, and deploy your chute," X added. "I want to see everyone in a stable falling position—no suicide dives."

X glanced at Ted, who nodded enthusiastically.

"Remember to keep your distance, both on the ascent and on the dive," X said. "Questions?"

Seeing no hands, he punched his booster. The orange training balloon shot out, filling with helium and hauling him into the sky. The other divers spread out, deploying their balloons at a safe distance.

While the horizon lit up with the rising sun, the divers rose into the clear blue sky.

Ted looked up at X and held a hand up. "Thank you for giving me this second shot," he said on a private channel.

"You're welcome," X replied. "Now, focus." He was glad Magnolia wasn't here to watch, because she would break his balls for allowing the guy back into the sky this soon.

But the need for Hell Divers outweighed any grief he would get for his decision.

Maybe being king did have benefits.

As the balloons pulled them higher, X took in the view of everything he was trying to protect. Rigs dotted the crystal-clear water, housing the last remnants of humanity. Securing the Vanguard Islands was the heaviest responsibility he had ever borne in his life, and not even his legendary days of diving had prepared him for the challenges he faced now.

The ships below grew smaller, and the rescue runabouts hardly appeared to be moving. He could tell only by the streaking white wakes.

He glanced at his HUD—time to release the helium. He gave the order over the comm channel. At fifteen thousand feet, he hit the booster's purge valve, deflating it. Then, as his upward motion stopped, he pulled the ring cable releasing the booster harness. It peeled off him as he pulled his arms and legs into stable position and plummeted earthward.

The training balloons' bright orange would be easy enough for the motorboats to track and receive when they drifted down to the surface.

As he began to fall, the other divers followed suit, releasing their boosters and going into free fall. A few seemed to struggle, especially Alberto, but Ted was one of the first to get it right.

The kid seemed determined to make up for his mistake.

"Lena, Hector, watch your six," X said.

The two divers turned and extended their legs just a bit, quickly getting fifty feet of separation, but Hector lost his stable position and did a barrel roll before finally managing to get stable again.

"Relax," X said. "Remember, you're light as a feather."

The water rose up to meet them, the two ships and many rigs once again coming into focus. X could already see the white landing zones on the decks. He took a moment to savor the thrill of falling.

Then he tracked toward the left vessel, keeping his eye on Ted.

"Slow it down, hot rod," X said.

The diver was falling a little faster than the others and catching up with X. They would be the first two on the deck of the first vessel.

"Lena, Hector, Alberto, take vessel two," X said. "*Tomen el barco dos.*"

All of their parachutes blossomed open without mishap.

"Easy, everyone, you got this," X said. The deck

rose up to meet his boots, and at six feet he pulled his toggles to slow his descent and stepped out of the sky.

Releasing the left riser, he spilled the air from his canopy and watched Ted.

The young diver performed such a graceful two-stage flare, X might have cheered if not for a scream over the comms. X turned to see Hector smack into the other ship's hull, just below the rail.

Lena and Alberto came in hot, both of them running, then tumbling in a shroud of tangled cords and chutes.

Two Cazadores dived over the side of the ship to retrieve Hector.

X ran over, pulling off his helmet on the way, ready to jump in himself. But the Cazador swimmers got Hector up to the surface. He thrashed in their grip—a good sign.

Miles came trotting over with Ton and Victor. They watched as the swimmers got Hector into a flotation litter and two others winched him up to the deck.

A pair of medics treated Hector for injuries.

"You're lucky," said one. "Your armor saved you from breaking bones."

Hector didn't seem to understand the medic, and the other translated. A grin crossed Hector's face, and he said something in Spanish.

"He said he's ready to go back up," the medic told X.

X smiled back at Hector. Then he walked over and patted Ted on the shoulder.

"Good work," he said. "Let's see if you can do it twice in a row."

He took them back into the sky for three more dives, and the team improved on each one. On the fourth, a speedboat showed up with Rhino, Samson, and Lieutenant Sloan.

Once the divers were safely on the deck, he ended the training and left Miles for Lena to take back to the capitol tower. The young woman had taken a liking to the dog, and both he and X trusted her.

After saying goodbye, X boarded the speedboat with Ton and Victor, and Rhino piloted it to a distant oil rig that the Cazadores had turned into a massive dry dock.

During the ride, Rhino filled X in on the night before and what had happened on *Elysium*. X stroked his graying beard. The jumps had cleared his mind—a good thing, because they were facing a slew of problems.

With the *Lion* sunk and *Star Grazer* deployed, they had only *Mercury* patrolling the barriers. *Elysium* remained operational but anchored for training. There was no way to contact the crew manning the second fuel outpost in Belize, and X wasn't willing to send either warship to check on the Iron Reef until they had another to replace it.

And the nagging question remained: What the hell had killed the crew at Bloodline?

The crew of *Discovery* may have the answer to that, but the electrical storms had kept him out of contact with Captain Mitchells.

At midmorning, they reached the docks surrounding the oil rig. The place looked like a rusted box in the water. Near the roof of the ten-story platform, streaks of bird shit had formed what looked like a white waterfall.

The sun gleamed over the horizon as they tethered the boat next to a score of others. Sergeant Wynn and his advance team of militia soldiers were already here.

"Area is secure," he confirmed.

Sloan motioned for X and the entourage, and they climbed a ladder up to the only platform overhanging the exterior of the rig.

Rhino went up first, then X. At the top, he turned to help Samson up, who seemed to be struggling even after losing weight.

"I ain't a spring chicken anymore," he grumbled.

X chuckled. "That makes two of us."

The old engineer took his hand and climbed onto the platform, filling his lungs with clean air.

"I hope this was worth the trip," he said.

"It is for me," X replied. "I've been wanting to see this place for a while."

The militia soldiers came next, and soon they were all on the platform, along with the four Cazadores in light armor guarding a steel door.

The soldiers held their spear shafts vertically. One of them unlocked the door and stepped aside. Clanging hammers and buzzing saws and grinders echoed through the cavernous space. Ten floors of interior platforms extended off the bulkheads that surrounded two warships moored inside the hangar doors.

Behind the ships were a container ship and what looked like an old cruise ship. Mezzanines and scaffolding, many of them occupied with workers, rose up the sides of the vessels.

A female voice called out in Spanish, and X looked up to see Carmela standing on the deck of the first ship, right above fresh paint that read, "*Renegade*."

The colonel wore leather today, forgoing her armor in the hot space. Judging by the grease streaks on her face, she had been here for a while, working alongside the mechanics and engineers.

She shouted down to Rhino and then walked out of view.

"What did she say?" X asked.

"To join her on *Shadow*," Rhino said. He waved for the group to follow him toward the metal spans extending over the water.

The militia soldiers watched the Cazadores working inside the facility. The men and women were hard workers, but in the eyes of the sky soldiers, they were also threats.

Many of the mechanics, engineers, and dock-hands looked as if they had been working through the night. They too seemed interested in the newcomers, and X found many of them staring at him, some of them glaring.

He was used to it, and unlike his guards, he wasn't worried about a security threat here. Sloan flashed hand signals, and several of the soldiers fanned out. Ton and Victor moved to a higher platform than the militia soldiers, to keep an eye on all levels at once.

Rhino led the way across another mezzanine over the water, to the second ship. This one was much bigger than *Renegade* and in much better shape.

The exterior looked like the one that he had rescued Magnolia from back in Florida—the ship where el Pulpo had skewered Rodger like a bug.

X pushed aside the memories and climbed with the others to the deck above. A crane operator smoking a cigarette looked down as he prepared to lower an armored turret.

Carmela raised a hand in the air, but not to the worker.

A white cockatoo with a yellow crest swooped down behind X to land on her shoulder.

"Pretty impressive shop they got here," Samson said, standing with his hands on his hips. "But the question is, when can these ships be ready to sail? They both look like shit, and that's coming from someone who spent most of his life working on the *Hive*."

Samson was right, of course. While *Shadow* looked better off than *Renegade*, much remained to be done, from overhauling the anchor capstan to sandblasting rusty scuppers.

"Ask Colonel Moreto," X said to Rhino.

Rhino and Carmela spoke for a moment.

"She says *Shadow* is rough on the outside but

the guts are good," Rhino said, "and the mechanical system wasn't damaged in the fighting. She thinks we can have it back in service in a week or two, max."

"What about that one?" X asked, pointing to *Renegade.*

"Our engineers need piston rings that we don't have, unfortunately," Rhino said. "We have to go on a scavenging mission to find them."

Carmela spoke again, and he translated.

"She says she has a crew of sailors and a team of soldiers ready and waiting to go on your orders, King Xavier," Rhino said. "They will take a smaller vessel to a location where we believe there are parts."

"Get it done," X said.

Rhino told Carmela, and she caught the eye of the soldier who had been shadowing her. He nodded and hurried off.

They weren't wasting any time. That was good, because X had a feeling there was none to waste. "I want to know the location where they believe there are parts," he said to Rhino. "Make sure it's noted on a map and brought to my quarters."

They continued the tour of the ship, going down the narrow passages. At the bottom deck, they entered a large bay that housed several old-world vehicles. Two were armored trucks with patched rubber tires, while the third was a transport vehicle with tracks.

Rhino pushed on, showing them several more compartments, until the crackle of a radio stopped them. Sloan pulled out her walkie-talkie.

"I'll go topside to see if I can make this out," she said.

X decided to follow her, sensing that it was something important. When they reached the weather deck, the transmission cleared with a message from a militia soldier monitoring the radio in the command center.

"Lieutenant Sloan, I've made contact with Captain Mitchells," said the man. "He wants to speak to King Xavier."

X grabbed the handset.

"This is X. You're going to have to coordinate the conversation, okay?"

"Okay, sir."

The soldier spoke into the radio equipment back at the command center, explaining that he had X on a mobile radio. X heard a faint response from Captain Mitchells in the flurry of static that followed.

"King Xavier," said the militia soldier, "Captain Mitchells said they know what killed the Cazador crew at the outpost. Something called the *skinwalkers*."

Rhino shot Carmela a glance.

"Captain Mitchells destroyed the rest of the outpost, and they are now on their way to Rio de Janeiro," the soldier continued. "He anticipates they will reach the target in four to five days."

"They destroyed the rest of the outpost?" Rhino asked.

"Confirm your last about destroying the outpost," X said into the radio.

"*Discovery* fired two missiles to destroy the fuel station," he replied.

"What the hell would they do that for?" X muttered.

"Shit," Rhino said, looking down.

"Captain Mitchells has a message from General Santiago to relay to General Rhino," said the soldier. "He says to firm up the borders. The skinwalkers could be heading to the islands."

Rhino glanced up, and X caught the flicker of fear in his eyes.

"Copy that," X said. "Tell Captain Mitchells to stay safe and to use only the encrypted line, and only if absolutely necessary."

"Roger that."

The line severed, and X handed the radio back to Sloan. Then he turned to Rhino and Carmela.

"Who, or what, are the skinwalkers?" X asked.

"Demon men who flay the hides off men and wear them as trophies," Rhino said.

X almost laughed, but this was no joke. Apparently, el Pulpo wasn't the worst of his kind.

"Come on," he grunted. "You've got to be screwing with me."

"I'm afraid not, King Xavier," Rhino said. "Five years ago, el Pulpo's bastard son, Horn, took the warship *Raven's Claw* and two hundred of his warriors on a raiding mission."

"Bastard son?" X said. "Isn't that something you should have mentioned?"

"He was thought dead," Rhino replied. "We still

don't know exactly what happened when the warship anchored, but when they didn't return, el Pulpo sent an expedition to find them."

X shook his head wearily. Of all the secrets the Cazadores had kept over the past few months, this was one of the craziest.

"We found a quarter of the crew murdered barbarically at the site of the target, and *Raven's Claw* missing," Rhino said.

"Like psycho, like son, I suppose," Sloan muttered.

Rhino didn't seem to understand the old-world reference and kept talking. "Many people thought el Pulpo sent his son to die on that mission. Perhaps that's why Horn and his comrades slaughtered their commander and those loyal to his father." Rhino ran a hand over his shaved head. "Others believed that Horn took *Raven's Claw* in search of treasure and would someday return."

"And you think Horn and his merry crew of demon assholes attacked the fuel station?" X asked.

"According to General Santiago, yes."

X lowered his head in dismay. "The shit keeps piling up and smelling worse. As if mutant beasts and man-hunting machines weren't bad enough, we have a demented army of skin … whatever the hell you called them, to worry about now."

"I wish I knew more about them," said Rhino, "but there are just two men alive who do. One is General Santiago, and the other is the sole survivor of that ill-fated mission."

"I thought you just said everyone died."

Rhino hesitated. "Not exactly …"

"God *damn* it," X said. "All these damn secrets and half truths are really starting to rankle my ass."

"I'm sorry, King Xavier. We found one former sailor from the mission alive, but I'm afraid he won't be much help."

"Why's that?" X asked.

"Come with me. I'll show you."

* * * * *

Almost four days of pushing through the skies at a little over fifty knots had taken its toll on Les. The thought of at least two days' travel still to go just made him tired, and knowing that the Vanguard Islands were facing another threat made the journey seem almost unbearable.

Les had thought his wife and daughter would be safe at home. The defectors didn't know the location of the islands, but the skinwalkers did, and from what General Santiago had said about Horn and his crew, they were a significant threat, even in small numbers.

If Les had to guess, el Pulpo's bastard son had fueled his warship and killed everyone in the outpost and was now heading to the Vanguard Islands for his revenge and to take the throne from his father.

Les massaged his temples, wondering whether they should turn back.

No, he thought, *X has it under control.*

He had too much thinking time on his hands.

Part of him wondered whether he should fly ahead to scope out Rio de Janeiro. But he wasn't keen on leaving the slower-moving *Star Grazer*, especially now that they had dropped the *Sea Wolf* off on the ship's deck with Sofia, Magnolia, and Rodger.

Thoughts of the skin sculptures at the outpost, the two-headed snakes, the defectors killing his boy, and Ada Winslow dropping a shipping container of Cazadores into the ocean all swirled in his head.

She's not your problem now. The disappointment and rage he felt toward the woman who had served as his XO momentarily took his mind off the threats to the islands and to his mission.

Ada was young, but she had done something that couldn't be forgiven.

He looked over at the other young woman now occupying the XO's chair.

"How you doing over there, Lieutenant Brower?" Les asked.

"I'm fine," Layla said with a smile. "Not going to lie, though, and tell you that I don't miss sunshine and clear water, but if we end up saving some people on this trip, it'll be worth it."

"Indeed," Les said.

He looked down the row of stations to Eevi. "Ensign Corey, have we heard anything else from that bunker yet?"

"Negative, sir, but I'll let you know the moment we do."

Les got out of his chair and decided to go for

a walk through the ship. "Timothy, you have the bridge," he said on the way out.

The ship's nuclear-powered engines rumbled softly in the bulkheads. He ducked under a low overhead into the mess hall for some grub.

Michael held a tray in his robotic hand, stacked with fresh fruit and some water.

"Hey, Captain, how's it going?" he said.

"Fine. Just thought I'd get something to eat and stretch my legs. How about you, Commander?"

Michael held up the tray. "I'm taking Layla some food."

"She probably could use some rest," Les said. "Tell her I've got the watch when I'm back."

"Will do, sir." Michael paused. "Sir?" he said.

"What is it, Commander?"

"We never talked about what happened in Jamaica."

"What's there to talk about? The machines killed my son."

Michael set his tray down on a counter. "Yes, but—"

"I don't blame you, Commander, if that's what you're getting at," Les said. "If I blame anyone, it's myself for not going down there with him. Maybe if I had, he would still be alive."

"Or you would also be dead."

"And I would make that trade in a heartbeat," Les said. "But there are no do-overs in diving. All Hell Divers understand the risk, and so do their families. Your father knew the risk, just as you know you might not come back from your next dive."

Michael's brow creased. He was obviously worried about leaving Layla and their unborn child behind when they got to Rio de Janeiro.

"I respect you for continuing to dive despite the risk," Les said. "Your mission of saving others out there is a selfless one, Commander. My son believed in that mission, and he died for it. In a few days, we will honor his memory by diving."

Michael smiled. "Yes, we will, Captain. You have my word."

"Good," Les said. "Now, go take Layla some food. You don't want her to get grumpy."

They parted ways, and Les walked over to grab an apple and some dried fish. He remembered Katherine's appetite when she was pregnant with Trey and Phyl. Always famished with weird cravings, but there were never enough rations to keep her satisfied.

Despite the lack of food and the darkness of their world on the *Hive*, he would trade anything to go back to that life.

At least, then he would still have his boy.

On his way out of the mess hall, an alarm blared.

Red lights strobed at the end of the passageway.

One of the hatches opened, and Edgar Cervantes walked into the passageway. His dreadlocks swung as he looked left to right, then focused on Les.

"What's going on, Captain?" he said.

"No idea," Les said as he took off for the bridge.

Halfway there, the public address system crackled with a message from Timothy.

"General quarters," said the AI. "All hands to their stations."

Rounding the next corner, Les nearly slammed into Alfred and another technician.

"Sorry, Captain!" Alfred yelled.

Les kept running until he got to the bridge. Layla, Michael, and Eevi were at the sonar station, studying the screen.

"What's going on?" Les asked.

Timothy's hologram emerged.

"Sir, we have multiple contacts on sonar," said the AI, "and it looks like they're headed right for us."

"What do you mean, 'contacts'?" Les asked. He looked out the portholes, a chill rushing through his muscles. All sorts of thoughts crossed his mind, from other airships to mutant winged beasts.

"Life-forms, sir," Eevi said. "On the surface."

"Timothy, turn on frontal beams and reduce thrusters," Les ordered.

"Aye, aye, sir," replied the AI.

Les checked their altitude and speed. *Discovery* was only five hundred feet above the water and cruising at just over fifty knots. He considered using the turbofans to climb, but he knew of nothing on the surface that could reach them at these heights.

He spotted *Star Grazer* sailing directly ahead of them. The beams hit the warship.

"Contact General Santiago on the encrypted line," Les said.

"Already have," Timothy said. "They are aware of the contacts."

The beeping from the sonar echoed in the quiet space.

"I don't see anything down there," Michael said, watching from a different porthole.

Eevi studied the sonar. "Whatever it is, it's big," she said. "And—oh, shit …"

"What?" Les said.

"Picking up another contact," Eevi said. "Three total now."

Les looked at the main screen that displayed the views from the cameras. The front beams captured something gliding through the choppy waters. The creature went right beneath *Discovery* and continued its trajectory without slowing.

"Captain," Eevi said, glancing up, eyes wide. "Whatever those things are, they're almost as big as *Star Grazer*."

"My God," Les said. "They weren't looking for us. They're after the warship!" He snapped into action. "Turn us around, Timothy. Full speed toward *Star Grazer*. And, Lieutenant, I want those weapons hot."

Les thought of the *Sea Wolf*, sitting on the deck of the Cazador warship.

It wasn't just Cazadores down there anymore.

There were Hell Divers on that ship.

SEVENTEEN

Rhino had planned to boat over to the trading-post rig to talk to his old teammate Mac. Instead, he found himself headed to the only maximum-security prison in Cazador territory—a place he loathed even more than the trading post.

The Shark's Cage.

With news of the skinwalkers, he didn't have much of a choice. Horn and his crew, whom most everyone had written off for dead, had him on edge, especially since the men likely had the warship *Raven's Claw*.

Rhino pushed the throttle forward, speeding away from the Vanguard Islands.

X stood beside him, wearing Hell Diver armor and helmet. Rhino was also in full armor today, and not just because of the water.

The place they were going to was one of the most dangerous rigs—home to some of the worst Cazadores ever to draw breath—and the home of the only man to survive an encounter with the skinwalkers.

Two boats followed them to the rig. One was filled with militia soldiers, the other with Cazadores. *Mercury* was still patrolling the barrier, and *Shadow* would be back out there soon, but he wasn't sure when *Renegade* would return to service.

Raven's Claw was one of the best warships ever in the Cazadores' fleet and could inflict a lot of damage on the islands if it returned.

The boat reached its top safe speed, its exhaust stacks jetting black smoke into the sky. They were approaching the invisible line between light and darkness.

A few minutes later, the boat broke through, and blackness swallowed them. Two miles into the darkness, rain pounded them, streaking down the windshield and his helmet.

"How much farther?" X yelled over the engine noise.

"Another twenty minutes, maybe," Rhino said. The rig was far enough away that if anyone ever did escape from the prison, they wouldn't be able to swim to the Vanguard Islands without being eaten by a shark first.

X folded his arms over his chest. Rhino didn't need to see his face to know that the king's mind was burdened with worry. He wasn't the only one.

"King Xavier, there is something I need to tell you."

"More bad news?" X said. "Sure, pour it on."

Rhino took his eyes off the ocean and said, "Sir, I believe that if General Santiago does not return from Rio de Janeiro with *Star Grazer*, you will be overthrown in a bloody battle. A battle I can't prevent unless drastic measures are taken—and a battle we can't win, even if I manage to put together a team, unless we act first."

"So you want me to kill Ada *and* start another war?" X said.

"This is not about Ada, King Xavier." Rhino twisted the wheel to avoid a wave. "This is about striking first, before our enemies do."

"Striking *who*, exactly?"

"Vargas, for starters. I almost killed him myself last night on *Elysium*. But Colonel Moreto is also a threat. She showed her hand at the Sky Arena, when she invoked the rights of the Black Order of Octopus Lords."

"If I remove them, won't *that* cause a war? Won't the soldiers under your command all revolt?"

"Very possibly. I would not be surprised if their supporters came to avenge them."

X uncrossed his arms. "So what would you have me do? Kill every Cazador soldier? Then what do we do when the defectors or these skinwalkers show up and start ripping people apart and stitching them into blankets?"

Rhino empathized. They both were warriors trying to be civilized in a barbaric world filled with monsters of every kind: mutant, metallic, and human.

"Tonight, I'm heading to the trading post to seek allies," Rhino said. "Then, with your permission, I will slit Colonel Vargas's throat in his sleep. No one will know who did it. I'll start with him and then take out Colonel Moreto."

"I don't know," X said. He stared ahead into the darkness, his knees flexing up and down, absorbing the shocks as the speedboat bounced over the swells. "Perhaps we should let the council weigh in when General Santiago, Magnolia, and Les return."

"King Xavier, I don't know how you did things in the sky, but on the Metal—*Vanguard*—Islands, we do not vote on matters such as this. And frankly, the odds of General Santiago returning are not good."

X grabbed the gunwale railing to brace himself but didn't respond.

"No one liked el Pulpo's bastard," Rhino said, "but if he still lives, he is a challenger to the throne. If he shows up, Colonel Vargas and others might join him. We *must* strike first."

X let go of the railing and faced Rhino. "You do what you must, then, and let *me* deal with my people."

A blue gash of lightning split the horizon. X gave a weary nod and stuck out his hand. Thunder boomed as they shook on it.

The bow lights finally picked out a shape rising above the waves. A lonely silo-shaped structure was the only oil rig outside the barrier of light. On the top of the flat roof, several rusted old-world helicopters perched like gargoyles, overlooking the tower walls.

Rhino eased the throttle back and steered toward the pier, where several spotlights raked back and forth, turning the dark surface bright as day.

"Why do you even have a prison?" X asked. "I

thought you guys liked killing each other in the Sky Arena."

"Some people are too crazy even for that," Rhino said. "Besides, the people here contribute to the economy by making our bombs and bullets."

"Has anyone ever escaped?"

"Once, a prisoner found a way to sneak explosive powder back to his cell. He saved up enough that he eventually blew his way out," Rhino said. "He got pretty torn up in the razor wire but managed to get to the water."

"And then?"

"No one saw him again. As you will see, this place was built to keep people inside."

"Can't wait."

A Cazador soldier in full armor slung his assault rifle over his shoulder, grabbed the side of the boat, and pulled it in.

X jumped out first, and the soldier standing sentry pounded his chest armor. While he tethered the boat, a second guard walked down to meet the other two boats. The group followed the two guards toward a gate blocking off a secondary steel door twice Rhino's height. The soldiers unlocked the first gate and pushed the double doors open. An alarm blared and red lights swirled over the metal decks.

Inside, a central guard tower rose all the way to the ceiling. Windows gave the guards inside a view of the prisoners on all ten levels.

Rhino looked up at the circular mezzanines

bordering the barred cells of each level, patrolled by guards with cattle prods. The double doors sealed behind the visitors with a thud, and the Klaxons and red lights clicked off.

"This level is for the guards," Rhino said. He pointed to one of two doors in the bulkhead. "That's the mess and barracks."

"Wonderful," X said, "but I came to see the prisoner that's going to tell me about the skinwalkers."

"Yes, of course, we'll head up in a moment," Rhino said. He took off his helmet, breathing in the steamy air and waiting while his eyes adjusted to the dim lightning.

Now, with the sirens off, nothing blocked out the bedlam of screams and howls. The guards shocked some of the more unruly inmates away from the bars, but they wailed on in Spanish and other tongues.

"Everyone but Sloan and Rhino is to stay here," X said to the militia guards. They fanned out on the open first floor, looking up at the prisoners, who gawked back at them from behind the bars.

Rhino ordered his team to stay behind, too. He followed the two main guards into a stairwell, and the sounds faded once the door closed behind them.

"The best workers are kept on these lower floors," Rhino said. "They are the most valuable to us."

"Let me guess, then," X said. "We're going to the top."

"Indeed."

As they went up, the shouting from the prisoners

grew louder until Rhino could hear them over the pounding of boots on stair treads.

On the ninth floor, the guards opened the door to a rusty mezzanine. Rhino nodded at the guard behind the tower glass. A ten-foot gap and an electric mesh fence separated the tower windows from the mezzanine.

Another guard gave an electric zap to a prisoner who tried to get a view of Rhino's team. The two guards accompanying the three visitors moved out toward their comrade at once, hitting the bars of the cells as the group passed. One man didn't let go in time and took a jolt. He hit the floor, baring his teeth like a wild beast.

The guards continued around the circular walkway. Many of the prisoners inside the cells were missing fingers, and a few had even lost a limb to the ordnance and bullets they made.

Halfway around the platform, the group stopped in front of a cell. The prisoner gripped the bars, looking at them in turn with sad, dark eyes. Both guards shouted for him to get back, and when he didn't, they used their prods. The electrical current didn't have the same effect on this sinewy Cazador. He made a grunting noise but did not scream like the others.

"What the hell is wrong with this guy?" Sloan asked.

The prisoner finally stepped back and opened his mouth as if to yell, but all they heard was another flurry of grunting noises. It was then that Rhino knew, they had their man.

"Gael, *estamos aquí para discutir a los cueros andantes*," Rhino said. To X, he said, "I told him we're here to talk about the skinwalkers."

"The guy's got no tongue," X observed. "How's he going to tell us anything?"

Rhino reached into his pack and pulled out a map and a pencil. Then he pulled out an apple and an orange.

"Fresh fruit," Rhino said. "Works like a charm." He held them up to the bars for the prisoner to sniff. "Now, get back and do as I say, and I'll give them to you."

Gael hesitated, then shook his head.

"You don't want this?" Rhino asked. He brought the apple up to his mouth but stopped shy of taking a bite.

Gael reached out for it, letting out another guttural noise.

"Back up, and I'll give you this," Rhino said.

Gael retreated to his bunk.

"Open it," Rhino said.

"Sir, that goes against procedure," one of the guards replied in English.

"Do it," X said.

The guard looked at X, then fiddled with the key chain on his belt. He opened the door, and Rhino and X went in, leaving Sloan outside. The small space was furnished only with a bunk covered in straw, and a small desk and stool.

Rhino tossed Gael the apple. He caught it midair and bit into it like a Siren with a fresh carcass.

"Why is he a prisoner?" X asked while the man inhaled the fruit.

"For fleeing the battle with Horn," Rhino said. "He deserted his comrades, which is normally punishable by death. But we kept him alive since he's the only one who knows anything about Horn. And he was a mechanic—knows how to make bullets."

"But he's never said what happened that day?"

"Only to el Pulpo," Rhino said. "And to my knowledge, el Pulpo never told anyone."

"Give me the orange," X said.

Rhino handed it over, and X peeled off the skin while Gael watched. That seemed to agitate the prisoner, and he reared away.

It then struck X that he was doing to the orange basically what the skinwalkers did to their enemies. As soon as he stopped, Gael stepped back to the bars.

"Show us what happened out there and where *Raven's Claw* went, and you get the orange," Rhino said in Spanish, holding up the pencil.

"Tell him if he does that, he can have a bucket full of oranges," X said.

Rhino relayed the message.

The prisoner's gaze flitted from Rhino to X. His hand darted out and snatched the pencil. Then he picked up the pad of paper and scribbled for several moments, drawing what appeared to be a crude map with a few lines of illegible text. With a shaky hand, he drew a line on the map, and then a circle. He glanced up, like a child looking for approval.

Rhino picked up the paper.

"What's it say?" X asked.

"Something about a great journey," Rhino said. "Horn took the warship to …" He held up the paper and pointed to what looked like a skull. "Then what is …"

Rhino looked closer at the map. The line did indeed go where he suspected.

"What?" X asked.

"He says Horn took *Raven's Claw* to the former colony that we abandoned many years ago," Rhino said. "A place we call la Escolta—the Outrider."

X pointed at the circle on the map.

"And what's that?" he asked.

Rhino swallowed. "The Vanguard Islands," he said. "Just as I feared, the bastard must be planning to come back for his throne."

* * * * *

Magnolia sat in the hot lower compartment of *Star Grazer* with six half-naked Cazador warriors. Sofia sat beside her on a crate, trying to explain the complicated game that involved dice, a deck of dog-eared cards, and a lighter.

So far, Magnolia wasn't having much luck, and not because of intimidation. The Cazadores had certainly tried clacking their teeth, pounding their chests, and yelling, but she didn't fear them. She had decided yesterday that if she was going to fight alongside them, she would get to know them. And what better way than by playing cards?

Rodger, by contrast, had no desire to know these people or join in their games. He sat in a chair across the open barracks, tongue sticking out in rapt concentration as he carved a wood figurine.

That was fine. She didn't want him to see her lose, and so far, she was doing little else.

"How about poker?" Magnolia said. "This shit is rigged."

"It's not rigged just because you suck," Sofia said.

Magnolia sighed. "You know, I was happy when Les sent you down here to make sure nothing happened to us, but now I'm not so sure." She squinted at Sofia's cards. "Are you cheating?"

Sofia laughed. "No!"

"We shall see …" Magnolia said. She was glad to have Sofia down here with them, but it wouldn't be for the entire journey. When they reached the destination, Sofia would return to the airship and join Michael's team.

Sudden shouting interrupted the game. Across the room, a Cazador pounded down the ladder, waving. He wasn't here to play cards.

"¡Vengan rápido!" he shouted.

The Cazador warriors all hopped off their crates and chairs.

"What's going on?" she asked Sofia.

Sofia shrugged. "No—"

Automatic gunfire jolted Rodger out of his chair.

"Armor up," Magnolia said. "We must be under attack."

The three divers threw on their armor and helmets, grabbed their weapons, and headed up the ladder.

The sounds of battle reminded Magnolia of the day the sky people had shown up at the Metal Islands to save her. Machine guns barked from the turrets, firing into the water as Cazadores ran across the deck toward their stations.

"What's going on?" she shouted.

"No clue!" Rodger yelled back.

The bow cannons boomed, and twin geysers erupted and then fell back to the surface.

After the next shot came a flurry of loud clicking sounds. But this noise wasn't from the weapons. It came from whatever they were shooting at.

Magnolia watched tracer rounds lance into the water. Whatever they were firing at was big. The possibilities raced across her mind.

"Come on!" Sofia yelled.

They ran up to the command center. General Santiago and Lieutenant Alejo were on the bridge, monitoring the battle.

"Sofia, find out what they're firing at!" Magnolia shouted.

As Sofia crossed the busy bridge, Magnolia and Rodger went to the port windows, where she switched on her infrared optics.

A red mass flashed across a large section of water.

That reading couldn't be real. The beast would be almost as long as the warship.

Magnolia bumped on her comm channel. "Captain Mitchells, do you copy?"

Static crackled in her helmet.

Les's voice came over the channel, faint but recognizable. "Copy. Mags, are you okay?" he said.

"What's in the water?" she shouted.

The gunfire outside made hearing difficult. She hunkered down to listen.

"Come again, I didn't catch your last," she said.

A momentary letup in the gunfire allowed her to hear the next response.

"Timothy believes it's some mutant version of a sperm whale," Les replied.

Magnolia stared at the gargantuan creature cutting through the water on the port side. She remembered reading about them when she was a kid and wondering what one might look like in real life.

But this wasn't what she had imagined, and she doubted this beast ate only fish and squid. It wanted to eat everyone aboard *Star Grazer*.

"There are more—"

The crack of gunfire made it impossible to hear the captain, and she stood back up just as the whale slammed into the hull.

Glass shattered from the portholes, and a computer exploded in a shower of sparks and electronics. Two Cazador officers fell to the deck.

As Magnolia pushed herself up, the vessel got slammed again, this time from the other side. Now she understood what the captain was trying to say.

There was more than one whale out there.

"We have to get to the *Sea Wolf!*" Rodger yelled.

Sofia looked down at a monitor next to Santiago. "We're taking on water," she said.

The general yelled at his crew, giving what looked like orders to abandon ship.

Another message came over the open channel with *Discovery*. "Get away from the windows!" Les yelled.

Magnolia pulled Rodger to the deck just as a missile came streaking through the sky. She didn't see the explosion, but she heard it. A few beats later, a curtain of seawater deluged the ship, and she heard thuds against the windows. Looking up, she saw that it wasn't just water. Blood and lumps of pink gore flecked the cracked glass.

General Santiago raised a fist in defiance at the whale bits sliding down the glass.

Rodger helped Magnolia to her feet. Two turrets on the bow rained machine-gun fire into the water, punching into the flesh of the biggest living beast Magnolia had ever seen.

The bullets seemed only to peck at the thick flesh covered in orange barnacles and scars from what looked like tentacles. The creature slipped back under. On the way down, it slapped the weather deck with a tail fluke, crushing one of the turrets like an old-world beverage can.

Santiago yelled something—a curse, no doubt—at the whale. He turned to one of his men and shouted more orders. Then he looked at Magnolia and Rodger and again waved them off the bridge.

This time, Magnolia obeyed. She pulled on Rodger and ran outside with him and Sofia. A ladder took them back to the deck where the *Sea Wolf* was secured to a davit.

Another missile streaked through the sky and hit the water on the port side. This time, she saw the geyser of water. And this time, no bits of flesh or blood rained down on the ship. *Discovery* had missed.

Not entirely, she realized. The missile had angered the giant cetacean. She braced herself as the beast speared toward them, its barnacled back above the surface.

"Incoming!" Sofia yelled.

Magnolia reached out to Rodger just before they both went flying through the air. She lost her grip on Rodger's hand and saw him slam into the rail, but she kept flying.

Right over the side of the ship.

She hit the water on her back, and darkness rushed around her.

Panic gripped her as she tried to move, and for a moment, she simply sank into the ocean. She could see the rusty hull of the ship cruising past.

Then she snapped alert and managed to bring her body vertical. She kicked toward the surface and pulled with her hands, all the while watching *Star Grazer* sail away.

Her heart skipped at the sight of the giant twin screws. They churned the water in front of her as the warship passed, and she went cartwheeling away into the depths.

Habits learned from years of Hell Diving kicked in, and she forced herself to relax. At last, she stopped spinning. After getting her bearings, she started kicking and pulling toward the surface.

Not being able to see her surroundings fed her fear, but the only thing that mattered right now was getting to the surface. She could then radio *Star Grazer* or *Discovery* to come pick her up before one of the whales spotted her and swallowed her for an appetizer.

She broke through the waves, pulling herself up while treading water. The armor made it tough, but she was well rested, and the fall hadn't injured her.

Turning in the water, she looked for the warship.

She spotted it to the west, but it continued to plow ahead. The one machine gun still operational rained lead into the ocean, piercing the vast surface with an audible *shick, shick, shick.*

Magnolia slipped back under the water and kicked back up, only to get slapped in the helmet by a wave. She fought back above the surface and glimpsed motion in the dark sky. A sudden beam shot away from the clouds as *Discovery* lowered.

The light covered the area off the ship's starboard side, where the whale had sounded. Magnolia bumped on her chin pad.

"Captain Mitchells, do you copy? It's Magnolia. I've fallen overboard!"

The only response was static.

Magnolia watched in horror as the monstrous

sperm whale surfaced off *Star Grazer*'s port beam. A rising wake followed the creature as it swam toward the bow. She could hear the crunch that was the beginning of the end for the warship.

Star Grazer swung around from the collision, giving Magnolia a view of the starboard side. Several boats were already being lowered from their davits. One snapped loose and fell into the water.

She hit her chin pad again, opening a line to Rodger.

"Rodger, do you copy?" she said.

White noise crackled in her ear. Then a voice. "Mags …"

"Rodger!" she yelled.

She slipped under the water but could still hear his faint response. He sounded hurt.

She kicked back up over the waves in time to see the warship begin to founder. Soon, the compartments would fill with enough water that it would drop like an anchor.

Discovery hovered over the sinking vessel, and another missile streaked away from the launch tubes. The blast sent a red-tinted geyser into the air. Les had found his target.

"Target destroyed," came a voice over the channel. "Magnolia, do you copy?"

"I'm here!" she yelled, raising her arms toward the sky. "South side of the ship, off the stern, a quarter-mile out."

Discovery rotated over *Star Grazer*, its frontal beam flitting back and forth across the surface. Several rowboats moved away from the warship. As it dipped, she saw that the *Sea Wolf* was still on the deck.

"Get the *Sea Wolf* first!" she yelled.

She wasn't sure there was time to save the boat, but it looked as if Les was going to try. Cables lowered from the belly of the airship.

"Rodger, where are you?" Magnolia said.

Panic whispered inside her as she treaded water, watching helplessly as *Discovery* tried to save the *Sea Wolf* before it sank with the warship.

She pulled herself into a front crawl, fighting the weight of her armor to keep above the waves. At least, she didn't have to worry about swallowing any water.

"Rodger," she said again. "Do you copy?"

"Mags," came a reply. "Sofia … she has me … where …"

About halfway to the rowboats, Magnolia rolled onto her back to rest her muscles. She couldn't make much sense of what Rodger was saying, only that he was with Sofia.

Seeing that *Discovery* had cables lowered and attached to the *Sea Wolf* also helped calm her thumping heart. She rolled over and began a front crawl when an expanse of warty, barnacled flesh slid through the water in front of her.

What in the wastes?

She flip-turned out of the crawl and kicked backward, away from the creature. What she saw under the surface was nowhere near the size of the whale that sank *Star Grazer*. The animal swimming parallel to her was the calf of one of the mutant sperm whales. It swam in a circle, coming back around.

Though much smaller than its parents, it was still big enough to swallow her whole. She didn't have her laser rifle, and she had lost her blaster in the fall.

She pulled herself back above the surface, where she again treaded water as she reached over her back. Her two sickle-shaped blades were still sheathed. She grabbed the hilt of one and pulled it out. Then she ducked under the water to look for the creature.

The calf continued circling her, studying her with one huge eye. Magnolia tried to guess where in that bomb-shaped body she should thrust her blade, and waited for her moment.

The beast opened a long jaw of conical teeth and gave a long, clicking sigh that she could easily hear underwater.

This wasn't the snarl of a predator. It was the sound of a baby that had just lost its mother. The orphan calf finally turned and swam away into the depths.

Magnolia kicked back up to the surface and sheathed her blade. She turned just in time to see the massive screw propellers of *Star Grazer* disappear below the surface.

A beam hit her from above. In the glow, she saw the hull of *Sea Wolf* locked against the belly of *Discovery*.

"Get me out of here!" she yelled.

EIGHTEEN

When the radio popped, X had dozed off. He nearly fell out of his chair reaching for the comms equipment.

A weak voice vied with the static crackling that filled the capitol tower's command center. Miles looked up from the deck, then quickly lost interest. Resting his head between his forepaws, he closed his eyes and let out a sigh.

"No, no, no," X muttered. He hadn't heard from Les or anyone else on the airship for almost two days and was starting to worry that something had happened.

Of course something happened.

"Captain Mitchells, do you copy? This is Xavier."

X waited for a response, lowering his head as if in prayer, but that just made him feel more tired. He glanced at the wall-mounted clock. It was well past midnight.

He rubbed his eyes and slapped his cheeks. For the past two days, he had slept only a couple of hours at a time, just as he had during those years back in the wastes. But instead of fighting for survival, he was fighting a more internal battle.

Mallory had hit a nerve the night of the funeral for her husband and son. Her assessment of his leadership had him wondering about his ability to protect his people. He certainly hadn't saved Rhett or DJ.

Since then, he was second-guessing all his decisions, from letting the Cazadores keep their army and navy to sending his people and the only airship back into the killing wastes. Hell, he was even starting to wonder whether decommissioning the *Hive* had been the right call. What if someday they needed to escape this place?

He tried the radio again. "Captain Mitchells, this is X, do you copy? Over."

More static filled the room.

X stood up, stretching his tired muscles. What he needed was a long swim.

No, you need sleep.

Candlelight flickered over the command center, just two floors below the Sky Arena. It wasn't a big space— just a few tables, two desks and chairs, and the bank of radio equipment—but it served as his war room.

A flat-screen computer sat on one of the tables, and rolled-up maps covered the other. Stacked on a desk were several books that Imulah had found documenting Cazador missions. X picked up the record of General Santiago's mission to find the skinwalkers—the mission that had turned up Gael. He thumbed to the page with the sketches: a beach, an old lighthouse, and what looked like an ancient fortress—nothing he hadn't seen before in the wastes.

But the bizarre scarecrow-like human remains that Horn and his crew had assembled were unlike anything X had encountered during his decade in hell. The barbaric nature of the kills was beyond even what Sirens did. Sirens killed without regard for their victims' suffering. But skinwalkers went out of their way to *prolong and intensify* the suffering.

And it was eerily similar to the defectors' ghoulish handiwork. *Why?*

It didn't matter, really. All that mattered was being ready to stop them if prisoner Gael was right.

The radio crackled again. "This is Captain Mitchells. Does anyone copy?"

"Giraffe!" X shouted. "This is X! What's your status?"

"Sir, we've got a major problem out here."

"What happened now?"

"Whales happened, sir. A group of them attacked *Star Grazer* …" Les paused long enough for X to deduce that the ship was now at the bottom of the sea.

"She's gone," Les confirmed.

X stared at the handset. Two Cazador warships gone in the same week.

"Survivors?" X asked after the pause.

"We rescued about a third of the Cazador crew and the *Sea Wolf*, but the vehicles and all the fuel are gone, sir."

"How about our people?" X asked.

"All present and accounted for."

"Good, and General Santiago?"

"Alive," Les said. "We've been trying to get ahold of you for days now. Should we come home, or proceed? Now that we're no longer caravanning with a slow-moving warship, if we continue at max speed, we can reach the target in only a few hours."

Just a few hours. His team was tantalizingly close to the target, to finding out whether there were indeed survivors out there. Or defectors …

"Sir, the skinwalkers—they could be sailing *Raven's Claw* to the islands," Les said. "Don't underestimate them, sir. What we saw was pretty horrific."

"I know, and I won't," X replied. "I've got our defenses squared away, I think."

"I can turn us around and be back in a day, sir."

An airship would certainly help mitigate the emerging skinwalker threat to the Vanguard Islands, especially now that they had lost *Star Grazer*. But *Discovery* was practically within pissing distance of its objective. X didn't want to scrub the entire mission without first doing some aerial scans to see what they were dealing with. And, of course, the defectors could be there, hunting down the survivors.

He couldn't abandon them now.

Static crackled from the speakers.

"Check out the signal," X said. "Find those survivors, and if defectors are there, destroy them. Then get your asses back here."

"Yes sir," Les said. "And, Xavier?"

"Yeah?"

"Look after my family. They're all I have left."

"I'll make sure nothing happens to them," X promised. "You have my word, Captain."

The door opened just as the line severed, and X got up to greet Lieutenant Sloan.

"Was that *Discovery*?" she asked.

X gave her the gist of the call.

"Damn," Sloan said.

X was sick of questioning his decisions, and he was even sicker of doing nothing. He scooped a handheld radio off a charger and handed it to Sloan.

"Deploy a team of soldiers to the *Hive*," he said. "I want two machine-gun emplacements on the roof, and one of our turret-mounted thirty-millimeter cannons."

"Protecting it from what kind of attack, sir?"

"From *Raven's Claw*," X said. "I want this by sunset." He looked at the clock. "You've got eighteen hours, Lieutenant. Can you make that work?"

"I'm not the one that's always late," she said, cracking a rare smile.

"Yeah, yeah," X said.

Miles got up and followed him out of the command center. He went left down the hall. Around the next corner a militia guard stood outside a door.

X went inside the former brig that his people had retrofitted into an armory. Their weapons were neatly stacked on shelves on the other side of the barred barrier splitting the quarters in half.

Behind the bars, a man named Dusty sat at a desk. He stood, shook his long gray hair back, and gave X a mostly black smile.

"You must be here for your new gun," he said.

Dusty walked back into the armory, past a shelf of militia armor and helmets. Stopping at the rifles, he bent down and picked up a modified AK-47-shotgun combo.

"Just sign here, sir," Dusty said, handing a clipboard through the window.

They had implemented the same rules governing weapons as on the airships: every firearm accounted for at the end of each day.

Dusty grinned as he walked over to the barred door. Unlocking it he proudly handed X the gun.

"Would love to see how it fires in person."

X took the rifle. It was lighter than he had expected. He raised it toward the ceiling, looking through the scope. Then he lowered it and put the strap over his shoulder.

"And the ammo?" X said.

Dusty threw his arms up. "Well, shit, can't forget that."

He returned a moment later with a bag of 7.62 mm magazines and double-aught shotgun shells. Miles sniffed the bag, then sat back on his haunches when he realized there was no food.

"All freshly made at the Shark's Cage," Dusty said. "Won't have any jams with those bullets or shells. Those Cazadores know what they're doing."

"Thank you, sir," X said. He left the room with his new weapon slung over his shoulder. Miles followed him to their next stop, three floors down.

The hatch opened to a crisp night, the moon

hanging high in the sky. X walked onto the platform where he had once surrendered to el Pulpo and his forces after a brutal fight.

He moved through the gardens, past the pool, toward the balcony overlooking the marina below. The burly figure of a soldier stood near the railing. X had a feeling this was where he would find the general.

Rhino was scanning the water for threats. He spun about when X stepped on a dry leaf. The blade of the spear flashed through the air and stopped just shy of his neck.

"Easy, there," X said, stepping back.

Rhino lowered the blade.

"I'm sorry. I did not know—"

"Forget it," X said.

He walked over to the balcony and took a moment to breathe in the salt air and admire the splendid view of white clouds scudding over gleaming water. Then he got down to business.

"General, I've ordered Lieutenant Sloan to prepare the *Hive* for battle," X said. "I've already got this tower fortified the best I can, but there is still something we need more of."

"What's that, sir?"

"Soldiers."

"Working on it, sir," Rhino said.

X unslung his new rifle. "We've got another problem," he said. "*Star Grazer* is at the bottom of the ocean."

Rhino leaned forward, his jaw hanging open. "What?"

"Sunk by *whales*, apparently," X said. "General Santiago is still alive, but the Cazador armada is hurting."

"Buckets of shit!" Rhino muttered.

"That also leaves us with the same problem of dwindling oil reserves," X said.

"I know."

"I'm authorizing *Mercury* to escort a tanker to the Iron Reef for fuel as soon as *Renegade* and *Shadow* are back in service. That place just became crucial. We must protect it at all costs." X sighed, dreading the answer to his next question. "How much fuel do we have left?" X asked.

"Not much, sir. Basically one full tank trailer."

X looked out over the water again, thinking of his next order. It would hopefully take one of his problems off the table.

"I'll have the militia secure that tanker," X said. "And I want Carmela to lead the expedition to the Iron Reef, to secure the fuel outpost."

"And Colonel Vargas?" Rhino asked.

"You dispatch him as soon as you can, General, and leave the security of the Vanguard Islands to me." He raised his new rifle. "If Horn does show his mug, I'll blow it off with double-aught buck."

* * * * *

"We're twenty miles from target," Timothy said. "Cricket has reached the shore."

"Good, hold us here," Les said.

Michael stood on the bridge of *Discovery* with Magnolia, both of them armored and ready for the mission. They had finally made it to Rio de Janeiro, but a storm sat right over the target.

"Performing scans," said the AI.

Les, Layla, Rodger, and Eevi sifted through the scan data streaming in. Using the new thrusters Michael installed on the journey over, the drone had flown to the shore, where it was now transmitting data back to the airship.

The door to the bridge whisked open, and Edgar Cervantes walked in with Sofia, both in armor. Edgar had a knife sheathed on his chest, and bandoliers of shotgun shells crisscrossing his body. He looked ready for a fight. So did Sofia, with her slung rifle and holstered blaster and pistols.

Behind the two divers were General Santiago and Lieutenant Alejo, also armored, though neither carried weapons. They wouldn't be given any unless the mission was approved.

"Commander Everhart, the divers are almost ready," Edgar said.

"Our team is ready to hunt," Alejo said.

Hunt ... Michael didn't have any reason to distrust either Cazador officer, but he still didn't like having them all on the boat with Magnolia and Rodger.

"Thank you, Lieutenant," Les said. "Head belowdecks and stand by for orders."

The men left, but Edgar and Sofia remained behind.

"General Santiago and Lieutenant Alejo aren't

stupid," Sofia said. "But if they suddenly get that way, I'll be the first to cut their hearts out."

Magnolia grinned. "I bet you will."

"How are the skies looking, Ensign Corey?" Les asked.

"There's a big storm over the entire coastline," Eevi replied. "It extends inland, which pretty much makes flying or diving too risky."

"Lowering the ship could get us blown out of the sky if defectors are here," Michael said. "We need a subtler approach."

"I've identified a potential pocket in the storm that we could fly through," Timothy said. "It will be bumpy getting there, but if we make it, the divers could jump. Take a look."

Eevi bent down. "That looks promising," she said. "But what about the *Sea Wolf*?"

"I've located a spot to drop them off a few miles from the coast," Timothy said. "Choppy seas, but they should be fine."

"What do you think, Mags?" Les asked. "You sure you're up for it?"

"Of course we are," Rodger said.

Magnolia laughed. "Who said *you're* going, bright eyes?"

He frowned, and she nudged him. "Just kiddin', Rodger Dodger. But you better not get seasick."

"Okay, then," Les said, "if the scans come back clean, we drop off the *Sea Wolf*, then move into position to drop Team Raptor in."

"I'm sorry, Captain, but there is one problem," Timothy said.

"What's that?" Les said.

"I'm afraid we need to get closer to shore to complete these scans. Too much interference from the storm to scan for exhaust plumes, and Cricket doesn't have the range."

"All right, plot us a course and do your scans," Les said.

The six thrusters fired, accelerating the airship toward the coast.

"Magnolia, Rodger, prepare to depart on the *Sea Wolf*," Les said. He looked to Michael. "You better get to the launch bay, Commander. Stand by for scans and orders."

Michael walked over to Layla, who stood at her chair, wincing slightly.

"You okay?" he asked.

"I'm fine. Bray's just been really active today."

Michael looked down at her belly and felt a twinge of anxiety.

"We'll be fine, and you will be, too," she said. "I love you, Tin."

"And I love you," Michael said.

He kissed her goodbye as the ship rumbled into the storm clouds. Lightning glanced off the bow, rattling bulkheads. By the time he got to the launch bay, the other divers were suited up.

"Listen up, everyone," Michael announced. "The moment we get the green light, we're diving. If you've changed your mind, I won't hold it against you, but you need to decide now."

When no one moved, he clapped his hands together.

"Okay, then, let's move it, people."

With the technicians' help, the team did their final gear preps. The blue slashes outside the porthole windows felt like a harbinger of things to come.

"Captain Mitchells, this is Raptor One," Michael said. "How we looking up there?"

"Almost in position, Raptor One. Stand by for orders."

Michael got the divers into a horizontal line in the middle of the launch bay. On his HUD, five beacons came online.

"Systems check," he said.

"Raptor Two lookin' good," Edgar said.

"Raptor Three, good to go," Alexander said.

Arlo and Sofia verified their suit and systems functions, and Michael uploaded their target and source of the SOS.

The airship groaned like a waking giant as it lowered into position.

"Stand by for biological scans, Team Raptor," Les said over the open channel.

Michael scanned his team. Though he couldn't see Sofia's or Arlo's faces behind the mirrored visors, he hadn't missed the tension in their voices. This was their first real dive. They would soon discover how ready they were for whatever awaited on the surface.

"Not picking up any exhaust plumes from the machines," Les confirmed. "We are picking up life-forms, however. Timothy believes it's mostly vegetation."

In a few seconds, he came back online. "All right, everyone, I'm giving the all clear for the mission. Taking the *Sea Wolf* down first."

The white glow of Timothy's hologram emerged in front of the launch-bay doors.

"What's Ghost Man doing here?" Arlo sneered.

"Cut the shit and get your head in the game," Michael said. "You don't want to end up a statistic on your first dive, do you?"

Arlo shook his head.

"I would listen to Commander Everhart," Timothy said. "Sensors are picking up a massive concentration of organic life in the zone marked on your HUDs."

A map emerged on the divers' subscreens. Most of the area showed red.

"What is it?" Edgar asked.

"I'd hypothesize that it is some sort of flora, perhaps a forest," replied the AI. "But it is unlike the readings from other zones we've explored."

"Great," Alexander said. "Let's hope this isn't the type of flora that eats humans."

Sofia twisted slightly toward him. "*Eats humans?* You left that out of training, Commander Everhart."

"I didn't tell you about the trees that eat people?" Michael replied. "Or the *vines* that eat people?"

"Uh, no."

"Don't worry, we'll be avoiding that area."

"Still not detecting any exhaust plumes that the DEF-Nine units produce," Timothy reported, "but I have located a hive of what could very well be Sirens."

Another rectangular map replaced the digital telemetry on his HUD.

Michael cursed when he saw how close the hive was to their drop zone, but it didn't surprise him—Sirens normally lived near where they were birthed.

"Please find me a new DZ, Timothy," Michael said. "I'm not risking those things spotting our battery units on the dive in."

"Already done, Commander. My suggestion is uploading to your HUDs … now."

Michael checked his subscreen. It was nearer the coast, which meant they would dive partly over water. He was okay with that, since it was how they had trained Sofia and Arlo back at the Vanguard Islands.

"All right, Team Raptor," Michael said, "we're back in business. "Prepare to dive."

He pushed the button to the launch-bay doors. They parted, letting in a rush of wind as the airship lowered the *Sea Wolf*.

With light cloud cover and little electrical interference with their systems, the divers could see part of the shoreline in the distance. Roads of pulsating purple and red glowed like a network of luminous veins throughout the city.

"Guess we know what your scans are picking up," Edgar said.

The ship jolted as the cables released the *Sea Wolf* onto the choppy water below. Michael caught a glimpse of it as it sailed away.

"Good luck, Mags," he whispered.

"Stand by to retrieve Cricket," Timothy said.

"Everyone, back," Michael said, retreating to the red line with the other divers. The robot emerged a few moments later, flying across the city's fractured skyline and then switching to hover modules to maneuver into the open launch bay.

"Good job, buddy," Michael said, patting the robot on its smooth armored side. It chirped and flew over to the wall-charging unit for some extra juice. Michael closed the launch-bay doors as *Discovery* ascended back into the clouds. The view outside darkened.

"Team Raptor, prepare for launch," Les said over the channel.

The airship slowed, and Michael reopened the launch doors. At twenty thousand feet, he couldn't see much of the city except for the glowing vein of flora that pulsed as if it had a beating heart.

Somewhere beneath that poisoned surface were the first humans Michael had personally ever come across in the wastes who weren't Cazadores. People who had lived underground for centuries.

On this mission, the Hell Divers' motto had taken on a new and terrible significance. They dived so humanity survived—by saving the remaining humans before the defectors could find and kill them all.

"All clear, Team Raptor," said Les. "Good luck, and Godspeed. Radio silence except in emergency."

"Copy that, sir," Michael said. He checked on Arlo, who gave a thumbs-up.

Michael shouted their motto and dived headfirst into the clouds. He pulled his body into stable falling position, arms out, elbows and knees at ninety degrees. Glancing up, he looked at the airship one last time, thinking of Layla and Bray. In his heart, he knew he would see her again and would meet his son.

A deep breath, and he put them out of his mind to focus on his team.

Edgar's beacon began moving in the subsquare of his HUD. Next came Alexander, Sofia, and finally Arlo.

Michael's suit whipped and rippled in his ears as he dropped through the clouds, eyes roving constantly between his HUD, the dark surface, and his aerial surroundings.

Fourteen thousand feet ... twelve thousand ...

At ten thousand, everything looked good. No lightning, turbulence, or rain. The cloud cover even seemed light. By all appearances, the pocket Timothy had discovered seemed to be a hidden paradise like the Vanguard Islands.

At eight thousand feet, one of the beacons on his HUD started picking up speed. It was Arlo, in a nosedive. For some reason, he was trying to catch up.

"God damn it," Michael muttered. He kept the radio link off, observing the captain's order of radio silence.

If defectors were down there, he didn't want them picking up any chatter—even though he wanted to scream and tell Arlo to pull out of the suicide dive. The kid probably thought diving into the wastes was easy, because they'd had an easy dive today. But conditions could change in a heartbeat.

Sofia closed in on the right flank of Edgar and Alexander, just as they were trained to do. When Michael looked down again, they had broken through the cloud cover at five thousand feet. The pulsing mutant flora lit up the surface in a network of red and purple that looked like a vascular diagram.

He had never seen anything like this before.

The vegetation provided enough glow that they may not even need their night-vision optics on the surface.

The wind suddenly grew shrill, almost like a human scream.

Not the wind, he realized. The scream came from his speakers. Someone had bumped on the comm channel. Rotating forty-five degrees left, he saw that Arlo had clipped Sofia after coming out of his nosedive, probably due to a pocket of turbulence, as Michael had feared.

Both spun away from Edgar and Alexander.

"Son of a bitch!" Michael shouted in his helmet to no one but himself. He glanced back again, resisting the urge to yell orders into the comm link.

While Arlo quickly pulled himself back into stable position, Sofia cartwheeled through the air. Extending his legs behind him, Michael let the relative wind resistance push him toward them, but he was moving too slowly to help.

Lightning flashed in the west, the direction they both were headed. He checked the HUD again. The drop zone was big but not boundless. If they drifted too far off, they could easily hit the edge of the storm.

But what could he do?

He couldn't reach them—he was already five hundred feet below both their positions.

Edgar and Alexander kept on the plotted course. It was the contingency plan should something like this happen. They couldn't risk the entire team trying to save one diver.

Michael quivered with rage. Arlo's stupid hotdogging was the reason for Sofia's off-kilter flight.

At three thousand feet, the blasted ancient city came into view. Shattered buildings and bridges and towering granite domes filled his vision. Mutant forests covered much of the landscape, hiding God only knew what kinds of fearsome creatures.

Michael checked one last time to see Sofia in a stable fall. The sight was a relief, but they weren't out of this yet. The two rookies were way off course. Once they landed, he would have to trek over and find them.

At two thousand feet, he pulled the pilot chute from its pocket on his right thigh. It caught air and dragged out the canopy, which billowed overhead, jerking him vertical. Reaching up, he grabbed both toggles and steered over a spire of rock. At its summit stood a colossal statue of an angel or a god, holding its arms out over the city. Gliding over, he saw that one of the arms had partially broken off, and a hunk of the head was missing.

He looked away, sailing toward the city and the shoreline beyond. Waves crashed against the eroded seawall surrounding the bay. He searched for the *Sea Wolf* but couldn't spot such a small vessel in all that ocean vastness.

According to his HUD, the DZ was right below him, but that couldn't be right. The ground below was a sinkhole, its depths glowing red like the eye of a defector.

He toggled right, and both Edgar and Alexander followed his lead. The three divers aimed for the rim of the hole, where several buildings formed a skirt of debris. Vines and bristly, leafless trees grew out of the rubble.

As Michael started to flare, he saw something moving on the surface near the scree apron, walking on two legs. He caught only a glimpse, but this didn't look like a Siren or a monster, and it was not a machine.

It looked like a naked human.

NINETEEN

Magnolia hated not being in radio contact with Team Raptor. By now they would have landed on the surface and would be trekking toward the rendezvous point.

The *Sea Wolf* wasn't even to shore yet.

When they made land, they would need to hide the boat and then find a way up the cliffs and into the city. Splitting up wasn't always a good idea, but this time it made sense. It improved their ability to discover threats, and the teams could back each other up if one was ambushed.

Although she did wish Sofia were here. With just Rodger and herself among ten Cazadores, she was feeling a little outnumbered.

Team Raptor needs her more than you do.

Magnolia and Rodger shared the boat's cockpit with two Cazador men she had to start trusting if they all were going to survive. General Santiago and Lieutenant Alejo sat to her right, on the other side of Rodger, who was watching the radar and sonar stations.

Somehow, Alejo managed to hold the map steady as the twin hulls pounded over the waves. He studied the chart while General Santiago spoke rapidly. There was anger in his tone, and Magnolia finally glanced over.

"What now?" she said.

Alejo looked up from his map. "He says this piece of shit is going to get us killed."

"This *piece of shit* saved our lives and got us across the ocean to the Vanguard Islands," Magnolia said.

Alejo translated for Santiago. The old general regarded her for a moment and then snorted.

"You're lucky we're giving you a ride," Magnolia said, instantly regretting her words.

"Let's hope there aren't any whales out here," Rodger said.

Alejo glared at Magnolia but did not translate her words to the general.

"Whales, sharks, octopuses, sea serpents, or anything else big enough to eat us," Rodger added. "Maybe these waters are free of monsters, or maybe they're all vegetarians and live on seaweed."

Magnolia laughed. They all knew the truth: that any animal bigger than they were probably wanted to eat them.

Beneath the waves dwelled beasts large enough to swallow the *Sea Wolf* without even chewing. She just hoped the boat could avoid detection. Sometimes, smaller was better, especially when you were trying to be sneaky.

She adjusted their bearing two points to westward.

They weren't far from shore now—what was left of it. Most of the coastline was gone. The tsunami that hit centuries ago had swept away all the lovely beaches in the old archival photos.

Cliffs rose above the rocky shore, and the sporadic lightning revealed the skeletal frames of high-rise buildings. The city was one of the biggest she had ever seen, and for the first time today she felt a raw stab of fear.

"Where are we going to park this rig?" Rodger asked.

"Any ideas?" Magnolia said to Alejo.

He looked at his map for several moments. Then he checked their location on the dashboard. Finally, he pointed east, and she followed his finger toward what looked like an inlet.

"I think that is the spot."

"What spot?" she asked.

"Where our expedition landed many years ago. Assuming my map is correct, there is a port there."

"The expedition that never came back?" Magnolia asked.

"*Sí*," Alejo replied.

"Yeah, no way. I think we should find a different place to dock."

"Do you *see* a different place to dock?" Alejo asked. "The only port out there is east."

"I'm with Mags," Rodger said. "Your idea just got a rousing no-thanks."

Magnolia swung the boat due west.

"What are you doing?" Alejo protested.

"The opposite of what you tell me, because I plan on surviving this mission, unlike your comrades. And because this is my boat. So, sit that ass down and shut up if you're not going to be helpful."

Rodger laughed, but his voice trailed off when Alejo glared at him.

"Easy there, buddy," Rodger said.

Santiago looked from his lieutenant to the two divers, clearly sensing the tension.

Magnolia took one hand nonchalantly off the wheel and let it hang inches away from one of the two pistols holstered on her duty belt. She could always use one of her curved blades or her new blaster if the Cazador lieutenant got terminally stupid.

Should have kept your mouth shut, she thought.

She had been telling herself that for years but never seemed to find her filter.

Fortunately, Alejo backed down, perhaps deciding that reacting to her mouth wasn't worth the risk of angering General Santiago.

A chirp on the sonar kept Magnolia from relaxing.

"Rodger, check that out," she said.

"Coming from the northeast," he said. "Not sure what it is, but it's big. Like *shark* big."

Magnolia looked right, the same direction that Alejo had told her to go earlier.

She kept her westward bearing and pushed the throttle forward, speeding in a diagonal line toward the coast.

"Tell your men on deck to get ready," she said, "just in case whatever that is decides to try us."

Alejo put on his helmet and moved outside, where eight Cazadores watched the sea. One was on the mounted harpoon gun, and two others manned a machine gun they had installed. If something out there wanted them, they would at least have a shot at killing it first.

She needed a place to dock the boat, but nothing looked promising. The rocky coast was close enough that she could see several buildings on the cliffs, and cascades of vegetation hanging over the bluffs.

The sonar continued to beep, and Magnolia scanned the waves, looking for a dorsal fin or a boat, but saw nothing.

"Go find out if they see anything out there," she said to Rodger.

He grabbed his rifle and left the command center in a hurry, leaving Magnolia with her favorite Cazador. The general stroked his long beard and muttered in Spanish as his eyes combed the water.

She couldn't help but wonder what those dark eyes had seen over the years, and what those callused hands had done. The man next to her was a murderer, and she had no doubt that if not for her people, he would have kidnapped, and perhaps eaten, the very people they were here to save.

How could someone like that ever change? It was a question she had pondered for months, all the while hoping the Cazadores had left their most barbaric traditions behind.

But one thing was certain: she could never fully trust him.

He suddenly raised his arm and pointed at the coast to her left. She followed the finger toward what looked like some sort of peninsula. Whether man-made or natural, it was better than anything she had seen yet.

She spun the wheel and piloted the boat toward the spit of land.

The sonar continued beeping, but a glance at the screen showed the unknown mass heading in the opposite direction now.

She put her other hand back on the wheel. If Santiago tried anything, she would just have to beat his old ass into submission.

Waves splashed the jagged eastern shore of the peninsula ahead. Magnolia eased off the throttle and switched to the twin battery-powered engines and began the curve around to the western shoreline.

A light flashed on the distant cliffs. Santiago saw it too, and pointed.

The white beam faded almost as quickly as it had appeared—just a flicker, like a signal.

It wasn't mutant plants.

She kept her gaze on the spot, but the flash did not recur.

The peninsula was coming up fast, and she had to focus on getting them around the rocky spit. Jagged rocks stuck out like spears from a fortress battlement.

The hatch to the command center opened, and Rodger stepped inside, dripping wet.

"Nothing out there," he reported.

Alejo joined him inside and closed the hatch. Both men shed their helmets.

"I think I found a spot to tie up the boat," Alejo said. He bent down beside Magnolia and pointed at the peninsula.

"On the other side," he said.

She turned the craft, giving a wide berth to any ripples or patches of sea foam that might indicate rocks below the surface. The depth finder showed twenty feet clear, but she didn't want to take any chances.

Curving around to the other side of the spiky landform, she saw what Alejo had spotted from the top deck.

A metal platform extended from the peninsula, anchored by two poles.

Maybe humans had been here after all.

"Well?" Alejo said. "Does this look good enough for you?"

Magnolia studied the terrain. The narrow peninsula led right to the cliffs, but she didn't see a way up. Worse, there were also plenty of likely spots for an ambush, with the defectors owning the high ground.

Not to mention that this was a lousy place to leave their boat. Even with its dark hulls, it would be easy to spot, but it was their best option so far.

"Tell your men to tie us up," Magnolia said. "We'll leave two sentries here to guard the boat."

She reversed the engine and, after lining up with the platform, maneuvered the boat carefully toward the docking platform.

Rodger stood right beside her, making her nervous.

"Give me some space, Rodgeman," she said.

He moved away, nearly bumping into General Santiago.

They were almost to the platform when a Cazador jumped off the deck above them, making Magnolia flinch. Another man on the upper deck tossed the mooring lines.

The soldier onshore grabbed the side of the boat and pulled them over to the dock, then tied the bow and stern lines to the metal poles.

She turned off the engine, unslung her rifle, and followed the men up onto the weather deck. Two Cazadores remained on the mounted weapons, the harpoon gun pointed at the water, the machine gun at the cliffs in the distance.

"Tell them to stay here and watch the boat," she said to Alejo.

He gave the order and then went to monitor two other soldiers carrying a wood plank, which they laid over the razor-wire-festooned rail.

Magnolia looked at the bluffs stretching in both directions. A low haze flowed like a ghostly smoke over the edges.

The Cazadores all turned toward Magnolia and Rodger. She unsheathed one of her curved blades and pointed it at the rocky ledges.

None of the soldiers moved. She then realized that they weren't looking at her and Rodger; they were looking at General Santiago.

"Tell them that treasure awaits," she said to Alejo.

The lieutenant translated her words to the other warriors, who raised their weapons but refrained from voicing their enthusiasm.

She resheathed her blade and raised the laser rifle, ready to meet whatever dwelled in the haze of this mysterious wasteland. And ready to fight by her side were soldiers who only months ago had been her enemies and captors.

* * * * *

Dinner was always the busiest time at the trading-post rig. In the moonlight, hundreds of Cazadores swarmed the five levels of shops like locusts. All of them played a role in the economy.

The farmers carried baskets of fresh fruit, picked from their rigs earlier in the day. Artisans carried handcrafted items to barter with those who ran shops on the rig's five shadowy levels.

Rhino climbed to the top level. When he got there, he spotted motion in the distance, where X was training the greenhorn Hell Divers. Canopies sailed down in the moonlight as the king guided the divers to the decks of several vessels. The warrior never seemed to rest, and for his sake, Rhino couldn't either.

He turned his attention to the bustling open floors

below. People traded every imaginable thing: eggs, jars of pickled fish, jewelry, medicines, fishing poles, fabric, knives, hats, and a thousand other things.

Every square yard of floor space was occupied. Even the sky people had booths now. Rhino spotted Cole and Bernie Mintel's watch shop, where they also sold wood carvings, chairs, and tables.

But not everyone was here to shop.

Some came just for the entertainment. The music of flutes and stringed instruments provided a backdrop for the early evening, rising above the babel of different languages that had survived over time.

Some people were here for other pleasures. Off the selling floors and away from the hawkers' cries, in the darker corners of the rig, were tents and booths where a man—or a woman, for that matter—could fulfill almost any desire in the sex trade.

And still others had come here to buy a different type of resource: people. The third floor held cages of indentured servants to be auctioned off to the highest bidder.

Rhino hated this place.

The rig was a cesspool of grifters, prostitutes, and food of questionable origins. But the man he was here to see loved the rig. The former Cazador warrior known as Mac had made his home here after retiring from the army.

Rhino finally spotted him in the throng below. Of the hundreds of Cazadores and sky people packed in the open area, it was not hard to pick out the one man missing both a leg and an arm. He walked with the support of a cane and had two metal prosthetic limbs.

Several rich merchants in their colorful, fancy clothes and dumb sailor hats walked toward Mac. Unlike the other customers, Mac made no effort to get out of the way. In fact, he waved his cane at the men as he shambled toward them.

Rhino wasn't deceived by Mac's ungainly posture or slow pace. He was one of the most skilled warriors in all the islands, and he could fight if it came down to it, even in his present condition. But not everyone seemed to recognize the man.

"*¡Fuera, pendejo!*" called out one of the merchants.

It was Tomás Mata, telling Mac to get lost and, worse, using profanity to do it.

Mac halted and turned slightly toward the councilman. He tapped his cane on the deck and started to walk over, but Tomás must have recognized him then. The merchant took off his sailor hat and gestured politely to convey that Mac could go wherever he pleased. They exchanged a nod and moved on.

Grinning, Rhino pulled his hood over his head. Mac had a reputation that scared even the richest merchant in the islands. With his features shaded, Rhino made his way down to the next level, which smelled of excrement and ammonia. Hogs grunted, and chickens squawked in their pens while potential buyers negotiated prices.

The next floor down held the indentured servants. Much like the animals above them, they were in cages and being scrutinized by potential buyers. In Rhino's eyes, they weren't treated much better than slaves. They were paid something for their labor, but not nearly enough for the scut work they had to do.

He avoided the sad gazes and grimy faces by pulling his hood close. He took a ladder down to the main selling floor. His nostrils filled with the reek of body odor and the oily smell of fish frying in pork fat.

The sweet scent of tobacco wafted to him from the next booth, and he almost stopped at the aroma. It was the one store Rhino would patronize if he were here to purchase goods. He liked a good joint from time to time, but he wasn't here to get a buzz.

The crowd thickened around him as he moved. Watchful eyes turned in his direction, noting the double-headed spear that he held vertically. The weapon drew stares, and he moved faster, trying not to attract any more attention than necessary.

Several Cazador soldiers, wearing leather vests and pants, patrolled the periphery, but none seemed to have spotted him yet. These men and women were not the best of warriors, which was why they got police duty and were denied the honor of going on raids.

They didn't worry Rhino, though he was concerned about Vargas's many spies. This wasn't the capitol tower, and the ambitious colonel had eyes deployed on this rig and others.

That was why Rhino had waited to come until night, when he was less likely to be spotted. He stood taller to look for Mac in the crowd. The old soldier had wandered away from the main booths and down an alley of grubby shacks and tents.

Rhino hurried through the crowd to reach him before he vanished into the interior of the rig. Unsurprisingly, the shanty shops lining the alley offered all sorts of taboo merchandise. Bottles of eel oil to increase sexual performance, shark's teeth that, crushed and boiled in soup, were said to boost one's fighting abilities.

It was all a load of crap, of course, but Mac had always enjoyed experimenting with things like this. Thinking back on the man's skills as a fighter and his charm with the ladies, perhaps there was substance to the claims for some of these products.

Rhino walked head down along the dimly lit alley. Several patrons talked to shop owners, but Mac kept going, his cane clicking, toward the open hatch at the end of the alley.

"*Shit*," Rhino muttered. He walked faster, nearly hitting a man who had backed away from a booth selling "surefire magical charms." Mac went through the hatch and closed it behind him.

Rhino got there a half minute later. He tried the handle, and it clicked open. He ducked through, into a narrow passageway that smelled like piss.

He had taken two steps when he heard a whisper of noise and stopped to look down at the blade poised inches from his throat.

But he wasn't the only one with a blade at his jugular.

Mac's gaze ran from the spearhead under his chin, along the shaft, to Rhino's grinning face.

"Mac, how you doing, you old wharf rat?" Rhino said.

After sheathing his sword cane, Mac shuffled forward and shook Rhino's arm. "Aside from getting old, well enough. I heard you made general."

Rhino looked back at the open hatch. The patrons at the stalls went right on with their business, not even glancing his way. He shut the hatch and motioned for his old friend to accompany him into the enclosed hallway.

A candle sconce at the end flickered over the rusted bulkheads.

"Things are not good," Rhino said, "and I need your help."

"Because of the sky people?"

Rhino shook his head. "Because of *our* people."

"Brother, our people are from Texas," Mac said, running his hand over his salt-and-pepper beard, "and don't you forget that."

A memory surfaced of that day when the Cazadores had invaded their underground home. The day Rhino, Sofia, and Mac were captured.

"That is true," Rhino said. "And that's exactly why you're the one man left I trust."

"Anything you need, Nick. I've got you."

"I need your help putting together a strike team and bringing the Barracudas back."

Mac swallowed. "I gave a lot to that team," he said, raising his prosthetic arm. "Almost gave it all."

"I know, and I'm sorry to have to ask you again, but—"

Mac put his hand, the real one, on Rhino's shoulder. "Don't be sorry. Like I said, I've got you."

"Good," Rhino said. "I'm also thinking about asking Isaiah."

A silver brow rose. "I think he just got back from a fishing trip a few days ago. Might need some convincing," he said. "You know Isaiah; he likes incentives."

Rhino reached into his robe and pulled out a bag of silver. He had come prepared. Isaiah was never a Barracuda, but he had helped train Rhino to be the fighter he was today. The old drill sergeant was the best of the best, despite his ripe old age.

Mac took the coins and nodded.

"I've got one more man I need to gather before our first mission," Rhino said.

"What's our first mission?"

Rhino checked both ends of the passage. A civilian had stumbled in. The thin man with a long and wispy beard came unsteadily toward them. Stopping halfway, he pulled his pants down, turned, and proceeded to urinate on the bulkhead.

"*Muévate*," Mac said in Spanish, tapping his cane on the floor.

The man grumbled and pulled up his pants, then stumbled past them, smelling like booze. At the end of the hallway, he stopped again and this time threw up.

"Shit," Rhino said. He motioned with his chin for

Mac to follow him back the way they had come, until they were alone again.

"Remember Colonel Vargas?" Rhino said.

Mac grimaced. "Of course. The bastard was almost as bad as el Pulpo. I still see him here from time to time, when he comes to visit the brothels. He killed one of the girls a few weeks ago. I would have killed him if it weren't for all his babysitters."

"Well, now's your chance," Rhino said. "I'm going to slit his throat while he sleeps."

Mac laughed. "You'll never get that close, old friend."

"That's why I need your help. I can't trust anyone else."

"What about King Xavier?" Mac asked. "Is he a good man?"

"Indeed, he is. I'll die for him if I have to, which is why I must kill Vargas."

"Why not just give the order to your soldiers?" Mac asked. "Send a battalion to smoke his ass."

"Because I'm not sure they will follow the order, and I do not want this coming back to us. I had the chance to kill him a couple of days ago—had his throat in my hands. If I'd squeezed a bit tighter for a few more seconds, he would be octopus shit."

Rhino was glad he had spared Vargas then. It would help him get away with killing him later. No one would see this coming.

"Vargas sleeps with those bug eyes open," Mac said. "I've seen it, and it is some weird shit."

"Then we'll find another way." Rhino handed him a chain with a key. "Meet me at the capitol rig tonight and show the guards this."

"Where you going?"

"To talk to the third recruit," Rhino said.

"Going to tell me who you got in mind?"

"Whale's boy," Rhino said.

Mac chuckled. "Which one?"

"Felipe. I fought him a few days ago. He's got skills. I just need to convince him to follow me like his father once did."

TWENTY

Michael hunched behind a concrete wall while Edgar and Alexander waited for his signal. They were a half mile from their drop zone, in a section of the city that had been reduced to mounds of rubble.

If he had to guess, the area had been shaken down by a massive earthquake long after the tsunami washed away the coastline. The flattened buildings and leaning ironwork left little protection for the divers, and plenty of places for an ambush. Sinkholes, deep fissures in the ground, and tunnels in the mounds were all potential nesting spots for mutant beasts or shadowed enclaves for the machines.

Michael slowly rose above the wall to scan the area for signs of life. The infrared sensors came back with multiple contacts, though mostly insects, lizards, and rabbit-sized rodents. Nothing the size of a Siren or a defector.

He still wasn't sure what the hell he had seen walking upright on the dive in, but he would bet his rank it wasn't a naked human. No one could survive out here without protective gear and helmets.

The radiation levels were in the yellow range, almost red, and his scans were picking up toxic fumes. The surface and air quality were little better here than at the fuel station where the mammoth snakes ambushed them.

Everything south of the equator seemed different, and they had little intel on what sort of beasts lived in this area. Thinking of all the possibilities brought a chill through his body. He switched his optics over to night vision again and hunkered back down, wishing he had Cricket to help look for threats.

But Les was right to recall the robot to the ship. With all its electronic parts, it was just too big a target for Sirens and defectors.

Michael raised his hand and flashed the "advance" signal to Alexander and Edgar. The two divers dashed to his position. Lightning flashed at the same moment, capturing both men in the blue glow.

They made it to the wall safely and took up positions on his right and left.

Thunder boomed, and Michael waited for the inevitable high-pitched wail. But the electronic cries of the Sirens did not come.

The beasts still didn't know the divers were here— at least, not his half of the team.

He checked his HUD for Sofia and Arlo, now less than a mile away. Their beacons were still idle, but they were active, which meant they were alive.

They appeared to be hunkered down and waiting, just as Michael had told them to do if they ever got separated. While he was glad they had followed orders, getting to them was going to be a struggle. The hive of Sirens Timothy had marked on their map was right between Michael and the two stranded divers.

Edgar peered over the top of the ledge to check for hostiles, but Michael kept prone, studying his HUD for the best route.

"Looks clear," Edgar said, bending down.

Michael didn't know how accurate the map on his HUD was, but it showed a road not far away. He decided the safest route was the one through the ruined structures beyond the wall they now hid behind. It was the long way, but it would avoid the potential Siren hive.

Also, one of the cardinal rules of diving was always to stay off old streets and out of view.

He took point and guided the divers along the foot of the first mountain of debris. Rebar and twisted steel beams stuck out of the fragmented concrete, but he didn't see any openings or tunnels here that could lead to nests.

He slowed down when they reached the outskirts of the destroyed city blocks. On the other side, several structures were still standing or, at least, hadn't finished falling down.

Roofs had caved in, windows were shattered, and each building had an apron of scree around its base. Nature had taken over—mutant trees growing through ceilings and vines worming their way out of windows.

A distant animal howl broke the silence.

It wasn't just flora here.

Michael raised a fist for the divers to hold position. They crouched down, weapons up and roving over the broken structures.

Another noise pierced the night, this one midway between a growl and a wail. He didn't know the sound—only that it wasn't human or Siren.

Michael raised the laser rifle scope up to his visor, then saw something on his HUD. One of the beacons was moving.

It was Sofia.

"Stay put, damn it," he whispered. He wanted to use the comm but couldn't risk breaking radio silence. Not yet, not for this.

He gave hand signals to Alexander and Edgar, who fanned out in combat intervals. If their HUDs were correct, Sofia and Arlo were just on the other side of the structures ahead. He had to get to them before whatever was making the noise found them first.

Michael kept a brisk but cautious pace to avoid stepping in any holes or snagging his hazard suit on anything sharp. There were plenty of threats. Tendrils grew out of the cracked dirt ahead, and bulb-shaped flowers opened slightly as he approached.

He changed direction and signaled his team to do the same.

Halfway across the stretch between the debris piles

and the buildings, he came across another cluster of foliage with the same tentacular limbs that he had seen turn an adult Siren into a deflated sack of mutant skin.

The divers moved around the plants but stopped at a meter-wide crevice in the ground. Vines covered the chasm walls like cobwebs, and he decided to take another route rather than jump across. He could make the easy hop, and so, probably, could the next diver. But after that, the plants would be awake and ready for the last one to jump.

Another eerie call broke the silence, rising into a long, melancholy moan. Sofia's beacon moved again as if in response.

Michael turned back and made his way around the carnivorous plants. A bug the size of a bread loaf crawled from under an uptilted section of curb in his path. The single eye atop its armored head swiveled back to look at him as it scuttled away.

The insect was small, but life out here was violent, and even the most benign-looking creature might kill a man. He carefully trotted the last stretch to the building.

Alexander and Edgar arrived a moment later and took up position behind a brick wall covered in blue, sticky moss that seemed to riffle in the breeze. But there was no breeze.

"What the fu ..." Edgar whispered after almost leaning against the wall.

Michael saw then that the moss wasn't moving after all. It was the bugs, ants, and flying insects trapped on the surface that created the rustling effect.

The team stepped away from the killing field of bugs, not wanting to be there when something bigger came along for a snack.

A mostly intact street separated them from the next building. Michael stopped at the corner to check his HUD again.

Sofia had stopped moving, and Arlo was still in the same spot, just past the structures across the street.

Crouching, Michael waited for another howl, but nothing broke the dead calm. He held up his wrist computer and tapped the surface to pull up a bigger map. To the south, he saw two new beacons outside the range of the smaller map on his HUD.

He smiled for the first time today.

Magnolia and Rodger had landed and were making their way into the city. That meant he needed to get moving.

"Alexander, you take rear guard; I'm on point," Michael said. "We need to move fast and stay low."

Alexander nodded back, and Michael led the way around the corner. The rotted hull of a car remained parked on the broken sidewalk, providing some cover. He decided to risk using the road and took off in a sprint for the vehicle.

Halfway to the first building, he spotted movement on the sidewalk.

With his chin, he bumped the night vision off to look at the blackened concrete with his own eyes. Fire ants the size of his thumb formed a long river of red from their den under the broken street. Several carried insects many times their own mass back to a hungry colony.

Michael decided to stick to his plan and took off running again. Leaping over the line of ants, he continued to the building and hugged the brick wall. Alexander and Edgar quickly joined him.

They stopped at the corner, and Michael looked around the wall. A listing metal fence blocked off a courtyard between the structures.

In the center, thick purple vines grew down the sides of a chipped fountain.

Michael considered crossing the open area, then thought about the hundreds of windows looking down into the courtyard.

Instead, he led the divers past the metal fence, to the next building. Remarkably, the scratched and dented metal door remained intact.

Michael kept low past the row of empty window frames and stopped at the end. Across the road loomed another building. Red vines spilled down from a huge hole in the side, like entrails from a gaping wound.

He did a scan unaided, then again with his infrared. Seeing nothing, he checked around the corner to the left, in the direction Sofia and Arlo were each hunkered down.

The street passed in front of two more buildings, then abruptly disappeared. A few more steps showed him why. A sinkhole had swallowed the entire city block.

He had a bad feeling that Sofia and Arlo had landed inside the cavernous hole.

Another hand signal, and the three divers were moving at double time. They didn't stop until he got to several overturned vehicles on the buckled pavement.

There were two ways to the sinkhole ahead: straight down the road or through the two high-rise buildings fronting it. Since Arlo and Sofia were not in the same location, he decided to break off.

He sent Alexander to the building on the left before following Edgar to the right. They ran fast and hard on the uneven concrete.

A large stone statue stood in a concrete alcove in front of the building. It reminded Michael of the huge god he had seen on the dive in, though this one still had its head.

Edgar moved behind a sunken stairwell where Michael joined him.

They stopped to listen and check their HUDs. Sofia was somewhere to their left, and Arlo was somewhere right ahead of them.

Michael wasn't eager to go inside the ruined building, but he wasn't sure he had a choice.

Thinking over his options, he looked back at the statue and suddenly recognized it.

This wasn't just an angel or a god. It was a sculptor's depiction of Jesus.

Edgar crossed himself. Like some sky people, he was a follower of Christianity. Michael had never been religious, but he did hope it would bring them luck. And if someone was watching over them, well, he would take all the help they wanted to give. So, he crossed his chest as Edgar had done, and gave the "advance" signal toward the stairs. The front door was gone, and sections of at least two lower floors had collapsed in a jumble of plasterboard, furniture, and twisted pipes.

Edgar took point, and Michael followed him over the broken tiles.

The first two rooms on the right were filled with debris, and in the second, Michael found skeletal remains. He stopped and angled his tactical light inside, playing it over as many as five scattered sets of bones. They were oddly free of mummified skin or other soft tissue.

A surprised grunt came from down the hall, and Michael turned to see Edgar with his hands in the air as if someone had him at gunpoint.

Shining his light on the unmoving diver, Michael suddenly understood. He slung the laser rifle, unsheathed his knife, and hurried over. Edgar was caught in a thick, translucent spiderweb. Michael sliced through the finer filaments, then sawed through the thicker radial cables. With one arm free, Edgar began pulling the sticky strands away from his armor.

"Thanks," he said quietly.

"Got to watch where you're going," Michael whispered. "And keep an eye out for the thing that made this web."

Edgar nodded, and the divers pushed on toward the end of the hallway. An opening in the wall gave them a window into the sinkhole. The bowl outside was the size of a large old-world sports stadium.

Five buildings surrounded the rim, and one other had lost the battle with gravity to spill a cataract of debris down the slope, all the way to the bottom.

Detecting movement in his peripheral vision, Michael looked left to find Alexander, waving from a second-floor balcony.

He wasn't alone.

Michael breathed a sigh of relief when he saw Sofia. She waved, too, and then pointed into the sinkhole. Edgar edged forward to take a look down.

"Not too close," Michael whispered, stepping up behind him.

They shined their tactical lights into the hole. Michael raked his back and forth, then stopped when the light captured a black canopy of a chute.

Sure enough, Arlo had parachuted into the sinkhole.

Their beams found him perched on a jutting shelf of sidewalk below. He waved at them frantically, and Michael quickly realized why.

"Shut off your light," he said.

Edgar did as ordered.

Michael turned on his infrared. A section of the pit lit up with red contacts, almost all of them roughly the size and shape of a human.

"Fuck a mutant's mother-in-law!" he whispered.

The Siren hive Timothy had noted on the map wasn't the only one. Dozens of bulbous nests lined the sloping walls of the hole. Even more of the beasts slept at the bottom, in a writhing mat of intertwined bodies.

Arlo had fallen right into their lair.

* * * * *

Team Raptor had a major problem on their hands, and Les wasn't sure how to help them. Standing on the bridge, he watched Cricket's video feed. Since the entire team seemed to be lying prone, he had decided to deploy the robot for a better look. Now he saw why.

The robot hovered below the clouds, using its advanced optics to see into a sinkhole quite literally crawling with Sirens. The beasts were sleeping right below the area where Arlo had fallen. Somehow, they still hadn't detected him. But time was running out.

Michael, Edgar, and Alexander had linked up with Sofia, and they were right above the sinkhole, no doubt trying to devise a plan to get Arlo out of there before fifty Sirens tore him to shreds.

"If only I could mount a missile to Cricket," Les said.

"Sir, that's actually not a bad idea," Eevi said. "What if we turn Cricket into a missile and slam it into the bottom of those nests? It could provide a distraction, at least."

"We also lose our only eye in the sky," Layla said. "And you destroy Michael's friend."

"Timothy, got any bright ideas?" Les asked.

"I have been tinkering with one, Captain." The AI walked over, scratching his perfect beard as if deep in thought. "Perhaps we could use the drone as a distraction, but not quite in the way that Eevi suggested."

Les moved closer to the main monitor. "Switch overlay to infrared," he said.

The screen imagery turned greenish, with red blotches scattered across it.

"Zoom in."

Timothy tapped into Cricket's cameras and magnified on the cluster of Siren nests. They formed a sort of honeycomb on the eastern and northern slope of the sinkhole.

At the bottom of the ten-story pit, a group of larger Sirens slept amid a graveyard of bones and carcasses.

Les walked up to the screen for a better look. Arlo was on the southeast side, almost directly above the sleeping beasts on the ground, backed against the wall and looking up at the other divers.

"Switch back to Team Raptor," Les said.

The camera climbed to the top of the hole, where Michael and the other divers were crouched down, still not doing anything to get Arlo out of there.

"Sir," Eevi said, "I've got movement on the drone's scanner."

"Where's it coming from?" Les asked.

"The bottom of that pit."

"Show me, Timothy," Les said.

The video feed returned to the sinkhole. In the mass of limp, slumbering bodies, several Sirens were stirring awake.

"We're running out of time," Layla said. "We've got to do something."

"The ones on the ground all seem to be males," Timothy said.

"What's your point?"

"They can fly," Timothy said. "What if we use the drone as a decoy and try luring them away from the sinkhole? That could give Arlo a chance to get away with Team Raptor."

"Or it wakes all the beasts and they swarm the divers," Les said.

He looked to Layla and then to Eevi. They both had loved ones on the surface, and he wanted them to weigh in.

"It's our best shot to save the kid," Layla said.

Eevi didn't seem so sure, but she finally nodded.

"Okay, do it, Timothy," Les said. "And take us down to one thousand feet."

"Aye, aye, sir."

The airship began lowering toward the ocean. Les returned to the captain's chair to watch the screen.

"If this doesn't get their attention, I don't know what will," Timothy said.

"If what doesn't?" Les asked.

Timothy smiled proudly. "I'm going to play some Led Zeppelin. I believe they are one of Xavier's favorite old-world bands, right?"

"If the defectors are hiding down there, they'll hear it, too," Les said. He thought on that for a moment. "Maybe that's another upside to using Cricket as bait.

If it draws out the defectors, we can take 'em out from the air."

"What about Team Raptor?" Layla said.

Eevi rolled her chair toward Les, waiting to hear his response.

"We won't put them at risk, don't worry," he said. "They are my priority, but if we have a chance to kill the Sirens, and especially the defectors, I'm going to take it."

He nodded at Timothy. "Proceed."

"Ladies and gentlemen, may I present 'Black Dog,' by the one and only Led Zeppelin," Timothy said. "I listened to these guys a few times in my day, back at the Hilltop Bastion."

His mood seemed to brighten at distant memories of his human past as the ancient song thumped over the speakers inside the bridge. Les checked the main screen footage from Cricket's cameras, which were now focused at the bottom of the pit.

The Sirens all seemed to jerk awake, their eyeless heads looking skyward. Dozens of the beasts stood, and then a flurry of motion filled the bottom of the pit as they took to the sky.

"Oh, shit," Timothy said. "Please pardon the expletive," he added, and his hologram vanished.

The feed moved as Cricket fired its thrusters away from the hole.

"Good luck, Commander Everhart," Les said under his breath.

He looked over to Layla, who watched the screen

with wide eyes, one hand on her tummy. This stress wasn't what she needed, but he knew that she wouldn't go and rest in her quarters even if he ordered it.

The drone's camera feed showed a skyline full of flying monsters. More beasts joined them from across the metropolis, taking to the air on leathery wings to pursue the drone.

"Sir, should I find a place to land Cricket?" Timothy asked.

"No," Les said. "Full speed ahead to our location."

Both Layla and Eevi looked over, and Timothy's hologram reemerged. This time, he was right in front of the captain's chair.

"Captain, you want me to draw them *right to us?*" asked the AI.

"Yes," Les replied. "Weapons hot, Lieutenant. I'm heading to the combat information center."

"On it, Captain," Layla said.

Les stood and walked across the bridge. "Timothy, you have the helm. If those Sirens make it past my gunfire, get us out of here."

"The Sirens are gaining, sir," Timothy said.

"How long until they're within view?" Les asked.

"Two minutes, sir."

"Can that tin can fly any faster?" Les asked. "I thought Michael souped up the thrusters."

"He did, but it still isn't fast enough," Timothy said. "I could shed some of the new armor, though; that might help."

Les thought on it for a moment. Losing the armor

would leave the robot vulnerable. Then again, if it got hit by a round from the 20 mm Miniguns, no amount of armor would save it.

"All right, lose the armor."

"Aye, aye, Captain," Timothy replied.

Les counted the seconds in his head as he dashed through the passageways. He made it to the launch bay within a minute and punched in his access code to open the hatch to the combat information center on the deck below.

A ladder led him into the operations center, which looked a lot like a large cockpit of an old-world airplane. He pushed a button on the dashboard to open the hatch over the windshield. Lightning forked through the dark, scalloped clouds, but he didn't see anything moving in the airship's wake.

"In position," he said into his headset. "Timothy, use the turbofans to start backing us away, but hold as steady as possible."

The airship began to reverse.

Les opened the hatches belowdecks to deploy the 20 mm Miniguns and then grabbed the controls. On the dashboard, a screen with crosshairs came online.

Multiple webworks of lightning sizzled downward, capturing motion on the horizon. The bat-like images swarmed behind a blue light, chasing it out over the open water.

Les moved the joysticks and lined up the targets with the two Miniguns.

He had done this only in training, but he had

scored high marks. It shouldn't be that different in real life.

I hope ...

"Timothy, hit them with the lights," Les said.

Several beams shot out from the ship, lighting up the strange, rubbery skin of the flying abominations. Black maws opened, and claws reached out toward Cricket as it led them on a merry chase toward the airship.

Les squeezed the triggers on the joysticks. Green tracer fire lanced away from the ship, punching holes through mutant flesh. The beasts spun away or simply blew apart in the sky. But those that evaded the first spray of lead dived or tried to climb.

Les went after them. Firing a hundred rounds per second from each weapon, he needed to conserve ammunition as best he could, and he had to be careful not to hit Cricket.

Swooping away from the fountain of tracer fire, a squadron of the beasts formed a V, following a powerful leader.

"Come on," Les said, taking two more down with short bursts. He aimed one of the weapons at the flock coming toward the airship. This time, even the fastest fliers couldn't avoid the spray. A one-second burst obliterated almost the entire V formation.

Within minutes, only three Sirens were still in the sky. Two batted their wings for altitude but couldn't outrun the bullets. The third turned away, flying back toward shore.

The next burst missed, and he considered letting the creature live, to save ammo. It wasn't a threat now, but it could always come back.

"Timothy, target that last bogey with a sidewinder and fire on my mark," Les said. He looked at the screen, and when the missile was red, he said, "Mark."

The projectile arced away from the airship and exploded on impact, blowing the Siren to hunks of meat that fell lazily through the air.

Les leaned back in his chair, watching with satisfaction as Cricket returned to the launch bay, where the techs would intercept it and begin the decontamination protocol.

"Timothy, run a scan for exhaust plumes," Les said.

"Already complete, sir. I'm not picking up anything on the surface."

Les was a little surprised to hear that, but also relieved.

"How about our divers?" he asked.

"The beacons appear to be on the move again, sir," Timothy said. "All five of them are together now."

TWENTY-ONE

"*This* is your strike team?" X muttered. He had just finished with the new divers and had taken Miles to the edge of the pier in the enclosed marina. Only one candle sconce was burning tonight, but the light was enough for X to see the two men on the old fishing boat.

"Not the *whole* team," Rhino said. "There's one more."

"Oh, so you recruited a whopping three total?" X said. "Well, that changes everything!"

Only one of the warriors standing in front of X could be considered a man at all. The other was just a kid. Felipe, son of Whale, stood with his muscular arms folded over his chest.

To his right, a dark-skinned man with almost as many scars as X used a cane to prop himself up in the bobbing boat.

"I thought this boy challenged you on *Elysium*," X said.

Rhino nodded. "This 'boy' lost."

"What makes you think you can trust him now?"

"If Nick trusts him, so should you, Your Holiness," said the guy with the cane.

X reared back. "*Holiness?*"

The man tapped his cane on the deck. "You are the king of these islands and, to some, a God. As for Nick, he has never let me down. If it weren't for his bravery in battle, I would have lost the other two limbs and my head, too."

"You must be Mac," X said.

"My birth name was Bill, but I've gone by 'Mac' most of my life." He reached out his hand to X in an old-world tradition. "Nice to meet you, King Xavier," he said.

X shook his hand. "You as well, but skip the 'holiness' crap. I'm about as holy as a Siren."

Mac's grip was strong, and if Rhino was right, the old warrior had a few tricks in his quiver. But of all the Cazadores on the islands, this was the best Rhino could come up with? Maybe he was saving the best for last.

"Nick killed twelve Sirens and then dragged me back to the boats that day," Mac said. "I owe him my life, and he will always have my sword."

"All right, then," X said, motioning for Miles to jump onto the boat. "Let's go meet the third member of the reconstituted Barracudas."

"You sure you want to come?" Rhino asked. "Colonel Vargas will have spies on the water."

X pulled the hood over his head. "Then you'd better not get us spotted."

He had thought this through. This assassination had to be discreet, so they couldn't use any militia soldiers. And he couldn't trust any Cazador soldiers other than Rhino and whatever team he assembled. X had considered asking Ton and Victor to join the team, but he didn't want to risk the life of anyone who had already suffered so much under the Cazadores. That left a very small pool of warriors Rhino could work with.

So far, X wasn't impressed.

Rhino swung the lever to open the port door, and Mac steered out into the night. Storm clouds blotted out the stars and moon. Not a bad thing, X thought. The rain and lightning would keep most boats off the water while keeping theirs hidden from any spies who might be watching the tower.

Rhino took over for Mac at the wheel, and X sat beside Felipe.

"*¿No hablas inglés?*" X asked.

"*Español,*" Felipe said.

"I'll translate if you have something to say," Mac said.

Felipe stared at X, but it wasn't the same hate-filled gaze that X had seen on *Elysium*. Whatever Rhino had said to the kid worked.

But X still didn't trust him.

"Tell him I appreciate him risking his neck," X said.

Mac told Felipe, who clacked his jagged teeth together.

The radio in X's pack buzzed. He had slipped away without telling Sloan where he was going, and didn't really want to debate the issue, but he answered just in case it was about the mission to Rio de Janeiro.

"This is X; go ahead," he said.

"X, this is Sloan. Where are you?"

"Busy. Why? Somethin' wrong?"

"I've completed fortification of the *Hive*. Thought you might like to take a look."

"I will in a bit," he said. "I'm not feeling so good after eating that pickled mullet earlier."

He could hear her snicker over the radio.

"Going to be on the can for a while," he lied.

"Okay, sir."

X signed off, then grinned at Rhino and pointed at the capitol rig with its decommissioned airship. The engineers had finally added the top platform over the curved rooftop, and put a fence around the entire rectangular perimeter. Massive vertical steel beams held up mezzanine walkways on each level. Hatches had been cut into the hull, allowing residents to walk out onto balconies overlooking the water.

"Take us that way," he said.

The boat swung around for a look. Enough lights were on inside the airship for them to make out two machine-gun emplacements and one cannon on the top level of the north side. The rectangular platform was supposed to be turned into a garden and rain catchment, but so far it looked like a military base.

A launch bay in the decommissioned airship was open, and another cannon was inside, with two militia soldiers standing guard. The weapon suddenly angled toward their vessel as they curved around the rig.

"Not too close," said X.

Rhino turned the boat back out into open water.

"I bet Colonel Vargas has seen our preparations," X said.

"I'd count on that," Mac replied.

"Everyone is preparing for Horn's return," Rhino said. "Especially the Black Order of Octopus Lords. And we can use that to our advantage. Vargas won't see this coming."

X reached down and rubbed Miles's chest. The dog normally slept easily on boats, but tonight he seemed agitated. He let out a low whine.

The journey took them another hour, and it was just after midnight when they finally reached the ancient fishing boat Isaiah called home.

The large vessel floated in the middle of nowhere, moored to an ancient tsunami sensor buoy. Tarps covered most of the deck, and a ladder of white rope clung like a cobweb to the mainmast with a crow's nest at the top. It reminded X of pirate ships in books he had read as a kid.

Reaching down, he stroked Miles again. "You've got to stay here, boy," he said. "I'll be right back."

They pulled up on the port side of the fishing boat, and Felipe grabbed a rope.

"Isaiah speaks English, but best to let me do the talking," Rhino said.

Felipe jumped onto the gunwale and practically

ran up the rope netting on the hull. At the top, he vaulted over the rail and secured the mooring ropes.

X was curious to see how Mac handled the netting, but he got up it surprisingly fast. Miles whined as X followed, but a quick hand gesture quieted him.

Next came Rhino, with his spear and a torch. On the deck, he lit the oil-drenched wick, and the four men waited, scanning the shadows as he moved the torch back and forth. The boat rocked, the ancient wood and metal creaking.

"Isaiah!" Mac called out. "You awake?"

"Up here," replied a gruff voice.

X looked up to the crow's nest, where someone had popped up with a drawn bow pointed at the men below.

"Easy, brother," Mac yelled up.

"It's just Mac and Rhino and a couple of friends," Rhino said. He held up the torch so Isaiah could see their faces.

The man in the crow's nest swung his legs over the side and slid down the mast to the deck. He unslung the bow and renocked the arrow on the string.

"Who are your amigos?" Isaiah asked.

"This is all of us," Rhino said.

Lowering the bow, Isaiah approached slowly, squinting in the torchlight.

"Ah, the new king?" he said.

This man was old, older even than General Santiago, with his receding hair pulled back into a greasy ponytail. A butcher knife hung in a crude canvas sheath from his hip.

He slung the bow over his back and dropped the arrow into the quiver. Then he reached out with a muscular, tattooed arm.

X shook his forearm in the Cazador way.

Isaiah smiled. "Welcome to the *Angry Tuna*," he said. His smile was surprisingly white.

"You know why we're here," Rhino said, "so I'll get down to business. I'm going to kill Colonel Vargas, and I need your help."

Mac pulled out a bag of coins and shook it.

Isaiah's green eyes flitted to Mac.

"You bring more?" he asked.

Mac nodded.

"How much?"

"What you asked for this morning," Mac said.

Isaiah smirked. "Unfortunately for you, I changed my mind this afternoon. I'm going to need double your offer if you want my help." Turning, he waved his arm around them. "As you can see, I need a new boat."

"I told you he was greedy," Mac said to Rhino.

"Actually I blame the sky people," Isaiah said with a snort. "Mr. Tomás Mata sent his goons out earlier this evening. Said he is raising prices on his fleet because of the battle that sank some of his trawlers, and I'm already behind on payment."

"Double it is then," Rhino said, "but you get half now, and half when the job is done. That work for you?"

Isaiah walked closer to X, scratching the stubble on his chin.

"I want to do two things before I make my decision,"

he said. "First, I want to have a good look at the king."

The Cazador soldier turned fisherman circled X, looking him up and down.

"You got the scars," Isaiah said, "and the reputation. But are you really immortal? That is the question."

"I'm just a man with a killer instinct and a high pain tolerance," X said.

"Perhaps a man with a lot of luck, too," Isaiah said, halting before X. "So tell me your brilliant plan to kill Vargas. His Praetorian Guards are seasoned warriors. They won't be easy to sneak up on."

"We infiltrate *Elysium* tomorrow night after Felipe here provides a distraction during dinner," Rhino said. "As soon as Vargas retreats to his quarters, we take him down in a dark passage."

"Isn't that how someone tried to kill you?" X asked.

"Yes," said Rhino. "Lucky for me, Wendig had my back."

"Well, she doesn't now, does she?" Isaiah said.

X didn't like Isaiah talking about Wendig. She had been a peerless warrior and deserved to be honored, not disrespected.

"No, but I do," X said.

Isaiah frowned, unimpressed. "You're talking about sneaking onto a ship with hundreds of warriors aboard," he said. "How do you expect to get away without being seen?"

"They're mostly just recruits," Rhino said. "You saw them with your own eyes, and Felipe is going to create a distraction among the youngsters, then sneak away to

NICHOLAS SANSBURY SMITH

help us. Besides, Vargas hardly ever leaves the warship, and when he does, he brings a whole entourage of guards."

"Wait a minute," Mac said. "Remember what I told you at the trading post?"

Rhino shook his head. "Which part?"

"Vargas patronizes the brothels regularly, and I know the owners. Maybe I could set something up where we don't have to sneak onto *Elysium* at all."

"That would be better," X said. "Way fewer threats on the trading rig."

Isaiah ran a hand over the chipped paint on the bulkhead.

X could still make out "*Atún*," but the other word was too faded to read.

"How many of us will there be?" Isaiah asked, still looking at the letters.

"Us, minus Xavier," Rhino said.

Isaiah's smile dried up. "I'll do it for the agreed price, but only if he comes too," he said. "I don't trust a man who pays others to do the risky stuff."

X looked at Rhino, who shook his head.

"No way," Rhino said.

"Not so fast," X said. "Count me in. It's been a while since I had a good fight."

* * * * *

An hour had passed since the Sirens took wing and headed out to sea. None had returned. *Discovery* had blown them all back to hell.

With that threat gone, Magnolia and the Cazador team pushed down the rocky shore, battling hard wind as they looked for a way into the city. Acid rain streaked down her visor.

She brushed it away, scanning the cliffs. A Cazador scout team had already tried to climb up in several spots, but the bluffs were too steep and crumbling.

The tsunami of two and a half centuries ago had created the natural barrier around the city, making it as impregnable as an old-world castle. Since then, the tide had eaten into the ribbon of shoreline left behind, narrowing the space between the water and the earthen walls.

And the tide was starting to rise again.

For now, the team was safe on the rocky, debris-strewn beach, but the clock was ticking. Magnolia stayed back from the encroaching waves and close to the bluffs that rose a hundred feet above them.

"Mags, take a look at this," Rodger said, pointing at a bone that stuck out of the wall. "Is it human?"

She nodded, spotting most of a skull in the rubble. Intermingled with the bones jutting out of the layers of earth, concrete, and rock were oxidized copper pipes and wrought iron, and twisted hooks of rebar. The raw ends were all potentially lethal hazards if any should snag her suit. It made climbing and falling all the more dangerous. They pushed farther down the shore, stepping over driftwood, the roof of a buried vehicle, and a flaking rusty hubcap.

Around the next corner, she finally saw a spot

that looked promising. The hundred-foot bluff had partially collapsed, leaving a slope of debris that cut the vertical exposure by half. It certainly looked better than the vertical cliffs, but the jagged and unstable hunks of concrete and metal would still make it dicey.

Lieutenant Alejo was already talking to the scouts with ropes and other climbing gear. They set off while the rest of the Cazadores formed a perimeter, rifles and machine guns up.

"If there is a way up, they will find it," Alejo said to Magnolia.

She kept against the rock wall while they went to work. The drizzling rain flecked her wrist computer as she checked Team Raptor's progress. Their beacons again showed slow but steady movement. Since the male Sirens flocked out of the city, they had gone nearly three miles from their drop zone. If she had to guess, Captain Mitchells or Timothy had used a decoy to help them get away from a hive of the beasts.

It must have worked, because all five Raptor beacons were still active.

Rodger bent down beside her. "How are they doing?" he asked.

"Good, I think," she replied. "They're moving along like nobody's hurt bad."

Lightning illuminated the two Cazador climbers. They practically scampered up the crumbly surface. Halfway up the slope, the men reached the first vertical slab of concrete. They threw a rope with a grappling hook over the top.

The crashing waves grew louder, bringing Magnolia to her feet. Ten-footers slapped down on the rocky shore, sending frothy ripples ever closer to the cliffs.

Magnolia gripped her laser rifle and scanned the ocean with her optics, leery of sea monsters that might use the opportunity to ride a wave in and snatch an unwary Cazador. She wiped her visor clean again and slowly scanned the water, finding nothing bigger than a shoal of fingerlings darting en masse this way and that.

Something larger was out there prowling, though. She had seen it on sonar on the way in. And she couldn't shed the feeling they were being watched from the bluffs.

A voice called out from above. She backed away from the cliff and aimed her rifle at two Cazador helmets looking down. Three ropes snaked over the side and down to the ground.

"I told you," Alejo said, grabbing one and offering it to Magnolia. "Would you like to go first?"

"I will," Rodger said. "Let me check it out first, Mags."

A Cazador started climbing each of the other two ropes, and Rodger took the third. He tried pulling himself up hand over hand, walking his feet up the slab, but his boots skidded down the rock right away.

"Careful," she said.

He tried again, this time grasping the rope between his ankles, and shinnied upward.

Behind them, the tide kept coming, each new wave sliding farther and farther inland. Magnolia turned back to the water, holding rear guard with the laser rifle.

This time, she saw something under the surface

about three hundred meters out. A dorsal fin cut through the water.

She backed away, nearly tripping over a partly exposed iron block that had once been a car engine. Screaming rang out above her as she staggered to regain her balance.

A heavy thump followed, and when she looked over, a Cazador lay at the foot of the cliff. The last few yards of the rope he had been climbing slithered down on top of him.

Normally, such a fall would have killed a man, but the armor had protected him to a degree. Magnolia rushed over.

Rodger had paused two-thirds of the way up, and so had the Cazador on the other remaining rope.

"Keep climbing!" Magnolia shouted.

"¡Sigan!" Alejo yelled.

The man who had fallen lay moaning on the ground. One leg pointed in the wrong direction, and his helmet had cracked open on a rock. Blood leaked onto the wet soil.

Alejo crouched, talking in a hushed voice and holding the soldier's hand. Then he looked up at General Santiago, who unsheathed his sword and plunged it into the fallen man's heart.

They dragged his body over to the cliff, out of sight from above.

Magnolia glanced up to the top of the wall, but the Cazador scouts were out of sight. They were going to get a good reaming for not anchoring the rope securely.

Rodger and the Cazador on the other rope made it

HELL DIVERS VI: ALLEGIANCE   371

over the edge, and Magnolia checked the ocean again before slinging her rifle. The large life-form had gone back under, and she didn't see a reading on her visor.

The encroaching surf lapped nearly to her boots. Turning to the wall, she grabbed the rope.

You got this, Mags.

As she inchwormed her way up the cliff, she tried to make out voices over the waves assaulting the shore. All she could determine was that their speech seemed frantic and faster than normal.

Electricity arced across the skyline, lighting up the swollen, dark clouds. They were moving in fast, dumping more acid rain on the toxic land.

Halfway up the wall, Magnolia looked down at General Santiago. Still banged up from the fight with the oil serpents back at the fuel station, he climbed slowly. He would get to the top, though, she had no doubt.

Below her, the surf lapped around the body of the fallen Cazador. When she looked again, the waves had lifted the body and slapped it against the wall. The crunch of armor against the rock spurred her on, as if she needed an incentive to avoid the Cazador's fate.

As she neared the top, Rodger reached down to grab her by the armor. She scrambled over the ledge and followed him to a brick wall.

Several Cazadores huddled around a helmet on the ground, but she didn't see a body. The rest of the soldiers had fanned out, pointing weapons out at the black terrain and the fog masking much of the city.

Rodger motioned for her to follow him over to

the stacked slabs of a collapsed parking structure. Lieutenant Alejo crouched there, talking to several of his men. One of them held up a frayed end of rope.

The pieces of the puzzle started coming together.

Their rope hadn't snapped or come untied. It was slashed, and whoever did it had taken the two scouts into the fog.

She unslung her rifle and brought it up, scanning the wastes. Behind the ruined structures and sunken streets, the purple and red flora pulsated, adding its glow to the wrecked cityscape. But there was no sign of any living creatures out there, nothing moving or howling in the silences between thunderclaps.

But for the bloody helmet a few feet away, she might have thought the two scouts had vanished into thin air. Whatever monster had taken them was long gone now, leaving behind no spoor of blood or tracks other than the helmet.

Rodger was lucky he hadn't fallen to his death too. She patted him on the shoulder as they looked out over the city. Storm clouds rolled in over the fog-shrouded devastation, and with the clouds came a dazzling display of lightning.

Alejo crouch-walked over to Magnolia and handed her the frayed rope.

"It's happening again," he said.

"What do you mean?" she asked.

"Cazadores are being hunted."

TWENTY-TWO

The wind howled outside the abandoned factory. The toxic monsoon pounded the roof, and lightning cracked in all directions. Water dripped from a hole in the ceiling to form a growing puddle behind a metal desk.

Traveling now was too dangerous, and Michael had ordered his team to find shelter until it let up. Outside the dark room, Edgar and Alexander stood sentry on the mezzanine. The other divers used the time to check their gear and study their digital maps. According to Michael's wrist monitor, Cricket was off the grid, which meant it had either perished at the hands of the Sirens or was simply too far out to get a signal.

He prayed it was the latter.

The robot had become like a friend, if such a thing was possible, and it had saved their lives at the sinkhole. Some quick thinking by Captain Mitchells and Timothy had also helped, but Michael feared it had meant the end for poor Cricket.

"We're pretty close to the target," Sofia said. She

took a seat on an I-beam next to Michael. Arlo joined them. His hands were shaking. He shoved them in his pockets, but Michael already knew how scared the young diver was.

"Magnolia and her team are hunkering down, too," Michael said. He punched his cracked wrist computer screen, bringing up their location. "Still three miles to our south."

Sofia looked at the ceiling.

Michael couldn't help feeling that they were wasting time, but going outside in the driving rain was an even greater risk than the lightning. Moving over to a shuttered window, he squatted down to look through a crack in the iron hatch that someone had installed after the war. The brass casings and the bullet holes in the walls led him to believe that people had used this place as a hiding spot centuries ago.

Michael wondered whether it had worked, and who or what the people were shooting at. Other humans? Monsters?

Defectors …

Michael felt his throat tighten at the memory of the last ambush. He had promised himself he wouldn't dwell on the tragedy in Jamaica and instead use Trey's death as motivation to save others. He wouldn't let his friend die for nothing.

Moving to the side, Michael looked through a different crack. Water cascaded down the sloped street, riffling past the hulls of vehicles still parked outside. The rubber tires were gone, and the plastic components brittle and broken. All that remained were iron engine blocks, rusted body metal, and some glass.

Thunder boomed in the distance.

"Reminds me of my birth," said Arlo.

He stepped up next to Michael. "Thunder sounds like a badass nickname, right? Well, it's not."

Michael let the kid talk—it would help with his nerves after he nearly ended up Siren food.

"Kids used to make fun of me when I was younger, but they didn't know the story," Arlo continued. "I was born during a storm, but I wasn't breathing when I arrived in this dark world. My dad gave me mouth-to-mouth, and for nine minutes, Dr. Huff said, I didn't breathe."

Arlo clapped his hands together.

"Quiet!" Michael snapped.

"Sorry," Arlo whispered. "I was trying to describe the thunder. When it clapped outside the airship, I gasped for air and saw my parents for the first time. That's why they called me Thunder."

"Cool story," Sofia said. "I'm still pissed at you for clipping me on the dive."

"I'm sorry," Arlo said.

"Do something like that again, and you won't be having any more fun with your lady friends, if you know what I mean."

Arlo hesitated and then looked to Michael.

"I'm sorry to you too, Commander Everhart," he said.

"You're forgiven," Michael said. "Just don't go pulling any more stupid shit."

"That's a promise."

"Commander," said a new voice.

Michael looked to the open doorway, where Edgar stood with rifle cradled.

"We found something you might want to check out," he said.

"Stay put," Michael said to Sofia and Arlo.

After leaving the two new boots in the office, he took the stairwell down to the first floor. Alexander was waiting there and led them across the factory floor. They stopped at a door to a bathroom, and Edgar pushed it open.

"Found some sort of maze," he said, shining his light inside.

Michael clicked on his beam and went into the bathroom. Broken tiles were strewn over the floor, and a row of sinks had collapsed. Cracked mirrors hung on the wall, their surfaces covered in gray-green moss.

He followed Alexander around a corner to the showers, and a hole in the center of the floor. The tile and concrete had been broken away, opening into an old sewer line.

"This is probably where the survivors fled to," he said, bending down. They shined their lights down a narrow passage littered with glass bottles, cans, and galvanized buckets.

"Want to see where it goes?" Edgar asked.

Hearing voices behind them, they found Sofia and Arlo at the entrance to the bathroom.

"I thought I said stay put," Michael said, trying to keep his voice low.

"I'm sorry, Commander," Sofia said, "but that growling we heard back at the sinkhole—it's back."

"I heard it too," Arlo said, clearly nervous. He shifted hands on his rifle. "Doesn't sound like Sirens. I think this is something else. Something *big*."

"Keep your voices low," Michael said.

They all moved back out onto the factory floor. Rain leaked through the ceiling, collecting on old metal tables and dripping on the machinery. Michael stopped to listen.

Sure enough, a few minutes later, low growling came through the sound of dripping and trickling water.

He looked at the ceiling. It sounded as though it was coming from above.

Michael motioned for the divers to fan out. They shouldered their rifles and crossed the space in combat intervals.

Michael moved toward the side door they had used to enter the building. It was the only entry point they had found besides a window on the second floor. The other entrances were all sealed off with heavy beams and equipment by whoever had taken refuge here in the past.

A loud bang across the room made him flinch. Alexander had knocked the sheet-metal hood off an old piece of machinery, and the duct clattered onto the floor.

Gritting his teeth, Michael waited.

It wasn't long before a piercing howl rose above

the pecking of rain on the roof. A thud rang out from the roof, and Michael pointed his laser rifle at a large dent in the metal. The other divers did the same, backing slowly away.

Heavy footsteps sounded on the roof.

"What is it?" Arlo said, his voice cracking.

Michael put a finger at mouth level on his helmet.

Whatever was up there had enough weight to make a dent with every step.

Another thump sounded to the left, and Michael swung his rifle toward the brick wall. An impact on the other side dislodged several bricks. One popped out and skidded on the floor.

Michael pulled one hand away from the laser weapon and gave the hand signal to retreat to the bathroom. They all turned and made a run for it, but Edgar's armor clipped a table on his way, knocking several empty cans to the floor.

A guttural howl answered, and Michael looked up as a piece of ceiling was pried back. Rain poured into the room, and lightning flashed overhead, silhouetting the beast looking down at them.

This was no Siren, but it did have some humanoid features, especially in the face. The knees snapped as the hulking creature bent down and looked into the factory. The thing was huge and covered with bony armor.

This was the same type of creature that killed Commander Rick Weaver at Hilltop Bastion. The monster the Cazadores called the *demon king*, or *bone beast*.

But this one seemed slightly different from the others. Barbed spheres protruded from the double-jointed kneecaps and elbows. The thick pectoral muscles under the exterior bones flashed orange with each beat of its heart.

Michael aimed his laser rifle at the chest, just left of center, where he hoped the heart was, and fired a bolt. The shot was perfect, an orange hole sizzling through exterior bone and muscle.

Roaring, the creature pawed at the floor, and when it pulled its hand away, Michael saw that the thick muscles and bony armor had stopped the bolt.

"Mother of God," he whispered.

The wall to Michael's left collapsed, and the monster's twin stormed through the explosion of bricks and dust.

"Open fire!" Michael shouted.

Laser bolts lanced into both creatures.

Michael ducked to avoid crossfire from Arlo, who hadn't pulled back from his scope to check his firing zone. Taking cover under a table, Michael crawled to the other side and then pushed himself up. He aimed his laser rifle at the beast looking down at them, but it jumped down at the same moment, landing on a table across the room and crushing it under its weight. The monster brought up black-taloned hands to shield its eyes from the flurry of rounds chipping away at its bony armor.

The creature on the left lumbered into the space, tossing a steel worktable aside as if it were balsa wood. Sofia rolled away before it could hit her. She came up on one knee and fired a blast into the creature's face, destroying an eyeball.

That seemed to enrage it even more.

Reaching over its shoulder, it pulled out a sharp-ended bone nearly two feet long and hurled it at her. She rolled again and took cover while Michael fired bolts at the humanoid face, trying for the other eyeball.

A laser punched through the armored biceps, and blood sloshed out. The creature staggered, gripping the injury with its other hand. It looked his way, and as the black maw opened to let out a roar, Michael fired a bolt.

The laser went through its mouth and out the back of its head, slinging hunks of bone and gore onto the wall. The beast slumped over, crashing against another table and onto the floor.

The divers turned their attention to the remaining creature, which had pulled several of the bony darts from its back. One after another, the spears whistled through the air.

Michael shot a rapid-fire stream of laser bolts, which tunneled through the thick chest armor on the right side, punching out the other side. The creature fell to the floor but pushed itself back up.

A roar nearly brought Michael to his knees. He needed just one lucky shot. The creature threw another bone arrow just as Michael fired a flurry of bolts into the center of its skull.

The weapon sizzled and locked up, overheated.

But the lasers had burned through the monster's bony face, melting away the hideous features. It slashed at the air before finally falling backward onto its double-jointed knees, then rolled facedown on the floor.

The entire building trembled from the impact.

Michael let the smoking rifle hang from its strap and pulled out the pistol X had given him. Heart thumping, he waited and listened. For the moment, it seemed, they had avoided death.

But then he heard a new sound over the patter of rain and the booming thunder. Many feet pounded the ground outside, sounding like a stampede of wild animals.

"What in the wastes is *that*?" Arlo said.

"Get to the bathroom," Michael said. He turned with the kid to find Sofia and Edgar at the back of the room, kneeling over Alexander.

Michael ran over as fast as he could, hoping the wound wasn't as bad as it looked. It was worse. The diver had taken a bone dart right through his stomach armor.

The pounding feet grew louder, shaking the floor.

Michael knelt beside Alexander, ignoring the sounds. The injured diver writhed in pain as Sofia rummaged through her med pack.

"We pull it out, patch the wound, and then patch the armor," Michael said. "Come help us hold him."

Edgar moved over, but Arlo stood staring in the other direction, trembling.

"We'll pull it out on three, okay?" Michael said.

Alexander nodded.

"One …" Michael pulled the shaft on two, and out it came. Alexander let out a long scream and then clamped his jaw shut.

As Sofia went to work on the bleeding wound, Michael gripped Alexander's hand.

"Hold on, man," he said. "We're going to get you out of here."

Edgar rejoined Arlo to provide cover. They aimed their rifles at the gap in the brick wall, and the hole in the ceiling left by the bone beasts. Rain sluiced in through the opening in the roof, pooling across the floor.

"Those things are almost here," Arlo said. He took a step back, his rifle shaking in his hands.

Choking noises pulled Michael's gaze back to Alexander.

Sofia worked faster, but the blood was everywhere.

"Commander …" Alexander coughed and then said, "Tell Eevi she is my rock and I will always love her."

He let go of Michael's arm and reached toward his vest, pulling up the leather flap to expose his battery unit.

"Get out of here," he grunted. "I'll hold them back while I can, and then I'll blow my battery unit."

Michael looked over his shoulder. The entire building seemed to shake from the approaching beasts. It sounded like an entire herd.

Alexander choked, and Sofia continued to work.

"I can save you," she said. "Just hold on."

"There's no more time," Alexander said, trying to sit up. He choked again and broke into a deep cough.

"Please," Sofia begged.

Alexander grabbed Michael's hand. "Save the rest of them, Commander."

"I will," Michael said. "I'll tell Eevi what you did."

Alexander nodded again.

Sofia finished taping a blood-soaked bandage, sobbing. Edgar helped Michael drag Alexander to a wall, and Arlo handed Alexander his dropped rifle.

"It's been an honor diving with you," Edgar said, squeezing Alexander's hand.

"I'm so sorry," Sofia said.

"Sorry, man," Arlo said. "You're my definition of bravery."

Michael led the divers back to the bathroom, leaving Alexander to face the beasts alone. He hated doing it, but it was either leave now, or they all would die.

A roar sounded as soon as they entered the room. Dust sifted down from the ceiling. Arlo, Sofia, and Edgar made their way around the corner, but Michael hesitated.

Gunfire cracked on the open factory floor, echoing over the first screech. Seemingly all at once, a dozen roars came from outside and above the structure. More thuds on the rooftop.

The divers ducked into the sewer tunnel, but Michael backtracked around the corner, keeping his laser rifle up to cover them.

The gunfire echoed in the other room, then went silent. He finally turned and climbed down into the narrow passage.

The divers moved in a crouch, their helmets scratching against the low ceiling. Michael turned and aimed his laser rifle at the entrance they had left behind. Destroying it would seal that side, so if they didn't find a way out, they were trapped.

He didn't get the chance to decide.

A thunderous boom came from inside the factory, bringing part of the bathroom ceiling down on the floor and crushing the tunnel entrance.

Michael flicked on his night-vision goggles and looked at his HUD. One of the beacons was offline.

Team Raptor was down to four members.

* * * * *

It was almost 2 a.m., but Rhino couldn't sleep. Apparently, neither could King Xavier. They stood at the southern rail on the capitol tower, looking out over the rigs. Unlike on the boat ride earlier, Miles didn't seem to have any trouble dozing off now.

He lay at their feet, snoring loudly.

Rhino tried to keep his mind off Sofia. She was risking her life in the wastes to find people just like herself and Rhino—survivors trying to scrape out a living belowground.

He should have been by her side, but he wasn't. He was here on the Vanguard Islands, and now it was time to fight for their future so that when she returned home, she wouldn't have to live in fear of another war.

X broke the silence.

"I really don't know about this plan," he said. "You're sure you can trust these men?"

"Mac will never betray me, and Felipe has sworn his loyalty."

"And Isaiah?"

"As long as he gets paid, we don't have to worry," Rhino said with all the confidence he could project.

"I've got a lot of other things than this to worry about, Rhino. We can't afford to make any mistakes."

"And we won't, sir. Mac will arrange everything at the trading post. They are his stomping grounds. No one on the islands is better for this mission."

"All right, General." X drew in a breath of cool morning air. "Much as I don't want to, I'd better tell Lieutenant Sloan of the plan now that it's set. I can't keep this from her."

He pulled out his radio, and a few minutes later, Sloan came jogging around the rooftop's plot of tropical forest. Rubbing her eyes, she joined them on the platform.

"Sir, you called for me?" she said.

X nodded. "We need to chat."

Militia soldiers, some of them smoking cigarettes, patrolled the rooftop.

"Assassinate Colonel Vargas?" Sloan gasped. "Are you *out of your tiny frigging mind* ... uh, sir?" Her lazy eye wandered toward Rhino. "This is your idea, isn't it?"

He started to reply, but Sloan was rolling. "If you want to get yourself killed, be my guest. But my duty is to serve King Xavier and to prevent the bloodshed of innocent sky people. Not to mention protect humanity. One wrong move could spark a——"

"Lieutenant," X interrupted.

Sloan looked at him but kept talking. "I will have no part of this, and the militia will have no part of this. If Cazadores want to kill each other, who am I to get in their way? But if X is caught killing Vargas at this point, it could start an all-out war."

"*Lieutenant*," X growled.

She finally clamped her mouth shut.

"The militia is sitting this out," X said. "And I'm moving forward with the assassination to *prevent* a war. If something happens to General Santiago out there, Colonel Vargas and his allies are coming after Rhino *and* me."

"By killing him, we end the threat first," Rhino said.

Miles wagged his tail, as if he were all for it.

Sloan shook her head. "This still sounds crazy to me."

X gave her a sly grin. "Crazy kept me alive in the wastes, and it's going to keep our people alive. You just have to trust me."

She took a moment to answer. "Well, shit, maybe I *should* help, because I sure as hell don't think you and three other soldiers are going to take down Colonel Vargas and his Praetorian Guard, even if you catch him with his pants down, so to speak."

"No, you are right about not involving the militia," X said firmly. "This needs to seem like it was all Cazadores, settling their differences."

"You should have killed him when you had the chance." Sloan growled the words, sounding enough like an animal to draw Miles's attention.

"Hindsight is always twenty-twenty, as they used to say," X said. "But I don't regret my decision. I did it to keep the peace. Now things have changed."

Sloan sighed.

"You just worry about security," X said. "Make sure the oil tanker, the *Hive*, and this rig are protected at all costs. If something goes wrong or if Horn shows up or if the defectors come …"

The threats facing them might have daunted someone else, but Rhino had lived his entire life with death knocking at the hatch. He was less fearful now than when he had served under el Pulpo.

"You keep our security tight, no mistakes," X said. "That's your job, Lieutenant."

"Don't worry, sir. Nothing's getting through."

"No tuna out of the net, Lieutenant," Rhino added. He normally didn't joke, but the woman needed to take the edge off.

To his surprise, she one-upped him.

"I believe the term is, 'security's as tight as a turd cutter,'" she said.

With a nod and a snort, she walked off to the command center with her orders.

"I really think you're starting to grow on her," X said.

Rhino laughed again, deeper this time. He admired the sparkling band of the Milky Way and thought of his love. *Discovery* was somewhere out there, under the stars.

"I hope they are doing okay," he said.

"The crew and divers are all experienced," X said. "If there are people out there, my team will find them and bring them home. And if they encounter the defectors, Team Raptor will destroy them."

He bent down next to Miles. The dog had gone back to sleep now that Sloan was gone.

"Come on, boy," he said. "Time to go back to bed."

The dog looked up and let out a whimper as X helped him to his feet. The hybrid animal was old, and Rhino feared it was nearing the end of its life.

Miles suddenly barked and growled.

Flashlight beams were flitting through the fence of tropical trees. Multiple voices called out in the night. Rhino grabbed his spear from where it leaned against the rail, and X unslung his new weapon.

Militia soldiers came running out onto the platform, machine guns cradled. Sloan was right behind them, running with a radio in one hand, her helmet in the other.

"What now?" X muttered.

"Sir," Sloan said.

"What's up?" X called out.

"A boat's been discovered drifting through the border," she said.

Sergeant Wynn joined her at the platform, and the other guards, including Ton and Victor, spread out. Rhino turned to see the machine-gun turrets and the thirty-millimeter cannons on the *Hive* already swinging around to the east as word spread over the comms.

"Is it the skinwalkers?" Rhino asked.

"I don't know," Sloan said. "It's just a skiff, but it could be a trap, sent in by Horn to distract us."

"Skiff?" Rhino asked.

"Yes," said Wynn. "On the side, it says 'Leon,' whoever that is."

Rhino's grip tightened on the spear shaft. "Who found the boat?"

"Rhino, what's it mean?" X said.

"Who found it, and are there survivors?" Rhino said to Sloan.

"A fishing boat that was trawling just off the border," Sloan replied. "Two survivors, but they're in bad shape."

"Fuck a bone beast!" Rhino groaned.

"Either this is a well-orchestrated trick, or those men have been out on the water for a while," Wynn said. "I've already dispatched two war boats to warn *Mercury*—figured we may need the help. Our people saw it heading out a few minutes ago."

"God damn it, what's 'Leon' mean?" X growled.

"*Lay*-OWN," Rhino said, keeping his voice low. "Spanish for 'lion,' King Xavier. Those men aren't skinwalkers from Horn's crew. They are Cazadores who somehow escaped when Ada drowned the rest of the *Lion*'s crew."

TWENTY-THREE

Magnolia snapped awake. The rain had stopped sometime in the early morning hours, but the dead city was alive with animal sounds. Electronic wails of hunting sirens, the thunderous roaring of bone beasts, and the cackles and squawks of the creatures the alpha predators hunted. The noises from the circus of mutant creatures echoed outside the underground shelter, taking her mind off Alexander's death for a moment.

She raised her wrist monitor and tapped the screen to bring up the location of the other divers onto her HUD, to make sure it wasn't just a dream.

Only four beacons of Team Raptor came online.

Her pounding heart ached for Eevi and for everyone else who had loved Alexander. He was a good man and a brave diver.

A screech, followed by a long wail of agony, distracted her. Magnolia recognized the sound of a dying vulture, probably being torn apart, wings and all.

She wanted to shut off her speakers and seal her

helmet to block out the noises, but she had to keep alert. They weren't safe here. The building with a sinking foundation was only a mile north of where they docked the boat, and they were still another two miles from their target.

Another guttural roar came from outside. This one was closer than the others.

She looked toward the sealed-off windows on the left side of the room. Rainwater cascaded under the sheets of metal, forming a lake on the far side of the basement.

"Those are really bone beasts?" Rodger asked.

"Yes," Alejo replied.

"Sounds like there are a lot of them," Rodger said.

Everyone in the basement knew that the beasts were more powerful and harder to kill than Sirens. Not even the hardened Cazador warriors, who lived for the hunt, were out there trying to bring one home as a trophy.

General Santiago was already down three men since they docked, and with two sentries remaining behind at the *Sea Wolf*, that left only five soldiers in the main group.

They weren't the only ones who had suffered a loss. Magnolia checked her wrist computer again to make sure the remaining four beacons were still online. They blinked on her screen, but they weren't moving. Like her team, they had ridden out the storm through the night.

She checked her suit battery again—still above

70 percent. Then she leaned her helmet on Rodger's shoulder to get some rest.

Several feet away, General Santiago and Lieutenant Alejo sat with their backs against the same wall. A third Cazador stood guard at the stairwell, the only entrance and exit to the space. He stood so still, she wondered whether he had somehow dozed off while standing up.

The other two men held watch on the upper floors, looking out over the streets for hostiles. Soon, Magnolia would take one's place, allowing him some rest before they moved back out in the morning.

She closed her eyes, trying to drown out the monsters' racket and the heartbreak of losing Alexander.

A deep roar sounded in the street, jerking her awake just as she was nodding off. The ground trembled, rattling dust from the dry ceiling. She pulled her head away from Rodger, grabbed her laser rifle from the wall, and walked to the center of the room.

"What is it?" Alejo whispered.

Magnolia pointed at the metal sheets strung up over the broken windows on the east corner. Footfalls thumped outside, pulverizing the cracked asphalt.

She motioned for everyone to be quiet.

The shadow of a massive beast moved across the metal window coverings, darkening the cracks and gaps.

Glancing over her shoulder, she motioned toward the window. The guard at the stairwell had moved down, rifle up, to stand beside General Santiago. It took Rodger a moment before he too raised his weapon.

The thudding footsteps continued past their hideout. A cracked, leaning wall was all that stood between the team and the beast. It stopped about halfway along the wall to sniff the air. Then it let out a roar so loud, it hurt her ears. Heart thudding, she aimed her rifle at the shadow, finger against the trigger guard.

The monster suddenly bolted away, but she kept her rifle up and her eyes locked on the windows. In her mind's eye, she could picture one of the beasts ripping away the metal sheets and squeezing into the room.

Outside, an animal screech ended abruptly. The bone beast had found other prey. With luck, whatever it was eating would tide it over and it would return to its lair.

She finally lowered her rifle and retreated to her spot against the wall, hoping for sleep.

A nudge woke her some time later. Gasping in alarm, she brought up her rifle, and the person who woke her fell on his butt.

"Mags, it's just me," said a voice.

She saw then that it was Rodger, and a glance around reminded her that they were in the basement of the shelter. Sorrow filled her when she also remembered that Alexander was dead.

Rodger held up his hands. "Mags, lower the gun," he said. "It's our watch."

A glance at her HUD told her it was just after four in the morning. Standing up as the confusion wore off, she stretched and took a drink from the straw in her helmet.

After relieving herself into the bag in her suit, she went up the stairwell with Rodger. The guard there nodded at them and joined Santiago, but Alejo followed them up the stairs to the first floor. Using hand signals, they moved out into a hallway.

The passage the team had used to enter the building was a narrow crawl space through a pile of rubble on the west wall. The first-floor ceiling had caved in on the north side of the building, dumping pieces of broken furniture, acoustic tile, and other debris into the rooms.

She walked with Rodger and Alejo to the east, toward a stairwell that opened to the second floor. They passed several rooms open to the elements, their doors long since broken off. She glanced into each, seeing more wreckage piled on the floors.

The only recognizable furniture was a slanted metal desk with a broken leg, and a lamp with no shade.

Voices came from the stairwell, and she moved behind Rodger to get a look.

The sentry, Ruiz, who was still injured from the snake attack at the fuel outpost, limped into view. His rapid, almost frantic speech and hand gestures to Alejo told her something was wrong.

She squeezed past Rodger and crept up the stairs.

"What's going on?" she asked.

Alejo looked back. "Ren is missing."

"What do you mean, 'missing'?"

"He's not at his post, and Ruiz couldn't find him when he went upstairs."

"Shit," Magnolia said. "Tell Ruiz to show us where Ren was posted."

Ruiz motioned for them to follow. He limped up two flights of stairs and entered a hallway. The walls were covered in splotches of reddish lichen. Ropes of the stuff grew in a web across the passage, but a doorway had been hacked through.

They slipped through, and Ruiz pointed to a room on the east side of the hallway. She brought her laser rifle up and crept toward the room. How had a bone beast, not known for their stealth and subtlety, sneaked through here and grabbed a sentry without waking everyone?

Another string of the sticky vines gripped her armored shoulder but broke away as she pressed ahead. Alejo followed her into the apartment where Ren had taken up his post. The wall separating the former kitchen from the living room had a hole through the middle. Bent and broken pipes stuck out in the shape of a smashed rib cage.

Rainwater covered the floor under the broken window frames in the next room. Muddy footprints led up to them. Magnolia bent down and looked them over. They were human.

Alejo whispered to Ruiz as she studied the tracks. She found another print, but it wasn't from a boot.

She shined her helmet light over what looked like another smaller footprint. Next, she raked the beam over the dark puddle. Finally, she ran the light up the wall, finding blood spatter.

"Shit," she muttered. Shutting off her light, she switched back to night vision and backed away with a shushing finger to her helmet. Alejo and Ruiz nodded in acknowledgment and raised their weapons.

Something had killed Ren and removed his body without their hearing it, just as it had killed the Cazadores on the shore and gotten away before they could even get a glimpse of the beast.

Alejo was right: something was hunting the Cazadores—which meant it was also hunting Team Raptor.

* * * * *

The lack of sleep made X feel as if he were drunk. He should be so lucky. Getting shit-faced would at least take his mind off all the problems facing him.

But that was the old X. He was responsible now for more than himself. Thousands of lives rested in his hands, and things were about to blow up.

An hour had passed since the two members of the *Lion*'s crew sailed into Vanguard Island territory. Now he waited to hear about their condition and what they knew.

He remained on the capitol tower, staring at the wake of the cigar boats packed full of militia soldiers, off to intercept the rowboat. Miles sat on his haunches, and Rhino stood beside X, not saying much but clearly nervous.

The big Cazador warrior finally spoke. "We have to kill them."

X glanced at the Cazador warrior. "Okay, now I have to go with Sloan," he said. "That idea is crazy as hell."

"If those two survivors explain what happened with *Discovery*, then forget killing Vargas—you're going to have to kill every Cazador soldier on these islands, and a few boatloads of civilians."

Now X *really* wished he were drunk. He cursed under his breath. Things had just gone from terrible to a damn sight worse in a matter of hours, and the sun still wasn't up yet. Meanwhile, *Discovery* was off on a mission over three thousand miles away.

"We have to hope your war boats get to that rowboat before *Mercury* does," Rhino said.

The breeze rustled through the beard X had grown. He rubbed his cheek, then pulled out his walkie-talkie.

"Sloan, X. Do you copy? Over."

She answered a moment later. "Copy, X. Go ahead."

"Have our boats reached that skiff yet?"

"Just got there. They are in the process of moving the two survivors onto our boats, but *Mercury* also just arrived."

"Shit," X said.

"You have to quarantine those men," Rhino said. "Do you have Spanish-speakers in those crews?"

"Sloan, do we have any Spanish-speaking members of the militia on those boats?" X asked.

"Roger that, sir."

"Tell them to explain that our team is taking the survivors to treat them for radiation poisoning."

"Will do, sir," Sloan replied.

"And what about the fishing crew?" Rhino said. "What if those two sailors told them what happened?"

"Then we're screwed," X said. "Either way, I'm planning for the worst."

He left Rhino standing there and nodded for Miles to follow him.

"King Xavier, what about Ada?" Rhino called out.

X stopped and turned slightly. "What about her?"

"You still haven't done anything with her." Rhino's chest puffed out, reminding him of a vulture calling for its mate. "You can't let her go without punishment, King Xavier."

X had anticipated this moment, when his friend and most trusted bodyguard finally lost patience about the former airship officer.

"I promise you this," Rhino said. "Pretty much anything you do to her will be better than what the Cazadores will do if they find out the truth."

"True," X said. He led Miles away from Rhino, needing a break to clear his mind. They walked toward one of the two machine-gun emplacements nestled at the edge of the rooftop.

The canopy of palm trees swayed lazily in the citrus-scented breeze. The smell made his stomach growl. He had skipped dinner last night, and on top of being exhausted, he was so hungry he could eat a mutant whale. But before he ate or rested, he had to make sure they were ready for whatever was coming.

X stopped at the machine-gun nest. It had been built on a platform with bags of rock positioned around the old weapon. Two militia soldiers sat on stools looking over the eastern horizon. They both stood as he approached, and in the candlelight, he recognized a young man and an even younger woman from the lower decks of the *Hive*.

"Sir," they said as one.

"Morning," he said. "How are things looking out there?"

The woman turned a helmet two sizes too big to look out at the water. She then looked back at X and pushed up the visor, revealing a pimply face.

Another kid. Like Felipe and so many others who were fighting for their people.

"Are we going to war again, sir?" she asked.

"I hope not, but if we do, I'll need you both to hold this position," he said. "That's your job: make sure no one gets to this tower."

"We won't abandon our post, sir," said the young man. He held a bolt-action rifle in his hand.

"You good with that?" X asked, reaching out.

The soldier handed it over. "I could shoot a crab off the *Hive* from here without puncturing the hull," he said.

X looked through the scope at the decommissioned airship. He could see light through several of the portholes. There was no way in hell the kid could hit a crab from here, but he didn't argue. Confidence was a good thing. It helped dull the fear.

He handed the rifle back to the soldier. "Stay sharp and watch the waters."

"For what, sir?" asked the girl. "Is it the machines?"

"Could be the machines, could be humans," X said. "Just make sure you're ready."

He had given the order to prepare for a battle without giving any details on who they would be fighting. Until he knew more about the two survivors from the *Lion*, he didn't want to get his people too riled up.

But he did want them ready. If *Elysium* and *Mercury* went on the warpath, they would inflict some serious damage on the *Hive* and the capitol tower before his people could stop them.

It would be the end of the islands, allowing Horn to sail in and claim the throne with little resistance.

All because of Ada.

The radio crackled as X left the two young soldiers. He paused a moment before answering. During all the time spent trekking through the wastes or sailing on the *Sea Wolf* to the Metal Islands, he had never felt such bad anxiety.

The entire fate of both peoples hinged on two survivors from the *Lion*.

"This is X, go ahead," he finally said.

"Sir, we have both castaways and are bringing them back to the islands," Sloan reported. "*Mercury* is following our boats but hasn't tried to wave them down, or anything."

"Let me know when they get here," X said. "I'm going to the shit can."

"Yes, sir. And I always appreciate you sharing such details."

X had to grin as he led Miles back across the roof and into the forest, where a hammock hung between two trees. It was tempting, but he wasn't going to sleep, and he wasn't going to the shit can.

He was sneaking off to pay a visit to Ada.

TWENTY-FOUR

Team Raptor moved through the sewer tunnel for three hours, walking mostly, crawling in some spots. To avoid the storm and the monsters, Michael had decided to keep moving underground.

Leaving Alexander was one of the hardest things he had done on a dive, but it had saved the rest of his team. There was no going back, only forward.

Around midnight, the four divers found an overfill area a mile from their target. Michael ordered the team to stop and sleep in shifts.

It was nearing six in the morning now, and he was wide awake, standing sentry and scanning for hostiles. Most of the bricks lining the bell-shaped room had broken away.

The members of Team Raptor weren't the first humans to camp here. Broken bottles littered the underground lair. Skeletons of small rodents formed a small pile. Next to them were several buckets filled with a hardened greenish substance.

There was other evidence of the former occupants. Michael picked up the legless head and trunk of a plastic doll, the hair long since gone. There was also a miniature metal fire truck, and a police car without wheels.

He thought of the families that had once tried to survive here. It was surely a bleak and fearful existence. Maybe not so different from the life of lower-deckers on the *Hive*. But on the airship, they didn't have to worry about Sirens, bone beasts, and toxic air.

It made him wonder about the living conditions for the people they had come to save. Anyone who had survived this long down here had to be hard as nails.

He hoped they were peaceful, but the threats down here made him wonder whether that was possible. They would surely know how to defend themselves.

Michael walked over and nudged each of the other divers with his boot.

"Wake up," he whispered. "We need to start moving again."

The other divers gathered their gear in silence. Everyone was feeling the loss of Alexander, but now was not the time to grieve. They needed to be fully present once they climbed aboveground again.

He checked his wrist computer—suit integrity was 100 percent and battery over 60. Next, he brought up the digital map of the city.

Rodger's and Magnolia's beacons were on the move again toward the target. Seeing they had made it through the night helped buoy his confidence.

"Everyone good?" Michael asked the divers.

Three nods.

"I'll take point," he said. "Keep quiet and listen for hostiles."

He brought up his rifle and ducked into the exit tunnel. Slick moss grew in clumps on the bricks. He wasn't sure what it was, but he had a feeling it was rife with bacteria.

"Watch for anything that could tear your suit," he said.

A spider scuttled across the ceiling and vanished into a crack. Michael pulled out his knife and slashed through the web ahead.

The sticky material was surprisingly strong. He crouched and signaled everyone to turn off their helmet lights. Absolute darkness enveloped the divers.

Michael listened for grunts or skittering claws but heard only the drip of water. A light flashed as he started to switch on his NVGs. He kept the optics off and stared into the blackness, waiting.

A moment later, the purple light flashed in the adjoining tunnel to their right. The glow was weak, but it came again and again.

He motioned for the divers to follow him into the intersection. They hugged the wall and moved with barely audible footsteps.

When Michael got to the corner, he aimed his rifle to the left side of the passage, switching on his NVGs and then his infrared. Seeing no evidence of life, he inched closer to the corner and glanced around.

The scan came back void of contacts, but he did

see the source of the light. It was coming from the ceiling. He had discovered a way out.

Pulling up his wrist monitor, he saw the first good news since they landed. The source of the SOS was a quarter mile away. The tunnels had led them safely under the city, almost to the doorstep of the bunker.

Excited, Michael gave the "advance" signal and took point again.

A mound of rubble seven or eight feet high formed a natural staircase of bricks and concrete leading out of the sewer. He aimed his rifle up through the hole, at clouds rolling overhead.

The rain had stopped, but lightning still flashed. That wasn't the source of the light, he realized as another flash of purple lit up the tunnel. They had reached the profusion of bioluminescent vegetation he had seen on the dive in.

Michael checked the debris, looking for footholds, and started up while the other divers waited. A few steps up, a brick skidded under the weight of his boot. He flinched at the clank.

The screech of a vulture answered, freezing him in place.

Two of the nightmarish birds sailed overhead and circled. On the second pass, one landed on the nearest rooftop and perched there. This was going to complicate things.

The vulture seemed to look in his direction but then turned. He kept moving cautiously. At the top of the mound, he poked his head up into the street.

They had emerged in what was once a heavily populated area. Large apartment buildings and commercial buildings, many of them still in relatively good shape, lined the street.

He looked around for his first up-close view of the purple-and-red flora. The vines, as thick as the bodies of the snakes at the fuel outpost, had barbs and spikes covering their flesh.

On one side of the road, reddish-hued trees grew out of what had been a park. Vines and foliage had almost completely hidden the slides and swings.

He looked back to the rooftop. The vulture was still looking in the opposite direction, and he motioned back into the tunnel for the divers to join him on the road.

While they climbed, he took up position behind the rusted hull of a car. He pushed the scope of his laser rifle to his visor and centered the crosshairs between the mutant bird's eye and ear.

Sofia emerged first, then Edgar, but when Arlo pulled himself up, he knocked a hunk of asphalt loose. It plummeted back into the tunnel, and the loud crack turned the vulture's head.

Michael pulled the trigger, blowing off the beak and the top of the head with a single bolt. He held in a breath, hoping the bird wouldn't fall to the street. It slumped backward, a single feather wafting away on the breeze.

The team bolted for cover inside a hotel atrium, entering through glass push doors that were cracked but strangely intact. They spread out, rifles up, and cleared the room.

"All right, we're close," Michael whispered. "We just need a better view of the area."

Edgar directed them around a pile of glass, formed when part of the dome ten floors above had broken away. A shard the size of a table had fallen like a guillotine, splitting the reception desk in half.

Michael went up a staircase to a second floor that looked out over the atrium. Despite the gaping roof, the hotel's interior remained somewhat preserved. He could even see the design of the tile floor.

A chandelier hung over the wide landing in front of two double doors, which were locked. They came to a door with a faded exit sign.

Michael grabbed the knob. It turned, unlocked.

Edgar led the way up to the fifth floor before they stopped to rest and listen.

Hearing nothing, Michael took point to the top floor. Wind gusted against his armor as soon as he opened the door. The second half of the hallway was broken away and open to the elements.

Across the street was another building, but it was only five or six stories tall. Most of the exterior on the upper floors was destroyed, exposing the interiors of apartments and offices. Not seeing any movement there, he tested the floor with his boot.

"Careful," Edgar said.

Michael moved cautiously out into the hallway for a better view. Jagged planks and broken beams jutted into space, and a flap of ceiling hung loosely overhead. He stopped a foot away from the planks and looked out at swollen clouds.

Rain drizzled from the sky, coating his visor. The vantage point gave him a look at the western city blocks and the flora consuming them.

The strange vines had completely overgrown another park and snaked through the ruins of surrounding buildings, crawling up the sides and in and out of windows. One city block appeared to have collapsed under the weight of the dense vegetation. Then he saw that the roots and trunks were actually coming from a sinkhole. He switched off his NVGs. The opening pulsed an angry red before fading into darkness.

The glowing flora made his infrared optics pointless, so he scanned the area with his rifle scope. He found a nest of vultures in a blown-out room of a building to the north, but no bone beasts or Sirens prowled the streets. Perhaps they had returned to their lairs to sleep. If so, then Team Raptor had its second stroke of luck.

He brought up his wrist computer. Looking out over the ruins again, he determined that the SOS was coming from under a building somewhere two blocks away, dangerously close to the edge of the sinkhole.

With his finger, he traced out a map on his wrist computer, then transferred it to their HUDs. He backed away from the edge.

"I've identified the target," he said. "Check your minimaps and follow me."

The divers went back down the stairwell, stopping at the closed door on the second floor.

"Stay quiet and stay low," Michael said. He looked at Arlo, who hadn't said much over the past few hours.

"You okay?" Michael asked.

"Not really, Commander. I thought I was ready for all this, but I'm scared shitless we're going to run into one of those things that killed Alexander."

"It's okay to be scared," Edgar said. "But you gotta keep your wits, man, or you're going to get yourself and all of us killed."

"Alexander sacrificed himself for us," Michael said. "Remember that."

Sofia patted Arlo on the back. "You're braver than you believe."

"Yeah, I know," Arlo replied.

Michael waited a moment, and when Arlo nodded again, he gave the order for the team to move out. Edgar went first and opened the door. Sofia followed, sweeping her rifle muzzle over the lobby below. Leaving the way they came in, they moved west down the street.

Keeping close to the edge of the building gave them some cover from the rain but not the lightning. A bolt struck a radio tower in the distance.

Michael decided to keep moving. They had to get to the target before the monsters came back out. This was their chance.

After sweeping the road, he turned onto the next block. A mesh of vines from trunks that had broken through the street clung to the buildings.

Michael led the team around the limbs and found a way under the arbor. A twenty-foot wall of crushed vehicles and rubble blocked off the route on the other side. Razor wire topped the barrier, stretching from one side of the street to the other.

He bolted for cover when he saw a machine-gun nest in the blown-out side of a building behind the wall. The team took up position behind a brick stoop. Michael peeked over to check the machine-gun nest. The mounted weapon was still there, but zooming in, he saw the rust. If he had to guess, this place had been abandoned for some time.

He scanned the wall again and noticed something he had missed earlier. A doorway had been broken into the mountain of cars. It looked about the size of a bone beast.

Michael stared at the wall. It was the only thing separating him from the bunker, and in a few minutes, he would see the home of actual live humans who were neither Cazadores nor sky people.

The thought triggered a tingle of adrenaline.

"What do you think?" Edgar whispered. "Should we contact Captain Mitchells now and have Timothy reply to the SOS in Portuguese to let them know we're here?"

Sofia squeezed up next to them. "We should wait for Magnolia and her team first, right?"

"We still don't know if defectors are down here," Michael said. "At the prison, they surprised us. I won't let that happen again. For now, we keep radio silence, and I want to take a look before Magnolia's team gets here."

Michael considered asking Edgar to join him on the recon. He was the most experienced diver besides Michael, and the best marksman. And that was why Michael needed him with the weakest link.

"Edgar, you stay here with Arlo. Sofia, with me."

"Got it, Commander," Edgar said.

Arlo didn't protest.

Michael hunched down and ran for the wall, with Sofia on his heels. They stopped at the doorway. Scratches and shards of metal confirmed his suspicions. A bone beast had ripped its way through.

He slipped into the opening. The tunnel through the cars and rubble was almost twenty feet long. A network of purple vines webbed across the cracked asphalt on the other side.

Michael raised a fist when he got close to the opening. The infrared scan picked up the flora but nothing else.

He switched back to his NVGs. A single building showed in the green hue. Four stories tall, with metal sheets and bars covering every window. Steel plates covered the front doors.

An overhang above the wide stoop of stairs read, *Polícia Federal.*

Barred gates ten feet tall sealed off a parking lot on the left side of the building, but the gates on the right side had fallen to the ground.

Moving just outside, he checked the buildings towering over the road on both sides. He found another abandoned machine-gun nest in the broken-out third floor of an apartment building but no sign of recent human activity.

Concrete blocks and other vine-covered obstacles created a maze from the wall to the barricaded front entrance of the police station. Several open windows in the side buildings would be perfect for snipers.

But where was everyone now?

"Commander, what do you see?" Sofia whispered.

"Nothing," he said. "Follow me and move fast, but mind your suit."

They bolted for a shattered door in a storefront. Along the way, Michael saw inside the parking lot behind the broken-down gate. Brown flags hung from three poles. He nearly tripped over a vine that caught his boot but managed to catch himself and continue into the shop.

He didn't stop moving until he was inside what was once a grocery store. Behind the counter with the cash registers lay upended shelves. Sofia followed him over to one of the counters for cover.

They waited, listening for hostiles, before he finally peeked over the edge. Using his rifle scope, he zoomed in on the flagpoles. The brown flags weren't flags. They were the hides of humans, with lips, noses, and other body parts stitched into them.

"No," he choked.

Team Raptor was too late. Again.

"What?" Sofia asked.

Michael checked the dark stains in the parking lot that looked fresh.

The defectors had beaten them here again.

His transmissions had gotten another bunker of humans killed, and now he feared he had doomed his team to the same fate as Trey.

"We have to get out of here," he said, ducking down. "When I run, you run, okay?"

"Why? What do you see?"

"Just do as I say," Michael growled.

Drawing in a breath and exhaling, he steeled himself. A moment later, he got up and ran back for the wall of cars. He hurdled a barbed vine and sprinted the rest of the way to the tunnel through the wall.

In the passage, purple flashes guided him and illuminated the street beyond, where Arlo and Edgar stood watch.

A muffled voice called out, and Michael moved faster, ducking under a ragged strip of body metal. Just as he emerged, he saw motion on the other side of the thick vines twisting across the road.

Several naked humans ran around the next corner. This time, he was sure of it.

He turned to look for Edgar and Arlo, but they were no longer holding their post.

The contacts definitely weren't defectors, but how could humans survive out here without suits or clothing?

"Where are Arlo and Edgar?" Sofia said quietly.

"I don't know," Michael said. "Come on."

He took off running and checked his HUD for Edgar's and Arlo's beacons. They were on the move, too. Michael hoped they were pursuing the humans, even though it meant they had disobeyed a direct order.

He rounded the next corner and halted at the sight of the sinkhole. Vines reached out into the nearby structures, twisting through the interiors and breaking through the tops.

Sofia and Michael walked toward the edge. One of the vines suddenly moved like a snake, slithering before their boots. But it was the beep on his HUD that made Michael stop.

He glanced at the minimap just as Edgar's and Arlo's beacons winked off.

* * * * *

Les knelt beside Cricket and shined his flashlight into the machine's guts. It had gotten safely back to *Discovery*, but at a cost. Not only had it shed the armor plating protecting its hardware; it had also lost multiple cameras.

Michael was not going to like it.

He had to get the robot back up and running as soon as possible. Not having Cricket in the field meant losing their tenuous connection to the divers and the Cazador team, and Les was getting more anxious with each passing minute. Over seven hours had passed since they received data from either team.

While awaiting news, Les had spent much of that time working with Alfred and his team to get the robot field-ready. They had replaced most of the wiring and two of the cameras and were preparing to add new armor using pieces of an old diver suit.

"You're practically a Hell Diver," Les said.

The robot chirped.

Alfred pulled the hood down over his eyes and bent down to begin welding the armor plating. While he worked, Les spoke into his headset.

"Timothy, how are things looking up there?" he asked.

"The storm is still interfering with our instruments, Captain," Timothy replied. "I haven't been able to get an update from any of the divers."

The AI appeared in the launch bay, his glow spreading around Cricket as sparks showered the deck.

"How is our little friend?" Timothy asked.

"Almost ready for action," Les said. "I'm sending him back out as soon as Alfred's team finishes up here."

Timothy clasped his hands behind his back and bent down to examine the robot. He said, "I wish I could transfer my consciousness into Cricket. It would be nice to move around again without my current constraints."

Les wasn't sure what to say. He had wondered what the AI thought of the drone, but figured Timothy was indifferent, just as a person might be to a pig or other livestock. After all, Cricket was a tool and had never been a person.

"I'll be back on the bridge soon," Les said. "Why don't you go see how Layla and Eevi are doing?"

Timothy nodded and vanished.

NICHOLAS SANSBURY SMITH

The technicians finished installing the frontal armor plates and moved to the back.

"After these plates are done, we just need to load the launcher with ammo," Alfred said.

Les opened a comm channel to the militia soldiers and ordered them to bring the grenades. He had gone a step beyond Michael's instructions and installed a grenade launcher on one of the robot's arms.

The militia soldiers arrived a few minutes later, carrying a secure crate.

"Almost done," said Alfred. His team finished the last of the armor and then connected patch cords to run diagnostics. Cricket chirped, moving its limbs up and down.

"Good to go," Alfred said.

"Nice work," said Les. "Load up the grenades and prepare it for launch. I'll be on the bridge."

"Aye, aye, Captain."

Les made a pit stop at his locker and grabbed his suit, armor, and helmet. He wanted to be prepared for anything, especially since he had no idea what was happening on the surface.

He made his way back through the airship, stopping to relieve himself and then to grab a coffee. The aroma of the fresh brew was intoxicating. Coffee beans, wine, tobacco, and other rare old-world staples had changed his people's life and opened an entire new world to them.

He drank down the cup, feeling the caffeine sharpen his senses as he walked. The mug was empty by the time he got to the bridge.

A militia guard stood sentry at the hatches. He saluted Les and moved out of the way.

Eevi was the only officer at her station. She swiveled her chair and smiled. "Good morning, Captain. Did you get Cricket up and running?"

"I did," he said. "Where's Layla?"

"Resting, sir."

"Good. She needs it."

"Why do you have your jumpsuit and armor?" Eevi asked, eyeing the gear in his arms. "Is something wrong?"

"No, just being prepared," Les said. He put the gear down and moved over to his chair. "What's our status, Timothy?"

The AI appeared at the helm, looking out the portholes at the storm that blotted out the horizon.

"We're currently hovering at twenty-one thousand feet, three miles from the coastline," Timothy said. "Skies are clear in our current location, but the storm over the target is intensifying, and expanding in all directions."

"Keep an eye on it," said Les. "And program a course for Cricket that takes it under the storm."

"Already done, sir. Uploading to the drone … now."

Les buzzed the launch bay. "Is Cricket ready to deploy?"

"Yes, sir," Alfred replied.

"Good. Launch on my mark."

Les turned on the robot's weapons system by typing in his pass code. He brought up the drone's cameras on the main monitor. Next, he accessed the data feed in a subscreen that would show them a minimap and location of the divers once Cricket got in range.

"Mark," Les said.

The bridge doors whisked open, and Layla entered.

"Just in time," Les said. "I just launched Cricket."

"Have you heard anything from Tin or Mags yet?" she asked.

"Not yet, but we're hoping Cricket can give us an idea of where they are within the next few minutes."

Layla brushed her braid over her shoulder and sat at her station. She smiled at Eevi, but Les could feel the tension in both of them as they waited for news of their men.

Les had tried not to think of Trey, but old memories surfaced unbidden as he waited. For some reason, he had a bad feeling about things on the ground, as if something terrible had happened during the night. He buried the thought and tapped his monitor to pull up the data on-screen.

Cricket lowered through the sky and then switched to thrusters, moving fast in the turbulent air beneath the storm clouds.

"Almost in position for a first scan," Timothy announced.

Les was starting to doubt that any defectors were out there. Avenging his son might have to wait. Right now, the most important thing was finding the survivors of the bunker and bringing his divers home safely.

The first stream of data from Cricket's scan rolled

across the screen. Magnolia's and Rodger's beacons were moving at a good clip. They both were still alive and nearing the target.

Next came the data for Team Raptor.

But that couldn't be right. Les saw only two beacons.

A moan of dread resounded through the bridge.

"No … no … This can't be right," Layla said. She looked over at Les, then to Timothy.

Eevi's eyes were glazed with tears. "This can't be real," she said. "Can't be real."

"Tell me that's wrong," Les said to Timothy, hoping the ensign was right.

The AI hesitated a moment before replying, perhaps to double-check or perhaps because he, too, was staggered by the data.

"I'm sorry, Captain, but the scan appears to be correct," he said. "Edgar's, Arlo's, and Alexander's beacons are offline."

Eevi stared ahead in shock.

"I'm afraid those divers have been killed," Timothy said.

TWENTY-FIVE

In the early dawn, Rhino trained his binoculars on *Mercury*. The warship's guns weren't pointed at the airship or the oil rig, and the soldiers on deck went casually about their tasks. If they knew the truth about what had happened to the crew of the *Lion*, they weren't showing it.

That was good, but Rhino had a feeling Carmela was plotting something. She was supposed to be preparing for the mission to the backup fuel outpost in Belize, but the trip was on hold until the team of raiders returned with engine parts for the warship *Renegade*.

Now she seemed very interested in the two survivors from the *Lion*. She stood outside *Mercury*'s command island, watching the capitol tower.

Rhino scanned the horizon for *Elysium*, but the largest warship in the remaining fleet was still out of view—another good sign. It meant that Colonel Vargas and Colonel Forge were waiting before taking any drastic measures.

But Rhino knew that the two societies were spiraling toward another clash and possibly even another war, and he was running out of time to stop it. Eventually, the sky people would need to hand over the Cazador survivors from the *Lion*, and unless X killed them and said they had died of dehydration and exposure, there would be hell to pay if the two sailors told the truth about what had happened out there.

Rhino couldn't take that chance.

He handed the binos back to a militia soldier and picked up his spear. Worried sick about Sofia, and worried sick about the Vanguard Islands, Rhino was about at his breaking point.

Across the rooftop, a platoon of militia soldiers patrolled in the rising sunlight. On the way to the stairwell, he passed another patrol. With so much security outside, it would be easier to get to the brig.

Rhino took the stairs down several floors to the cells. As he had suspected, no one was guarding the entrance. Part of him wished there were a guard, someone to stop him from doing what he had to do—from doing what X should already have done. Ada had to pay for her crime, and it fell to him to exact payment.

His heart pounded with adrenaline but also with fear as he waited outside, considering his decision one last time. He never felt like this before battle, not even when facing monsters. But this wasn't a battle. This was murder.

"No," he said aloud. "This is justice."

Rhino opened the barred gate to the cell-lined corridor and walked inside. Ada was the only prisoner being held here. No one but her to see what he was about to do.

He leaned his spear against the wall and pulled his knife from the sheath on his belt. The long sawtooth blade had killed dozens of men, but he had never used it to execute someone in cold blood, let alone a young, defenseless woman.

He looked for the key ring near the door but didn't see it on the hook. Then he checked the dark passage between cells and saw the key ring, hanging from one of the cell doors.

"Ah, shit!" he said, hurrying over to the unlocked door.

"I knew you'd come," said a familiar voice from inside the cell.

X lay on the bed, hands behind his head, staring at the ceiling. Miles lay on the floor, head between his paws.

"King Xavier," Rhino stuttered.

X sat up. Then he stood up and let out a sigh.

"Where is Ada?" Rhino asked.

"Gone," X said.

Rhino opened the rusting door and stood in the entry. "Gone where?"

"I gave her a rifle, gear, provisions, a map, and a boat with oars and some fuel," X replied. He walked over to stand in front of Rhino. "I decided exile is the best punishment, but you have to understand, I couldn't kill her in cold blood."

Rhino stepped closer to the king.

"That's not my way," X said. "That's not *our* way."

They came face-to-face. This wasn't their first time. The last time was on the boat, just before the battle for the Metal Islands, before they were bonded by bloodshed. He had wondered whether X was going to kill him then, and he wondered the same thing now.

"She escaped justice," Rhino said.

"Justice," X said with a snort. "There is no justice here. There will never be justice when you have the Sky Arena, and people owning other people."

Rhino didn't step back.

"She'll probably die out there," X said, "but I gave her the same chance you give your people in the Sky Arena, without risking more bloodshed."

He shook his head wearily and looked back to the barred window. "Ada killed the soldiers who killed Katrina," X said. "It was cowardly, and it was wrong, but it's done."

"You shouldn't have let her go."

"I could have let her rot here, but I knew you would come for her, and if you had killed her, then whatever bond we have would be broken. So I removed the opportunity, and we'll leave it at that."

Rhino clenched his jaw, suppressing the flash of rage that made him want to knock the king's lights out. He had sworn loyalty to X, but the guy was driving him crazy with some of his decisions.

"Consider her dead," X said. "Chances are, she won't last long out there."

Rhino's eyes narrowed. He still believed in the old warrior's vision for rebuilding the islands and expanding the economy to provide food and shelter for everyone. But Rhino wasn't sure the two societies could live in peace, even with the common threat of the defectors and, now, the skinwalkers.

"You planning on using that knife still?" X asked, looking down at the blade.

"Not on you," Rhino said. "Guess I'll save it for Vargas."

The moment of tension passed. Rhino wondered whether X was going to punish him. Did X even still trust him?

But the king just shrugged and said, "Better get a move on it. We've got some planning to do, I've got Hell Divers to train, and I have a ton of other shit to shovel before I head to the trading post with you and your four badass Barracudas."

Rhino stepped to the side, letting X and Miles pass. When they were gone, he looked at the empty cell and bed. He knew he had to let the past go, but he had a feeling it was still going to haunt him, one way or another.

* * * * *

Magnolia ran, dripping tears and sweat. Arlo, Alexander, and Edgar—all dead. And so were most of the Cazadores.

Another soldier had vanished an hour ago. Now

it was just her, Rodger, General Santiago, Lieutenant Alejo, and the injured grunt soldier, Ruiz.

Something was hunting them, taking them quietly, one at a time. A Siren, perhaps, maybe something else. Rio de Janeiro was a haven for Sirens, bone beasts, and a zoo of other mutant creatures, along with some truly bizarre plant life. One thing was clear: this was their turf, and the divers were unwelcome guests. Or welcome, perhaps, as meat on the hoof.

Coming down here in two teams had been a mistake. They should have stuck together all along. Then they might have had a chance to reach the target.

They were only two blocks from the location. Michael and Sofia weren't far, but their beacons were moving at a crawl.

Magnolia's group was no longer moving in combat intervals, but in single file, keeping close so the monsters couldn't snatch anyone else away into the darkness.

The electronic wail of a Siren echoed in the distance. The beasts were active again. She still thought those were the predators picking off her team one at a time. Maybe there was an alpha unlike any they had come across in the wastes.

The defectors wouldn't take them out individually. Neither would the bone beasts. One of those things could kill their entire group if it managed to trap them in a room. But the Sirens were stealth hunters.

Magnolia slipped around a fallen door lintel into a space overgrown with vegetation. The purple-and-red vines had run riot inside the office building, pushing over desks and breaking through walls. The team kept clear of the spiny bulbs that grew like bark on the scaly skin. She didn't want to find out what would happen if they got too close.

Broken glass doors led to a business that had served coffee. She looked at the faded green mermaid logo on the ground. Paper cups and plastic spoons were strewn about as if a hurricane had blown through. Two tables remained standing. Everything else was upended or smashed.

Alejo waded through the debris to the missing front door, to check the street. Glowing vines pulsated on the road, rhythmically lighting up and dimming the twilit room.

"I think the divers are somewhere out there," Magnolia whispered, pointing.

"And the target is around the next block," Rodger said. "We should link up with Michael and Sofia first, then—"

Alejo cut him off. "We link up with your divers; then we get the hell out of here," he said. "Pray our boat is still waiting with my men."

"*My* boat," Magnolia said.

Alejo's helmet rotated toward her. "Maybe you haven't noticed, sweetheart, but the mission has failed. We're getting picked off like flies."

"And what's the general have to say?" Magnolia asked.

Alejo spoke to Santiago in a hushed voice. The old

warrior cradled his double-barreled shotgun and said, "*Sigamos. Cumplamos la misión.*"

Alejo gave an exasperated snort. "He says we complete the mission."

"Good," Magnolia said. "We're almost there."

"I'll take point," Rodger said.

"Not a chance." She got up and moved toward the exit before he could get out in front.

Rain drizzled onto the slick sidewalk just outside the door, and lighting flashed over the skyline. The thunderclap came a moment later, followed by the high screech of a Siren.

She hesitated in the open doorway, looking, but saw nothing. There was no sign of monsters, and no sign of Michael or Sofia.

How was that possible? According to her HUD, the other divers should be right across the street. The building there had collapsed, but the data put the two remaining divers on Team Raptor somewhere in the area.

She brought up her scope just to make sure, zooming in on the pile of debris. As she scanned, brown flesh darted past the crosshairs. She tried to follow, but it was too fast.

"What?" Alejo said quietly.

"Siren, maybe, but the flesh looked darker."

"Maybe we should find another route," Rodger said.

"No, Michael and Sofia should be right out there," Magnolia said. "We just have to find them."

She waited another moment before signaling

the team to follow her out on the sidewalk. The new vantage provided a view of the demolished structures on both sides of the road, but no Michael or Sofia.

Baffled, she looked at the tangle of vines stretching across the asphalt. Could they be crawling *through* the thick flora?

She followed the beacons on her HUD over to the closest vine, wrapped around a slab of concrete. Stepping onto the slab, she looked over the edge. The lip of a sinkhole was a few feet away.

Michael and Sofia weren't inside the vine or in the buildings, she realized.

They were under the road.

She stood looking down at the trunk of vines that wound deep into the cavernous hole. The roots flashed, spreading a dull glow over the muddy slope and the multiple footprints going down it.

But why in the wastes had the divers gone down there?

Unless some beast took them ...

She signaled the team to join her. Rodger and Alejo were already moving low across the road. Santiago stepped away from the wall, but Ruiz suddenly squirmed on the sidewalk, his arms tight at his sides.

Before anyone could help, Ruiz was yanked off the sidewalk and pulled up the side of the building.

Magnolia brought up her rifle and aimed at the rooftop, where two naked men were pulling the Cazador up by the rope they had lassoed him with.

"Ambush!" she yelled.

Something whizzed past her before she could pull the trigger, and she jumped away. Another projectile thunked into the vine in front of her. An arrow. A third hit one of the bulbs, which blew out droplets of sap.

Magnolia rolled away from the toxic spray and bolted for the safety of the building as the naked men on the roof fired more arrows. The four remaining members of the team all took cover against the wall. Rodger brought up his assault rifle, but Alejo pushed the barrel down.

"Don't fire," he said. "It will draw the beasts. We have to run."

"Screw that, man," Magnolia said. "We're sitting ducks down here."

Something crunched down on the pavement outside of the coffee shop. Rodger let out a yelp and backed away from a splash of blood and gore.

"Dear God," Magnolia whispered.

The hunk of meat on the concrete was Ruiz—or, more correctly, the upper half of Ruiz. The naked humans, or whatever they were, had cut him in two at the waist.

"We have to get inside the sinkhole," Magnolia said.

Alejo nodded and relayed the plan to Santiago.

"The laser rifle is quiet," she said. "I'll lay down covering fire."

"Get down!" Alejo said.

Magnolia dropped, and Alejo threw his knife over her head. She heard a dull smack and turned to see a naked man crumple to the ground not twelve feet away, the knife buried in his chest.

As if on cue, a dozen more men came rappelling down the sides of the buildings and running over the debris piles across the road.

Arrows bracketed the wall around Magnolia's team.

In a few seconds, they were surrounded.

Alejo, too, must have realized they couldn't win this fight.

"Don't shoot," he growled.

She moved her rifle from target to target as they moved in with bows. She counted fourteen, all of them dark-skinned and naked.

But as they got closer, she saw that their skin looked odd, dried out. Perhaps, these were the people from the bunker, who had somehow adapted to survive in the toxic conditions here.

The leader of the group carried an axe in either hand. Both blades were caked with dried blood. He was almost as big as Rhino and had a horn sticking out of the center of his forehead.

"What are they?" Rodger stuttered.

The horned man walked over, and in a prolonged lightning flash, Magnolia saw that he wasn't one of the people from the bunker after all. He was *wearing* the people from the bunker.

Dried, shriveled flesh covered his armored body from head to toe.

"Skinwalkers," Alejo said.

"*!Hijo de la gran puta!*" Santiago yelled. Magnolia knew this one from gambling with the Cazador warriors—something about a son of some great whore.

The big man did not speak but simply gestured for them to lower their weapons. Alejo kept his rifle trained on him, and so did Magnolia and Rodger.

An arrow crunched through Alejo's armored shoulder, knocking him backward. A second hit his weapon, knocking it from his hand. Rodger and Magnolia finally lowered their weapons.

Santiago laid his shotgun on the ground and drew his sword. The skinwalkers fanned out into a circle around him but did not riddle him with arrows as Magnolia had expected after the insult.

"*Saludos, general,*" Horn said in a voice that sounded almost robotic. "*Nos encontramos de nuevo.*"

Santiago replied in only a few words that Magnolia understood, but she didn't need a translator to know that the two men were about to fight to the death.

She subtly glanced at the sinkhole, gauging whether she could make a run for it with Rodger and Alejo, but two bowmen had already flanked them and nocked their arrows.

She crouched beside Alejo to check his wounds. Blood trickled down his armor. He snapped the end off one arrow.

"The *pinche cabrón* must have heard your radio messages to the people in the bunker," he groaned.

"I thought the Cazadores don't use radios," she whispered.

"They don't transmit, but that doesn't mean they don't listen."

Alejo stumbled, then rested his back against a wall. He was done for unless they got him patched up soon, and the only way to do that was to get into the sinkhole.

"We led him right to the bunker, didn't we?" she said.

Alejo nodded. "And now they are going to fillet us like fish unless General Santiago pulls off a miracle."

Metal clashed against metal as Santiago's sword met Horn's axes. The leader of the skinwalkers jumped backward, avoiding the next sword stroke. He swung one of his blades at Santiago, following it with the other axe.

The second blade clipped the armor covering the general's right arm but did not penetrate. He thrust his sword at Horn, and Horn parried the blow with an axe.

A screech sounded. The clanging weapons had alerted a male Siren. The beast swooped down to examine the noises, only to crash into the debris pile, bristling with arrows.

Magnolia used the distraction to tell Rodger to get ready to run. He nodded back, but Alejo shook his head.

"You won't make it," he said.

"We have to try."

The dying Siren somehow managed to push itself up on the sidewalk. Six arrows stuck out of the wrinkled flesh. Two skinwalkers ran over with swords drawn.

The beast slashed at the air, but one of the men cut the taloned hand off, and the two went to work, stabbing until it finally stopped moving.

The general slashed at Horn, who brought up his axes together, deflecting the blade and pushing Santiago backward several feet.

Horn then swung with his right axe, very nearly slicing Santiago across the gut. Old but still agile, the general back-stepped, following with a jab to the face. But his adversary twisted, and the horn cresting his helmet deflected the thrust.

The miss knocked Santiago off-kilter, and he staggered, allowing an opening. This time, the axe got through, crunching into his ribs. The general screamed in pain as Horn yanked the blade free.

Santiago bent over, gripping the gushing wound.

The other skinwalkers looked at the sky and streets for hostiles, knowing that the scent of fresh blood would draw them.

This was Magnolia's chance. "Rodger, NOW!" she said.

Scooping up her rifle, she got off two quick bolts, through the chests of both distracted soldiers on their flanks. Then she grabbed Alejo and helped him to his feet. He pulled a pistol and fired, dropping a bowman.

One of the faster skinwalkers let an arrow fly. Alejo stumbled behind Magnolia from a bolt to his side. He took down the shooter with his pistol and then looked over at Magnolia as several arrows cut the air between them.

"RUN!" he shouted.

Two more arrows hit him in the chest, and another went through his thigh. He went down on one knee, screaming a war cry.

Magnolia dashed after Rodger while looking over her shoulder. Lieutenant Alejo killed two more of Horn's men before they finally brought him down. It took seven arrows to finish him off.

A last glance over her shoulder showed Santiago on his knees, gripping his bleeding side. Horn brought up both axes to finish the last of the Cazadores who had sailed with the sky people.

Arrows hissed past her and Rodger as they zigzagged toward the vines. They were almost there, but any second now, she would feel the inevitable stab. Even if the bolt didn't kill her right away, the tear in her suit would.

She gritted her teeth and prepared to jump. Rodger tripped on a vine, falling just as an arrow streaked over him.

Magnolia reached down to help him, firing the laser rifle for cover. A skinwalker went down from a blast to the face, but the others closed in with their bows.

In a stolen moment, she saw Santiago's slumping headless body, with twin geysers of blood jetting out of the neck.

Horn raised a bloody axe in the air, then pointed it at Magnolia and Rodger. She grabbed his hand and pulled him up. As they stumbled for cover, a flash came out of the sky.

Then a second flash.

Behind the skinwalkers, a projectile detonated, blowing pieces of two men skyward.

Using the brief window, the two divers hopped over a thick braid of vines and into the hole. Rodger skidded down the side, screaming all the way down, while Magnolia ducked behind the wall of flora and fired her laser rifle at the two men pursuing them.

Both went down with smoking holes through their torsos.

"Mags!" Rodger called out from the bottom of the hole.

The skinwalkers took off in all directions as the divers' savior swooped down, firing a blaster and a grenade launcher.

It wasn't *Discovery* coming to their aid—it was Cricket.

The little Hell Diver was doing what Team Raptor and the Cazadores couldn't do. It was killing the killers.

TWENTY-SIX

"Vargas is going to see his whore in an hour," Rhino said. "Mac says his advance team of Praetorian Guards is already at the rig."

X stared at the radio equipment in the command center, his hands shaking. The news of their good luck with Vargas did nothing to lighten the weight of the news he had just heard from Captain Mitchells.

"King Xavier, this is our chance," Rhino said. "Mac and Felipe are in the port, waiting for us in a boat."

"Better come inside," Sloan said.

"What's going on?" Rhino asked.

She shut the door behind him. "We just got a message from *Discovery*," she said.

"Shit. It's bad, isn't it?"

X got up from the chair facing the bank of radio equipment. He looked down at Miles, who looked back at him with eyes clouded by cataracts. The dog's tail thumped against the floor, anticipating a belly rub or perhaps a treat. He had no idea what had happened, but his tail went still.

"It's okay, buddy," X said. He gave the dog a piece of fish jerky and leaned down to look at the maps of Rio de Janeiro, the Iron Reef outpost in Belize, and Outrider, the colony the Cazadores had abandoned thirty years ago—the place where Horn had apparently spent the past few years preparing to retake his throne.

"King Xavier, what's happened?" Rhino asked, his voice tense with worry.

"The mission has failed," X said. "We've lost half the divers."

"Sofia," Rhino said, stepping closer.

X could see the dread in his general's face. "She's still alive," he said.

"Thank the Octopus Gods."

"Don't thank them yet," Sloan said.

"The Cazadores are dead," X said. "All of them, as far as we know. Killed by Horn and his skinwalkers."

"*Horn?*" Rhino took a shaky breath and let it out. "The skinwalkers are there?"

X nodded. "Captain Mitchells saw them on the drone footage."

"General Santiago …"

"Dead."

Something seemed to shift in Rhino. "Then there is no time to waste," he said. "We must strike Vargas today."

"Hold up, big guy," Sloan said. "I want to know how Horn knew about our mission."

X looked to the radio equipment. "He must have been listening to our transmissions. First to the fuel outpost, then to the bunker."

"But they were encrypted," Sloan said.

X slapped himself on the forehead. "Yes, but the response from the bunker wasn't. And to have known about the fuel outpost, he must be tapped into the Cazador channels."

"Horn and his demon men," Rhino said. "Traitorous filth."

"Could they be working with the Black Order?" X asked.

Rhino pulled on his nose ring. "Possibly, but—"

"I doubt Vargas or anyone else in the Black Order has cracked our encrypted channel with *Discovery*," said Sloan, "but if they have, they'll know soon what happened. You were both right. We must act now."

X walked over to the locker and took off his white T-shirt, trading it for a brown robe that went over his shorts. Then he grabbed his duty belt of weapons and finally his sword.

Sloan said, "If Colonel Vargas and his pals don't know yet what's happened out there, they will when the airship returns without any Cazadores aboard."

"There isn't a single Cazador survivor?" Rhino asked.

"No, but that could actually help us after we kill Vargas," X said. "I'll have video footage to prove to the Black Order that the skinwalkers, not us, killed General Santiago."

X finished securing his gear and weapons.

"Maybe you should let us handle this, King Xavier," Rhino said.

"Big guy's right," Sloan said. "You shouldn't be seen."

X flipped the hood over his freshly buzzed head. "I won't be seen," he said. "Just look after Miles while I'm gone, Lieutenant. Okay?"

She muttered a curse. "You're never going to listen to me, are you?"

X grinned. "Probably not." He pointed at the radio. "If Captain Mitchells sends another transmission, be careful what you say, just in case our enemies are listening."

"Understood, sir."

X patted Miles on the head. "I'll be back soon, buddy."

Rhino opened the door, and they stepped out into the sunshine. A short walk brought them into a stairwell they took down to the boat port. A fishing boat waited in the shadows near the back of the moorings, past the fancy boats.

Mac sat behind the wheel. In the seat beside him, Felipe honed a blade. Both men wore hooded anoraks with long sleeves. Rhino put his on as soon as he got in the boat.

"Isaiah moored the *Angry Tuna* there this morning," Mac said. "He's already in position."

X took a seat between Rhino and Felipe as Mac fired up the engine. He was surrounded by Cazador warriors heading out to kill more Cazador warriors. It seemed crazy that keeping humanity alive required so much killing.

There was a reason the world had ended, and this was it, X thought to himself. The machines may have helped speed up the process, but basic human greed had all but doomed his species. He had never understood this simple truth before now.

X gripped the sword that Katrina had used in battle against the Cazadores. She had given her life to save their people, and Michael and Les were out there doing what they had to do. Now it was his turn. If it meant slicing open Vargas's throat, so be it. He probably should have done that on day one.

The boat sped away from the capitol rig in warm sunlight. X kept his hood pulled up to hide his face from curious eyes. He didn't look over his shoulder, afraid that if he did, he would change his mind about this crazy scheme.

"Listen up," Mac said. "This plan is simple, but we all have a role."

Felipe tilted his head, and Rhino translated.

"Once we get to the rig, we enter through a ladder on the eastern side," Mac said. "From there, we go through the inside of the rig, avoiding all the open trading areas."

The boat hit a wave at an angle and slewed a little sideways. Mac straightened out and backed the throttle off a notch. "The brothel Vargas visits is just off an open area, and there are two floors above it that give a clear view of the front entrance."

"That's where Isaiah is going to be?" Rhino asked.

"Yes. He'll take out the front guards with his bow while we enter through the back. There will be at least two more guards there, maybe three, that we have to kill before we get to Vargas, who should be busy when we arrive."

"You're sure he isn't a thirty-second kind of guy?" X asked. "He always seemed like one. I ask because that gives us a very small window."

Mac laughed. "The shop owner is a friend of mine. She said Vargas typically goes for the full treatment, including a long massage."

"And the girl?" X asked. "Is she in on this?"

"No, but I'll make sure she gets a really good tip and doesn't say a word."

X didn't like that she would see their faces, but that was the least of his worries right now. The Praetorian Guards were all skilled in close-quarters fighting. They had to surprise these guys and kill them fast. Sure, he could go in blasting with his new weapon slung over his robe, but there were too many civilians in the area for a shoot-out. This would require precision and sharp swords.

"We do this clean," X said. "Clean and fast."

Rhino explained the rest of the plan to Felipe. The young man grinned and went back to honing an already razor-edged small knife with a curving blade. An identical blade was sheathed on his belt.

"Heads up," Mac said. "Almost there."

The trading-post rig appeared small on the

horizon, but even at this reduced speed they would be there in minutes. X used the time to rehearse everything in his mind.

He prayed that Michael, Magnolia, Rodger, and Sofia made it back to the airship safely, but the horrific losses filled him with a deep dread. Looking out at the horizon, he also wondered where Ada was.

X would never admit this to Rhino, but when he went to visit her, he had actually gone there to kill her. But he couldn't bring himself to do it, so instead, he had helped her escape.

"Come back in five years," he had said, "and I will welcome you back to the islands."

It was half the time he had spent alone on the surface, and if she survived as he had, then he would forgive her for her sins.

The map he had given Ada was to the place in Florida where he had lived several years. If she could get there, she would have access to the resources that had kept him alive until the sky people landed and rescued him.

But he doubted she would make it that far. In a way, X *had* effectively killed her by sending her out there.

"Here we go," Mac said. Felipe hopped up on the bow and eased the craft into a mooring between two tethered boats.

Notes from a guitar and several wind instruments drifted away from the trading post. The tone was calming, beautiful even.

This was it. Time to fight again. And as always, he would rise to the occasion, ready to fight for humanity even if it meant losing more of his own.

* * * * *

The vines had burrowed deep inside the earth, forming tunnels wide enough for a person to navigate. Michael and Sofia had scrambled into one of them but now had to crawl as it narrowed.

After an hour, they finally came to a chamber that let them get off their bellies. Michael managed to get into a crouch, and Sofia came up on her armored kneepads.

"We're lost," she said.

"I know that."

Sofia twisted and stretched her torso. "Now that we can turn around, maybe we should get back topside," she said. "Edgar and Arlo are gone. You have to accept that, Commander."

"I have, but I haven't given up on finding the people who took them."

"Why? What's the point? Are you going to kill them? Kill the people we came to save?"

Michael wasn't sure what he was going to do. He just knew he wanted to find the survivors, even if they turned out to be Edgar and Arlo's killers.

He looked at his wrist computer, checking to make sure Rodger and Magnolia were still alive. Both their beacons came online. They appeared close. In fact, they seemed to be somewhere right above him and Sofia.

"How is that possible?" Michael whispered. He considered using the comm channel, but he didn't know who might be out there listening.

Sofia wiped grime and sap off her visor and said, "Commander, my battery's at forty percent and I'm almost out of water. I could use something to eat, too."

Michael checked the data on his subscreen. The radiation and air toxicity were surprisingly much lower underground than above and kept getting better the deeper they descended.

He pulled a sealed energy bar from his vest pocket. "You should be okay to open your visor for a minute or two," he said. "Go ahead. I'm going to eat something, too."

Over their chewing, they began to hear the faint sound of voices echoing in the passage.

"Do you hear that?" Sofia said.

Michael nodded and shut off his helmet light. She did the same. Darkness swallowed the divers, but it wasn't the pitch black that scared him—it was the voices.

"Can you make out what they're saying?" Michael asked.

"Sounds like Spanish, but I can't make it out."

"I thought the people we came here to save spoke Portuguese."

"Maybe not all of them," she said. "And Portuguese sounds a lot like Spanish, only softer."

"Turn on your NVGs and follow me. I want to check it out."

Michael crawled out of the chamber into the narrowing tunnel, moving on his knees and hands. It wasn't long before he saw the pulsing red light of vines winking in the passage. The glow seemed to be coming from a hole in the rocky wall. Several branches from a vine had broken through, curling inside the tunnel.

He pried back the mat of vines to look into a large cavern. No, a *huge* cavern.

Roots and stems stretched away from the floor and extended into dozens of tunnels in the walls above. All the roots seemed to connect to a bulb the size of a small house on the cavern floor. Helmet-sized barbs covered the mass like huge, spiky warts.

"It's the heart," he whispered.

"Heart?" Sofia said.

He got out of the way so she could take a look.

Sofia looked down and then jerked back into the shadows as more voices echoed.

Michael moved over and pulled back the vines again.

Sure enough, to the right of the heart were two naked men, walking with arrows nocked on their bowstrings. He strained for a better look at what appeared to be a steel door in the cavern wall.

"Holy shit," Michael whispered. "I think this is the back way to the bunker."

Sofia didn't say anything, which told him she

wasn't keen on the idea of going down there to check it out.

"This is what we came here for," he said. "Why our friends died. We have to check it out."

He thought of Layla and Bray and everyone else back on the airship and the islands. They weren't the only ones who had spent their lives in the darkness before finding the light. He didn't know whether the people down there were good or bad, but he had to find out more. For all he knew, the defectors had killed them and his divers. If that was what happened, then his people were likely responsible for the transmission that led the machines here.

"We have to finish what Team Raptor came here for," Michael said.

A whimpering sound came over the voices in the chamber. Michael checked again but couldn't see the source.

"Come on," he whispered.

Sofia hesitated, then followed him down the sloping tunnel. They were descending at a thirty-five-degree angle now, and they had to be careful not to slide along the steep, rocky floor.

As they descended, the whimpering began to sound more like sobbing.

He counted at least three, maybe four, voices over the noise. Another opening in the tunnel wall provided a view inside the chamber.

He turned so he faced up, toward Sofia, who had stopped on her knees. The window into the chamber revealed even more naked men with bows, and they weren't alone.

Two more men, both in black clothing, hung from ropes around their ankles. Blood dripped from their hair onto the floor.

Michael pulled back into the shadows and let Sofia scoot down for a view.

"Edgar and Arlo," she whispered.

It made sense now. Their beacons had switched off when these wrinkly men removed their armor.

Michael took another look. Even from a distance, it was obvious the divers were in bad shape. Beaten and possibly cut or stabbed, judging from the sheer amount of blood on their jumpsuits and flesh. Neither appeared to be conscious. The sobs were coming from someone else.

He moved again to check the door to the bunker and saw another group of people huddled together against the wall right below him and Sofia.

The plastic filtration masks they wore hid their faces, but he could tell that most of them were emaciated. He also spotted kids in the group. The entire lot wore gray outfits: jumpsuits, pants, and shirts with a logo of some sort.

The people from the bunker.

But who the hell were the six naked freaks who had taken his divers captive?

Michael thought back to the skin flags he had seen aboveground. He had seen something similar at the fuel outpost, but they also looked like what the defectors left behind in Jamaica.

If the machines weren't here, then it could only be …

"Skinwalkers," he whispered.

These naked men had to be part of Horn's group.

Michael crouched and brought up his laser rifle, zooming in on the biggest of the guards. The guy was a brute, easily Rhino's size. He held a long needlelike blade and walked around Arlo and Edgar, studying them the way a scientist might look at a caged animal.

Zeroing in on his face, Michael saw what looked like stitches in the wrinkled brown flesh, all the way around the chin and skull. It wasn't just his face. His entire body was covered in the stitched-on skin—even his damn boots.

Before Michael could react, the man jammed the needle blade into Arlo's side, but Arlo hardly made a sound.

"No!" Michael blurted in a voice just shy of a shout. His voice echoed, turning several heads among the skinwalkers.

He sank back into the shadows, heart thumping against his ribs.

Sofia, still on her knees, brought up her rifle and trained it on the opening in the wall. They waited several moments, but the arrows and excited shouts never came.

He moved slightly for a look farther down the sloping tunnel. It had to come out somewhere, and he had a feeling it wasn't far.

"We have to do something," Sofia said.

Michael was glad they were on the same page. He raised his rifle and said, "Let's kill these demonic fucks."

She nodded. "Just tell me when to fire, Comm—"

More voices cut her off. These were louder and seemed to come from new people entering the cavern. He sneaked a glance. The six men had turned into twenty, maybe more. Some were wounded, limping along or clutching wounds in their torsos. Others had armor showing through charred, wrinkled skin.

A man with a horn on his helmet strode into the cavern, carrying two axes. Walking past the heart, he raised one of his blades at Arlo and Edgar. The brute with the stiletto reached up and sliced through the ropes around their ankles, dropping them to the ground.

Michael counted another dozen soldiers flooding into the cavern behind the leader with the axes.

"*Siren shit*," he whispered.

The man with the horn spoke rapidly in a muffled voice. Burned skin hung loosely off his helmet. He wiped a shred away from his eyes.

"What's he saying?" Michael asked.

"He says to kill the rest of these people and skin them, then head back to their boat. It's time …" Sofia's words trailed off.

"Time for what?"

"To go to the Metal Islands and take the throne from el Pulpo," Sofia said. "He must not know that X is king."

"We have to stop him," Michael said.

"But so many …"

"I know, but we have guns and they don't," Michael said. "You stay and shoot from here. I'll head down and fire from the floor, okay?"

She hesitated, then nodded.

"Thanks for sticking with me," Michael said. "Good luck."

"Good luck."

He squirmed around and moved back down the tunnel. As he suspected, there was another opening in the wall, this one much bigger than the others.

A skinwalker stood on the other side, facing the group of people from the bunker. Michael pulled the knife from his sheath and jammed it through the back of the man's neck, up into the brain.

He slumped over, and Michael raised his laser rifle, choosing his first target, the big bastard who had stabbed Arlo. He now had an axe in hand and was preparing to bring it down on Arlo's neck.

Lining up the sights, Michael whispered, "Hello and goodbye, asshole."

The brilliant line of blue light flashed through the man's helmet and into the rock wall. He dropped with a thud onto the ground between Arlo and Edgar.

Michael roved to the next target, who was nocking an arrow on his bowstring. The laser ripped through his neck. The next bolt sizzled into another helmet.

In just over ten seconds, Michael had killed four men, but the others quickly homed in on his position. Arrows flew, and gunshots rang out from Sofia's position.

More gunfire joined the echoing din. Michael cursed their luck. These fuckers had guns too, and that changed the calculus. He expected rounds to start pinging off the wall over his head, but none came.

Not only gunfire but also laser bolts were coming from the other side of the chamber.

Oh, hell yes!

Magnolia and Rodger must have been stalking this second group. That explained why some of them were injured. But where was the rest of their team?

He helped them by laying down covering fire.

The skinwalkers fanned out, launching arrows in all directions. The people from the bunker tried to wriggle away, but they were all bound with rope.

Michael slid down into the chamber and started to cut their bonds. He freed a man and handed him a knife, motioning to cut the others free. The guy understood and went to work.

Another prisoner had already broken out of his restraints somehow and ran with outstretched hands at a skinwalker. The soldier turned and loosed an arrow into the guy's gray suit.

Michael took the shooter down with a laser bolt that cut his bow in half and flashed through his chest. Then he looked for the leader with the unicorn helmet. He was making his way toward Arlo and Edgar, both axes in hand.

"No, you don't," Michael said, firing a bolt that sent one of the axes spinning away.

Screams echoed through the chamber as two skinwalkers ran at Michael with swords drawn. He cut them down with laser bolts; then his gun overheated again.

Michael drew the pistol X had given him and

aimed for the leader, but by the time he spotted the man again, his men were trying to pull him away. A third joined in, grabbing him while Michael fired several bullets.

The group of skinwalkers fell in behind them, shooting arrows and guns to cover their leader's retreat. Michael got down to avoid the fire. He squeezed off more shots, thinning out the rear guard, but they whisked the leader away into a side tunnel.

Across the chamber, another ally had joined Magnolia and Rodger. The tall figure fired an assault rifle, picking off stragglers.

Michael got up and ran over to Arlo and Edgar, changing the magazine of his pistol along the way. When he got to them, Edgar was unconscious, but Arlo was awake. He drooled blood and looked up, his perfect smile ruined by several missing teeth.

"You came back," he mumbled.

Michael ripped into his med pack and began pulling out dressings to stop the bleeding from Arlo's side.

"You're going to be fine, man. Just hang on."

"I'm sorry," Arlo said with quivering blue lips. "I screwed up."

"You screwed up only if you die." Michael pushed gauze against the wound and taped off the sides. "Just breathe, okay?"

Arlo nodded. "Sir …"

"Don't talk."

"But, sir … I really wanted a new nickname."

"If you live, I'll give you one," Michael said.

Sofia ran over to help Arlo and Edgar, giving Michael an opportunity to call in support. He bumped on his comms for the first time on the mission.

"Captain Mitchells, this is Raptor One," he said. "We need evac as soon as possible. We have multiple wounded, and …" He looked at the survivors on the ground behind him. "… at least thirty people who need transport, over. Maybe a few more."

"I'm already here," said a voice.

Michael looked across the chamber, past the glowing floral "heart." The tall figure he had seen earlier was wearing Hell Diver armor.

"Captain," Michael said. "You're a sight for sore eyes."

Magnolia and Rodger ran over.

"The airship is topside," Les said. "We have to get everyone out of here fast, before the monsters come back."

Michael wasn't sure which monsters he was talking about this time: human or mutant.

He looked back at the bunker survivors, huddled in their gray jumpsuits and staring at the Hell Divers as if they were gods, like the statue they had passed on the dive in.

To a society that had known only demons, perhaps they were.

TWENTY-SEVEN

The trading post was doing a brisk business. It swarmed with people of all ages. Young and old browsed the offerings of stalls packed with fresh produce and fish. Neat rows of sea bass were displayed in one booth, under an overhang protecting them from the warming temperatures. Buckets of live shrimp and lobster made up the next stall. Antennae stuck above the rims, waving back and forth as if beckoning potential customers.

A woman with a hatchet cut the head off a chicken that continued to squirm and flap on her chopping block. Another seller handed lettuce and radishes to a sky person who had come to shop.

Rhino looked away, distracted by thoughts of Sofia. She was still alive out in the wastes, and he held on to hope that she was going to come home safely. If he wanted to see her again, he needed to focus.

Just focus on the plan.

They had already modified it once after coming up a ladder to an interior passage guarded by a patrol of grunt Cazador warriors. That forced them into the open trading areas. Rhino tried to stick close to a group of scribes and monks wearing the same clothing as the Barracudas. The sky people in the crowd, wearing longer clothing to cover their sensitive skin, also helped them blend in.

But Rhino didn't like being out in the open with the masses. His size could give him away, even without his armor. At least, he had managed to fit his double-headed spear in two pieces beneath his robe. Carrying it would have gotten him a lot of looks and whispers.

The scribes went left down a passage, and Mac led the team into another alley. He navigated the familiar corridors for the group, and Felipe followed, grinning. The young man was happy to be away from *Elysium* for a few days and eager for his first kill.

Rhino kept a reasonable distance, and X trailed just behind, head down.

They worked their way through the third floor, toward a stairwell that would take them down to the outer booths of the main trading floor. Most of the cages here were empty today, but several contained indentured servants who hadn't sold in last night's auction.

A group of potential buyers had already gathered to inspect them. The skinny men were going to be a tough sell. In this shape, they wouldn't make good laborers or warriors. If they were lucky, they would end up on a fishing trawler or working in a garden.

Mac entered a stairwell and led the team to the first floor, and from there to an alley between some of the less popular booths. It was close to the area where Rhino had found him a few days ago.

Signs hung from the bulkheads and shop fronts in the next passage, which intersected with another alleyway. Mac stopped to buy a skewer of seasoned shrimp. He bit one off and handed the skewer to Felipe, whose sharp teeth stripped off another shrimp.

"They got shine here?" X asked, stepping up beside Rhino.

"Not the type you're probably used to."

"If you're talking about wine, you're right," X said. "Tastes good, but it's basically old fruit juice if you ask me."

"I'm sure we both will need a drink or ten after this is over."

"But can you keep up?" X raised a brow. "Nah, highly unlikely."

You'd be surprised, Rhino thought. He felt relieved that the king wasn't holding a grudge, but now was not the time for jokes.

Mac took them past tin-roofed shacks to a corridor the size of an old-world street. Shop fronts framed both sides on the first level, but the three floors above were mostly apartments and single-family dwellings.

Open shutters revealed potted flowers and herbs growing on windowsills. An elderly woman sucked on a cigarette, watching the Barracudas.

Rhino spotted Isaiah through an open window, wearing a hood that shadowed his eyes and covered his greasy hair. He nodded as Rhino passed underneath.

Ahead, Mac opened a hatch to an interior hallway. As the four men entered, Rhino got a view of two Praetorian Guards standing sentry under a crooked wooden sign that read, "The Purple Pearl."

Though helmetless, the Cazador soldiers wore full armor and held spears. Swords hung from their belts, and red capes draped their shoulders.

Rhino recognized both scarred faces and steeled himself. These warriors knew how to wield sword and spear. The men inside would as well, but they would be no match for Isaiah's arrows, the Immortal, and the Barracudas.

Mac and Felipe stopped just before the intersection with the next alley. After sneaking a glance around the edge, Mac held up three fingers, indicating the number of Praetorian Guards at the back entrance of the Purple Pearl.

Rhino squeezed past Felipe. "I'll lead the way," he said. Opening his robe, he pulled out the two shafts of his double-headed spear and joined them together with a click.

Mac hit a button on his cane, bringing out the blade, and X unsheathed his sword.

Rhino gave the nod. This was it. Time to kill that bag of shark chum.

Felipe came strolling around the corner—just a guy heading for the brothel.

"*¡Alto ahí!*" shouted one of the three guards.

Footsteps clanked on the metal deck, and two guards strode through the intersection, spears in hand.

"Hey, bub," X said. "That whorehouse clean?"

Both guards stopped and peered into the shadowed alley. Rhino thrust his spear through the chest of the guard on the left, and X slashed the other across the neck. Blood spurted out, painting both Rhino and the king.

Felipe had turned and came running back. He threw both of his daggers. Rhino heard a muffled cry, then another thud.

By the time Rhino rounded the corner, the third guard was dead, and Felipe was wiping the two knives on his tangerine cape.

Mac moved ahead of the group, pulling out a key to the back entry of the brothel. He unlocked it and gently pushed the door open.

Rhino's spear tip went inside first. Felipe drew a cutlass and went next.

Candles lit the corners of the dark room, illuminating a dozen stalls cordoned off by drapes. An empty desk and two couches occupied the front of the room. Curtains covered the only window, and the metal front door was closed.

By now, Isaiah would have taken down the guards in front and would be on his way to help. That meant they had only one Cazador left to kill.

The Barracudas filed inside the brothel. Rhino used the tip of his spear to pull back a drape of the first space on the left, while X did the same going the other direction.

Rhino found a mattress and bedside table but no Vargas.

Rhythmic grunting came from across the room, and Mac pointed his cane at a draped stall.

Nodding, Rhino took point, X on his right flank.

Killing a man while he got his rocks off wasn't the bravest way to do it, but it would save a lot of problems later on, and Rhino didn't feel any compunctions whatever. Ending the threat Vargas posed would save many lives, and when Sofia did return, they would be closer to the freedom they both had dreamed of. His heart thumped at the thought of seeing his woman soon.

He approached the drape where the grunting was coming from. Reaching out with his spear shaft, Rhino prepared to pull it back with the blade, but movement just behind the bottom of the drape stopped him. He could see boot soles in the half inch of space just underneath. Not just one pair.

"Back!" Rhino shouted.

He ducked as several arrows burst through the drapes and cut through the air. With his spear, he swiped under the curtain hard enough to sever a foot.

An agonized scream rang out as the drapes of other stalls opened. Cazador soldiers poured into the room, raising swords and spears.

Two men rushed out of the room in front of Rhino, and he swung his spear, taking a head off clean. Then he back-stepped away from the wide swipe of the other soldier's sword. The man stumbled out of the enclosed space, right onto Rhino's spear.

He had taken three Cazadores out of the fight in

twice as many seconds. When he turned to help his team, everything seemed to slow down.

X and Mac fought back to back in the center of the large room. Both had arrows sticking out of their robes.

Felipe had lost his cutlass and threw one of his daggers into a soldier slashing at him with a sword. Then he sidestepped a low jab from a spear and stabbed the wielder twice in the neck.

The front door swung open, and in rushed the two Praetorian Guards Rhino had seen out front earlier. Following them in was a third man with an arrow nocked on his bowstring. He aimed it at Rhino and let fly.

The shaft caught Rhino in the shoulder. Adrenaline kept the pain at bay, but he did feel the deep cut of betrayal of his old friend and trainer.

Isaiah took another arrow from his quiver and shot it into Rhino's other shoulder. At this range, he shouldn't have missed the heart. That told Rhino the old man was disabling him so Vargas could finish him off.

Screaming in rage, he thrust at a Cazador soldier who came from the side with sword upraised. The spearhead ripped through the man's exposed chest, opening him from navel to sternum.

The two Praetorian Guards moved in front of Isaiah to intercept Rhino, and Rhino jabbed at the one on his left. The soldier tried to parry but hadn't given himself enough room. He backed into Isaiah, knocking a third arrow from his bow.

Rhino impaled the guard, through the stomach and out the back. He jammed it farther, hoping to get Isaiah on the same skewer, but his wily old mentor had jumped away.

As the other guard drew back his sword to strike, Rhino clicked the button in the middle of the shaft and twisted, disconnecting the two halves of his spear.

Leaving the top three feet of spear stuck through the first guard, he thrust the other half up under the second man's chin, through his palate, and into his brain before he could bring his sword around.

Rhino was down to the knife on his belt, but instead of drawing it, he pulled the arrow from his left shoulder. Isaiah was renocking the arrow that the staggering Praetorian Guard had knocked loose. He managed to bring it up and release it, but nerves must have thrown off his aim, and the arrow sailed past, an inch from Rhino's face. Rhino used the opportunity to slam into Isaiah and knock him to the ground.

"No!" Isaiah yelped as he squirmed under Rhino's weight. "Rhino, please, don't!"

Rhino wrestled Isaiah onto his back and raised the arrow he had plucked from his shoulder.

"No!" Isaiah yelled again.

With both hands, Rhino jammed the bolt into the center of his chest. He heard a satisfying crunch, then gurgling as blood filled Isaiah's lungs.

"Why?" Rhino grunted. "Why did you betray me?"

A voice in Spanish answered, "Because I paid better."

Rhino turned to see Colonel Vargas sitting on a bed

in one of the small rooms, watching with a bemused smile.

The fighting outside the stalls had all but ended. Six Cazador guards stood in the open space, their weapons pointed down at X and Mac, who lay on the floor, bleeding from the arrows and sword and spear wounds.

Felipe was the only one still on his feet, fighting two soldiers near the back exit. But he was down to one dagger, and both men had swords. He kicked the leg out from under one soldier, ducked the other's sword stroke, and jammed his knife into the face of the downed man.

Then he punched the second guard in the temple and jumped on him, knocking him down. His sharpened teeth clamped down and ripped the man's throat out.

Vargas gestured toward the young warrior. "I want that one alive," he said.

Two guards left X and Mac to help subdue Felipe. They tackled him to the floor, but he fought on, biting and head-butting. A third soldier finally went over and hit him in the head with his sword hilt.

Rhino remained on top of Isaiah, knowing that he would soon draw his last breath here in this grubby brothel. In trying to ambush Vargas, they had walked right into a trap. All because of the waste of air that now lay trapped and dying under Rhino.

Isaiah's lungs rattled as they filled with blood. Rhino finally pushed off him and stood. Unsheathing the long blade on his belt, he bent down and sliced his old mentor's throat from one earlobe to the other.

Isaiah looked up at him, but Rhino didn't give him the honor of looking into his eyes. He wiped the blade on Isaiah's robe and turned to Vargas, who finally stood and walked over to Mac and X.

"I'd say you fought bravely," he said. "But trying to kill a man while he's fucking is below cowardly."

Vargas drew his sword and angled the blade at the king's neck. An arrow stuck out of X's right arm, and another protruded from under his collarbone.

"I should have killed you when I had the chance," X growled.

Vargas smiled. His bulging eyes flitted to Rhino. "Since you showed me such respect by trying to kill me with my pants down, I won't give you the honor of a good death."

He gave a nod, and two of the men guarding X and Mac moved cautiously toward Rhino, while a third stepped away from Felipe.

Rhino threw off his robe, and the men stopped as if daunted by the sight.

"¡Mátenlo!" Vargas yelled.

The men advanced, and Rhino held up his long knife. Both shoulders throbbed from the arrow wounds despite the adrenaline rushing through his body.

He deflected the first sword blow, but the next two left a long, curving gash across his ribs, and a deep cut to the opposite hip. He staggered backward.

"No!" X yelled. He fought to get up, but the Cazadores clubbed him back down with their spear shafts and kicks to his gut.

Rhino locked eyes with X just before the three soldiers swarmed. They weren't cautious, however, and moved with haste. He jabbed his knife into the mouth of a man in the act of stabbing Rhino in the belly. The other two men stabbed from the side, finding little resistance.

The man Rhino had killed slumped onto him, and Rhino held on to the corpse as the other two men stabbed again and again. The heat turned to ice.

Pushing the corpse off him, Rhino then grabbed one of the swordsmen by the neck. The other guy jabbed Rhino's belly again, but before he could pull the sword out, Rhino reached down with his other hand and grabbed the man's arm and held it.

Rhino crushed the windpipe of the soldier he was holding and dropped him in a heap. He punched the remaining guard in the face, crushing his nose, then dropped to his knees with the sword jutting from his gut and an arrow in his shoulder. He knew that his many wounds were too deep and too many to survive. He would never see his sweet Sofia again. All he could do now was try to save his king and his men.

Only four soldiers remained in the room—easy odds if he weren't bleeding like a speared Siren.

Vargas gave the nod to finish off Rhino. The first warrior approached uncertainly, eyes wide with fear. He brought his sword up, but before he could deliver the final stroke, Vargas ordered him to stop.

X mumbled something that sounded a lot like "Go fuck yourself."

The guards, who had stopped beating him, gave him a few more kicks to shut him up.

X still managed to nod at Rhino, and Rhino nodded back.

"I changed my mind," Vargas said. "I do want to be the one to kill you."

He walked over and raised his sword in both hands, his crazed eyes looking as if they might pop out of his skull. And then, to Rhino's astonishment, one did.

Vargas crumpled to the floor as X turned a small pistol on the other guards.

The crack of gunshots filled the room, and one after another, the remaining Cazadores fell. Mac thrust his sword cane into the groin of the last soldier, and Felipe got up and ran over to Rhino.

Blood pooled around his body as the young warrior tried to stop the flow. X and Mac scrambled over to help.

Rhino looked at Vargas's ruined face and cracked a smile. His eyes went back to X, who could only see out of one eye.

"King Xavier, tell Sofia she will always be my queen," Rhino said. He slumped to his side, but X caught him under the arm.

"Breathe, General," X said. "You're going to be okay; just stay with me, and don't stop breathing. You're a beast, man. These are just little flesh wounds."

Rhino smiled one last time at the man he respected above all others in this world.

"I wish I was immortal like you, King Xavier, but alas, I'm just a man," Rhino said, his voice growing faint. "I will always serve you. Even in the next life, I will be watching over you while you fulfill the prophecy."

TWENTY-EIGHT

The assault rifle jammed again when Les tried to fire at a Siren. Cursing, he worked to free the round as more beasts closed in from the sky, buildings, and road.

The predators were drawn to *Discovery*'s nuclear-powered engines and the noise of the battle raging inside the tunnel.

"Timothy, don't let up!" Les said over the comms.

The twenty-millimeter Miniguns on the bottom of the airship raked the sky with tracer rounds, catching the beasts as they swooped down for the fresh meat.

There was plenty of it to be had. Team Raptor had evacuated over thirty survivors from outside the bunker. From their frightened faces, most of these people had never been aboveground. A few, however, pitched in to help carry Arlo and Edgar. Both divers were conscious and had their armor back on, but neither was in any condition to fight.

Once they made it out of the tunnels, they had decided to make their stand above the sinkhole. For the past half hour, Les and the uninjured divers had held their ground and waited for an opportunity to board the ship hovering five hundred feet above them.

But they were running low on ammo, and the time for getting these people into the air was running out. Timothy couldn't bring the ship down without first clearing the landing zone. The sheer numbers of hostiles meant that many of the injured would never make it aboard if they made a run for it, even with help from the others. And the people from the bunker weren't wearing much protection aside from the gray jumpsuits and plastic filtration masks.

"Sir, we've got a mass of hostiles heading your way from the south," Timothy reported.

"Fire the missiles!" Les yelled back. Giving up trying to free the jammed round, he let the rifle hang over his chest and pulled his pistol to fire at a Siren making a run at them. Three rounds took it down, and it skidded into a mass of vines.

A missile streaked away from the airship, and a loud boom rocked the next block. Following the noise came the alien shrieks of dying Sirens, and the cries from more of their comrades flocking toward the area.

Les went back to working the jammed round free as he scanned for Horn and his skinwalkers. The fiends were still out there, probably watching and waiting to make their move.

But they weren't the only monsters to worry about. The roar of a bone beast cut through the thunder and the chatter of automatic gunfire.

Les finally managed to free the round and aimed at a Siren swooping toward the airship. He fired a burst into its spine, sending the beast spiraling to earth.

"Changing!" Rodger shouted.

"Down to my last magazine!" Sofia yelled.

Michael shot a gliding Siren with a bolt to the chest, and it augered into the earth.

A burst of automatic fire cracked next to Les as Rodger started on his fresh magazine.

The city sounded like a war zone.

The silhouetted figures of more Sirens emerged on buildings fronting the roads. Others swooped in from the sky. The twenty-millimeter rounds from the turrets on the airship cut them to pieces, but ever more of them came on, like sharks to a bleeding carcass.

Les knew they couldn't wait any longer to get to the ship.

"We have to make a run for it!" he yelled.

Michael waved the group forward and set off on point, firing his laser rifle to clear a path.

"Timothy, bring *Discovery* down," Les ordered. "And open the launch bay when you're about to touch down."

"Copy that, sir," replied the AI.

The airship began to lower, the wash from the turbofans blasting down onto the street. Les fired three-round bursts at the beasts climbing over the piles of rubble.

A pack of twenty had already reached the landing zone. They bounded over the carcasses littering the broken asphalt.

"Take them down!" Les yelled.

Bullets and laser bolts brought down more and more of the beasts. But each time one fell, another took its place, black maw open, jagged teeth dripping ropes of saliva. The ravenous creatures seemed crazed for a chance at food.

Muzzle flashes lit up the sky under the lowering airship. Tracer rounds, looking like mini laser bolts, sprayed outward as Timothy worked both Miniguns, blowing apart the mass of the Sirens.

That did the trick. The beasts scattered in all directions, some of them bolting, others limping on the ground, dragging mangled wings.

The launch-bay doors parted, and a platform extended downward. The turbofans clicked off, and the ship's landing feet crunched against the ground.

"run!" Les yelled.

He turned and waved, his heart racing at the sight of Sirens flanking them from the sky across the sinkhole. Others came pelting down from the ruined buildings, and now that the ship was grounded, the Miniguns couldn't fire on any of them.

"Mags, Sofia, get these people to safety!" Les yelled. "Michael, Rodger, on me! We have to hold those Sirens back!"

The three men formed a line, laying down covering fire while the rest of the group made a run for the launch bay with the injured. Gunfire cracked in that direction as Sofia and Magnolia took down any beasts foolhardy enough to try picking off a human.

"I'm out," Rodger said, drawing his handgun.

"Sir, I can't get a shot with the Miniguns," said Timothy, "but Alfred has rearmed Cricket with grenades."

Les looked over his shoulder as the drone flew out of the launch bay, its arms extended with the blaster and grenade-launcher attachments.

"Instruct Cricket to fire at the flanking Sirens," Les said.

"Ay, aye, sir," Timothy replied.

As the drone joined Les and team, the fired grenades detonated around the sinkhole, collapsing the edge and burying many of the beasts on the ground.

More grenades hit the crushed building on the right side of the road, ripping apart the Sirens streaming over the pile.

Les and the other divers, meanwhile, concentrated their fire on the creatures coming in by air. Together, with Cricket's help, they held back the horde while the last civilians loaded into the launch bay.

"Captain, we're in!" Magnolia said over the comms. "Get back here!"

Les checked his six and then tapped Michael on the shoulder.

"Rodge, let's go!" Les said.

The men ran and Cricket followed, still launching grenades to cover them. The ground rumbled from the impacts, and the air filled with the cries of wounded and dying Sirens.

They were halfway to the launch bay when something burst out of a shop entrance on the right side of the road. The thing shook dust and concrete from its massive frame of muscles and bony armor.

"Bone beast!" Michael yelled.

The hulking mutant stormed out onto the sidewalk. A black-taloned hand ripped a steel signpost from the ground. Holding it like a spear, the beast hurled it through the air.

The projectile hit Cricket, breaking off the arm with the blaster and knocking the drone off-kilter. Sparks rained from the machine's broken limb. A flurry of chirps followed as the robot tried to stay airborne.

The divers opened fire on the bone beast, but the bullets did nothing against its bony armor and only pecked away at the muscular flesh. It held up a wrist to protect its eyes from Michael's laser bolts.

"Come on!" Magnolia shouted, waving from the launch bay. Alfred and the militia soldiers joined her, firing rifles at the monster.

The flurry of bullets drew its attention, and it pulled a bone dart from over its shoulder. It hurled the missile at the open launch bay, hitting a militia soldier and knocking him backward.

"Over here!" Les shouted, waving.

Michael fired a flurry of bolts that hit the beast in the shoulder, breaking away armor and burning through flesh. When he pulled the trigger again, the gun sizzled.

"It's overheated!" he yelled.

"Get to the launch bay!" Les shouted.

"No way!" Michael said.

Rodger took off running, leaving them both alone.

But they weren't alone.

Cricket moved overhead and launched a grenade at the storefront. The explosion blew out the overhang and dumped debris over the monster, pinning it to the sidewalk.

Les jammed the last magazine into his rifle and ran over to the struggling beast. Michael joined him, still waiting for his gun to cool.

The creature swiped at them as they approached. Michael distracted it, giving Les an opportunity to move in from the other side. He jammed the barrel of his machine gun against an eye and fired a burst.

The rounds punched through the brain, and the creature went limp.

"Watch out!" Michael shouted.

Raising the handgun X had given him, he fired at the top of the ruined building. Les moved back, but too late to avoid the Siren that jumped down. The creature landed on him, crushing him to the ground.

He tried to move but couldn't, and wondered whether his back was broken. Maybe that was why he couldn't feel claws ripping into his flesh. Blinking, he saw blood trickling from a hole in the thick skull. Les tried to get out from under the limp carcass, but the big dead son of a bitch had him pinned.

A robotic hand grabbed his shoulder armor and hauled him out from under the beast. "You okay?" Michael asked.

Les wobbled. His limbs felt like jelly. He put an

arm around the commander, and Magnolia ran over to help the three divers get back to the launch bay. Cricket covered their six and then joined them going up the ramp. Once inside, Michael hit the button to retract the platform.

Les collapsed on the deck, and Michael bent over, hands on his knees, panting like Miles. The doors began to close behind them as the ship rose off the ground. Before they shut, Les spotted what Magnolia was pointing at. A herd of perhaps twenty bone beasts ran down the street below, tearing into the Sirens and letting out their monstrous roars.

The airship thumped as winged Sirens crashed into the hull.

"Get us out of here, Timothy!" Les shouted.

The turbofans lifted them higher into the air as the legs retracted. More thumps sounded against the starboard and port sides as Sirens latched on.

Les knew they weren't safe yet. He pushed himself up and, with Michael's help, stood.

The ship shook again, knocking both divers back to the deck.

"Everyone, hold on," Timothy said over the public address system. "We're leaving this monster-infested hellhole."

The ship continued to ascend, but the thumps from Sirens banging on the hull only grew louder and more frequent.

Les got up on his knees and looked at the new faces in the launch bay. The thirty-odd people from the bunker were all looking at him and Michael. The kids were wailing; the adults just stared. Several had taken off their plastic masks, revealing shocked and mystified faces.

A crack sounded across the launch bay as a Siren slammed its clawed fist against one of the portholes. Another beast head-butted the glass over and over until it cracked in a bloody halo.

"Faster, Timothy!" Les yelled.

"Activating thrusters," replied the AI.

The ship jumped forward, rattling the launch bay. Les tried to keep his balance, but the acceleration shoved him back down to the deck.

Screams rang out around him.

"Everyone, hang on!" Magnolia yelled.

The ship climbed, the nose spearing through the clouds. A Siren's eyeless face filled a porthole, slamming against it before being ripped away into the darkness.

Discovery gained altitude and speed, and one by one, the Sirens outside were peeled off the hull.

"Almost clear," Timothy reported.

Lightning flashed outside the portholes, capturing a single Siren still holding onto the hull. Its black hole of a mouth opened, smearing spittle across the window, where it froze.

And then it was gone, torn away into the sky.

"All clear," Timothy said.

Les heaved a sigh of relief. "Timothy, see if you can find the *Sea Wolf*. I'm not going home without her and the two men who might still be alive down there."

"Roger that, Captain," replied the AI.

Michael clapped Les on the back. "Thanks, Captain," he said. "Thanks for coming down here after us."

"Thanks for saving my ass," Les said. He almost smiled, but that somehow felt like disrespect toward all who had died on this journey.

But they had succeeded in part of their mission, anyway.

Les checked on the people from the bunker. They were safe now, and soon they would see sunshine, but they were busy enough trying to wrap their minds around the inconceivable present. Most of them appeared to be in shock. The medical team and technicians fanned out to check them for injuries.

Alfred had already put a blanket over the militia soldier killed by the bone beast. The bone spear lay on the deck beside him, its sharp end covered in blood. Les said a silent prayer for the man and moved over to help the living.

The doors to the passage outside the launch bay opened, and Layla ran inside. Michael slung his laser rifle and ran over to meet her. They embraced in the center of the room.

"Timothy, I need you to translate for me in the launch bay," Les said. He took his helmet off and stood in front of the survivors huddled on the floor.

Timothy's hologram emerged, offering a warm smile.

Les pointed at his own armored chest and said, "My name is Captain Les Mitchells." Then to Timothy, he said, "Tell them this airship is called *Discovery*, and it is taking them to their new home."

Michael pulled away from Layla and walked over, holding her hand. He smiled wider than Les had ever seen him smile.

"Do you want to say something?" Les asked.

Michael nodded. "Timothy, ask them if they are ready to see the sun."

* * * * *

X awoke on a boat thumping over the waves. Ton, Victor, and Lieutenant Sloan were with him, all of them wearing the same worried look. Another militia soldier piloted the boat toward the capitol rig.

Sloan looked down and said something, but X couldn't hear her over the motor. He tried to remember why his body was covered in blood. The sight of an arrow sticking out of his upper chest brought back a flood of memories from the Purple Pearl.

They came crashing over him like waves. He recalled the ambush and the brutal fight that followed. And then he remembered how it ended, with Rhino dying in his arms after promising to watch over him always.

A platoon of militia soldiers had stormed into the Purple Pearl not long after Rhino took his last breath. The gunshots had also attracted Colonel Forge and a small army of Cazadores.

What happened after that was fuzzy in his mind. He vaguely remembered Sloan, Ton, and Victor carrying him through a back alley, where his memories ended.

"What happened to Mac and Felipe?" X said.

Fear stabbed his heart, questions swarming his mind. Had the militia soldiers engaged the Cazadores? Had he just started the war he was trying so hard to prevent?

He tried to sit up, but Sloan pushed him back to the deck and said something that he couldn't hear. Ton and Victor both tightened their grip on his legs and arms to keep him down.

"No, move, King," Victor said. "Please."

Looking up at the blue sky, X tried to calm his thumping heart. He could hardly see out of one eye, and he was pretty sure he had a broken rib. And, of course, there were the stab wounds and the arrows.

Sloan pulled out her radio and brought it to her mouth. X tried to listen and managed to make out a few things. Something about Captain Mitchells and *Discovery*.

X sat up and grunted. "Tell me what the hell is going on, damn it."

Sloan, Ton, and Victor looked down at him with varying expressions of disbelief.

"Samson is in contact with Captain Mitchells," Sloan said. "That's all I know."

"What about Mac and Felipe and the militia?"

Sloan pointed to the back of the boat. X twisted, wincing in pain, and saw the two men sitting in the back, getting patched up by two militia soldiers.

"And Colonel Forge?" X asked. He was hoping the scene of death in the Purple Pearl would look like what it was: a power struggle between Rhino and Vargas. He was also hoping Rhino's sacrifice would help bury the hatchet between the sky people and the Cazadores, especially now that Colonel Vargas and General Santiago were dead.

Though he had been too thick to realize it until now, it at last dawned on X that Rhino had been trying to do just that—and had paid the ultimate price making it happen.

Sloan brought her radio back up, this time talking to Sergeant Wynn. Her voice trailed off, or maybe X just couldn't hear her. He grimaced from a fresh wave of pain.

"Wynn has the situation under control," Sloan finally said. "There's been no further fighting."

The news filled X with energy, and he sat up straighter, the lapse in pain allowing him to focus his mind. The boat glided through the open door of the marina under the capitol tower.

A group of people waited on the pier inside.

Dr. Huff was among them. He climbed into the boat, carrying a bag. For a moment, he simply looked at X.

"What the heck happened to you, Xavier?" he finally asked.

"He made a mess, that's what," Sloan said.

"I need to get up to the command center and talk to Captain Mitchells," X said.

"Sir, all due respect, but you need to get to the medical ward, pronto," Huff said. "You have *arrows* in your chest and arm!"

X looked down again at his wounds. Bandages covered most of them, but the arrows were still in his flesh.

A memory of Rhino being stabbed over and over flashed across his mind. Gritting his teeth, X grabbed the end of the arrow and broke off all but the first four or five inches protruding from his right arm.

"I'll be fine," he growled. "Now, help me up."

Huff looked at him in awe. "Sir, you need—"

"Take care of Felipe and Mac, and then hide them," X said. He looked over at Sloan. "Let's go, Lieutenant."

Ton and Victor helped X to his feet and off the boat. They followed Sloan to the internal door, where she hesitated.

"Better take the cage," she said. "No way you can get up those stairs and still be alive at the top."

X didn't argue.

Sloan still didn't move. "King Xavier, I beg you to listen to the doctor," she said. "You're hurt really bad and should get—"

"I need to get to the radio in the command center," he said as firmly as his weakened condition would allow.

Sloan finally nodded at Ton and Victor, and they all set off for the door that led to the outer pier. From there, they took the elevator cage.

The beautiful view of teal water and purple sunset did little to relieve the anguish overwhelming X. He had been hurt worse than this before, but losing Rhino cut as deep as anything he had ever known.

Sloan spoke to Wynn over the radio again—a welcome distraction from the dreadful thoughts plaguing him.

"Sergeant Wynn said Colonel Forge has left the Purple Pearl," Sloan said. "Our team is cleaning up the bodies now and will have Rhino sent to the capitol rig."

Suddenly light-headed, X leaned against the cage. She reached out to help him.

"I'm okay," he lied.

The cage clanked to the top level, and she opened the gate. From there, they took several flights of stairs up to the command center, stopping twice for X to catch his breath. Victor and Ton practically carried him up the last flight.

"Sorry," Victor said when X cried out in pain.

He was hurt bad, all right, and would need surgery to remove the arrows. But it was nothing he hadn't experienced before. It just meant more scars and more stories.

This one was a tale he wanted to forget, though. Seeing Rhino beaten and stabbed like a Siren was too much to bear. A tear welled in his eye as Ton and Victor helped him off the top landing.

Sloan opened the door to the room, letting Miles out. The dog rushed over, barking and then brushing against X.

Samson rose from the radio equipment to stare.

"Rads and lightning, man!" said the engineer. "You look like you just fought an army."

Miles whined and licked X's hand.

"It's okay, boy," X said, giving the dog a feeble scratch behind the ears.

"*Did* he fight an army?" Samson asked Sloan.

"Yeah, pretty much," she replied.

X staggered into the room and waved Ton and Victor off. They stepped back, and he fell against the table. Both men reached out to help, along with Sloan, but X waved them all back.

"I'm fine," he said.

Even the dog wasn't buying it, and he let out a low whine. X sat on the chair in front of the radio equipment, and Miles came to sit beside him. X reached out for the receiver, and Samson handed it to him.

"Captain Mitchells, do you copy?" X said.

Static crackled; then a voice came on.

"King Xavier, I copy," Les said.

"What's your status?" X asked.

"Sir, I'm not sure what Samson has told you," said the captain, "but we're on our way back with thirty-one survivors from the bunker. We've sustained some major losses rescuing them."

X steeled himself and listened to Les rattle off the losses of Cazadores, a militia soldier, and Alexander, plus all the equipment and *Star Grazer* itself. The captain went on to list the injured, including Edgar and Arlo.

Overall, the mission had been a success, though at a steep cost, especially for the Cazadores. But at least they had two survivors to tell the tale to their comrades when they returned home.

"We retrieved the *Sea Wolf* with two of General Santiago's men," Les said. "The surf had taken them out to sea, which saved them from the skinwalkers."

"Where are the skinwalkers now?" X asked.

"Licking their wounds, but I have a feeling Horn will come for the throne once he recovers. Sofia overheard him saying that was his plan."

"Let him come," X said.

"There's something else," Les said.

X winced from a rush of pain and blinked away the dots in his vision.

"Timothy has been talking to the survivors we rescued," Les said. "They know more about the defectors than we do."

Static broke over the speakers, blocking the rest of the transmission.

"Les, come again," X groaned.

The channel cleared, and Les came back online.

"I said these people know more about the defectors than we do," he said, "and they claim to know how to shut them down."

X's shaking hand lowered the handset. He took a moment to think. Raising it back to his mouth felt like lifting a fifty-pound anchor.

"Is Tin there?" X asked.

"Yes, right here. Hold on."

"X?" said a voice.

"Hey, kid, good to hear you."

"You don't sound so good," Michael said.

"I've got a few more scars, but I'll be fine." He wanted to talk about Rhino, but couldn't find the words to describe what had happened. "General Rhino didn't make it."

White noise filled the room.

"Michael," X said.

"Yeah. Holy shit, X. What happened?"

"We averted a war." X couldn't say much more over the radio, and Michael must have sensed that.

"But there's another war coming, kid," X said. "A different kind of war that's going to require Hell Divers."

"We dive so humanity survives, always," Michael said. "It's what we do."

The door to the command center opened, and Dr. Huff entered. X turned back to the radio, stars bursting across his vision like little bombs going off.

Samson bent down to grab the receiver. "I've got it, X," he said.

"I got to go, Tin," X managed to say. "I love you, Michael."

"I love you, too, Xavier."

Sloan and Huff helped X out of the chair while Samson sat back down at the radio equipment. Ton and Victor clasped forearms and carefully picked X up under his legs to carry him, and he finally let his body weight go while his burdened mind grappled with the future.

In a few short months, Layla and Michael would welcome Bray to the Vanguard Islands. There was a lot to do between now and then.

Rhino had given his life to help pave the way for peace. But more threats were closing in on their new home, and before X could face them, he had to rest and heal. He would need his strength more than ever for this next fight.

COMING
SUMMER 2020

HELL DIVERS VII

Don't miss the next installment
of the Hell Divers series with
Hell Divers VII!